THE
BOOKSELLER

The First
Hugo Marston
Novel

MARK PRYOR

SEVENTH
STREET
BOOKS™

59 John Glenn Drive
Amherst, New York 14228–2119

Published 2012 by Seventh Street Books, an imprint of Prometheus Books

Cover image © 2012 Shutterstock.com/Eskemar
Cover design by Grace M. Conti-Zilsberger

Inquiries should be addressed to
Seventh Street Books
59 John Glenn Drive
Amherst, New York 14228–2119
VOICE: 716–691–0133
FAX: 716–691–0137
WWW.PROMETHEUSBOOKS.COM

16 15 14 13   6 5 4 3

Library of Congress Cataloging-in-Publication Data

Pryor, Mark, 1967–
    The bookseller : the first Hugo Marston novel / by Mark Pryor.
        p. cm.
    ISBN 978-1-61614-708-2 (pbk.)
    ISBN 978-1-61614-709-9 (ebook)
    1.Americans—France—Paris—Fiction. 2. Missing persons—
Investigation—Fiction. 3. Booksellers and bookselling—France—Fiction.
4. Embassy buildings—Security measures—Fiction. I. Title.

PS3616.R976B66 2012
813'.6--dc23

                                                                    2012019017

Printed in the United States of America on acid-free paper

To my wife, Sarah.

AUTHOR'S NOTE

As much as I love Paris, I have been forced to take occasional liberties with its history and geography. Events have been created and streets invented to suit my own selfish needs. All errors and misrepresentations, intentional and otherwise, are mine and mine alone.

CHAPTER ONE

The largest of Notre Dame's bells tolled noon just as Hugo reached the end of the bridge, the brittle air seeming to hold on to the final clang longer than usual. He paused and looked across the busy Paris street into Café Panis. The yellow carriage lights above its windows beckoned as dim figures moved about inside, customers choosing tables and waiters flitting around like dancers.

Hot coffee was tempting, but this was the first day of a vacation Hugo didn't want, with nothing to do and nowhere to go, and he didn't much want to sit at a table by himself and think about that.

He squared his shoulders against the wind and turned right, leaving the café behind, heading west alongside the river. He glanced over the parapet as he walked, the growl of a motor launch floating up from below as the boat's propellers thrashed at the icy waters of the Seine. On cold days like this he wondered how long a man could survive in the river's oily waters, struggling against the deceptively strong current before succumbing to its frigid grip. It was a grim thought and one he quickly dismissed. After all, this was Paris; there was too much boat traffic, too many people like him admiring the river from its multitude of bridges, for a flailing man to go unnoticed for long.

Five minutes later he spotted a riverside bookstall, four green metal boxes bolted to the low wall and crammed with books, their colorful spines like the feathers of a bird fanned out on the shelves to attract passersby. The stall's owner was stooped over a box, the hem of his worn, gray coat brushing the pavement. A shoelace had come undone but the man ignored it, even as his fingers scrabbled through the post-cards, inches away.

A barrage of shouting made the seller straighten and both men looked toward the voices, ringing out from a stall about fifty yards away, across the entrance to the Pont Neuf bridge. A man, squat and burly, poked a finger and yelled at the stall's owner, a crimson-faced woman who was bundled against the cold and determined to give as good as she got.

The old man shook his head and turned back to his box. Hugo coughed gently.

"*Oui, monsieur?*" The seller's voice was gruff, but when he looked up and saw Hugo he cracked a grin. "Ah, it's you. Where have you been, *mon ami?*"

"*Salut*, Max." Hugo slipped off a glove and took Max's proffered hand, warm despite the chill of the day. They spoke in French even though the old man knew English well enough when it suited—like when pretty American girls were shopping. "What's all the fuss about?" Hugo asked.

Max didn't respond and together they turned to watch. The woman was waving an arm as if telling the stocky man to leave her alone. The man's response shocked Hugo: he grabbed her wrist and twisted it hard enough to spin her around, and in the same movement kicked her legs out from under her. She dropped straight onto her knees and let out a plaintive wail as she threw her head back in pain. Hugo started forward but felt a strong hand holding him back.

"*Non*," Max said. "It's not for you. *Une affaire domestique.*"

Hugo shook him off. "She needs help. Wait here."

"*Non*," Max said again, grabbing Hugo's arm with a grip the American could feel through his winter coat. "Let her be, Hugo. She doesn't want your help, believe me when I say that."

"Why not? Who the hell is he?" Hugo felt the tautness in his body and fought the desire to release it on the bully across the street. Something in Max's plea had resonated, the implication that by getting involved he could make things worse. "What's it about, Max?" he repeated.

Max held his eye for a long moment, then let go of Hugo's arm and looked away. The old man turned to his stall and picked up a book, then put on his glasses to read the cover.

Hugo turned to face him and saw that the left lens was missing. "Jesus, Max. Please tell me that guy didn't pay you a visit."

"Me? No." Max ran a sleeve under his bulbous and pockmarked nose, but didn't meet Hugo's eye. "Why would he?"

"You tell me." The quai was front and center for crazies, Hugo knew, drawn like mosquitoes to the water and tourists that flowed through the heart of the city. And the *bouquinistes* were easy and frequent targets.

"No reason. If you're worried about my glasses, I just dropped them, that's all." Max finally looked Hugo in the eye and the smile returned. "Yes, I'm getting old and clumsy, but I can still take care of myself. Anyway, your job is to keep your ambassador safe, protect your embassy, not worry about old men like me."

"I'm off duty, I can worry about whomever I want."

Again Max put a hand on Hugo's arm, this time reassuring. "I'm fine. Everything's fine."

"*D'accord.* If you say so." Hugo looked across the street to see the woman on her feet again, the man's arms flailing all around her, but not touching. Reluctantly, Hugo decided to leave it for now. He turned to the books on display. "This is how you take care of yourself, by fleecing tourists, *oui*? Do you have anything actually worth buying? I need a gift."

"I have key chains, postcards, and *petit* Eiffel Towers."

"It's for Christine."

"Ah." Max raised an eyebrow and waved a hand at his stall. "Then nothing I have out here."

"You keep the good stuff hidden, eh?" Hugo looked over his friend's shoulder and watched the burly man stalking down the quai, away from them, hands in his pockets. His victim, the bouquiniste, looked unsteady on her feet and Hugo saw her collapse into a canvas chair beside her stall, her face sinking into her hands. As Hugo watched, she reached into a plastic bag beside her and pulled out a clear, flask-sized bottle.

When he looked back, Max was watching him. "That, in her hand, is her biggest problem," the old man said. "But around here, it's best to mind your own business." He gestured toward his books. "So, are you buying or just wasting time? And by that, I mean mine."

Hugo turned his attention back to Max. "A gift, remember?"

"*Bien*, let me see." Max picked up a hardback, a book of black and white photographs of Hollywood stars from the 1920s to the 1970s. He showed Hugo the cover, a picture of a smiling Cary Grant, all teeth and slick hair. "Looks like you, *mon ami*."

Hugo had heard that before, from his wife, though he assumed she was just making fun. The caption said Grant was forty-one at the time of the picture, a year younger than Hugo. At six foot one inch, Grant was also an inch shorter than Hugo. But the men shared the same thick hair, though Hugo's was a lighter brown—light enough to camouflage a few recent strands of gray. His was thick hair that had never been touched by the globs of gel, or whatever those guys used. In the picture, Cary Grant's eyes glittered like jewels, a hard look Hugo could emulate when he needed to, but normally his eyes were a darker and warmer brown, more thoughtful than magnetic. The eyes of a watcher, not a player.

"Here." Max took the book back, then stooped and lifted a stack of newspapers off a battered leather briefcase. "I have some books in there. Help yourself."

Hugo knelt, unzipped the case, and peered in. "An Agatha Christie?"

"*Oui*," Max nodded. "A first edition, so *très cher*. A humble diplomat like you cannot afford it, I fear."

"I expect you're right, but I know someone who would love it."

Max grinned. "Someone who might love you for giving it, you mean."

"Maybe so." Hugo turned the novel over in his hands. He wasn't quite an expert on rare books but he knew as much as many of the bouquinistes who peddled their wares along the river. This one was a beauty, a 1935 first edition of *Death in the Clouds*, one of the Hercule Poirot mysteries. It was bound in full maroon Morocco leather, banded, and lettered in gilt with marbled endpapers, and it looked to Hugo like it had the original cloth backstrip. He spotted a short tear to the gutter of the final advertisement leaf, but overall he was impressed. It was clearly a fine copy. Hugo held it up. "How much?"

"For you, four hundred Euros."

"And for everyone else?"

"Three hundred, of course."

"In America we cheat strangers," Hugo said, "not our friends."

"You're not in America." Max's eyes twinkled. "You are a big man, Hugo, big enough to throw me in the river. I would not dare cheat you."

Hugo grunted and pulled another old book out of the bag. Covered in dark blue cloth, it exuded antiquity, and a quick check inside confirmed that: 1873. Gold lettering on a red panel on the spine read *On War*, then the word *Clausewitz*. "The first English translation?"

"*Merde!*" Max hurried over and snatched the book from Hugo's hand. "This one isn't for sale."

"Why not?"

"Because." He clutched the book to his chest, then held up a hand in apology. "*Je m'excuse*, it's important. I just have to look at it more closely, before I decide."

"Let me look at it for you, be happy to advise," Hugo said, his tone intentionally light to mask his curiosity. It wasn't like his friend to be obscure, to guard his words.

"*Non.*" Max held the book tight. "It's not about the book, its value. Look, if I decide to sell it, I'll hold it for you. *D'accord?*"

"Sure." Hugo nodded. "Thanks."

"*Bon.*" Max smiled and pointed to the cowboy boots on Hugo's feet. "You are the only Texan who knows books, *mon ami*. But you haven't lived in France long enough to find a good pair of shoes?"

"No compliment without an insult. Sometimes I think you're an Englishman."

Max spat in disgust and muttered something unintelligible.

"Let's see," Hugo went on. "What else do you have?" He dug back into the case and pulled up a slim volume encased in a protective plastic envelope. Hugo inspected the book, which appeared to have its original paper cover. It was off-white, slightly pink perhaps, with a thin black line in the shape of a rectangle about an inch in from the edges, within which the book's information was presented. The name of the author and publisher were also in black type, but the title was in block letters that would once have been blood red.

"*Une Saison En Enfer*," Max said, looking over his shoulder. *A Season in Hell*. "By Arthur Rimbaud. That is not a first edition."

"No? The only collector's copy of this I've seen is an early edition of Zelda Fitzgerald's translation," Hugo said. He also remembered reading about Rimbaud on a train to Paris from London, a couple of years back. "Can I open the plastic?"

"Have I ever let you?"

"I know, I know. I can open it when I buy it. Can't blame a man for trying."

"If you say so," Max said. "The friend who gave it to me said it is in good shape, which you can see, but that it has some scribble in the front." Max waved a hand. "But he is almost blind, so maybe you'll be lucky and find the author's signature."

Hugo thought for a moment. It was an important book, in the literary world if not the reading one. An extended poem first published in 1873, it was as influenced by the author's choice of drug as it was by his passionate homosexuality. "Christine does have a thing for Oscar Wilde," he said. "This is close enough. How much?"

Max looked at him and shrugged. "Hard to say. I haven't looked it over, it may be worth a lot or nothing."

"Very helpful. How about I give you five hundred Euros for both books?"

"How about you just pull out that gun and rob me, eh?"

"Then you tell me." Hugo smiled. "You negotiate like a fox, Max."

"A thousand for both. First you pay and then you thank me for the privilege of paying."

"I'm on vacation," Hugo said, digging into a pocket and pulling out his wallet. "I was thinking about a trip to the states, deliver these in person, but you're taking all my travel money. If I decide to go, I'll have to walk from the airport."

"Ah, but you will have something to read when you rest along the way."

"People don't read rare books, Max, you know that." Hugo handed the old man a wad of cash. "This is all I have on me. I'll bring you the rest later?"

"The ones who don't realize they are rare are the ones who read them." Max took the money but didn't count it. "We have banks in France, you know."

"Then if you can wait thirty minutes, I'll go find one."

Max spread his hands. "Where else would I be, but waiting for you?" He paused, eyeing Hugo. "You really think you're going to America?"

"Why not? The mad romantic dash isn't really my style, but nor is sitting on my ass for two weeks."

"You don't want time off from work?"

"Use it or lose it, they tell me. Not that I mind losing it, but the State Department is convinced my mental health will suffer if I go to work because I want to, not because I have to."

"You Americans." Max shook his head. "How you came to rule the world, I have no idea."

"We have big guns," Hugo said. "And we don't surrender every time the Germans invade."

"*Touché*," Max guffawed, then pointed again to Hugo's feet. "*Alors*, if you decide to go, bring me a pair of those cowboy boots, and next time I'll give you an even better deal. Size forty-one, *s'il vous plait*."

"*Bien*." Hugo looked at his watch. "I'll go rob a bank, make a phone call, and hopefully be back in less than an hour."

"You are welcome to pay me another time. To consider those books a gift, Monsieur Hugo, for now anyway. If I change my mind, I know where to find you."

"No, you might disappear to some beach somewhere, and I don't like owing people money. I'll be right back."

They shook hands and for the second time Hugo saw something in Max's eyes. But the old man looked quickly away, up at the clouds. "I think it will snow soon," Max said, his voice flat.

Hugo glanced at the sky, gray and heavy, and started back the way he'd come, books in hand. Thirty yards later he looked back at Max. The old man was shuffling along the quai toward his neighbor and, as he crossed the street, Max glanced over his shoulder as if someone might be following him, or watching.

The wind tugged at Hugo's hat, seeming to rise around him and shift direction, placing its cold hands on his back, propelling him along the quai. He walked slowly at first, then his footsteps quickened and he shivered as a chill settled around his neck, cold fingers spreading down his spine. He approached a middle-aged couple dressed in identical blue ski jackets, the man holding a camera and looking hopefully around him. On any other day Hugo would have stopped, offered to take the photo, but he strode past without catching their eye. Their need to capture a moment in time for their kids or grandkids was no match for the disquiet that crowded in on Hugo, the cold wind at his back, the leaden sky above, and a rising fear that he should have pressed Max harder, made sure that everything really was all right.

CHAPTER TWO

An hour later, Hugo stood on the curb of the Quai Saint-Michel, roughly a quarter-mile from Max's stall. He waited for a break in the traffic before hurrying across the street, heading in the direction of his friend. He kept his head down against the breeze but looked up every so often, trying to catch a glimpse of the old man, but soon the cold wind blinded him with his own tears.

Max was fine, he told himself. An angry man at a nearby stall and a pair of dropped glasses, and maybe Hugo's own need to find action where none lay. He'd known Max several years, they'd shared meals and more than a few cups of coffee, swapping stories about Paris and Texas, finding common ground in their love of books and their slightly jaded view of the world. Hugo still felt a tug of urgency, but logic had slowed his walk and reminded him he was in Paris, a place to stroll, not stride.

To his right, an engine sputtered as a tourist boat cast off from the far bank. Hugo watched as the *bateau-mouche* chugged slowly into the middle of the river, its passengers huddled together on the open deck, blobs of color on a bleak winter's day. France had endured a drought since the summer, particularly to the south of Paris, and the little water that escaped the thirsty wine regions left the tourist barges sitting low in the river, almost too low for those on board to see over the embankment and take in the majesty of the Grand Palais and the Musee d'Orsay. As the boat passed by, he saw a little boy on the deck clinging to his father for warmth. Hugo bunched his hands deeper in his pockets. He'd find some coffee after paying Max.

He walked on beside the river, eyes watering when the breeze whipped into him as he made his way toward Pont Neuf. His path was blocked momentarily as two old ladies, bundled against the chill, held onto each other's arms and kissed hello. Their red noses bobbed from side to side, but their little bodies were too cold or too stiff to complete the second *bisou*, so they abandoned it with nods and waddled away, arm-in-arm.

As he approached Max's stall, Hugo felt a sense of relief. The old man was folding his camping chair and stowing it beside one of the metal boxes. He looked over at Hugo. "I assumed you'd run off. *Alors*, I meant to ask before, when you mentioned her. What is happening with Christine?"

"Well, I'm not sure really," Hugo said, glancing over Max's shoulder. The bouquiniste across the bridge had packed up her stall and gone. "Chrissy's in Texas, I'm here, and that was pretty much the end of it. I just called, though, and left a message about going over to see her, to talk about things."

"That's something," Max said.

"It's a long plane ride, is what it is." But with two weeks of vacation to endure, a last-minute dash to Dallas actually seemed plausible. Or only slightly idiotic. "We'll see what happens," he said. "Anyway, here's the rest of your money."

"*Merci*." Max's hand swallowed the roll of bills like that of a practiced pickpocket. "Need a receipt?"

"No, if I need one later, I know where to find you." Hugo hesitated, then put a hand on his friend's shoulder. "Hey, you'd tell me if something were going on around here?"

"Going on?"

"With your neighbor. And I've never seen you drop anything, Max. A book, money, your glasses. Call it a feeling."

"*Ach*." Max turned away and shrugged. "You should have feelings for Christine, not me. Anyway, I'm thinking about retiring. Getting off the street. This job, I live around so many crazies I sometimes feel I might become one."

"You, retire? Are you serious?"

"Why not?" Max picked up a small bag of key chains and grinned. "Get a nice place in the countryside and write a novel. How about that?"

"Sounds wonderful. But I'm not sure I believe you."

Max looked past him, along the quai, then met his eyes. "Everyone must know when to quit, Hugo. An old man can't battle the forces of evil alone, you know, not for long anyway."

"Forces of evil sounds a little dramatic. Are you serious?"

"*Mais oui.*" Max spat and then rubbed his chin. "The cold in winter, the heat in summer, the miserly tourists, the bums that harass me for my hard-earned cash every day." He looked away. "There are many evil forces, you should know that."

Hugo shook his head, unsure how serious Max was, and stood there for a moment watching his friend fuss in front of his stall. They both looked up as a seagull squawked low over the parapet, whirling down to the water. Hugo thought about Christine and being impetuous. Maybe he should go.

"It will be snowing within the hour," Max said, a finger jabbing toward the sky. "I see it and I feel it."

"Then you should pack up, old friend." Hugo patted him on the back. "And maybe I'll go pack a suitcase."

But Max was no longer listening. His eyes were fixed at something over Hugo's shoulder, his old face drawn tight. His hand opened of its own accord and the bag of key chains fell to the sidewalk.

Hugo turned sideways, alert, the back of his neck tingling as though the devil himself were breathing down his neck.

"*Bonjour*, Max."

The man was tall and broad with an angular, chiseled face and deep-set, dark eyes. He wore a beige raincoat and a fedora much like Hugo's, but his was tilted low over his brow. He seemed to be ignoring Hugo on purpose, an artificial posture that heightened Hugo's image of the man as a comic-book bad guy.

Max licked his lips and stood as tall as he could, a conscious effort at bravery. "Nica, what do you want now?"

Nica stared at the bookseller for a moment, then appeared to notice Hugo, turning his head just slightly to meet Hugo's gaze. For five long seconds neither man looked away. Then Nica smiled and turned his eyes on Max. "Just to talk. Do you have a moment?"

"Say what you have to say," Max said. "I am busy."

Nica gestured to the stone steps ten yards from the stall, stairs that led down to the walkway beside the river.

"We should talk in private," Nica said.

"I can't leave my stall."

Nica looked at Hugo and smiled again. "Your friend can look after it. This won't take long."

"I don't think he wants to go anywhere," Hugo said.

"And I don't think this is any of your business."

"*Ach*, Hugo, my busybody American. *Ça va*, it's no problem." Max nodded to the stairs. "Come on then, let's talk."

Hugo watched them disappear down the steps, Max's old shoes scuffing loudly on the stone as he descended, and Hugo fought the temptation to spy on them. He forced himself to unfold the old canvas stool and sat on it, a temporary bouquiniste in a cashmere coat and cowboy boots.

He sat for a full minute, his mind busy but his feet numbing as he worried about Max. Using the cold as an excuse, he got up and walked to the stone balustrade, and looked down to the walkway. At first it seemed empty, but then voices rolled out from under the Pont Neuf. He leaned over the parapet and saw them in the shadows of the arch. He listened for a moment, unable to hear the words but recognizing the harsh tone.

He hesitated. Nica had said that this was none of his business and Max had wanted him to butt out, but it wouldn't hurt to wander down there, just to be sure. After almost twenty years in law enforcement, inserting himself into other people's disputes was second nature, sometimes an urge he couldn't resist—especially if the dispute seemed one-sided. Whether that urge was to protect the innocent or catch the guilty didn't much matter anymore.

Hugo started down the stairs. At the bottom he heard them again, Max's voice plaintive now. His quickened his step and looked past the men as he heard a low grumble from further under the bridge where a motor launch bobbed in the river behind them. Its propellers churned the gray water into white as an invisible hand throttled it against the current, keeping it close to the bank.

He was barely a dozen paces away when Max raised both hands, his old voice cracking, "Nica, *non.*" But Nica ignored Max's pleas and grabbed the bookseller by his lapels, pulling him close until their noses brushed.

"Hey!" Hugo called out. He tried to control his anger, to keep his voice calm. Better to diffuse than inflame, he told himself. "What's going on?"

Nica released Max and turned. "I told you, this has nothing to do with you. Go away."

"Fine," said Hugo. "But if you're all done, I'll walk monsieur back to his stall." He held the man's dark stare and when he got no reply, added, "I saw some postcards I want to buy."

The movement was fast and unexpected, a blur that ended with Nica holding the ice pick high, as if he were proud of his flourish. He held the tip between Max's eyes, then pointed it at Hugo. "Go. Take all the postcards you want. They are free today."

Hugo hesitated. He could take two steps back and pull out his gun but, for as long as he'd carried a weapon, he'd never started a fire fight, and he had no desire to start one now. And if he wasn't quick enough, Max could be hurt, perhaps killed. Even if he did win a shoot-out he'd pay dearly, justified or not: his job was to protect the ambassador and visiting dignitaries, not play Wyatt Earp with riverside hoodlums.

But he looked at his trembling friend and knew that he wouldn't just walk away.

"If this is a question of money," Hugo began, "I owe monsieur a little and would be happy to—"

"Enough." Nica spat the words and a sneer crossed his face as he turned his head to look at the boat behind him. Without warning, he shoved Max against the high stone wall and started toward Hugo, moving like a boxer with his shoulders hunched forward, his steps small and quick, the ice pick circling. Hugo resisted the impulse to back away, instead turning sideways and taking one tiny step back as the man reached him, the point of the pick spiraling toward his chest. Hugo waited a split-second more, then stepped in close, blocking Nica's thrust with his forearm, bringing the palm of his hand up sharply into the soft flesh under his assailant's chin. Nica's head snapped back and his knees buckled, and Hugo swept his legs from under him to make sure he hit the stone walkway hard. Nica rolled on the ground, clutching his throat, the ice pick on the ground between them.

Hugo started forward, reaching for his gun, just as Nica propped himself on one elbow. His other hand flashed out toward Hugo, who stopped in his tracks, his eyes drawn to Nica's sharp features, smug behind the silver pistol in his fist.

"If this had a silencer, you'd be dead," Nica snarled. Still watching Hugo, Nica climbed to his feet and waved an arm at the boat, which had drifted a hundred feet or more from them. The engine barked and the bow lifted a fraction as it lurched forward, its windows black in the shadow of the bridge. Nica grabbed Max by the scruff of the neck and put the barrel of the gun against his temple, narrowing his eyes at Hugo. "Stay here until I can't see you anymore. You try to leave, he goes in the water." Like crabs locked together, the two men edged backward toward the boat, sidling at the edge of the walkway. "Until I can't see you," Nica called out. "And I will watch."

Hugo looked at the face behind the gun and felt adrenaline course through his body, urging him to act. But he knew better than to challenge an armed man, he'd seen the results of that before, so he just clenched his jaw and nodded, committing Nica's features to memory before looking one more time at the terrified Max, whose eyes implored Hugo for help.

In less than a minute the men were on the launch, leaving Hugo helpless on the walkway, his hands twitching for his gun, or at least his phone. But he couldn't risk consigning the bouquiniste to the slick gray water, so he did as he'd been told and watched as the boat revved loud and swung away, heading east against the current, passing in the lea of Notre Dame.

He was a statue on the walkway, turned to stone by the figure at the stern of the boat, the sharp-featured man who stood watch over him and also over his victim, the huddled form of the old bouquiniste at his feet. Hugo glared back, his eyes fixed on the boat until it finally rounded the tip of the Ile de la Cité and disappeared from view.

CHAPTER THREE

Hugo stood by Max's stall and told his story to the first gendarme on the scene, a waif of a man who spoke no English and kept his pen and notepad busy as Hugo talked. A small crowd gathered behind the policeman, wide-eyed but wary, drawn like moths to the blue light that flashed atop his little white car.

"Wait here please, sir," the policeman said. "There is a detective *en route*, he will take your statement."

"Look, forget the statement. Right now I want your river police looking for that boat, maybe a helicopter, too. A man with a gun just kidnapped a friend of mine, in broad daylight and—"

"I heard you, sir," the gendarme interrupted. He looked over his shoulder as an unmarked car pulled up behind his. "*Voila*, the detective. Talk to him about that, I don't have the authority."

The detective was tall and lean, with the dark skin and hooked nose that spoke of Arab descent. He wore a green woolen sweater under an open overcoat and a matching ski hat that was pulled low over his ears. He slammed his car door, then looked up at the sky, sighed, and walked slowly over to the gendarme. He stood frowning as he listened to the hurried briefing, his hands deep in his pockets. When the gendarme had finished, the detective nodded and walked over to Hugo. He drew a hand out of his pocket and offered it to Hugo. It was ice cold.

"I'm told you are one of us, *mon ami*," he said. He spoke in French, his voice low and worn as if he'd spent all day smoking the unfiltered cigarettes that Hugo could smell on him. "My name's David Durand."

"Hugo Marston. What do you mean, 'one of us'?" Hugo asked.

"Law enforcement." He nodded toward the gendarme. "He says you work at the American embassy, speak French fluently, and carry a gun."

"Former FBI, now security chief at the embassy," Hugo said. "Look, I don't mean to be rude, but—"

"I have given the order for our river police to look for the boat you described. If a helicopter can be found, we'll send one up to help. But it will be dark soon and the pilots complain when we make them fly at night, especially so close to the center of the city. Not safe, they say." He shivered and looked around. "Can you wait for a few moments? We have some witnesses I need to talk to."

"Of course," said Hugo, watching Durand approach a small group of onlookers. Hugo was comforted by the assurances of police boats, and maybe a chopper, but equally irritated by the man's languid attitude, his unhurried walk, as if this were a burglary with the intruders long gone.

Hugo turned and looked out over the water, picturing Max out there somewhere. He acted the gruff, tough guy, and maybe he once was, but Max was no longer young. Hugo had no idea what the thug Nica had wanted from his friend, but it wasn't some random shakedown. He wanted something specific and Hugo wondered what he would do to get it. His face flushed with anger as he imagined them hurting Max, beating a weak old man. Even if he had the mental toughness to resist, Hugo knew that violence to someone Max's age, even a minor assault, could prove too much for an old heart. Whoever had Max, whoever wanted something from him, could kill him without meaning to. Without even trying.

Hugo spun around when he heard the detective behind him. Durand had a frown on his face and dark green eyes watched Hugo intently. "*Monsieur, un problème*. I have spoken to two people who say that your friend got onto the boat of his own free will."

Hugo stared at the detective, wondering if he'd misheard or if his mind had somehow mistranslated. "What did you say?"

"Two witnesses, monsieur. They say your friend left of his own free will."

"*Non*, that's not possible, it's not . . . Who are the witnesses?"

"Why? Do you plan to make them change their stories?" It was said lightly, but the watchfulness in Durand's eyes remained.

"Of course not." Hugo bit back his anger. "Look, the man had a gun, I can give you a description, I can pick him out of a line up. And I can assure you, Max did not go with him voluntarily."

The detective looked out across the water, a black ribbon in the gathering dusk. "*Bien.*" He turned to the gendarme. "Make sure you have a full statement, every possible detail. I will go supervise the search. If they are still out there, we will find them."

"*Oui,* monsieur," said the officer, flipping open his notepad.

Durand took a last look at Hugo, then turned and walked to his car, the word "if" hanging between them.

Max had been right—the snow began to fall twenty minutes later as Hugo was walking home. He crossed the street into Rue Jacob and paused for a moment, bemused and angry by what had just happened, somehow unwilling to enjoy, perhaps undeserving of, the warmth and comfort of his apartment.

He took off his hat so the flakes could tickle his face and opened his mouth like a child, letting them fizz on his tongue. He walked on, the sense of unreality that had settled around him magnified as the falling snow muffled the sound of his footsteps on the sidewalk. He paused again, once, and thought he could hear a hiss as the snow hit the ground and melted. The flakes were large, though, and stuck to his coat and hair, so he knew they'd stick to the ground soon enough.

At the door to his apartment building he stopped and looked up and down the street. A hush had descended, the quiet that comes with the start of a heavy snowfall. He turned, wiped his boots on the large mat, and went into the foyer, nodding at the Cretian concierge who sat at the reception desk with a novel in his hand.

"*Salut*, Dimitrios." Hugo took off his hat and batted the snow from it.

"*Bonsoir, monsieur.*" Dimitrios sprang to his feet. A wiry old man with a brush moustache, he looked after his tenants as though his life depended on it. "How are you? Friday night plans?"

"No, I've had my excitement for this week." Hugo shook his head and kept moving. "Have a good night, Dimitrios."

"*Merci. Vous aussi, monsieur.*"

Hugo trotted up the stairs to his apartment, passing straight through the living room and into his bedroom. He dropped the Rimbaud and the Agatha Christie on the bed and unholstered his gun, a Glock 19, and laid it next to the books. Then he knelt in front of a safe that he'd had specially built. Disguised as his bedside table, it was essentially a steel box with an elegant mahogany facing, and it was bolted to the wall beside his bed. He opened the safe and put his gun on the narrow shelf next to a larger, wooden-handled Smith & Wesson.

Hugo checked the time, six o'clock, so midday in America. A good time to call Christine again, but he had some things to do first. He wanted to call Max's home, go there in person just to prove to himself that what he'd witnessed really happened, that Max hadn't been a party to his own kidnap. But he realized that he didn't even know Max's last name, let alone his address or phone number. A vague recollection that they'd swapped last names, sure, probably over coffee or beer at their favorite dive, Chez Maman, but it wasn't close to the tip of his tongue, and he felt a little ashamed about that. Instead, he dialed the police prefecture and asked for Detective Durand. Three dead-ends later, a man's voice came on the line.

"Monsieur, you are looking for David Durand?"

"*Oui.*"

"*Alors*, he is not available. Can someone else help you?"

"Is he on duty and not available, or gone-home-for-the-day not available?"

The voice hesitated. "I'm not sure. Unavailable is all I know. Would you like to leave your name and number?"

"That depends," Hugo said tautly. "When will he get the message?"

"I can't say for sure. When he is available, I suppose. I know he works on Sundays."

Hugo hung up the phone, swore under his breath, and thought about calling his boss, the ambassador. But he had no real reason to pull strings, not yet at least. As far as he knew, Durand was out searching for Max, directing a manhunt on both sides of the Seine. But when he pictured the lethargic detective, he couldn't help but doubt it.

Instead, he perched on the bed and took a calming breath. He was not used to being shut out of an investigation, either by intent or through bureaucracy, and it was especially frustrating when his friend was the one who needed help, who needed very badly to be rescued—and soon. He looked at the phone. If he couldn't help Max, he thought, then maybe he could do something positive about the situation with Christine.

He picked up the phone and dialed. When her cell phone sent him to voicemail, for the second time that day, he tried her home number.

A man answered. "Hello?"

"May I speak with Christine, please?"

"Certainly." The familiar voice paused. "Is this Hugo?"

"That's Mr. Marston to you, doc."

"Look, I'm glad you called. I never had a chance to explain—"

"There's nothing to explain," Hugo interrupted. "You had an affair with a married woman who also happened to be your patient. And my wife. Now hand her the phone because there's nothing you have to say that I want to hear, and anything I have to say will be uncivil."

A moment later, Christine came on the line. "Hugo?"

"Howdy. So is the good doctor a permanent resident now?"

"I'm a divorced woman, remember. You don't have the moral high ground anymore."

"Funny thing, Christine. Even when I had the moral high ground, you were the one who acted outraged." He took a breath. "I'm sorry, I didn't call to argue with you."

"Good, I don't want that either. Your message said something about coming over."

"Yes, but I can't now. Something's come up."

A moment's silence. "Well, there's a surprise."

"Take it easy, Chrissy, it's not my fault."

"It never is." She sounded weary now. "That's just how it works in your world."

"And yet still you blame me."

"You chose that world, not me."

"I don't want to rehash old arguments, Chrissy, I'd just like to be able to come over and talk to you. If this . . . situation gets sorted out."

"Hugo, no. I'm sorry, I really am. But . . . I've moved on."

"Moved on? I suppose I shouldn't blame you for that."

"Thank you." He could hear the sadness in her voice, but tempered by a smile. "You always were insufferably understanding."

"Thanks, but I'd like to know if there's any chance of you moving back."

"No, there isn't."

"You're not even willing to talk about it?"

"No, Hugo. I really have moved on, so there's nothing left to talk about. I'm sorry."

He thought, for a few seconds, about pushing harder, but he knew her well enough to take her at her word. "Well, you can't blame me for trying," he said. "You were quite a catch."

"Were? Thanks a lot."

He smiled at her mock outrage and looked down at the two books beside him. "Hey, this may sound weird but I bought you a couple of presents. OK if I mail them to you?"

"Oh. No, I really don't think—"

"A couple of books for your collection. One's a Hercule Poirot mystery, first edition, and the other is . . . kind of like an Oscar Wilde, but more personal."

"You're very thoughtful. But you're right, it would be weird. Please don't send them." Her voice caught and he knew she was about to cry. "Please, I thought I'd got past all this, you're making it difficult again."

"OK, don't worry about it. I'll keep the books."

"I'm sorry. I really am."

"Me too. Take care of yourself."

He hung up and dropped the phone on the bed. He picked up the Rimbaud and looked at the cover, then set it back down. He didn't feel much like homosexual love poetry, either.

But what had he expected from Christine, really? They'd been matched up by socialite friends after their first marriages had ended, and they'd talked about being in love because of the fun they had, and the sex. But had they ever gotten around to falling in love? Marriage had seemed easier the second time around, especially without the pressure of new careers to distract them. And the gloss had been thick. His job as security chief in Washington, DC, had been prestigious and was followed by an exciting two years as head of security at the London embassy, with parties and meetings with heads of state and celebrities from all over the world.

And, of course, his stories from the FBI. All this had entertained Christine, kept her starry-eyed and impressed. She had been, too, an intelligent and attractive companion, someone he could discuss international politics with until their third or fourth martinis drowned all semblance of coherent thought.

It took a while for him to discover that everything she knew came from books or television. Not until the last year had he realized that, despite all her wonderful traits, a sense of adventure was absent. And adventure, the curiosity to explore a place or thing in person, to lay hands on it and see it with his own eyes rather than just read about it, that was what drove Hugo Marston. They had traveled, sure, but with her family wealth they had done so in comfort, even when in Mumbai or Windhoek. Perhaps especially then. Hugo, from a modest background, had been seduced by this comfort and had slipped into his wife's travel habits. He hadn't noticed until too late that he'd not inhaled the scents of the Cairo markets, or haggled poorly with a vendor in downtown Delhi, but instead had watched from the car as their driver did it for him. But even knowing all this, he'd still believed they had a chance because knowing someone was more important than what the movies and novels described as love.

He picked up both books and put them on the bedside table. As he did so, the Agatha Christie fell open and a business card fell to the floor. He picked it up: it was the card of a Paris bookseller, one Hugo had visited once, maybe twice, over the years. It bore the seller's name, address, and hours of operation. Hugo looked down at the books. He would have liked to add them to his meager collection, but the damn things had just become keepsakes of a marriage ended, and they were unhappy reminders of what had just happened to Max, too. As he imagined selling them, his mind searched for reasons not to, and came up blank. One thought, a vague one, was that they might be connected with Max's kidnap, but it was a possibility easily dismissed: bouquinistes weren't kidnapped for books worth a few hundred dollars—if they were, a seller would go missing every day. And if the man called Nica had been after one of the books, Max would simply have told Hugo to hand it over.

Hugo ran a hand over his face, frustrated and tired, and thought about running a hot bath. That's what he needed now. Tomorrow morning he'd try again to find answers about what had happened to Max. He lay the card on top of the books and headed into the bathroom.

CHAPTER FOUR

It was still dark when Hugo called the prefecture the next morning, Saturday, hoping that a shift change might also mean a change in attitude. After five minutes on hold he was told, politely this time, that Durand had gone off duty.

"There is no one in charge of that investigation, monsieur. It has been flagged in the system as a hoax or mistake."

Hugo slammed the phone down and sat staring at it for a long minute before sinking back onto the bed. *Hoax or mistake?* They hadn't even looked for Max, let alone found him, and fear for the old man rose inside Hugo. The first twenty-four hours of an investigation were the most crucial, and too many hours had already been squandered. He knew that, in reality, Max's captors would be the ones to determine whether he turned up safe.

The phone rang beside him and he grabbed it, hoping desperately that it was a return call from the prefecture, or Durand himself, an apology for the confusion and an update on the search. It took him a moment to recognize the voice on the other end, but the words were familiar enough.

"Hugo. Fuck me, is that really you?"

"Yes. Is this . . . Tom?"

Tom Green had been his friend ever since they shared a room at the FBI Academy in Quantico, almost twenty years ago. A wisp of a man, Tom was a law school graduate with three pairs of spectacles, more books than clothes, and an unexpectedly foul mouth. At first his language shocked the well-mannered Texan, but they shared a dry sense of humor and a certain skepticism of the more gung-ho recruits.

Tom sailed through the academic portions of the training, but probably wouldn't have made it on the firing range and the physical training course without Hugo's help.

"Damn right. What time is it over there?"

Hugo glanced at the clock. "Six in the morning."

"So it's midnight here. Couldn't be bothered to look at my watch. Thought I'd call you instead."

"Where are you, Tom? Is everything OK?"

They had both been assigned to the LA field office straight out of the academy and they stayed in touch even when Hugo left the bureau for the State Department twelve years later, recruited to run security at the US Embassy in Pakistan. Hugo had turned down several such offers before, but when his first wife, Ellie, died in a car accident, he jumped at the chance to put himself in harm's way. Tom was the only one to recognize that his friend was looking for an excuse to get blown up, but he drove him to the airport anyway. A month later Tom left to work for the CIA, unable to tell Hugo where he was going or what he was doing. They'd not spoken for over a year, and Hugo regretted that every time he thought about Tom.

"Stateside, don't worry. Half asleep on the couch, if you want details."

"You can't afford a bed these days?"

"I'm in America, Hugo. An old, fat guy asleep on the couch is nothing new."

Fat? He didn't used to be, and there was more than sleep in the voice. Slurring. "Are you drunk, Tom?"

"Not yet. I was waiting for you."

"Funny you should say that. I just spoke to Christine, I'd been hoping to come over, maybe try and patch things up."

"Hookers getting too pricey for you?"

"We're talking about me here, Tom," Hugo grinned. "Anyway, she doesn't want me coming back."

"That sucks. She found someone else already?"

"She hooked up with her shrink."

"Shit, Hugo, I'm sorry."

"Thanks. It can't be helped."

"Living in the same fucking country might have helped."

"Yeah, Christine already mentioned that."

"She's right. You want to come over anyway? I got plenty of time and plenty to drink."

"I'll think about it. Something odd happened yesterday I have to deal with. If everything works out OK, then maybe." Hugo hoped so, very much. "Wait, how come you have so much free time? Get fired?"

"Fuck you." There was a pause. "Actually, I'm now retired. Retired and getting bored out of my mind."

"Seriously? I didn't get the party invite. When did that happen?"

"Well, it's a half-assed retirement. Occasional consulting, mostly sitting around waiting for the phone to ring. You spend years learning how to pick locks, follow spies, and torture Arabs and then, when you know what the fuck you are doing, they give you a wristwatch and tell you to fuck off."

"Was it a nice watch?"

"Screw you. Anyway, I begged them not to do it so they put me on the Europe desk, as a consultant like I said. Right now they have their eyes on a couple of corporate-espionage douche bags in Marseilles, so I might pop over and see you one of these days. And I have all my access codes and a fancy new computer at home, so if there's anything I can do to help out with your stuff, just call."

"Thanks. I don't think there's anything right now, but you never know."

"OK. Genuine offer, so call if I can help."

Hugo heard an unfamiliar note in his friend's voice, a mix of disappointment and entreaty, like a kid finding his second most-wanted toy under the tree at Christmas. Hugo prodded, gently. "You sure you're OK?"

"Yeah, just a little bored. Didn't mean to be needy, but you know how it goes; seems like geezers of our generation are all getting pulled out of the field, one way or another. Most spooks my age are retired or dead, and as a reward for staying alive they gave me a crappy desk job."

"Staying warm, dry, and safe isn't so bad. That's what I do."

"Yeah, I keep telling myself that. Trouble is, I'm not listening. But shit, I'm lucky to be around still, so I'm fine, just letting off steam."

Hugo heard his friend yawn. "OK," he said. "Then I'll let you get to sleep."

"Yeah, I need your permission for that. Anything else?"

"Yes. I like the idea of you coming to see me sometime. Call if you can make it. Or just show up, OK?"

Hugo opened the large windows in the living room and stepped out onto the small, iron balcony that overlooked Rue Jacob. He had willingly paid extra to live on the fifth floor, wanting to be high enough so that the noise of foot and road traffic could be shut out or allowed in whenever he wanted. He inhaled deeply and let the crisp air drift past him into his apartment. Raised on a ranch outside of Austin, city living had taken some getting used to. No matter the weather, he preferred to have fresh air in the apartment. It was one of his quirks that Christine, always cold, had failed to appreciate.

The street lay under a blanket of white, and the snow on the few parked cars showed that a good four inches had fallen in the night. The gray sky was tinged with blue now, and a breeze blew the occasional puff of white from the rooftops. Someone nearby had a fire going and the air was scented with wood smoke. After a minute he shivered and went inside, closing the windows behind him. He put on a second pot of coffee and, as it brewed, he stood by the gas fire in his living room, thinking about the day before.

Who had said Max got on the boat voluntarily? Had the cops been to his apartment and found him alive and well? He wanted to go there himself, but without help from the police he had no real way of finding out where the old man lived.

Tom. *Of course!* Hugo dialed his friend's number, suddenly excited at the chance to do something, but after five rings it went to voicemail and Hugo snapped his phone shut in frustration. He looked around the room, as if inspiration lay waiting to be discovered, a feeling growing within him that he had to be doing *something*. He remembered the business card from the Agatha Christie novel, fetched it, and carried it into the spare bedroom, which he'd converted into his office. Another frustration. The store on Rue Barrault, advertised on the card, wasn't open yet and wouldn't be for three hours.

Hugo sat at his desk to do some embassy work. It didn't need doing, it could wait until after his vacation, but until he could do something for Max his mind needed the distraction.

An envoy from Zimbabwe was coming to Paris to meet with select American and European dignitaries. As the United States had never colonized any part of Africa, the US Embassy was often a good place for those types of meetings, free from the taint of history. Ironic, Hugo always thought, given America's leading role in the slave trade and more recent financing of certain political leaders in the Congo. But it wasn't his job to worry about the politics. He had to make sure the various security details coordinated so that there weren't fifty bodyguards and twenty armored cars for three dignitaries. Especially at the US Embassy, he liked to have his men take on the close supervision. In truth, most of the third world visitors liked it, too. They knew how well-trained his men were and, sometimes, they didn't entirely trust their own.

He worked slowly, with several breaks for coffee and visits to the balcony to enjoy the cool but slowly warming day. It took him two full hours to synthesize the schedules of the visitors, and to rearrange those of his chief agents to make sure each one managed a shift for the five days of the visit.

At eight-thirty he switched off his computer. Still an hour until the book store opened, but there was somewhere he needed to go first. Just to see.

Outside the street was empty except for an old couple brushing snow from their car with their sleeves. They paid Hugo no attention as he passed, heading toward Rue de Buci. Ever the Texan, he still had an urge to greet people on the street, but after years of being ignored or looked at as if he were selling something, he'd learned to do as the locals did: tuck his head down, watch his step, and mind his own way.

As he rounded into Rue de Buci he caught the aromas of its market. Most compelling was the stall of fresh fish. Row after row of cod, haddock, and octopus, and behind them the wiry fishmonger eyeing passersby as he wielded a bloody hatchet over his chopping block, a purple scarf wound tightly around his neck. Hugo had always been amused that beside the fishmonger's was the florist's stand, bursting with wild and greenhouse blooms. A weekly battle of the senses, with the dead fish always triumphing over the dying flowers.

He stopped at a café and bought a croissant and a cup of coffee, swallowing both at the bar, then headed back outside.

At the end of Rue de Buci he turned left onto Rue Dauphine, named for the son of Henry IV roughly four hundred years before, and headed north toward the Seine. This street was busier and Hugo turned up his collar to fend off the melting snow blown from the trees, whose branches waved and rustled overhead as the wind gathered itself.

He picked his way past the slush and melting ice and five minutes later was back at the Quai des Grands Augustins, waiting for a break in the traffic. He crossed, his heart quickening as he spotted a figure at Max's open stall, a man taking money from a young lady who labored under a backpack that was roughly the same size as she was. Hugo hurried toward them, hardly daring to hope for the impossible.

Thirty yards away he stopped and his heart sank.

The man had turned away from the girl toward Hugo, a smirk on his face. He was smaller and thinner than Max, and considerably younger. He looked a little like the mailman Hugo had known as a kid, a man nicknamed by his parents (rather unkindly, he'd always thought) the Weasel. Hugo started forward again, taking in the man's features. He had a delicate and very un-French nose, a weak fulcrum for the man's thin lips and close eyes. His whole face seemed narrow, Hugo thought, as if he'd spent his life with his head in his hands.

As Hugo drew nearer, the man looked him up and down without subtlety.

"*Bonjour, monsieur*," the man said, his eyes on Hugo's clothes. Hugo wondered if the man was counting the threads in his coat as a proxy for the fullness of his wallet. "Are you looking for anything in particular? I have plenty of rare books, you see, and a few items of a more . . . mature nature, if monsieur is interested."

Towering over the man, Hugo decided to employ one of the most powerful tools of the interrogator—silence. Hugo ignored him as he scrutinized the stall, leaving the little man to flit around, trying to appear busy yet available to serve at the same time. "*Vous avez choisi, monsieur?*" You have chosen something? His accent, Hugo thought, was not Parisian. He rolled his Rs almost like a Spaniard.

"*Non*," said Hugo. "Tell me, where is Max?"

"Max?" Something closed down in the seller's eyes. He took a step back and began to caress his chin. "I don't know any Max, monsieur." The man picked up a stack of postcards from a battered card table and began to sort through them.

"No? You're working at his stall." Hugo looked around. "He is your *patron, non*?"

"I am my own boss." The man's tone was brusque, and he stopped what he was doing to look at the American. "*Alors*, who are you?"

"A friend of Max's." Hugo took a step forward. "And you know who he is. This is his stall."

"*Non*, this is my stall." The seller was not to be intimidated, despite the difference of a foot and fifty pounds. "You are not the police, are you?" He moved closer to Hugo and his thin mouth drew into a slight smile. "I think not, and I also think I do not have to answer your questions, monsieur. So unless you want to buy a book or maybe some postcards, please leave."

Hugo took off his hat and brushed the brim. *Fine, then we'll do it this way.* He looked at the man and took a step back.

"I apologize for my rudeness," Hugo said. "I am tired, and a little disappointed not to find *mon ami*." He flashed his most disarming smile. "I have many friends looking for books, I will be sure to refer them to your stall, monsieur . . . ?"

The man shifted from foot to foot, his suspicions softened by the charm and sincerity of a student of behavioral sciences. "Chabot. Jean Chabot."

"*Alors*, Monsieur Chabot, thank you for your time and please accept my apologies for any rudeness." Hugo executed a quick bow and turned on his heel before Chabot could respond.

Ten yards from the bouquiniste Hugo's path was blocked by another pedestrian, a tall, thin man in a trench coat carrying a bone-handled cane. He wore gloves but no hat, and stared at Hugo without moving. It was an unusual moment of aggression, asserted passively in a city where people moved out of each other's way as a matter of course.

Unable to help himself, Hugo took a moment to appraise the fellow. Many years ago, while at the bureau, he had taken a course that touched on phrenology, a technique premised on the idea that you can tell something of a man's nature by his skull. Had it not been a discredited pseudoscience, the guy on the sidewalk could have been the instructor's first slide.

He had, Hugo thought, one of those faces that you couldn't help but stare at, and not because it was beautiful. He was completely bald with large and very round eyes, set in deep, dark circles beneath a broad forehead. Below a prominent nose, his wide mouth dipped down at the edges as if he'd grown used to frowning at life's disappointments. Actors had made their livings with this face, Hugo thought, playing the gaunt and chiseled crook whose head made you think *skull*.

Hugo stepped around the man, but close enough so their coats brushed, the American unwilling to give ground completely. Once past him, Hugo smiled at his own machismo. *Christine would have rolled her eyes and made some comment about dick measuring*, he thought.

He reached Pont Neuf and looked back at the stall, surprised to see the bouquiniste pointing toward him. The man with the cane stared in his direction while the bookseller spoke animatedly. Hugo hesitated, wondering if he should go back. Maybe the seller was asking who Max was, which meant this guy might know. But as he watched, the tall newcomer drew back his hand and slapped the seller across the face.

The response was as surprising as the blow: Chabot held up both hands as if he were apologizing.

Hugo forced himself to keep walking. As curious as he was, he had no desire to insert himself into whatever dispute existed between these men. And, more importantly, he needed information before risking a confrontation with either one. Despite his earlier clumsy attempt with Chabot, blundering into a situation was not the way he usually worked.

He looked across the street, but Max's colleague, the red-faced woman with the bottle, had not opened her stall, perhaps put off by the previous day's encounter or, maybe, by the cold. He wanted very badly to talk to her about her "*affaire domestique*," to find out if that confrontation had anything to do with Max, and to see if she'd been one of the "witnesses" who gave a false story to the police. He'd come by again later and, hopefully, see her then.

As Hugo crossed the street and walked away from the river, a darkness settled about him and the traffic, the people, faded from his immediate consciousness. All he could think about was a friend taken from him, literally, a friend no one seemed to know or care about, and a crime that wasn't even close to being in his jurisdiction.

CHAPTER FIVE

The bookstore was further than Hugo had thought, partly because he opted for the more interesting walk down Rue Saint-Jacques over the busier Rue Monges, where the snow would be gray slush already. It took an hour, with a quick stop at a timbered café for to-go coffee and a *pain au chocolat*, to reach Rue Barrault.

A bell jingled quietly as he walked in, and as the door closed the familiar and distinctive aroma of once-loved books swept over him, the musty smell of paper and dust like incense, a welcoming cloud of calm and serenity. Hugo looked around. Heavy wooden book cases lined the side and back walls, filled with a colorful array of mostly leather-bound books that looked like they had been arranged by size rather than subject. Several small tables took up floor space, each bearing one or two glass cases in which the more valuable tomes were displayed under lock and key. The two ceiling-high bookcases at the back of the room sat on either side of a closed door. Hugo walked around the shop, looking at the books on sale.

"*Bonjour, monsieur.*" The door at the back opened and a man stood there smiling. He was short and probably fifty years old, with a full round belly and a closely trimmed white beard. "I thought I heard someone come in," he said. He stepped into the room and closed the door behind him. His movements were precise, careful, as if he were maneuvering in a tiny library where the books were in precarious stacks, not tucked away on shelves. He wore a pair of baggy corduroy pants and a paisley vest over a shirt that Hugo assumed had once been white. On his feet, a pair of slippers. When he spoke, he crinkled his nose so that his tortoise-shell spectacles shifted upwards and he was able to see his subject. His voice was as delicate, and his diction as precise, as his movements. He spoke in French. "Are you just browsing, or may I be of assistance?"

"*Bonjour.*" Hugo held up the two books. "I wanted to ask you about these, if you don't mind."

"*Bien sur.*" Of course. The old man cocked his head and spoke in English. "American?"

"Yes," Hugo said. "You?"

"English. Couldn't stand the weather so I popped over here and started a book shop." The man walked over and offered his hand. "Peter Kendall. That was thirty-two years ago, and I still hate the English weather."

"Me too," Hugo smiled, shaking his hand. "Hugo Marston."

"I think you've been here before. So, what do you have there?"

Hugo showed Kendall the covers, looking to gauge the man's response. It was minimal. "I wondered if you'd seen these books before."

"Let's have a look." Kendall took them and walked over to the window where the light was better. "Mind if I take them out of their plastic covers?"

"Not at all. I don't know if they are worth much, but I'm sort of curious to know whether I . . ."

"Got ripped off?"

"Got a good deal, let's put it that way."

"Very good. Follow me." Kendall started toward the door at the back of the room and Hugo followed him into his office, which was half as big as the store itself and dominated by a large mahogany desk. As Kendall rounded it and sank into his chair, Hugo picked one of the two wing-backed seats opposite. Kendall opened a desk drawer and pulled out a magnifying glass and a letter opener. "Do you mind if I ask where you bought them?" he said.

"A bouquiniste," Hugo said. "I know one of the sellers pretty well and sometimes buy from him." Hugo watched the man closely, teeing up his question and waiting for a reaction. "Do you know a bouquiniste called Max?"

Kendall furrowed his brow, but his hands never moved and his eyes showed nothing. "I might. By Pont Neuf?"

"That's him."

"I've bought a few things from him, yes. Can't say I know him well, but I will say he seems like one of the few out there who gives a hoot about the books he sells." Kendall sat back and looked at the ceiling. "Just sold him a few books about the war, come to think of it. Old, rather dry tomes, though I'm buggered if I can remember what they were."

"That's OK." Hugo nodded toward the Agatha Christie. "I ask because your card was in that book."

"Ah, yes," Kendall smiled. "She's one of my favorites and her books are a specialty of mine, you might say. She was friends with my mother, you see, back in the old country."

"I'm also asking because Max has disappeared."

The smile fell from Kendall's face. "What do you mean?"

"I wish I knew," Hugo said. "I'm just . . . concerned about him."

"I'm sorry." He spread his hands wide. "I don't know what to tell you, I haven't seen him in weeks."

Hugo believed him. His body language, his open face, both rang as true as his words. So: dead end.

Hugo looked at the books. "Can you tell if they're worth much?"

"I can hazard a guess."

Hugo watched as Kendall wielded the letter opener like a scalpel, opening the wrapping of the Agatha Christie with deft flicks of the wrist. "Well, this is a first edition, as I'm sure you know. Like the ones I have out there. I'd guess it'd sell for about three hundred Euros. Give or take. It's a nice copy for sure, and being an Agatha Christie it should sell fast enough."

"Good to know."

"Now, let's have a look at this one." He picked up the Rimbaud and eased it out of its sleeve and onto the desk. He reached for his magnifying glass and studied the book, front and back, for a moment. "That's odd." He looked up at Hugo. "Did you say how much you paid?"

"I didn't. I paid a thousand Euros for both."

Kendall leaned over and switched on his computer, picking up a pair of thin white gloves as he turned back to the book. He put them on and opened the front cover, leaning over it with his glass. "Well, that's something."

Hugo remembered Max's words. "There's some scribble in the front."

"There is." Kendall hunched closer over the inside cover. "I assume it's scribble, anyway."

"What do you mean?"

"Did he tell you it was a first edition?"

"What?" Hugo leaned forward. Max had said it wasn't, surely he'd have known.

"I agree that it seems unlikely," Kendall said pensively. He turned to his computer and spent a minute browsing and clicking. "You know, I think it is. And from what the Internet tells me, a good quality first edition of this book will sell for between twenty and forty thousand US dollars. I imagine thirty thousand is realistic."

"Seriously?" Hugo said. For some reason, he couldn't help but picture the boots he would like to buy Max. Hell, for that money he could fly him to Fort Worth, first class, and let him choose his own.

"Now then." Kendall held up a finger. "Your copy is in good condition but it appears to be missing the original box in which it was sold. You don't happen to have it, do you?"

"I don't."

"Shame." Kendall stroked the front of the book with his gloved fingers. "Even so, Mr. Marston. Well, let me do some research but I think you have a treasure here."

"Look," said Hugo, "any chance you could do your research and then handle the sale for me?"

It was a snap decision, the kind Hugo rarely made. But suddenly the books seemed like bad luck. Since he'd laid hands on them, Max had been kidnapped and Christine had closed the door of their marriage in his face, forever. His urge to get shot of them was a gut reaction, not a logical decision, and he knew that. He simply didn't want to see these books, touch them, ever again.

"Me?" Kendall chuckled. "I run a book shop, Mr. Marston, not Fort Knox. The most valuable thing I have here is worth less than a thousand Euros. I just don't have the security to house this sort of gem. Now, I do know people at the auction houses, so I could put you in touch, if you like."

"Honestly, I'm happy to trust you with them. Your store is as secure as my apartment, which is where I'd be keeping it." Hugo pictured his specially-made gun safe, knowing that security wasn't the issue for him, not really. "And I'm not that worried about the money side of things, even though it's a lot. If you handle it, I'm happy to pay you a good commission."

"Well, it might be fun." Kendall stroked his beard with his finger-tips. "And it's not like people break into used book stores very often. It's only happened here once and they raided the cash register, not the books."

"Perfect, just hide it in plain sight on one of the shelves."

"Very well then," Kendall said. "I'll have to consult with a fellow I know at Christie's, but I do think an auction is your best bet."

"I'll leave it to you."

"Very good, let me just get you a receipt." A minute later, he handed the receipt, containing a full description of the book, the date, and his own signature, to Hugo. "I hope that will suffice. If it's of any consola-tion, I don't just do this job for a living, Mr. Marston. I do it because I enjoy seeing book lovers get the books they want." His eyes twinkled. "What I am trying to say, is—"

"That my book is safe in your hands. I understand." Hugo smiled. "I appreciate your assistance, although I would be more comfortable if you would take a decent percentage."

Kendall thought for a moment, then reached for the receipt. "I shall add here that I may deduct expenses and keep a fee of . . . shall we say one hundred Euros?"

"You can say a lot more than that, if you like," Hugo said.

"A hundred Euros it is," Kendall said, finishing with a flourish of the pen. He looked at Hugo and smiled. "Just to handle a book like this is its own reward, I really mean that. Do you want me to put the Agatha Christie on sale, too?"

"Yes, please. I assume that won't go to auction."

"Probably not."

"Thank you." The men shook hands and Hugo reached into his wallet for a business card. "This has all my contact information." He rose. "Let me know how it goes."

"I will. And Mr. Marston?"

"Yes."

"Please, if you get news of Max I'd be grateful for a phone call. Like I said before, I don't know him well but he's . . . I don't know. A dying breed, perhaps. One of a kind. You know what I mean?"

"I do," said Hugo. "He is. And when I find him, I'll call you."

Hugo spent the rest of Saturday trying to find Max's house. Tom was still not answering his phone, but one of the other bouquinistes gave Hugo Max's last name, or what he thought it was: Cloche. But four hours on the Internet, running free searches and using pay sites, gave him nothing.

CHAPTER SIX

On Sunday morning, Hugo stationed himself on the busy Boulevard de Palais, near the exit to the metro stop closest to the Prefecture de Police. He walked in large circles, the police station always in view, hoping that the mid-morning tourist traffic and his hat and coat collar would give him the element of surprise.

He saw his man as soon as he emerged from the metro, the thin figure sporting the familiar heavy overcoat and woolen ski hat. Hugo hurried across the street and caught up to him at the front steps of the prefecture.

"*Excusez moi,* Detective Durand," he said.

The detective turned, his hooded eyes taking a moment to make the connection. "Ah, Monsieur Marston. How can I help you?"

"A progress report would be nice." Hugo decided to gauge Durand's response before mentioning the so-called hoax/mistake investigation.

"Not much to say, sadly." Durand frowned and looked down, as if thinking. "We searched the river that night but found no boat matching the description you gave. No one of the alleged victim's description turned up, either, in the hospitals or morgue." He turned his eyes onto Hugo. "And of course, we still have those witnesses who say your friend went onto the boat voluntarily."

"I suppose you're not willing to give me the names of those witnesses," Hugo said, forcing himself to remain calm.

"I cannot, I'm sorry."

"You can," Hugo said. "I'm one of us, remember."

"*Non. Je m'excuse.*" Durand started to turn away but Hugo gripped his sleeve.

"So the investigation is over?"

"*Non*. The description of your friend, and the boat, remains with our men on the street. If an unidentified person shows up in an ambulance or hearse, that person will be checked to see if it is him. Now, unless you know something you are not telling me, I don't quite see what more I can do."

"You can start by changing the designation of the investigation. It's neither a hoax nor a mistake."

Durand raised an eyebrow. "Who told you that?"

"What difference does it make?"

The detective stepped closer and Hugo smelled the stale cigarettes on his breath, saw the little flecks of gold in the angry green eyes. "Monsieur. I appreciate you are not used to being in this situation and that usually you are in my shoes. However, I have done my job and will continue to do it. Now, please let go of my arm. Right now."

A new voice snapped out behind Hugo. "What's going on here?"

Durand stiffened, his eyes wary now.

So the newcomer is your superior. Hugo turned to look at the man who'd spoken. He was short and fat, with a polka-dot bow tie scrunched under the lowest of several round chins. He immediately reminded Hugo of the wily Hercule Poirot with his dark, watchful eyes and balding, egg-shaped head. He also had the moustache, though this man's was a thin line rather than the thick and oiled specimen worn by Agatha Christie's sleuth.

"Just trying to get some information," Hugo said. "No big deal."

"I am Capitaine Raul Garcia," the man said.

"Hugo Marston."

"A tourist?"

"Head of security at the US Embassy. I live here."

Garcia nodded and watched Hugo for a moment, then his eyes slid down to Hugo's hand, which still gripped Durand's sleeve. Garcia smiled, like a conjuror withholding the secret to a magic trick. "*Bien*. Pleased to meet you. However, I'm sure you appreciate that even an American colleague has no need to lay hands on one of my detectives."

Hugo held his eye. This was an olive branch, a chance for Hugo to back off. Behind the soft words, though, it was clear whose side Garcia would take.

Hugo released Durand's sleeve and opened his mouth to say something, but Garcia brushed past him and, with a flick of his wrist, directed his junior detective into the prefecture. Hugo clenched his jaw and started after them, but another gesture from Garcia sent two uniformed gendarmes to block his way. Hugo didn't feel like a fight, and being arrested by the French cops would take some explaining to his own boss.

He walked away from the prefecture, avoiding the riverfront even though he knew all the stalls would be closed up for the day, Sunday being a day of rest for Christians, sinners, and bouquinistes alike.

At his apartment, he left messages at the ambassador's home and office, hoping his boss would be able to pull strings, get an investigation moving. Two hours later, neither call was returned.

Work kept his mind busy the rest of the afternoon, drafting shift rosters and approving vacation time until he could slip into a hot bath with a cold scotch, the events of the past two days seeping back into his mind after the impenetrable barrier of embassy business. A sadness crept through him, a feeling of hopelessness that had come to replace the urgency he'd felt immediately after Max's kidnapping. He tried to suppress it, tell himself there was still a chance, but he knew that hope was fading. If Max was free, uninjured, he would have sought out Hugo by now. And if he wasn't . . . Eventually, Hugo climbed from the tub, his body sapped of energy by the worry, the warm water, and the drink. He fell into bed long before midnight but slept fitfully.

Hugo woke early on Monday. He was glad to be active and walked the mile and a half to the US Embassy, thinking about Max every step of the way, wondering what he could do—should do—to help find his friend. A dark thought pressed in on him, reminding him that finding people wasn't all he was good at. When those who'd gone missing couldn't be found, all that was left was to catch those who'd harmed them. Given Max's age and the coldness in Nica's eyes, Hugo knew he had to face the possibility that finding Max was no longer his priority.

The snow had receded from the roads, pushed back by a warm Sunday and the workers who had scraped and brushed the city streets all weekend. Piles of graying slush lay at intervals on the sidewalk, watery at the edges, creating webs of rivulets that streaked the pavement and disappeared into the gutters. After yesterday's warmth it had turned cold again, temperatures hovering a couple of degrees above freezing, and Hugo wondered if the frigid day would turn the wet streets into ice rinks.

He used a side door at the embassy, showing his credentials on the way in and passing through the least busy of the metal detectors. It was a formality; he'd known the two marines guarding that entrance for over a year.

Inside, Hugo walked down the quiet hallway, hearing the murmur of voices and the clicking of computer keys behind closed doors, glad not to see anyone. He didn't particularly want to explain why he was not out enjoying his vacation or on his way to the States, the usual holiday destination for embassy employees. But if he wanted to use his office, seeing his secretary was unavoidable.

In another era, Emma would have been described as handsome, and it would have been a compliment. In her late fifties, she had the erect posture and even features that gave her a timeless appeal. Her shoulder-length brown hair knew its place, always, and she wore just enough make-up to let you know she had made an effort. They had worked together for two years, but other than her never-failing promptness and efficiency, Hugo knew little about her. He had access to every law enforcement tool in existence and no doubt could have learned plenty, but he'd respected her privacy the way she respected, and protected, his.

He pushed open the heavy wooden door labeled *US Embassy Security* and stepped in, smiling at Emma when she looked up. He waited for the raised eyebrow, the lingering look, knowing she wouldn't ask about his unscheduled presence directly.

"Surprise, surprise," Hugo said, closing the door behind him.

"Why, yes it is." Emma put down a magazine, the *Economist*. No fluff for her.

Hugo nodded to it. "Nothing to do while I'm away?"

"Plenty. I just don't want to do it." She held his eye. "Is everything OK?"

"Mostly. I was hoping I'd need the help of the embassy counsel to undo my divorce, but that didn't work out."

"Oh, Hugo." Emma's mouth tightened. "I'm sorry."

"Thanks." Hugo smiled to let her know it wasn't that bad. "Perhaps later in the week you could arrange for a couple of young ladies to come by my place and make me feel better."

Emma frowned and tsk-tsked, but Hugo's attempts to be outrageous had become a routine, part of their dynamic and even more reassuring than his smile. "You are a horrible man, Hugo Marston."

"Thanks, I try. Anything I need to know about?"

"Yes. In the few hours you were away from the office, all of the embassy's weaponry was stolen, the ambassador was eaten by a lion, and immediately after that we were invaded by Martians." She shrugged. "It happens every time you leave."

"I see. Well, unless some of those creatures are in my office, I shall get to work."

Emma tutted again as he went into his office and closed the door. He rounded the desk and sat down, switching on his computer. It wasn't work he intended to do, it was research. First, to learn about bouquinistes. He'd always meant to get the history of this Parisian phenomenon from Max over a drink, but their conversation had always been about other things—mostly books. He hoped he hadn't missed his chance.

The first site he visited, a travel guide, told him the basics. The term *bouquinistes* came from the Dutch word *boeckin*, meaning "small book." Made sense. The first sellers, he read, used wheelbarrows to transport and sell their goods, and fastened trays to the parapets of the bridges with thin leather straps. After the French Revolution, business boomed when entire libraries were "liberated" from nobles and wound up for sale cheap on the banks of the Seine. In 1891, bouquinistes received permission to permanently attach their boxes to the quaysides. Hugo was struck by the line: "Today, the waiting list to become one of Paris's 250 bouquinistes is eight years."

Hugo's phone rang, and he let Emma pick it up. A moment later, his intercom buzzed. "It's a Peter Kendall. I told him you were on vacation but he said you'd told him to call."

"I did, thanks Emma. Can you put him through?" The line clicked. "Mr. Kendall, Hugo Marston here."

"Good afternoon, Mr. Marston, I have news."

"Good or bad?"

He heard a chuckle from the other end of the line. "I'd call it good. After you left I got straight onto my friend at Christie's. Been selling books all his life. He asked me to take some pictures and e-mail them to him. I would have walked it over, but with the snow . . . Well, I just e-mailed him, and you'll never guess."

"It is a first edition?" That was no great surprise given Kendall's earlier opinion, but Hugo thought he heard excitement in the bookseller's voice.

"Yes, it is. And . . . and that scribble in the front. It's Rimbaud's signature." Kendall cleared his throat. "Actually, it's more than that, which is what threw me off."

"I don't understand," Hugo said.

"I saw the name Paul written inside the front cover. I assumed that someone named Paul had owned and written his name in the book, but my friend is convinced that Rimbaud inscribed the book to his lover."

"Paul Verlaine."

"Exactly, very impressive, Mr. Marston. It turns out that Rimbaud did indeed inscribe three copies of his book for Verlaine."

"And this is one of them?"

"Yes, it is."

"Incredible. So what does that mean?"

"It means, Mr. Marston, that your book is worth a great deal of money." When Hugo didn't respond, Kendall coughed gently. "I am told that at auction you can expect something in the region of a hundred thousand dollars. Maybe more."

Hugo was stunned. "Are you serious?"

"That's what they told me, Mr. Marston. Unless you wish to keep the book."

"No." Hugo almost laughed. "If someone wants to pay that much for a book, Mr. Kendall, then they want it a lot more than I do."

"In that case, I shall take it over to Christie's myself. There is an auction the day after tomorrow, Wednesday. They normally like to advertise the lots that are for sale in advance, but my friend assures me that a few well-placed phone calls will bring in the right bidders for a piece like this."

"Not many at that price, I'm guessing."

"A dozen or more, or so he tells me. You'd be surprised what the idle rich will pay for a book."

"Yeah, I would. OK, that sounds fine. Is there anything I need to do?"

"If you would be kind enough to fax me handwritten, or at least typed and signed, authorization to handle the sale. I hate to be a pedant, Mr. Marston, but . . ."

"A hundred thousand dollars is a lot of money," Hugo said. "Give me your fax number."

Ten minutes later, Hugo had entrusted the most valuable possession he'd ever owned to a secondhand bookseller in a Paris back street. He wondered for a moment why it bothered him so little, but he didn't want to think about bad luck so he dove back into his research on booksellers. A hundred thousand dollars made him a lot more intent on finding Max. Most of that money rightly belonged to the old man.

He began to read more on the history of the bouquinistes and was surprised to see that they were tightly regulated, even today. At least, in theory. From what he was seeing, they were initially prohibited from selling anything but books, but with the advent of international tourism they had banded together to form a semiofficial union, Le Syndicat Des Bouquinistes de Paris, or SBP. With more than two hundred members operating in the most tourist-friendly parts of Paris, and with the weight of history behind them, the government had relented on this rule and allowed them to sell souvenirs—as long as they carried three times as many books as they did mini-Eiffel Towers and postcards.

Apparently the SBP had managed to keep their rent low, too, a nominal amount. Hugo was no economist but he knew a good deal when he saw one. Low rent, prime location, and an ever-renewing supply of customers. No wonder there was an eight-year wait to become a bouquiniste. It also explained how the Seine's band of booksellers were able to undercut the book shops and tourist boutiques.

A knock at the door interrupted him, and he stood as Ambassador Taylor came in.

Rotund, balding, and somewhere around average height, one could walk past J. Bradford Taylor on the street and, assuming you noticed him at all, would imagine him to be a bank clerk or accountant. Actually, Hugo had joked with Ambassador Taylor over brandy one night that he'd make a master criminal—utterly unrecognizable and hugely intelligent. Typical of the ambassador, he'd taken the joke as a compliment.

"Morning, sir," Hugo said.

"Morning to you. Aren't you on vacation?" He gestured for Hugo to sit, and plopped down in a chair opposite him.

"Yes and no. Something came up."

"So I heard. I got your messages and made a couple of calls."

"Thank you."

"Don't thank me, Hugo, I'm not going to be any help."

"How's that?"

"I talked to a couple of people and they say there's nothing much to investigate. Which confused me. What the hell's going on?"

Hugo leaned forward, the last hope of official cooperation evaporating before his eyes. "Ambassador, a friend was kidnapped in front of me. A man with a gun took him from his book stall by Pont Neuf."

"You saw this?"

"I was right there, I couldn't do a damn thing except call the police afterwards. The detective made all the right moves but never really . . . I don't know." Hugo sat back. "It's hard to explain. He went through the motions, but since a couple of people told a different story, he's just thrown up his hands and stopped looking."

Taylor stroked his chin. "That's very odd. Why would he do that?"

"I have no idea, but I was hoping you might be able to find out."

"I'm sorry Hugo, but this is one of those jurisdictional things." He held up a hand as Hugo started to protest. "Yes, I know, we both hate that kind of talk, but the fact remains. If they don't want to investigate, there's nothing you or I can do about it. And I know what you're thinking, but don't. We have a sensitive conference coming up, our friends from Zimbabwe, and this isn't the time to be ruffling French feathers."

"Honestly, ambassador, right now I don't care about French feathers."

"Well I do," Taylor said, standing. "And you better start because that's your job. I'm sorry about your friend, Hugo, I mean that. But if the locals are satisfied there was no crime, then what can I do? Between nothing and very little. Which," he added, holding up a warning finger, "is what I want you to be doing."

"Meaning?"

"Meaning you stand down, vacation or not."

CHAPTER SEVEN

Wen Emma walked into his office with a cup of coffee, Hugo was staring into space.

"Hugo, you look pale. Are you OK?"

"Yes, fine. Just thinking, that's all. I just had some . . . news."

"Oh dear. Bad news, from the look on your face. And the look on the ambassador's when he walked out."

Hugo looked up. "Oh, I'm not worried about him. He has a job to do. No, this is something else, something good but mysterious, you might say."

"Care to share? We could use some excitement around here."

"Lions and Martians not enough for you?" He thanked her for the coffee and, when she left, he turned back to his computer.

What had that bouquiniste said his name was? Ah yes, Jean Chabot.

One of the things Hugo had done as embassy security chief was to negotiate access for himself and senior members of his staff to the databases of France's foreign intelligence agency, the Direction Générale de la Sécurité Extérieure, or DGSE, and the databases of the French version of the FBI, the Direction Centrale du Renseignement Intérieur, or DCRI. If he'd wanted to, he could also tap into Interpol's global communications system, known as I-24/7. He'd try that next, if nothing came up.

He first logged into the DCRI's system. The latest generation of crime-fighting software, it could search for crimes or criminals using the barest of details. A name, a place, a date, or even a *modus operandi* would bring back results. Not always fast, it was nonetheless thorough, and his first thought was to have it track down that bastard Nica. But his fingers hovered over the keyboard. Presumably the man's first name, but short for Nicolas? Nicholas? Nikolas? Too many possibilities. Instead, he filled two search boxes with the names "Jean" and "Chabot."

Then he sat back, lifted his boots onto his desk, and took a careful sip of Emma's hot coffee. Perfect, as always. Why he couldn't make it this good at home, he'd no clue. Even using her written instructions, and the exact same beans and coffee-concocting equipment, he ended up producing either a witch-thin potion or a bitter, burnt-tasting brew.

He took another sip and watched as a thick bar on his computer screen filled up from left to right. It paused at ninety-nine percent and then flashed up twelve hits on Frenchmen named "Jean Chabot." Only three were in Paris, so he started with those. The first was a bust: a black male killed in prison two years ago. The second and third Jean Chabots were also not his man, a quick glance at the pictures showed that much. He ventured further afield, choosing a Chabot from Toulouse. Not him. The next one was from Pau, a town Hugo knew from following the Tour de France religiously every year. Down near the Pyrénées, one of the mountain stages of that race usually began or ended there.

This Jean Chabot *was* his man, the too-close eyes and thin mouth unmistakable. He had six convictions, all for theft-related offenses, the most petty was a shoplifting charge when he was twenty and the most serious an armed robbery, for which he spent four years behind bars. What struck Hugo was that each of Chabot's crimes was in southwestern France, three in the city of Pau itself, two more in Biarritz, and the other one in Lourdes. Nothing at all in Paris.

Which meant that Hugo now had two questions that he couldn't answer.

First, why would a humble bouquiniste get kidnapped? Second, how did a not-so-petty criminal from the Pyrénées-Atlantiques Department end up in possession of one of the most coveted bookstalls in Paris? He didn't believe that Chabot didn't know Max, or at least know of him. But if Chabot wasn't talking, there wasn't a lot he could do about it. Yet.

The next step, he knew, was to try harder to find Max himself. His

fingers hovered above the keyboard, the cursor blinking in the empty
search box in front of him. Max was a friend and looking up his criminal history seemed like an invasion of privacy, a step too far. He didn't
know why, but he felt sure that any wrongdoings would be ancient
history, from a youth that Max had left behind long ago. Hugo was still
not sure he wanted to know, but he couldn't think of any other way to
find the old man.

All he had was his first and last name, and even the latter he
wasn't sure how to spell. He tried multiple variations on the spelling of
"Cloche" and then, when he got nothing back, he tried variations on
the name. After more than a dozen tries, running every name he could
think of that began with "Cl-," he sat back and ran his hands through
his hair. He thought for a moment, then checked his watch and smiled
at the realization that time didn't mean the same thing to Tom as it did
to everyone else. He dialed his friend's number.

Tom's voice came on the line after four rings. "I spy a French
number, so Dr. Marston, I presume."

"Well done, Sherlock."

"Silence 'lo these many years, then you can't get enough of me.
What's up?"

"You remember I said I had a little thing going on here?"

"And here's where I make a joke about your little thing."

"Wouldn't be the first time. Anyway, you near your CIA gadgetry?"

"Happens I am. It's the only way I can access global porn. The
classy Malaysian stuff."

"Naturally," said Hugo. "I need some information about someone,
but I don't have much to go on."

"Hang on." Hugo heard the clink of glasses, or perhaps bottles,
being moved. "You've tried your local databases I assume?"

"Yes, Tom, I managed to think of that."

"Good man. So what can you tell me?"

"Max is the first name; I'd thought his last name was Cloche but I
ran it, and every other name beginning with those first two letters, and
came up empty."

"What else?"

"No date of birth, I'd guess he's in his late sixties. He's a bouquiniste."

"OK. Anything else?"

Hugo searched his mind for more clues, for some deeply buried memory that might point to Max's identity. "If I think of something I'll let you know."

"OK," Tom said. Hugo could hear his friend's fingers working a keyboard, then Tom's voice, talking himself softly through the process. "Max and all its variations, in Paris, bookseller. Probably a union member, being a frog."

"Yes. And the bouquinistes have a union–"

"I know," Tom interrupted. "The SBP, I found it already. In his sixties, you say?"

"Yes." Early in the friendship Hugo had asked Max his age. The old man's response had been so colorful that Hugo had understood the meaning without recognizing many of the words themselves.

"Let's see," said Tom. "I have two candidates but I'd guess … crotchety looking fellow, with a rubbery nose?"

"You found him?" Hugo sat up. "I'm at my computer, can you send me a picture?"

"Just did. That him?"

Hugo opened his e-mail account and clicked on the attachment to Tom's message. "You're a genius, Tom. That's him. Can you send whatever you have?"

"Actually, not allowed to. The CIA retired me, I can't have them firing me, too. But you can take notes while I talk."

"Then talk."

"Maximilian Ivan Koche. German or Dutch I'd guess. Has an apartment on Rue Condorcet. Know it?"

Koche. Dammit. Hugo got up. "Hang on," he said, walking over to the large map on his wall. He found it just west of the Gare du Nord, the station that served routes to the north and to the United Kingdom. Just above Rue Condorcet was the Pigalle district, home to the famous Moulin Rouge cabaret and a multitude of sex shops. It was also home to many of the city's prostitutes, women and men who plied their trade in the winding side streets that led up to the tourist-heavy Montmartre district. "Near Pigalle," he told Tom. "What else?"

"According to this, he was born in 1938, which makes him over seventy years old." Tom hummed as he clicked several times. "I was right. Again. Your buddy Max is German, born of a Hungarian mother and a German father, both Jews, in Dortmund. Looks like they lived there for a few years, until 1942, when their house was raided by those Nazi bastards. The whole family was arrested and sent to an internment camp at Le Vernet, in southern France."

"I've heard of it," said Hugo. "Where the hell are you getting this stuff?"

"Can't tell you that," Tom said. "But you'll see in a minute why someone kept a file on him."

"Good. Go on."

"OK, so they were at Le Vernet for two years, alive and together, but in July of 1944 they were loaded onto a train and shipped east to Dachau." Tom's tone changed, and Hugo knew that even his world-weary and flippant friend felt the weight of that period of history. "According to this, Max was the only one to survive and was liberated from Dachau in 1945. He was adopted by a French colonel and his wife and raised in a suburb of Paris." Which explained why Hugo had never detected a foreign accent. "But then more shitty luck," Tom went on. "When Max was twelve, in May of 1950, his adoptive father and mother were killed in a car accident while the family was on vacation in Brittany. Max was the only one to survive."

Hugo shook his head. So much about the old man he hadn't known. "Go on. I'm still curious why you guys have a file on him."

Tom chuckled. "Not technically our file, but we're coming to the interesting part. In 1963 Max attended the marriage of lawyer Serge Klarsfeld to his wife, Beate. Those names ring a bell?"

"Yes, but I can't place them."

"Two of France's most famous Nazi-hunters."

"And the reason that file exists," said Hugo.

"Right. Moving on. Max spent the '60s with the Klarsfelds chasing

Nazis, including those responsible for wiping out his family. According to this, French authorities suspected that Max helped the Klarsfelds abduct former Gestapo chief Kurt Lischka in 1971. No proof, although when the couple was arrested for the kidnap, Max led the campaign to free them from jail. That happened pretty quickly, a lot of people joined the campaign, and they went back to work once they were released, Max helping the couple with more Nazi captures, including Klaus Barbie and Jean Leguay."

"Nice work," Hugo said.

"Yeah, until Leguay was let go without facing trial. This says Max lost heart after that."

"Who was Leguay?" Hugo asked.

"A high-ranking police official in the Vichy government, and one of the most senior collaborators with the Nazis during their World War II occupation of France. A second set of charges was filed against him in 1986, but he was let go before trial. Again."

"Amazing," Hugo said. "I had no idea."

"This Max guy is a friend?" Tom asked. "He in trouble?"

"Yeah. Most definitely."

"Anything else I can do to help?"

"Not right now. But I'll let you know if that changes."

They hung up, and Hugo sat with his elbows on his desk, staring into his now-cold coffee.

Rarely did a human being surprise him. Twenty-plus years in law enforcement saw to that, and with his behavioral training and experience in the field he usually found himself able to predict most people's odd behavior, or spot someone with a colorful history. But not this time. What stories the old man must have. And Hugo found himself pleased, somehow, that in a manner of speaking they were in the same line of work: catching bad guys. He'd failed his friend, let him be kidnapped, and that was reason enough to track Max down. But now the old man's compelling history added to Hugo's already fierce determination to find his friend.

Not to mention, of course, Hugo owed him a pair of cowboy boots.

CHAPTER EIGHT

That night, Hugo walked along the left bank of the Seine. It was almost eight o'clock and the green metal boxes attached to the stone walls were closed and locked tight, the sellers all gone. The air sat heavy and cold around him as he walked, and once he slipped on a patch of black ice on the sidewalk. He'd already paid a visit to Max's home, getting there by taxi an hour after talking to Tom. No one was there, either in Max's apartment or in any of the other four in the building. He'd brought his tools and could have picked the lock, but there were too many people still around, it was too early for that kind of clandestine activity. Reluctantly he'd left the place, knowing he'd return with a plan, a definite way to get through the front door. Now, he avoided Max's stall by cutting down the narrow Rue de Nevers. It made no sense, but he didn't feel ready to see it again. He felt as if it were a crime scene and, by returning to it full of questions rather than answers, the metal boxes might become contaminated and never give up their secrets.

He turned left again, making his way onto Rue Dauphine, heading toward his apartment. He wasn't ready to call it a night, though; he was restless and needed to be around people. Even if that meant sitting alone in a bar. He slowed, gazing into the windows of the tiny stores that made up these narrow streets, one-room boutiques that sold not much to hardly anyone. There were dozens of them in this *arrondissement*, and he often wondered how they paid the rent.

He found an empty table under a heating lamp at a café on Rue Andre Mazet. It was busy for a Monday night, but it pleased him to be out in a crowd. He ordered a scotch, and when the waiter returned he opened his wallet and took out a ten Euro note. The woman at the small table next to him stared at his wallet. She tried to be subtle about it but the edge of her table touched Hugo's, and their chairs were just inches apart. And, Hugo would have to admit, her presence had already attracted his attention, the moment she walked into the café. He sipped his drink and took the opportunity to look at her a little more closely. She was a few years younger than him, maybe mid-thirties, with light brown hair that she wore short, an almost-bob. Stylish and pretty, but with a hardness to the face that almost certainly dissuaded strange men from making conversation.

As he put his glass down, she caught him looking. He was about to apologize, when she did.

"*Je m'excuse, monsieur*," she said, nodding at his wallet. "I noticed your badge. You are a cop?"

"*Non*. Not exactly." So it wasn't the money. "I work at the US Embassy, in security."

"*Bien*. You speak French very well." She looked at his wallet again and switched to English. "You should know better than to carry so much cash." A smile accompanied the reprimand.

He patted the bulge under his suit and returned the smile. "The US Embassy, remember."

"Ah yes, you Americans and your guns. Perhaps I can help you lighten your wallet."

"Excuse me?" America or France, Hugo knew that a certain type of working girl, usually the more attractive ones, plied their trade in bars, restaurants, and cafés rather than on the street. But he'd never actually been propositioned before, and he wasn't even sure if that's what was happening now.

"By buying me a drink," she said, putting out her hand. "Claudia Roux." She put her other hand into her bag and pulled out her own credentials. "A journalist."

"I'm sorry, of course, I thought . . . I'm Hugo Marston," he added hurriedly.

"I know what you thought, Monsieur Marston, and I'm not sure whether to be flattered or appalled." Her eyes reflected neither, though the slight curl at the corners of her mouth suggested amusement.

"I'm sorry," he said, "I should be appalled, not you." He caught the waiter's eye and when he came over, Hugo turned to his companion. "What would you like?"

She spoke directly to the waiter. "*Un whisky, s'il vous plaît.*" She held up a hand, stalling the young man. "Have you eaten yet, Monsieur Marston?"

"Actually, no."

She turned back to the waiter. "*Alors, deux omelettes. Vous avez les cepes toujours?*"

"*Oui madam. Deux omelettes avec cepes?*"

"*Oui.*" She smiled at Hugo. "You are married, I take it." It was a statement, not a question.

"Why do you say that?" Hugo asked.

"You should see your face. You are not used to having a woman order for you."

He nodded. "That's true." His southern belle, Christine, would have let them both starve before she ordered for him at a restaurant. "But I'm not married, not anymore."

She watched him closely as he spoke and Hugo couldn't help but hold her gaze. She had hazel eyes, utterly flawless, and once he'd noticed them the toughness she carried about her like a cloak softened considerably. Her eyes matched perfectly a thick stripe of color in the scarf wound around her neck. Hugo wondered whether that was intentional, perhaps the gift of an observant friend or lover.

"Not anymore?" she said. "Then we are either celebrating or commiserating, no? Either way, we should order wine with dinner."

"Fine by me," Hugo said. "So what exactly did you order? Omelets, yes, but 'cepes'?"

"A type of mushroom. The best type. The Italians call them porcini but the ones they grow around Bordeaux are different, I would swear to it. Much better. We're a little late in the season but some chefs keep a good supply, and it seems we're in luck. You've never had them?"

"Not that I know of." When they arrived, he discovered that she was right. Rich but light, without the meaty, overpowering taste of other mushrooms, such as the ubiquitous portabella. Cooked in butter and garlic, he guessed, and only now did he realize how hungry he was. The waiter arrived with another basket of bread.

"So what kind of journalist are you?" Hugo asked between bites.

"Newspaper. A police reporter for *Le Monde*. Robbery, rape, murder, all that stuff. Drugs, too, that's my current interest. The cops are seeing a lot more of that lately, which means I'm writing about it more." She smiled and tore a piece of bread in half. "The whole European Union thing. You open the borders up to tourists and trade and guess what else you get."

"That makes sense."

"Believe me, the dealers think so. The cops are starting a new anti-drugs task force. I'm kissing a lot of butt to get info about it, get an exclusive or two." She was switching between French and English and had used the slang *cul* for "butt," which made Hugo smile. The way she said it, the language and her soft voice, it actually sounded elegant.

"I see." Hugo poured them more wine. "And are drugs more interesting than robberies or murder?"

"Usually. More back story. A murder or a robbery just happens and that's it. They're not like on television, the murders we have here. They're quick and senseless, almost always. But with drugs there's often intrigue, drama, and real people touched by them. Plus, I'm tired of looking at dead bodies."

"I understand that." He told her a little about his time in the FBI, working out of the Houston office as a profiler, showing up to murder scenes and having to dispassionately evaluate why the killer had gouged out the eyes of the victim. Too often a child. He'd had his successes, but success for him usually meant catching the bad guy after the event, not stopping him before. And that kind of success took its toll, which is why, he told Claudia, when he'd been offered the chance to get out of the trenches and travel a little, he jumped at it. No need to mention Ellie.

"But I think you miss it, no?" Again the cocked head as she looked at him.

"Maybe I do. A little." He looked at Claudia. "So you have good contacts at the prefecture?"

She batted her eyelids dramatically. "What do you think?"

He laughed. Of course she did. "Good. Do you do favors for American cops?"

"That depends on the favor." She forked the last bite of her omelet into her mouth and chewed. "And it depends on what's in it for me."

Hugo laughed gently. "I think you'd do this cop a favor even if there was nothing in it for you."

Delicate eyebrows rose high. "Why is that?"

"Just guessing. How about I pay for dinner?"

He did, and afterwards they went to Hugo's apartment, where they drank brandy by the fire. She was a more enthusiastic listener than talker, mentioning only her "humble roots," a father with some health problems who was turning to religion in his later years, and the lack of a mother growing up. She'd had a short marriage but didn't say whether it ended well or badly, and then she peppered him with questions about Texas. When they had exchanged enough background information and small talk, they went to bed.

Her lovemaking was adept, intense, her breath sweet with the night's liquor and her body as firm as he'd imagined it. He felt out of practice, because he was. She, without meaning to be, was like a dance instructor, guiding her talented but rusty student, and somehow he didn't mind the direction because he knew it meant she was getting what she wanted, and that was what he wanted.

She left in the night, thinking he was asleep. He watched her silhouette glide about the room gathering clothes and then dressing. She paused by the bed before letting herself out, just for a moment. She didn't leave a phone number or e-mail address.

A cop and a journalist would be able to find each other, if they wanted.

When he awoke, Hugo was glad to be alone. He hadn't thought about the morning after but as he made coffee he did, and the idea of awkward chatter disturbed him. Far better to part without diluting the memory with idle pleasantries. Then again, it'd been a while since this apartment had heard a female voice, so maybe the chatter would have been bearable.

It was Tuesday now, almost nine o'clock when he closed the apartment door behind him. He had three tasks for the day. The first was to find a bite to eat and some more coffee, the second was to ask Claudia for that favor and maybe arrange lunch or dinner together, and the third was to get inside Max's apartment on Rue Condorcet. But food and coffee first.

He strolled down the normally busy Boulevard Saint-Germain, crowded on weekends with tourists and in the week with commuters. It was at its quietest right now, the lull between the morning rush hour and the lunch-time exodus from offices and stores. He bought a crepe with lemon juice and sugar at the stand beside the Church of Saint Germain des Pres, then passed by the famous cafés of Deux Magots and Café de Flore, where the artists and writers of the previous generations congregated. He kept walking northwest toward the Seine until he got to Rue de Bellechasse, where he turned right and went into Café Rubais. There, the coffee was just as good as anyone's, and it was a few Euros cheaper. It was served quickly and he drank it almost as fast, impatient to begin his day's work. With a few sips left he reached for his phone. Emma answered on the second ring.

"Can you get me the number for a journalist at *Le Monde*? Name of Claudia Roux."

"Of course. But would it help if I reminded you that you're on vacation still?"

"Not really."

"OK. You have a pen?"

"Yes, but can you connect me?"

"I can conference us then hang up," she said, sweetly, "if dialing a number is too much trouble for your poor little fingers."

"Much too much trouble."

"Fine, but you'll have to hold while I call her, if you can stand the inconvenience." Before he could reply, the line went dead and stayed that way for a full minute. Emma reappeared and said, "Here she is, Your Majesty. Call me if you need anything."

Claudia was smiling when she said "*Bonjour*," he could hear it in her voice. "I hope I didn't wake you when I left," she said.

"No," he replied truthfully, "you didn't."

"Good. And I hope you weren't offended."

"I'm a big boy, Claudia, it's OK."

"Can you meet me for dinner tonight?" she asked, before he had a chance to.

"Yes." He paused. "Hey, can I ask you about that favor?"

"*Mais oui*, what is it?"

"I have a friend, a bouquiniste. He's disappeared and I'd like some help finding him."

"Disappeared?"

For no reason he could think of, Hugo didn't want to tell her about the kidnapping. Perhaps because he'd failed to stop it, perhaps because the police had refused to believe him. There was something larger going on, he was sure, but until he knew what it was, he would parcel information sparingly.

"Yes. At least temporarily. I'm going to his apartment later just to check but . . . well, I'll tell you about it tonight."

"*D'accord*. Give me his name and address, I'll see what I can do. We have our own investigators here, they're plugged into all kinds of resources, the same ones the police use."

"*Merci*." He gave her the information and added a physical description, just in case. "I checked the DCRI database but they didn't have anything recent."

"They probably wouldn't, ours would be better for a missing

person. I can check easily enough." She paused. "So, tonight. Let's eat early, I'll pick up some things and cook at your place, say seven o'clock?"

"Perfect." Hugo hung up, dropped money on the saucer for the waiter, and picked up his hat. With jobs one and two out of the way, it was time to visit the home of an old friend.

CHAPTER NINE

Max's apartment on Rue Condorcet was on the upper floor of a four-story building. The only visible entrance was at the top of six granite steps bordered by an iron railing, a black door that looked like it had recently been painted. For the second time in two days, Hugo climbed the steps and pressed the highest doorbell. He cocked his head to listen but heard neither ring nor movement, so he tried again. Still nothing. He tried the lower buzzers, hoping someone might let him in, but again got no reaction. He was digging into his pocket to bring out the little bag of tools he'd brought to his new job from the FBI when the front door opened and an old woman, carrying empty shopping bags in one hand and a cane in the other, let herself out. Hugo retreated down the stairs so as not to startle her.

"*Bonjour, madam.*" He took off his hat and gave a slight bow.

"*Monsieur, bonjour.*"

"*Excusez moi, je cherche un ami*. Max Koche."

"*Oui, monsieur*, he lives here. The top floor."

Hugo smiled. "Yes, I tried but got no answer. Have you seen him lately?"

"*Oui.*" She put a hand on the iron rail and started down the stairs. "Just last week. Is that recent enough? I don't get out much."

"It's hard when it's this cold." He smiled. "Actually, I was hoping you'd seen or heard him in the last day or two." He tried to keep his voice casual but the old woman was perceptive.

"Heard him? What an odd question, monsieur. Is he alright?"

"That's what I am trying to find out."

"Well, as I say, I've not seen him this week. Or heard him." She looked at Hugo and cocked her head. "You have an accent, you are not from Paris."

"I'm American."

A smile crossed her face. "*Vraiment! J'adore les Americains.* After the war, during the Liberation, I had quite a romance with a young colonel." She winked at him. "At least, he said he was a colonel, I never bothered to check."

"I'm sure he was."

"Pah!" She waved a hand. "I'm sure it doesn't matter." She reached the last of the stone steps and paused. "Talking of accents reminds me. A few days ago I came outside because I heard a dog barking. A man was leaving and he held the door for me."

"He had an accent?"

"Yes. I thought perhaps he was Italian or Spanish. He was very polite when I thanked him."

"Do you think he'd been to see Max?"

"That's why I mention it. I live on the ground floor, the one above me is empty, and the couple who live in the apartment above that are in Africa for three months. They do missionary work, you know."

"I didn't know that. Very noble."

She waved the hand again. "*Non, monsieur,* they are in some cult. Nice but . . ." She shrugged.

"I see. And when did you say this was?"

She frowned. "I have trouble remembering sometimes. But it was probably Saturday, perhaps Sunday. I wanted to go to bed and the noise was stopping me, so about nine in the evening. But I didn't see Monsieur Koche." She eased past him and nodded at the front door. "I didn't lock it. Go in and knock, if you like. *Au revoir, monsieur.* If I see him, can I tell him you came by?"

"Of course. *Je m'appelle* Hugo Marston. Just tell him 'the big American.' And thank you for your help."

"*Le grand Américain.*" She straightened up, a smile on her lips. "You are welcome, monsieur, and thank you for reminding me."

She started to shuffle away down the street, but Hugo had one more question. "Madam. Do you remember what the man looked like? The man with the accent."

"*Oui*, of course. He looked like a foreigner, monsieur. Small and thin, with dark skin. You know, his face made me think of a rat. And he kept rubbing his chin." She started to turn away, then looked back. "Ah, *mon colonel*, how long since I've thought of him." She smiled wistfully and continued on her way.

Chabot. That bastard had lied. Not only did he know Max, but he'd been to his apartment.

Hugo looked up and down the empty street, trotted up the stone stairs, and went inside. To his right was the door to the old lady's apartment, ahead of him a staircase with a worn runner, faded and dirty, inviting him up. The stairs creaked underfoot and even though he knew the building was empty he moved as quietly as he could. Instinctively he touched the weapon under his arm, a matter of reassurance rather than necessity. At the second-floor landing he passed the door to the empty apartment and kept going until he reached the third floor where, straight ahead of him, was another door. The couple in Africa. He barely paused, crossing the landing and continuing upwards.

Max's door was at the top of the staircase. Hugo stopped to catch his breath, irritated that his breathing and heart rate were faster than he would have liked. He stepped forward and knocked on the door. Silence. He looked around and saw a small wooden table on the landing, not even knee high. It bore no plant or ornament, just a thin layer of dust.

Hugo shook his head, a slight smile on his lips. It was an apparently pointless piece of furniture, but Hugo had learned over the years that very few things were without reason. He walked over and picked up the little table. He turned it upside down and inspected it. He then flipped it onto its side and found what he was looking for. Taped under the rim was a key. He peeled it off and inserted it into Max's door, paused for a second, and then felt it turn cleanly in the lock.

The door swung open silently and Hugo stepped into Max's living room and looked around. The room was large and bright, with three windows to his left that looked out over Rue Condorcet, and filled with furniture that would have cost Max very little but would last a lifetime, dark and heavy. And everywhere, books.

Obviously, someone else had gotten there first. While the furniture was still upright, the floor was awash with the contents of the room, mostly books. Some lay alone on the floor, their covers flung open like the outstretched wings of dying birds. Others had been tossed into piles, making untidy pyramids beside, and on, the furniture. Opposite Hugo was a long sofa piled high with them, several precariously balanced at the precipice edge of the leather seat.

A wing-backed armchair sat beside the couch, near the windows and at an angle to the room, its seat one of the few spaces free of literature. A pair of round end tables flanked the chair, books piled five and six high, and some spilling onto the floor. Directly to Hugo's left was an armoire, its doors open. He moved further into the room, intentionally keeping away from the large windows, and looked inside.

Max had inserted some cheap pine boards to hold more books, but the shelves of the armoire were mostly empty, their contents scattered on the floor at Hugo's feet. He looked down at them and his boots crinkled the discarded plastic envelopes that had once protected these books from the elements. With the bent covers and torn pages around him, the empty sheaths seemed like discarded body bags, too late to do any real good other than carry away the dead.

The plastic covers told Hugo one thing, though: the books tucked away in the armoire had been Max's more valuable ones. He knelt and sifted through them. No more Rimbauds, and he didn't see *On War*.

Standing there, in Max's home for the first time, he felt the familiar buzz of the crime scene. His senses and training were reactivating for the first time in years, absorbing and channeling information, processing what he saw into a coherent story. He crisscrossed the room, touching as little as possible, his eyes raking over everything. By the time he'd finished scouring the room he knew one thing: someone had searched Max's place, quickly and quietly. But there had been no fight in here.

Hugo moved to a half-open door in the far corner. It led into a short hallway, off of which sat a tiny kitchen on the right and a bathroom on the left. The hallway ended at Max's bedroom, the door open. He trod quietly, again out of habit as much as necessity, glancing into the kitchen and bathroom for further signs of intrusion. Nothing.

At the entrance to Max's room, he paused.

The bedroom was a person's greatest sanctuary, the place where he did his thinking, his sleeping, his loving. Walking in uninvited gave Hugo pause. He had, or hoped he had, always treated these rooms with utmost respect. So many of the bodies that he'd seen were in bedrooms; Austin's axe murderer hacked his victims to death as they slept, and he'd killed half a dozen before Hugo caught him a thousand miles away, sound asleep in a disused box car that sat at the back of a Cincinnati rail yard. Children, too, he'd found in bedrooms, though not usually their own.

He stepped inside. Facing the door was Max's queen-size bed, the blankets pulled up. At its foot sat a low, wooden trunk, its lid open. Hugo's chest tightened as he moved toward it, but he found it empty, blankets dropped carelessly in front after it had been searched. He turned to the closet on his left. The floor creaked as he walked to it and the door creaked, too, as if in sympathy. A string hung from a light bulb and Hugo tugged it. In the harsh light he saw two brown leather suitcases, open and empty. Beside them was a large duffel bag, panels of green canvas stitched together with heavy thread. Military, thought Hugo, and also empty. He ran his hands over the shirts and jackets hanging in the closet, then looked over the half-dozen pairs of pants on a high shelf.

Hugo heard a gentle click from the hallway. He snapped the light off and instinctively put a hand under his jacket. He heard the noise again. Had he closed the apartment door behind him when he came in? Locked it?

Hugo moved slowly out of the closet, staying close to the wall so he wouldn't be seen, and because that was where the floor was less likely to creak. He approached the back of the open bedroom door and peered through the crack between door and jamb. He saw a thin sliver of the hallway. He watched for a second, but saw no movement. His fingers closed around the butt of his gun.

"Anyone there?" he called out. If he was to startle someone, it should be from somewhere safe, from here. But no response.

He stepped around the door and moved quickly into the hallway, eyes darting from the kitchen to the bathroom. He ghosted against the wall when he heard a noise from the bathroom, a light brushing sound. He slid the gun from its holster and spoke in a low, calm voice. "I am an officer from the US Embassy and I am armed. Please remain where you are and identify yourself."

His heart hammered in his chest and his grip tightened at a light thump from the bathroom.

He raised his gun and aimed it at the door.

With a gentle bump the door swung open and a black cat wandered into the hallway and looked up at him. It meowed once, licked its lips, and then sashayed into the living room. Hugo let out a breath that he hadn't known he was holding and reholstered his weapon. He'd always preferred dogs.

He stepped into the bathroom. A simple pedestal sink and bathtub, but no shower. Beside the bath sat two saucers, both empty. Hugo knelt and touched them. Dry, so whatever milk or water Max had left for his cat was long gone. He stood and opened the vanity above the sink. A razor, shaving brush, and a little pot for the cream stood together on the shelf. Beside them, a plastic beaker holding a toothbrush and toothpaste.

He tried the kitchen, hoping to see something to change his mind, to challenge the disturbing and obvious conclusion that was settling in. The waist-high fridge held an open tub of paté, a large block of cheese, several plastic containers of unidentifiable leftovers, an unopened bottle of Sancerre, and a half-container of milk. He pulled it out, sniffed it, and almost retched. He went to empty it into the sink but the policeman in him said to preserve everything, so he put it back, silently irritated that he'd put his fingerprints on the carton.

Hugo looked over the rest of kitchen and noticed a loaf of bread protruding from under a dish cloth, so he picked it up and tapped it against the counter. Hard as a rock. He grimaced and moved back to the living room, where he found the cat perched on the top of Max's armchair.

He realized that he'd been hoping, despite everything he'd seen, that Max had been taken against his will but was staying away of his own accord. That hope now seemed ridiculous. The stale bread and sour milk made it clear that Max had been away from his apartment for several days at least, and the luggage and clothes still in the closet meant he'd not gone away of his own accord.

But what to do? He couldn't very well call the police. "*Bonjour.* Hugo Marston here. I just broke into someone's apartment and would like to report someone breaking in a day or two before me." Hardly.

There was one person he could call. He pulled out his phone and dialed Emma.

"Hey, it's me," he said.

"Well hello me, everything alright? You sound tense."

"I'm fine." How did she always know? She was better at reading people than he was. "Can you connect me with that journalist again? Claudia Roux."

She sighed, and he knew what she was thinking. *I don't believe that everything's fine, but if you won't tell me what's going on, I won't push it.* "I should have the number written here somewhere. Got it. Hold on and I'll connect you."

Twenty seconds later, Hugo heard two clicks and Claudia's voice.

"'*Allo*? Hugo?"

"Claudia, I know you're busy today, I'm sorry to bother you."

"Are you OK?"

"Yes. Listen, I'm at Max's place."

"He's there? You found him?"

"No. I found his cat."

"His cat? I don't understand."

"Neither do I. I let myself in and—"

"You broke into his apartment?"

"Claudia, *ça va*. It's OK. I had a key."

"A key. Since when?"

"That's not important. Listen, someone was here before me, they went through his books. But all his personal things are here like he just stepped out to buy bread. Claudia, I didn't tell you everything before. Max was kidnapped, I saw it with my own eyes."

"What? Why didn't you—"

"I know, I know. I'll fill you in later, but the point is, I was hoping that whoever had taken him had let him go, then told him to clear out of the city. But his stuff is here, clothes and suitcases, and his bread is stale and his milk sour. He hasn't been back."

"*Merde*, I'm sorry, this is terrible. Why would someone break into his place?"

"I'm not sure. Did you find anything out?"

"Oh, Hugo. I'm sorry. I haven't had time. That new drug task force I mentioned, I've been meeting with them all day. But I'll do it before I come over tonight, I promise."

"Thanks." Hugo swallowed his disappointment. Max's kidnapping hadn't worried the detectives at the prefecture, and a man gone from his apartment for a couple of days in Paris wasn't going to register with even the lowliest gendarme. He shouldn't be surprised that Claudia hadn't gotten to it. "No problem," he said. "I was just here so I thought I'd call. I'll see you tonight, OK? You remember the way?"

She laughed. "If I get lost, I'll ask a policeman."

"I'm going to take one more look around here, then I'll head home."

"*Bien*. Oh, Hugo. Feed him, will you?"

"Who?"

"The cat. Feed him before you go. Just in case."

CHAPTER TEN

At seven that evening Claudia appeared with a shopping bag in each hand and a peck on both cheeks for Hugo. He took the bags and she followed him into the kitchen where they started to unpack.

"You like snails?" she asked.

"*Mais oui*," he said. "As long as the garlic is pressed not diced and is just as fresh as the bread."

"Then you're in luck. Open some wine and watch me cook."

She must have gone home to change before coming over, Hugo thought, because her tight jeans were not made for field work, even for a journalist. Her top was simple, black and silky, dipping low down her back. As he watched her glide about the kitchen his appetite increased, but it was her that he wanted, not the food. He moved behind her and closed his arms around her waist. She laughed. "I see it's not just the bread and garlic that are fresh."

"They can wait a few minutes."

She dropped the butter and snails into the already-hot frying pan, turned the heat to low, then swiveled in his arms and put her lips against his ear. "I'm hungry too," she whispered.

He carried her into the bedroom as they kissed, and they left the snails to simmer for longer than any real chef would.

When they finally ate, they did so in the kitchen, both half-dressed and ravenous. They spoke little but smiled a lot, comparing snails for size and then devouring them, tearing each other hunks of bread from the rapidly shrinking baguette.

As Hugo got up to open a second bottle of wine, Claudia let out a small burp. "*Pardon.*" She held out her glass. "Before we finish this one, we should talk about your friend Max."

Max. Hugo hadn't mentioned, him but the old man had been with him all evening, a gnawing in his gut and a hollow echo in his mind. He'd wanted to ask what she knew the moment she stepped through the door but didn't want her to think he was using her, a childish thought and maybe an excuse for being overtaken by her presence. But now he was all ears.

"You found something?"

"No, that's just it. Nothing. I checked hospitals, morgues, and even the jails." She shrugged. "No Max Koche. Can you please tell me what's going on?"

He poured the wine and started with Max's kidnapping, with the bizarre response from the police on scene. She sat wide-eyed and unmoving as he filled her in on the old man's history, and how they'd become friends.

"The whole thing is . . . crazy. And what do you think is going on?" Claudia said. "That someone kidnapped him because of his past?"

"I have no idea."

"What about that book, the Rimbaud? You said you'd only just bought it from him."

"Yes, not even an hour—" Hugo stopped talking as his mind went into overdrive. *No. It couldn't be. The book?*

"I don't know everything you know," Claudia said. "But is it possible the book has something to do with it?"

"It crossed my mind originally, but it didn't make any sense. No one gets kidnapped over a book, and if that was what the man wanted Max didn't even have it. I did. All Max had to do was tell me to hand it over, no?"

"Maybe. Maybe he thought if he played dumb the guy would leave him alone. Was there anything unusual about it, or him selling it to you?"

"No, I don't think so." Hugo shook his head, then looked up. "All I can think is that . . . he didn't know the book's true value."

"Maybe someone else does," Claudia said. "Maybe that's what they want?"

"A book?"

"Sure, a valuable one. People have been killed for a lot less. But like you said, when he was kidnapped Max didn't have the book. You did." She lowered her wine glass and put a hand on his. "That means whoever took him knows that he doesn't have it, especially now that they searched his apartment. But they might know he sold it to you."

"Yeah, that just occurred to me."

"Don't play the hero, Hugo, you might be in danger."

"Possibly. Look, I don't have jurisdiction here, not officially. Do you think one of your cop buddies would open a missing person's file and go talk to that bouquiniste Chabot?"

"I will ask tomorrow, sure," she said. "But why would they shut down an investigation like that?"

"They found people who said nothing happened. Two or three Parisians versus one American." Hugo shook his head. "I don't know, maybe they thought I was drunk?"

"Were you?"

He shot her a look.

"Sorry," she said. "About the book. If it has something to do with his disappearance, you might want to think about getting it back. Can you?"

"The book, shit. Yes, I hope so." He slapped the table, annoyed at himself for not thinking of it. "If someone has Max and all they want is the book, then it's an easy swap."

"And if someone comes after you and you can give it to them, it's better than having a gun under your armpit."

"No reason I can't have both, is there?" Hugo stood and kissed her forehead. He felt better now that they had a plan. "I'm pretty sure I saw you sneak a mille-feuille into the fridge," he said. "Are you ready for some dessert?"

"Always. I'll get it while you call the bookseller."

She left in the night again, this time whispering into and kissing his ear, apparently not caring if she woke him. It was two in the morning when the door closed behind her and Hugo lay on his back, something tugging at his mind, something he was supposed to do.

The book. He'd not been able to reach Kendall, the business card having just the shop's number. He'd left a message and tried to put it out of his mind. He couldn't see how the book could really be behind Max's kidnapping, but he'd follow up in the morning and call off the sale anyway, just to be sure.

He tossed and turned until five, then gave up and rolled out of bed. He started a pot of coffee and then padded into his study. Hugo dialed the number for Kendall's store again, hoping that the Englishman was also an early bird. On the sixth ring, the store's voicemail kicked in. Hugo left another message telling Kendall to pull the book from auction and hang on to it for him. Then he looked up numbers for Christie's and left it on the screen as he went to the kitchen and poured the coffee. He'd have to wait for the auction house to open; he didn't trust voicemail to get the job done there.

He called Christie's at eight and, after explaining his needs to the receptionist, was put through to a junior auctioneer who specialized in French literature.

"Paul Goodson, how may I be of service?"

"My name is Hugo Marston, and your receptionist tells me that a book I own is being auctioned there this morning."

"I see. And what can we do for you?"

"I need you to pull it from auction."

"Pull it—"

"Yes," Hugo said. "Immediately."

"Very well, sir. I can try." The man sighed, clearly intending to let Hugo know how busy he was. Too busy for book owners who couldn't make their minds up about selling. "The auction starts in an hour, so

I'll need you to send in a written authorization, signed and notarized, describing the item and your relationship to it."

"Jesus, man. The item is a book, and we aren't having a relationship. I own the damn thing." Hugo took a deep breath. "Look, I'm the head of security at the US Embassy and I need you to pull that book from auction."

"This is State Department business?" The little ass was less sure of himself now.

"As far as you know, it is. I'll wait on the line, you go do your thing."

"Tell me your name again, I'll check."

Hugo gave him his name and the name of the book, and waited. It was a good five minutes before he heard the phone being picked up.

"Sir, I'm back."

"Did you find it?"

"Yes and no."

"Meaning?" Hugo said through clenched teeth.

"Well, the book is up for auction here." Hugo could hear the tension in the young man's voice. "Thing is, Mr. Marston, you are not listed as the seller."

Of course not, he'd authorized Kendall to handle it.

"Look, Peter Kendall is the man who put it up for sale for me. He's a bookseller here in Paris, you should know that. Just ask him. In fact, if he's there, bring him to the phone."

"Sir, no one is here yet. And I do know Mr. Kendall, which is why I can't pull the book without his permission. We do a lot of business with him."

"When does the auction start?"

"In less than an hour. And you should hurry if you're trying to contact him because we do the expensive pieces early. Our wealthy clients don't like to be made to wait."

Of course they don't. "I'll get back to you." Hugo hung up and tried Kendall again, leaving another message and then sending an e-mail. Too much to hope the guy carried a Blackberry.

He spent the next hour and a half hovering by his computer and the telephone, drinking coffee and crunching on a toasted, stale baguette made palatable by globs of black cherry jam. Every time he walked into his study he willed the phone to ring, and it did just before ten. He gave Kendall no reasons, just asked him to call and take the book off the auction block. Kendall apologized for not getting back to him before, he'd called Hugo's office by mistake. Kendall rang off with a promise to call back as soon as he'd canceled the sale.

It took another fifteen minutes, and when the bookseller called his voice was apologetic.

"I'm really sorry, Mr. Marston. The book sold already."

"Shit." Hugo's teeth clenched tighter. "Who bought it?"

"I asked but they wouldn't tell me. The buyer wanted to remain anonymous, and they have that right. Especially when they paid so much for it."

Dammit. Hugo thought quickly. "Look, is the buyer still there, do you know? If they'd just let me talk to him . . ."

"Oh no," said Kendall, "sorry, I should have said. He attended the auction by telephone. The wealthier clients tend to do that."

"And I don't suppose they'd give me his phone number, would they?"

"No, I don't think so." Kendall sighed. "I'm sorry Mr. Marston, I really am. Maybe if there is some compelling reason, I could ask someone there to make contact?"

Hugo didn't see his reasoning being too persuasive, and he didn't like going through intermediaries. He asked Kendall to fax a letter to Christies explaining that he'd put the book up for auction on Hugo's behalf. Kendall apologized again and said he'd send the letter immediately.

Hugo waited fifteen minutes before he called and asked for Paul Goodson.

"Hugo Marston again," he said. "You got the letter from Peter Kendall?"

"Yes, I have it in front of me."

"Good. He explained to me about the anonymous buyer."

"Yes, sir. As I'm sure Mr. Kendall explained, we can't give out any information about the buyer."

"So I gather," Hugo said. "So assuming that's your position, if you'd be kind enough to put me through to your boss. No offense, it's just that I need that privacy policy bent a little out of shape, and I'm guessing he's the one to do it."

"I can get him," Goodson said. "The thing is, it's not a policy. Assuring this buyer's privacy is the only way we can get him to bid, so it's always in our contract of sale. Which, as you know, is signed already. I'm sorry Mr. Marston, but God himself couldn't persuade us to give up this client. Could you get a court order, maybe? We would have to release the name then."

Hugo thought of the paperwork required to get an order from a judge. An American asking to make an international corporation give up confidential information and, possibly, make a wealthy French citizen give up an item he'd bought legally. And all for a crime that, even if it existed, had nothing to do with Hugo Marston or the American Embassy. No chance. "I'll look into that," he said. "Do me a favor in the meantime, would you?"

"I'll try, Mr. Marston."

"Get a message to your esteemed client. Tell him that if I don't get that book back, a man may die."

"Are you serious, sir? I don't—"

"Yes, I'm serious. And truthfully, I'm not sure how or why. That's why I need the book. Tell him he'll get his money back, every penny."

"That reminds me, sir. Do you want to know how much it sold for?"

Hugo realized he'd not even thought about the sale price. "Sure."

"Five hundred and thirty thousand Euros. That's almost three-quarters of a million US dollars."

"Yes," said Hugo, his voice a whisper, "it is."

"Several bidders pushed the price up. We honestly didn't think it'd go for more than three hundred thousand Euros. Good news, wouldn't you say?"

CHAPTER ELEVEN

W hen Eric Ambler wrote that Paris had "the macabre formality of a steel engraving," he could have been sitting at the
window of Hugo's apartment those early hours of Wednesday morning.
A steel engraving because the buildings and streets had a uniform gray-
ness, dulled further by an endless low cloud that hung above the rooftops, flattened the light, and drew the color right out of the city. And
macabre because Hugo had just seen a significant clue, and possibly a
lifeline, disappear into the hands of a remote and anonymous buyer. He
was furious with himself for selling the book in the first place. Would
he ever, *ever*, have been so careless with potential evidence in the past?

After he'd calmed himself he refocused and wondered, just for
a moment, whether the buyer was somehow connected with all this.
But the idea was impossible to explore in any rational sense, and so not
worth thinking about. For now, anyway.

He called Claudia but hung up before she answered. Two minutes
later, the phone rang and he smiled. Of course, her cell phone had reg-
istered his call. It was hard to change your mind in the modern world.

"Miss me?" she said.

"*Mais oui*. I miss Max, too."

"I didn't know you felt that way about him."

"Hush." Hugo couldn't help but smile. "You're not too big to go
over my knee, you know."

"Oh, Hugo." He could hear the smile in her voice. "I think I'd fit
rather nicely."

"Tell me, my crime reporter, what's the word on our new
bouquiniste?"

"Nothing yet. I called a detective friend and persuaded him to send over a couple of uniformed men."

"Thanks." He'd never been good at asking for favors. "Any idea when they might report back yet?"

"*Non*. But it's only just eleven."

"Oh right. I've been up too long." He told her that the book had sold already, heard the sharp intake of breath when she heard how much it went for.

"Maybe this *is* about the book," she said. "Did you ever look inside it?"

"You mean for something hidden?" He thought for a moment. There was the card in the Agatha Christie but the only time he'd seen the Rimbaud open was at Kendall's store. "No. But it's not a big book, it would have to be something small."

"Like invisible ink or something?"

"Silly, if it was invisible ink I would never have seen it. I meant like a piece of paper, or words underlined."

"Whoever bought it at auction, would he have known beforehand whether there was something inside?" she asked.

"I don't see how, he bought over the telephone."

"Maybe someone looked it over for him before the sale."

"Maybe," Hugo said. "That's a lot of money for something you haven't seen."

"Although you bought it without inspecting it."

"I didn't pay half a million Euros."

"Fair point."

"Look, can you get away for lunch? Or dinner? I don't mean to sound needy but I do like your cooking."

"Oh, I can't." Her voice was suddenly distant. "I have plans already. Let me call you this afternoon when my gendarmes return. And I will see you tomorrow, I promise."

Hugo hung up, feeling like a foolish teenager. He'd not imagined he would feel disappointment at such a slight rejection, yet he did. They barely knew each other, why wouldn't she have other plans, even other lovers? Because he didn't? Hugo almost laughed at himself. If the world's inhabitants matched their sex lives to his, it would be a world with few children.

He looked at his watch. Nothing he could do about finding Max right now, but he had to do something. Not work, he didn't want to go to the embassy and have Emma read in his face . . . what, disappointment? Frustration? Whichever emotion he was feeling, he'd never get to his desk without Emma spotting it, without her seeing through him. He didn't feel like dealing with that today. Plus, he was on vacation.

Lunch would be a good start, a catalyst for what Hercule Poirot called "the little gray cells." He could still taste the garlic from last night's snails and thought that a salad might be just the thing to cleanse the palate. He set off down Rue Jacob, glancing up at the solid gray sky and expecting to feel the spit of rain. He didn't mind, content that a hat, a coat, and the occasional doorway would offer enough shelter.

He meandered through the Sixth Arrondissement, never tired of the tight streets and small, cozy boutiques. Overhead, window boxes spilled red geraniums, brightening the stone façades of the two-star hotels that catered to the not-so-wealthy Americans and weekend visitors from Britain, tourists who wanted to be in the center of Paris and didn't mind tiny rooms, or didn't know they were getting one.

By the time he reached the Seine, he'd forgotten about eating. Across the Quai de Conti lay Max's stall. Hugo stood by the crossing light, impervious to the mass of cars rushing by just feet away. He fixed his eyes on the slight man moving back and forth in front of the open green box, adjusting his wares and occasionally looking up to spot potential customers. Something about the way Chabot moved galled Hugo, as if he'd been there for years, as if this was and always had been his territory.

Except it wasn't. It belonged to Max.

Hugo wanted to go over and shake the truth out of the man. He knew Chabot had lied about Max and he wanted to know why. But he also knew that there was a better way. Two decades of FBI training and experience had taught Hugo that rushing in before thinking could be the death knell for an investigation. Evidence could be missed, spoiled, or contaminated, witnesses scared off. And if it did become a police matter, maybe even get as far as a courtroom, he didn't want to be the one to screw it up. Not for his sake, and not for Max's.

And yet he had to do something.

He pulled out his phone and dialed his office. Emma picked up promptly.

"Hi Emma, fancy doing some research?"

"Sure. Fancy telling me what's going on?"

"What do you mean?"

"Well, you know I don't like to pry. And you know that sometimes I can't help myself."

"It's OK Emma, curiosity is a sign of intelligence."

"It's also a sign of nosiness," she said.

Hugo gave a wry smile. "And?"

"Well, obviously things didn't go well with Christine, but what's with the journalist here? The bookseller calling? Now the research? This is not like any vacation I've ever seen. And where are you? I can barely hear you for the traffic."

"Sorry, it is loud." Hugo retreated down a small side street, pausing beside a post office he'd never noticed before, and the roar of midday was instantly muffled. "Better? Look," he said, "I'm not up to anything, but if I am, I'll let you know."

"Thanks Hugo, that makes perfect sense." Her grudging respect for his privacy and sharp tongue were two of her best assets.

"I knew you'd understand. Now, I need a number, and contact name if possible, for the Syndicat Des Bouquinistes de Paris."

"Syndicat Des Bouquinistes? I never knew there was one."

"Me neither."

"Give me a few seconds here. Syndicat Des. . . . Here you go. Cecilia Roget seems to be its head. No, wait, Bruno Gravois. Took over a year ago."

"Thanks," said Hugo. "Where are they based?"

Emma gave him an address in the Seventeenth Arrondissement, on Rue Nollet. "Closest metro stop is Place de Clichy," she said. "Hugo, are you going there now?"

"Yes, why?"

"No reason. Sometimes I have the urge to tell you to be careful and I don't always know why."

"Because in a former life you were my mother?"

"If I'd been your mother, Hugo, I would have been reincarnated as a saint, not a secretary."

"But you are a saint, didn't you know?"

"Oh hush. Anything else you need me to do?"

"No," he said. "No doubt I'll call you tomorrow for something."

"No doubt," she said, and rang off.

Hugo walked back onto the Quai de Conti. He looked toward Jean Chabot's stall and saw two gendarmes talking to him. *Thank you, Claudia.* He resisted the urge to trot across the street and eavesdrop, or butt in completely, and instead turned east and headed alongside the sluggish roll of the river, walking toward the metro stop at Les Invalides, which, if memory served, would take him directly to Place de Clichy station. And the thirty-minute walk would give him time to come up with some sort of plan.

After exiting the metro station at Place de Clichy, Hugo walked northwest on Rue Biot against the traffic into the Seventeenth Arrondissement, which sat just to the west of the hopping Montmartre area. The Seventeenth was one of those truly French parts of Paris that rubbed shoulders with, but never quite got to know, the tourists who shuttled between the Place Pigalle, the Sacre Couer, and the arrondissements that sit either side of the Seine. A business hub since the 1970s, only the most avid historian would travel to this part of Paris and recognize the village of Batignolles, where in the 1870s painter Edouard Manet and his *groupe des Batignolles* captured the busy cafés and local parks on canvas.

As he walked, he noticed the windshield wipers of a few cars ticking back and forth, but under hat and coat he felt no rain. He spotted a small park on his left, the direction he wanted to go, and crossed the street toward it.

He pushed open a waist-high gate and heard it squeak as it swung shut behind him. The metal latch clattered, catching the attention of two Arab men playing chess on a nearby bench. They quickly returned to their game—he was of no interest to them. A gravel path led him between two rectangles of brown grass, each bordered by the entrails of lifeless plants, inert but preserved by the Paris winter.

The grass soon gave way to a large square of gravel where half a dozen men played or watched *petanque*, some standing and some sitting. The eldest, a stooped little man with an impossibly red nose, stood just inside a small green shed and brewed coffee, a line of tin mugs on a table by the door. Another of the men, as French as a postcard in his blue beret and baggy canvas pants, turned his palms upward to gauge the rain. Unimpressed by the feeble spatter, he went back to the game. A row of players awaited their turn on one of the worn park benches, cooing and nodding their approval of the action like a row of pigeons on a tree branch. Wraiths of smoke greeted Hugo as he approached, the pungent, raw aroma of unfiltered tobacco so much more pleasing to him than the sharp, clinging smell of the thin cigarettes smoked in the bars and clubs of the Fifth Arrondissement.

Hugo watched the game, too, for a moment, wondering if he could tell anything about these men from the way they spoke and what they wore. He gave up after a couple of minutes, amused by his own pretensions. All he could tell was that they were content and that they hoped that the sun might eventually come out.

The park let him out at the corner of two streets, the larger one being Rue de Dames. Diagonally across from him, kitty-corner as his grandmother would say, was Rue Nollet. Like a thousand other streets in Paris, it was part residential and part business, apartments stacked three and four high on top of stores, and the occasional heavy wooden door leading to a courtyard surrounded by more numerous, and more expensive, apartments. There were few people on the street—lunch and the chill bluster of the afternoon had seen to that.

He looked for number twenty-three and found it sandwiched between a bakery and a small store selling handmade linens from Provence. He stopped at the window of this store and looked in, trying not to think about Claudia and which design of napkins she might like. As if either of them were the napkin-buying type.

The door Hugo wanted was dark red, and beside it was a brass plaque, screwed into the brick, announcing it to be the home of the Syndicat Des Bouquinistes De Paris. A piece of paper with neat, flowing handwriting let visitors know that the bell was broken and that they should let themselves in.

Hugo did so.

Inside, a long staircase led up to the offices of the SBP. He took his hat off and started up, the thick carpet on the stairs making his entrance a silent one. At the top was a landing where the carpet turned into creaking floorboards, old but polished and a little slick underfoot. An unmanned desk sat to his left, guarding the two closed doors of the SBP. He walked up to the desk, looking for a bell and listening for the sound of voices or typing. He heard a phone ring and the door on the left swung open. A dumpy, middle-aged woman with a beehive hairdo bustled out carrying a stack of letters. He thought she hadn't noticed him but, without looking up, she dumped the mail on the desk and said, "*Oui monsieur*?"

Hugo gave his name and broke into his clumsiest French. "I am a journalist, American, and wanted to write an article about the bouquinistes."

It wasn't much of a plan but he couldn't play the policeman and, in his experience, the only people who could ask questions without raising suspicion were cops and journalists.

"You should make an appointment and speak with Monsieur Gravois," she said, still avoiding eye contact.

"Monsieur Gravois, yes," Hugo said. "The thing is, I'm only in Paris today and tomorrow, then I head to Belgium. Chocolates and beer." He shrugged. Americans. What can you do?

"*Un moment, s'il vous plait*," she said, apparently unimpressed by chocolates, beer, or Americans. She looked over her shoulder at the door she'd just come through, then at the phone on her desk, then at Hugo. She stood and walked back to the door, knocked tentatively, and listened for a response. Hugo didn't hear it but she did, and she slipped into the room and closed the door behind her, as if an unwelcome dog were trying to follow. Or an unwelcome visitor. A minute later she opened the door wide and stood holding it, bidding Hugo enter.

When he did, Hugo got two surprises, only one of which he chided himself for. The first came when he saw the man behind the desk, the bald head and gaunt features, the large eyes staring at him and ready to take in everything about his visitor, but giving nothing in return. Bruno Gravois was the man who had slapped Chabot.

The second surprise was the office itself. Three metal filing cabinets stood against the wall opposite the door, each drawer labeled in neat type, and to his left Gravois sat behind a desk that knew no clutter. Two sheets of paper lay on a blotter, and as Hugo moved closer Gravois laid his pen down between them, his movement as deliberate as that of a surgeon. No computer that Hugo could see, not even a telephone. Three prints hung on the wall, two placed precisely over the gaps between the filing cabinets and the third behind the desk, and as far as Hugo could tell, squarely in the middle. The book case to the right of the doorway was full but not stuffed, and even a brief glance told Hugo that every book had been placed according to its category.

Gravois rose and narrowed his eyes just a touch, trying to remember where they'd seen each other before. Hugo pictured their sidewalk stand-off and scrolled his mind back over their encounter, remembering nothing that would directly contradict his journalist story. He decided to take the initiative, to make it a non event.

"At the book stall by Pont Neuf," Hugo said. He leaned across the desk and extended his hand. "I believe we saw each other there a few days ago. I'm Hugo Marston."

"Yes, I remember now." Gravois nodded slowly. "You were asking questions." Despite the warmth of the office, he wore gloves and, as if to explain, said, "I am undergoing treatment for cancer, I have to be careful about infections."

"I'm sorry to hear that," Hugo said. That explained the baldness and lack of eyebrows. "As I told your assistant, I am a journalist. I'd been told that a bouquiniste called Max worked at the stall, that he'd give me an interview."

"*Ah, oui*? About what?" He spoke slowly, his voice deep and gravelly, his words as deliberate as his movements.

"About the bookstalls. Their history, what it's like to work at one, what they think of tourists."

"*Alors*. Sit, Monsieur Marston, please." Gravois directed his guest to one of two identical seats opposite him and sat down himself. "Tourists pay the bouquinistes' rent, what do you suppose they think of them?"

"True," said Hugo. "But they don't have to like them."

"And you think," Gravois said, "that my bouquinistes are stupid enough to tell you they don't like Americans?"

"No, no, you misunderstand. That's not the focus of my article at all."

"And who is your employer? Do you have credentials?"

"I'm freelance. I hope to sell to one of the airlines, actually. They pay the best."

"And your credentials?"

"Unfortunately," Hugo shrugged, "you only get those when you work for a news organization. We freelancers have to rely on our charm."

"Indeed." Gravois shifted in his seat. "What do you want from me?"

Hugo pulled out the notepad and pen that he'd bought at a *tabac* en route. "I've always wondered how the bouquinistes get their stalls."

"Like Monsieur Chabot, for example?"

"Monsieur . . . ?" Hugo played dumb, as good at this routine as anyone. But Gravois was inscrutable. He would make a great interrogator, Hugo thought, you had no idea what he knew, but you suspected he knew a lot.

"No matter." Gravois waved a hand. "Bouquinistes have been around for many years, over a century. How the stalls are passed along varies, Monsieur Marston. Sometimes father to son, sometimes friends."

"Sometimes the SBP?"

"Yes. We are a resource for our members in many ways. That is one of them."

"What else does the SBP do?"

"Many things." Gravois looked away from Hugo for the first time, checking the alignment of his pen. Almost perfect but not quite. Gravois straightened it, then looked up again. "We are a lobbying organization. If the government tries to oppress our members, we represent them. We provide supplemental health packages for those who do not want to rely on the current system."

"And for that your members pay a fee?"

"Like any union, yes, of course." Gravois smiled, but there was no change in the eyes. "Even journalists have unions, you know."

"So I've heard," said Hugo. "Just not in America."

"No? America is an interesting country, I should visit one day."

"You should." Hugo cleared his throat. He knew he would have to choose his words carefully, that for some reason suspicion was already aroused. That fact alone told Hugo plenty, about Gravois if not about what he was doing. Fastidious and suspicious, and either his temperament or some position of power allowed him to slap a man in public and fear no recrimination. It probably didn't matter if Hugo got thrown out as a fraud, but until he knew where Max was, he had no desire to antagonize anyone. "Are all bouquinistes members of the SBP?"

"Yes. It is, as the English say, 'a closed shop.' Your French, by the way, is excellent. For an American."

"Thank you." Hugo ignored the slight. "Let me ask you this, do you suppose Monsieur Chabot would give me an interview? Background on the SBP is of great interest but so too are the daily activities of your members."

"You did well to come to me first, monsieur. I think that few bouquinistes, none perhaps, would talk to you without my . . . our permission. You must understand that the police, government officials of several kinds, they go around looking for petty violations. Those spots are valuable real estate and I think some bureaucrats resent that we get them so cheaply. To them, money is more important than tradition. It's a shame."

"Yes, it is. But with your permission, I can interview Monsieur Chabot?"

They locked eyes for a moment, each man trying to read the thoughts and intentions of the other. Gravois spoke first.

"No. I think it is better that the bouquinistes retain a little mystery about them, don't you?" A thin smile. "You are free to write whatever pleases you, but I would prefer it if you did not bother my members, monsieur."

The interview was clearly over but Hugo made no attempt to get up. "Then one last question, Monsieur Gravois. How exactly did Monsieur Chabot come to be in possession of that stall?"

Again the deliberate pause. "Why your interest in him?"

Hugo shrugged. "When I spoke to him he didn't seem to know much about books. He seems young and I'm not sure he has the highest ranking in, or respect from, the SBP." *Yes, I saw you hit him.* "And yet he suddenly comes into possession of what must surely be one of the best stalls in Paris."

"Suddenly?" Gravois stood. "What makes you say it was sudden?"

"Just something Chabot said." Hugo flipped his notebook closed, well aware that Gravois had been looking to see if he'd been taking notes. He had. "I don't remember what exactly, he just left me with that impression."

"I hide nothing from you, Monsieur Marston, when I tell you that he is a stupid man. But even stupid men need to make a living, no?"

"Of course." Hugo reached for his hat as Gravois limped around the desk, leaning on it for support.

"I expect that with his limited intelligence and your good but imperfect language skills, there was a miscommunication." Gravois picked up his cane and walked to the door. He opened it and waited. "That is, of course, another reason why an interview is not a good idea. It would benefit no one for you to misrepresent their words in your article. Good day, Monsieur Marston. And *bonne chance.*"

Hugo paused in the doorway and turned to face Gravois, close enough to smell stale tobacco on the man's breath. Funny, he hadn't noticed an ashtray in here. It was an intentional invasion of space and Hugo felt satisfaction when Gravois shifted his weight to his bad foot.

"Do you know where Max Koche is, Monsieur Gravois?"

"Max Koche?" His face was impassive. "I'm not familiar with the name. We have several hundred members, I do not know them all."

"Then maybe you can look him up. Jean Chabot is running his stall."

"*Au revoir* Monsieur Marston. And as they say in America, 'take care.'"

CHAPTER TWELVE

It wasn't much of a café, and wasn't one at all except for those who knew it was there. On a narrow street less than a block from the Seine, a weathered board spelled *Chez Maman* in peeling black letters and hung over an entrance that showed no particular sign of welcoming strangers. It was five o'clock, a good time to find a table and some peace, and maybe wash away the bitter taste that had settled in his mouth in Rue Nollet.

Hugo put his shoulder to the door and stepped into a small room filled with trails of smoke that rose past the blank, tired faces of men who stared into cups of coffee, beer, and shot glasses of amber liquid. A scarred stone floor and the heavy elbows of the bar's patrons made every one of the dozen or so tables wobble, though no one was moving much. Above Hugo's head dark beams striped the low ceiling, the plaster stained yellow from a hundred years or more of cigarette and cigar smoke.

Hugo closed the door behind him, then looked over and saw the owner behind the bar, the woman known simply as Maman. She was short and squat and unwilling to pour anything but beer, wine, and the occasional whisky—if you didn't mind being horribly overcharged. Sixty-something, maybe seventy, but always there, and no matter how crowded and smoky the place got she was visible, shuffling up and down behind the bar with her bright orange head of hair that was a slightly different shade every week. She laughed plenty but never for long—the bar's smoke had stained her lungs, too, and jocularity inevitably devolved into a rasping, hacking cough that her customers pretended not to hear. For those moments she kept a canister of fresh

93

oxygen behind the bar, always within reach, and never far from the cigarette that burned in her fingers.

But her coffee was hot, strong, and served faster and cheaper than
anywhere else in Paris. And, if she recognized your face, most of the
time it came free when you ordered something stronger. It was a place
for bouquinistes who needed a moment of warmth or shelter and for
the men, and occasionally women, who worked nearby, sweeping the
streets and emptying the tourists' trash cans. Hugo had been here at least
once a month for the past two years, for the coffee and the atmosphere.

He'd been introduced to the place, and to Maman, by Max a
couple of months after they became friends. Hugo wasn't the most avid
book collector, but twenty years in law enforcement, mostly with the
FBI, had meant a discerning and distrustful eye when it came to buying
goods from the side of the road. He'd first met Max on a quick trip over
from England, chancing across his stall and buying a book about late
eighteenth-century serial killers. He'd reconnected with Max when he
moved to Paris and soon found him to be one of the few sellers who
derived joy not from the money he made from a sale, but from the very
act of pressing a collector's item into the hands of an appreciative cus-
tomer. Most of the time Hugo stopped by his stall to chat and bought
something on a whim, often not paying until the next time he stopped
by.

Once, Max had presented him with a set of first-edition books by
Eric Ambler, Hugo's favorite author. Hugo had not found out until
much later that the old man had squirreled them away one by one,
seeking them out among his colleagues for months before presenting
them with a flourish one summer morning.

There had always been something about the old man, his disin-
terest in money, a habit of deflecting conversation about himself with
a wave of his hands, and the occasional far-off look that started in his
eyes and quickly shut him off from the world. They were friends, Hugo
knew, good friends, but whatever lurked within Max always had to be
offered by the old man himself, not extracted. And, now that Hugo
knew about his past, he understood why.

"*L'Américain.*" Maman said it every time he came in; a year ago with mistrust, but nowadays just to let him know she knew.

"*Maman.*" Hugo nodded and asked for a shot of her whisky. He'd soak it up with a sandwich later if he had to, but the burn of Maman's overpriced rot-gut was good for right now. He perched at the bar and slammed the first one, nodding at Maman for a second. He wrapped a hand around it and smiled his thanks as she shuffled over and slid a cup of coffee in front of him. He sipped from the glass, then stood to make way for two men who'd just entered the bar, rubbing warmth into their hands.

He found a table at the back of the room, sat down, and began to run Max's abduction back through his mind, step by step, trying to reduce it to a training-ground exercise to take the sting out of a real man's kidnapping, maybe his murder. He knew there was little more he could have done to save his old friend, but that didn't stop him from trying to think of something, or from finding fault with himself for letting it happen. At the very least he should have abided by the seven-foot rule: the minimum distance between an agent and a hostile, enough distance to draw a weapon before a man with a knife became dangerous. A rule he'd forgotten, or at least forgotten to observe. *Too long out of the game*, he thought.

He was staring into his coffee, watching the steam rise slowly over the black liquid, when a newspaper slapped down on the table and he heard a voice behind him.

"You like look a miserable bastard. Buy me a drink and I'll cheer you up."

Hugo turned in his seat and a smile spread over his face. "Tom! What the hell are you doing here?"

"Tourist." Tom grinned back, then looked around the bar. "Nice place you got here."

"Isn't it? How the hell did you find me here?"

"Let's just say you have a lioness for a secretary."

"A toothless one, apparently." He'd told Emma about this place a long time ago; he couldn't even remember why. But she knew he came here with Max, must have guessed he'd be here now.

Hugo resisted the urge to put his friend in a bear hug. Chez Maman was a place where men nodded and shook hands with each other, then sat down. Hugs were reserved for after midnight when the orange-haired lady's hooch could be blamed.

Hugo gestured to the chair opposite him and stole a second look at Tom as he sat. Time had softened Hugo's own figure, but regular weight workouts and the occasional run had ensured that a core strength and fitness remained. Tom, on the other hand, had ballooned. The wiry figure of old had been obliterated by Tom's natural distaste for physical activity and his penchant for good food. And alcohol. Hugo knew better than to say anything, but seeing his friend huff his way into the chair, hearing the air whistle through his nose, was decidedly disappointing. He could probably get away with a comment on the thinning hair, but somehow his friend's shabby look and his watery, blood-shot eyes saddened Hugo and served to silence him.

"That's better." Tom settled in and looked around again. "I don't see any cocktail waitresses."

"You won't," Hugo smiled. "And don't try ordering from back here, either. What are you having?"

"Same as you. Load us up."

Hugo went to the bar and brought back two beers and two double shots of whisky. A moment later Maman herself dropped a cup of coffee onto the table in front of Tom.

"On the house," she said with a wink.

Hugo nudged Tom's shin with his foot as their eyes followed Maman's weighty shuffle back to the bar. "Never seen her do that before," Hugo said. "You got something to tell me?"

"I don't kiss and tell. I sure as hell don't kiss that."

Hugo sat back and his fingers played with his whisky glass, a smile on his face. "I can't believe you're here, Tom. It's good to see you."

"Well, you sounded all sad and needy on the phone, plus I have this Marseille thing." He smirked. "And playing in Paris is always fun."

"You still like to play, huh? Why does that make me nervous?"

"You'll survive. What about you, still doing your Sherlock Holmes party trick? You used to pretend to hate it when I made you do that for the ladies."

"Pretend?" He'd minded when Tom made him perform, but not too much. It looked like a party trick, that was true, but mostly it was a result of Hugo training himself to observe. And it was also true that he'd gotten the idea from Sherlock Holmes, who was able to startle people with his accurate deductions about where they'd been, or where they were going, through simple observations.

"Come on, you've not seen me for ages. Tell me something about myself."

Hugo rolled his eyes. "Later maybe. I have something more interesting to talk about first."

"The guy sounds like a control freak." Tom had drained his whisky, half his beer, and was onto his coffee. "His office, the way he looked and talked, everything by the sounds of it. Jeez, the only person I know of who slaps people in public is you."

"Funny."

"Look, Hugo, it's also possible he was just fucking with you. He may not know anything at all, just hates nosey American reporters. And there ain't no sin in that."

"Maybe. But he's definitely a control freak, I'd say actively paranoid. I just got the sense that he was hiding something. Correction: he was clearly hiding something."

"That's the definition of paranoid, Hugo. They hide shit when they don't have to, they hide shit they don't even know about."

"Yeah, I know." Hugo sipped at his own coffee, now almost cold.

"So what the fuck can I do to help?"

"Do you think you can find out who bought the book? Get it back?"

"Dude, I can find the buyer. I can have him disappear in a car accident somewhere in Monaco if you like."

Hugo looked at his friend and knew that he was only half-joking. Maybe not even half. "Let's keep it legit. He can have his money back and if the book turns out to have nothing to do with this, I'll give him first option to buy at a discount."

"You sweet man. And if he doesn't want to give it up?"

"I rely on your discretion and powers of persuasion," Hugo said.

"You got it."

"You remember I said legit, right?"

"Yeah, you did say that. Anything else?"

"Yes, one thing. Think you can dig up anything on this Bruno Gravois?"

"Honestly Hugo, if there's anything on him then it's probably on the DCRI or DGSE databases. I'll look, but all these agencies now, CIA, FBI, and Interpol," he snorted derisively, "they're all touchy feely, into sharing information and open access. Which means that we gather it, they use it. It's bullshit if you ask me, but of course no one does."

"Of course." Hugo drained his coffee. "Now, if the lecture's over, let's head out. I have work to do in the morning."

"Work?" Tom raised his beer glass. "Fuck work."

"Ah yes, you had something else in mind."

"Meaning?"

"You're hoping I'll go to the Moulin Rouge with you tonight."

Tom slapped the table with delight. "Now we're talking! Go on, do your thing."

"For old time's sake, but I'm a little rusty so this is an easy one. We'll start with the fact that you are tech savvy, which means you get your news online. And yet you come here carrying a newspaper. It's crumpled, so you've finished with it, but you didn't read it here, obviously, so you probably got it from the airport or train station."

"Airport. Free in the business class lounge."

"And yet you still have it, so I have to presume that you saw something that caught your eye and made you want to hang on to it. Otherwise, obviously, you would have disposed of the paper long before you got here."

"So far so good."

"So, knowing you, the something that caught your eye will either be drinkable or have long, sleek legs. Rule out booze because I can't think of anything drink-related that would cause you to hang on to a newspaper for hours. Which leaves us with the legs. Now, regular strip joints don't advertize in major newspapers, so I'm guessing it's something higher class and aimed at tourists, which brings me to the Moulin Rouge."

"Impressive."

"I'm not done, because you can go there any time you like, so why the newspaper today? That's made easier because I also know that you're a cheap bastard, which makes me suspect there's a coupon or discount advertized for tonight. Maybe tomorrow night."

"Fuck, I've missed you." Tom was grinning broadly, unfolding the paper to the full-page ad. At least half of the page was taken up by the long, bare legs of a dancer. "Her name is Mimi and she's a goddamn marvel, a star as good as any from the past. For her show tonight it's buy one ticket, a friend gets in for free. Shall we?"

"She is beautiful. But you know that buying a ticket doesn't entitle you to sleep with her?"

"My dear friend," Tom wagged a finger. "I think that's for her to decide, not you. Well?"

Hugo stood and patted his friend's head. "Good to see you, too, Tom. No dancing girls, but I do have booze at home. You coming?"

CHAPTER THIRTEEN

I t was early afternoon the next day when Hugo fixed himself a sandwich and flipped on the coffee maker for his third cup, and Tom's first. More whisky, several pints of water, and a host of war stories had kept them up well past midnight and neither man's body had seen fit to stir before the noon bells clanged.

As the coffee brewed and Tom took a shower, Hugo turned on the computer in his study, now Tom's bedroom, and was logging in when the doorbell rang. Hugo checked his security monitor, wondering if Claudia had decided to stop by rather than return the message he'd left with her. Instead, he saw a young man with the beginnings of a Mohawk fidgeting on the doorstep. He wore a blue parka with an insignia on the breast and blue nylon pants with a black stripe down the sides. Delivery boy, and apparently Dimitrios wasn't at his station to let him in. Hugo picked up his phone and unlocked the door remotely. A minute later he opened his apartment door and took an envelope from the young man, thanked him with some coins, and retreated back inside.

The envelope, unmarked, was between white and cream in color and so expensive it was almost cloth. Thin, too, so no more than a letter inside. The thinner the safer, Hugo knew. He went to his desk and searched for his letter opener, an ornate wooden knife given him by the head of a Namibian delegation who'd been impressed by the size and efficiency of the security detail Hugo had provided. He slipped it into the corner of the envelope and scythed it open. Inside, as he'd suspected, a single piece of paper. He pulled the letter out and sat down to read.

It was written in English, in an elegant, sloping hand. From the broadness of the letters and the lack of indentation on the back, Hugo could see it was written with a fountain pen. No doubt an expensive one. The paper was embossed with raised, silver lettering and, of all things, a coat of arms belonging to one Gérard de Roussillon, le Comte d'Auvergne. On the page was written:

Monsieur Marston:

Please forgive the short notice, I am not in the habit of imposing without a fair degree of warning. However, if you find yourself available I would be very grateful if you could spare me and a few of my friends an hour or two of your time. In a poor attempt to make amends for my late invitation, I will send a car for you at seven o'clock. Please dress for dinner.
    I look forward to meeting you.

It was not, Hugo knew, as much an invitation as a summons. And he had no idea why it had come to him. He tried but failed to remember an official function at the embassy involving a count. But he'd come across a lot of people whose names and backgrounds he didn't know, people who often wanted to curry favor with Americans. This guy could be one of them.

Hugo turned back to his computer and typed his host's name into a search engine, but other than a few links to books on French nobility, there was nothing of note on the first page of results. Hugo clicked onto the second page and saw a reference to "G. de Roussillon." The description indicated that, assuming it was the same man, le Comte d'Auvergne was a client. Hugo clicked on the link and the image of worn, leather-bound books appeared. It was the website for the bookshop belonging to Pierre Vasson, perhaps the most expensive and connected of the country's sellers of "*livres anciens et d'occasion.*" Hugo had been there several times, more to browse than buy, such were the prices. The image of the Rimbaud sprang into his mind, the connection too obvious not to rear its head. Not another coincidence, surely.

Hugo had loved books since he was a child, but they were starting to give him a headache.

He considered calling Emma to get more background on de Roussillon but couldn't face the inevitable questions in her voice, so he
dialed Claudia's number instead. Again no answer, and when he rang
off he felt a little foolish. The last thing he wanted to do was chase her
away by appearing overly eager.

Dating games. Jesus.

And that line, *Dress for dinner*. Where Hugo came from that
meant jeans and cowboy boots, but in embassy-speak it meant black
tie, though he could have guessed that a tuxedo was required just from
the silken stationary. Still, he didn't own shiny black shoes and didn't
feel obliged to rush out and buy any at such short notice, so the cowboy
boots would stay.

Tom emerged from the shower and Hugo excused himself, having
already seen too much of his friend. When he handed him hot coffee
five minutes later, Tom also took the letter.

"Am I your date?" he said.

"Not the kind of place where excessive drinking and swearing is
welcome, by the looks of the envelope."

"Fair enough," Tom said. "I got my list of things to do from you
yesterday, anyway. Want me to look into this guy first?"

"No," said Hugo. "I kind of like surprises."

The car was there at ten minutes before seven, a black Mercedes
chauffeured by a willowy man in his sixties wearing a gray suit and a
white, neatly trimmed mustache. The driver opened the rear door for
Hugo with the merest of bows and drove in silence, in a cautious but
assertive way that told Hugo he'd received police or military training
once upon a time. They headed west, gliding alongside the Seine, the
water drifting in and out of view as the night's fog folded itself around
it and them.

After a couple of miles they slanted northward, and Hugo's sense of
direction was rewarded when they passed the Memorial to the Martyrs.

They were headed to Nueilly-sur-Seine, one of the wealthiest areas in Paris, not far out enough to lose cachet as a suburb but not close enough to suffer the trials and tribulations of impermanence, which was the frequent result of tourist fluctuations. The families and some of the homes in the neighborhood had been there for hundreds of years and, God willing, would be there hundreds more.

The driver slowed and turned onto Boulevard D'Argenson, a boulevard in every sense, and not by chance did it intersect with Boulevard Chateau. Wide but quiet, the road was as straight as an arrow, perfectly spaced plane trees a first line of defense against traffic. The trees shaded the road and a broad cobbled sidewalk, on the other side of which ran a continuous stretch of bushes and shrubbery that provided color, and privacy, to the expensive homes behind. A minute later the car slowed again and crunched into the gravel driveway of one of the homes, a miniature chateau in stone that had a square, three-story tower at each corner. To his right, a pond lapped at the corner of the house, almost moat-like, deep green under the security lights. *Impressive*, Hugo thought, *even for this street*. He couldn't help notice the absence of gates on these driveways, a lack of security Hugo had observed ever since he'd taken the job in Paris. The French did not believe in preemptive measures, he'd found—an attitude that took some adjusting to, but that was also somehow reassuring.

Two other cars were in the driveway, parked as if they belonged there. An ancient but clean Range Rover and a spotless Bentley, also pre-1990s. Hugo wondered whether he was the only guest, but thought it more likely that everyone else attending had chauffeurs, all of whom were off somewhere smoking and grumbling about their bosses. His driver slipped out of the car and opened the passenger door for Hugo, who stepped out and thanked the man in French. Hugo turned to look at the house, admire really. The curtains were closed in all the windows and they glowed golden in the dark. He smelled wood smoke from one of the chimneys.

"This way, monsieur," said the driver. They started toward the front entrance, two heavy wooden doors set back and atop three stone steps.

As they got close, one of the doors opened and light from inside spilled out, the shape of a person momentarily just a silhouette.

Hugo saw that it was a woman and stopped in his tracks when he recognized Claudia. The driver, unsure, hovered. Claudia walked down the steps, high heels clicking on the stone. She wore a dress that was tight and simple—black velvet, Hugo guessed. A diamond necklace crossed her throat, and from it an emerald pendant nestled against her chest.

"*Jean, merci*," she said to the driver. "You are excused for now. We'll call you when Monsieur Marston wishes to return home."

You are excused? *So she lives here*, Hugo thought. *Nice house for a journalist.* Behind him, Hugo heard the heavy clunk of the Mercedes door and he turned to watch it pull through the circular driveway and into the street.

"Can't have a nice driveway like this cluttered with cars like that," Hugo said.

Claudia started toward him but wobbled when her high heels hit the gravel. He put out an arm. "Damn shoes," she said.

"Do you mind telling me what's going on?" he asked, glancing over at her. She was chewing her lip as they walked to the foot of the stairs, but didn't respond. Hugo turned to face her. "Claudia, was that invitation really from you?"

Claudia finally looked at him, and sighed. "I kept meaning to tell you," she said. "But it never seemed like the right time."

"Tell me what, that this is where you live?" Hugo waved an arm at the mansion. "Look, we've only known each other a few days, you are allowed to have secrets."

"I know, Hugo. Tonight wasn't my idea, believe me. I mentioned you to my father and . . ." She turned to face him as footsteps approached from inside, and Hugo instinctively stepped back.

A man's silhouette appeared in the doorway, paused for a moment, then trotted lightly down the steps, a hand extended toward Hugo. The man had perfect white teeth and manicured gray hair, and when he reached the foot of the steps Hugo saw how slight he was, in height and build. *Probably sixty*, Hugo thought, *maybe sixty-five*. And not wearing the uniform of the evening, rather a pale yellow sweater, blue pants, and a light blue cravat held in place with a gold pin. Hugo shook his hand.

"Gérard de Roussillon," the man smiled.

"*Enchanté*," Hugo said.

"Welcome to my home; please come in and meet some of my friends." Roussillon spoke in English, his accent almost undetectable. No doubt, Hugo thought, from years of tutoring, followed by vacations and social engagements, and maybe business ones, too, with his aristo-cratic counterparts from across the English Channel.

Roussillon sprang up the first two steps and then paused. "Monsieur Marston, I apologize for my attire, I have not yet had a chance to change for dinner. Perhaps you will accompany me upstairs while I dress?"

Hugo looked at Claudia and thought he detected the slightest of nods, but it might have been a trick of the light. "Certainly," he said. "And I appreciate the invitation."

"Of course, of course!" He waved away the thanks. "I do love to throw a party. Claudia, not so much, but she knows I am—how do you say it in America? Ah yes, a 'party animal.' No, it is I who should be thanking you, for coming at such short notice."

Roussillon stood aside to let Claudia and Hugo enter the reception hall, which was circular, stone-flagged, and unfurnished except for a round table, teak maybe, right in the center. It bore a ceramic vase brim-ming with wild flowers. Looking down from the walls were four large paintings of rural scenes. To his immediate right a small door opened into a closet, now a cloakroom, and Roussillon disappeared inside for a second with Hugo's hat and coat.

"No butler?" he murmured to Claudia, who responded with a tight smile.

Hugo could see the main room through an archway ahead of him but Roussillon turned left, up a curved, wooden staircase. He followed his host up the stairs and down a long, wide hallway until they reached what he announced was his dressing room. He pointed to an ancient oak door, its iron hinges stretching like arrows across the broad panels.

"I'd like to show you my little turret," Roussillon said. "It's my sanctuary, a sort of private place where I can meditate and exercise. No one
may disturb me in there, and only Jean is allowed in." He smiled. "My
only house rule."

"I see." Hugo wasn't sure what else to say or where this was going.

"Maybe later, I should not ignore my guests for too long. Please
sit." Roussillon gestured toward an undersized chintz armchair. *More
for decoration than comfort*, Hugo thought, but he sat anyway. Roussillon unpinned and slid off his cravat, then took off his sweater and
dropped them both on his dressing table. He opened a mirrored closet
and inspected two tuxedo jackets. "I do have a penchant for white tails.
People never seem to wear those any more, I don't know why."

"Monsieur." Hugo knew little and cared less about the fashion
habits of the elite. And he certainly didn't care to watch them undress.
"I am a little confused as to why you invited me."

Roussillon unbuckled and kicked off his pants, revealing plum-
colored, silk boxer shorts over thin, white legs. He turned and looked
at Hugo. "You Americans are known for speaking bluntly. We, and even
more so the English, tend to say in a paragraph what can and should be
said in a sentence. So you will not mind if I speak openly and honestly
with you?"

"I would prefer it, actually." *And I'd also prefer you to be in pants*,
he thought.

"*Bien.* This discussion requires, I think, that we arrive at a clear
understanding." Roussillon turned back to his closet and pulled out a
black tuxedo. "You are a behavioral scientist, yes? A profiler?"

"I was, yes. For the FBI."

"You consider yourself good at reading people, then."

"A misconception," said Hugo. "I consider myself good at reading
crime scenes."

Roussillon turned and held Hugo's eye. "Then it will come as a surprise to learn that I am gay?"

"This whole evening," Hugo said with a smile, "is turning into a
surprise. That isn't one of them."

Roussillon chuckled. "Monsieur Marston. My daughter is a desirable woman, attractive, and intelligent. All of her life I have guided and helped her, provided for her basic needs. Are you with me so far?"

"I think so."

"What am I telling you, Monsieur Marston? I am telling you that I am very careful about who I let near to my daughter. I do not mind if she has boyfriends or girlfriends, but I do not like her to fall in love with any of them." He looked at Hugo. "And I do all I can to discourage them falling in love with her."

Hugo raised one eyebrow. "I thought Paris was the city of love."

"*Mais non.*" Roussillon's tone lightened. "The city of *loving* is more accurate."

"Either way," Hugo said, stretching his legs out, "I have known Claudia for less than a week. Love is not an issue, believe me."

"Good." Roussillon slipped on a starched white shirt. "Understand that my protectionist concerns aren't merely those of a fussy father. Claudia is, in my view, particularly susceptible to a damaged heart."

"How do you mean?" Hugo asked.

"Did you know she has been married before, yes?"

"Yes, she told me."

"And did she tell you how it ended?"

"None of my business," Hugo said.

"Maybe not. But I'll tell you anyway." He turned his cool eyes to Hugo. "They were very much in love. He was a policeman, a young detective, handsome and clever and on his way up. On the way up until he was shot by the same type of people that Claudia is writing about now. They'd been married less than two years and she hasn't, to my knowledge, dated anyone since. Your name is the first she has mentioned to me, that much I can say."

"I didn't know any of that. And I'm still not sure it's my business."

Roussillon smiled. "And even knowing this, you think it strange that I vet the men in my grown daughter's life?"

"I am not a father, Monsieur de Roussillon. One of the reasons for that is my job, the things I have seen, the things I do, and the people

I meet. If I haven't had children because of the way the world is, I can hardly fault you for protecting yours so carefully," Hugo said. "And as I told you, we've known each other less than a week. You don't need to worry about it being love just yet."

"You have been married before?"

"Yes. Twice."

"Of course, you are from America, where marriage is like a fine suit. You wear and enjoy it for a while, then discard it when it becomes worn or uncomfortable."

Hugo clenched his jaw but kept his tone even. "My first wife was killed in an accident. And my second decided she didn't like the French enough to stay married to me and live here."

Roussillon turned and looked at Hugo. "*Je m'excuse.* I should not have assumed the worst. Forgive me."

Hugo nodded. "As I said, you are a father. I don't blame you for being protective. Even if she is a grown woman."

"Not to me." Roussillon smiled, then turned and went back to buttoning up his shirt. "She didn't tell you about me, about being a Roussillon?"

"No. And I confess the name would not have meant much to me anyway."

"That is often part of the problem, from where I stand. We do have to be careful, you know, because the name, the title, they can attract a certain sort of man."

"I can imagine," Hugo said.

"And forgive me for appearing to be rude, but I had imagined my daughter marrying a man of . . . well, a Frenchman, anyway."

"A man of what?" Hugo knew the answer and was amused at this glance into social elitism. He also felt a slight jolt of surprise that marriage would even occur to Roussillon at this stage because neither he nor Claudia had broached the subject of exclusivity, let alone matrimony. And he doubted it was something she'd gone to her father about for discussion or advice.

"Of nobility. Of a certain class." Roussillon grimaced. "Someone who recognizes the family name, at least. You find all this amusing?"

Hugo stifled his smile. "I'm sorry, really. But hearing you espouse a very traditional view of marriage is, you have to admit, a touch ironic. And, I have to say, a little preemptive."

"Maybe, but such things are nevertheless important to me."

"Are they as important to Claudia?"

"I can hope. I had thought so." Roussillon turned to him again. "And since you touch upon the subject, you are not wondering how a gay man has a daughter?"

"Again, that's hardly any of my business."

"No, it is not. But I want you to know that she is my flesh and blood. As a straight man can experiment, so can a gay man, especially when one is told that straight is the only way to be." Hugo didn't respond, and Roussillon asked, "You will continue to see her?"

"Normally I'd say that it's none of *your* business. But since we are sharing . . ." He shrugged. "If she wants to, of course."

"Yes? She will not be disappointed."

"But you are."

"We shall see. I suspect she will be disappointed with me for interrogating you." Roussillon wagged a finger. "And that will not do at all."

"That's between you and her," Hugo said, standing. "Now, if we're still speaking frankly, I could use a drink."

Roussillon picked up two boxes containing cufflinks and made his selection. "I am a terrible host, Monsieur Marston. Word will spread at the embassy about such rudeness. Forgive me for not offering before."

"No problem. I can find my way downstairs."

"I will be right down, monsieur. I trust we will have a rewarding evening together."

Hugo nodded. Rewarding? And a look in Roussillon's eye told Hugo that their conversation, one way or another, would be continued.

CHAPTER FOURTEEN

He found Claudia beside the walk-in fireplace, a glass of champagne in her hand and a worried look on her face. When she saw him, she started forward. "Hugo, I'm so sorry, are you angry?"

"I haven't decided," he said with a frown. "But I'm sure as hell thirsty."

Claudia glanced over his shoulder and, with a slight inclination of her head, summoned a waiter. "Champagne?" she asked Hugo.

"Scotch," he said, then looked at the waiter and spoke in French. "Large. I do not have to drive myself home tonight."

"*Oui, monsieur.*" The waiter smiled. "We have Laphroaig, fifteen years old, or a Talisker, I think twenty-one years."

"Either will do fine. Perhaps whichever is fastest. And no ice."

"Right away, monsieur."

The waiter turned and slalomed his way through the room with his head down, avoiding eye contact with, and thereby interruption by, the other guests. *Nice work—shame the French don't tip*, thought Hugo. He turned back to Claudia.

"So Ms. Roussillon, were you going to tell me?" He kept his voice light, amused rather than annoyed.

"Hugo, of course." She was having trouble meeting his gaze. "I should have told you right away, I am sorry. I want to know if you are upset."

"For humble roots, I wasn't expecting this," he said, gesturing to the room. Forty men and women, mostly middle-aged or older, stood holding drinks and napkins, some nibbling delicately at the corner of various hors d'oeuvres that Hugo couldn't recognize. Mostly things wrapped in pastry. All of the men wore bow ties, and most in tuxedoes, but a few wore tails. The women, as rich women do, looked comfortable in their tight-fitting dresses and heavy jewelry. But this wasn't just the rich set, Hugo saw, it was the rich and beautiful set. The conversation bubbled all around them and Hugo was aware that Claudia kept her distance from him. Roussillon's friends may know about his homosexuality, they may even keep it secret, but Hugo guessed that they'd still love to gossip about his daughter and an American.

"Believe it or not, this place *is* humble to some of these people," Claudia said, as if reading his mind. "And I think you'll like them, too."

"I have no reason to doubt it. I'm curious about your father, though. He could have stopped by my apartment to give me his little speech."

"That's not his style." Claudia shook her head, smiling. "And yes, he is a good man, too. But he does like to impress. I think he wanted you to know that he is important."

"Influential, you mean."

"That too. You know, Hugo, he's only protecting me."

"Because you can't do that yourself?"

"He's my father, reality doesn't enter that equation." Claudia looked at him, serious. "I would like to talk about it," she said, "sometime soon."

"We can. We will." Hugo's drink arrived on a silver tray. He took it with thanks and downed half the glass. The burn was less than expected, always the trouble with good whisky. "So did your gendarme friends find anything out today?"

"My . . . ? Oh, that." She looked disappointed. "You want to talk about that now?"

"Of course," Hugo said. "Seems like a safe topic, no?"

"*Bien.*" Her smile was thin. "Well, they talked to Chabot and said they were pretty firm, pressed him for a while." She shook her head. "I'm sorry, but he told them the same thing he told you: he didn't know Max."

"Did they ask how he came into possession of the stall?"

"I don't know, probably. They didn't tell me what his response was, though. If any. I'm sorry, they did try."

Hugo frowned into his drink. If you want something done right, do it yourself. And he'd do just that tomorrow.

"So," he said, nodding toward the busy room, "how does this work? Should I be meeting your friends?" The idea was less than attractive. He knew he had little in common with these people, none of whom probably worked for a living. He watched as a well-preserved woman in her fifties clinked glasses of champagne with a lookalike, their noses almost touching, an amusing secret just shared. The men in their black and white, the plumage on the women, and the little zookeepers in their white coats stopping to feed and water their charges all made Hugo feel claustrophobic.

But he was just a little bit curious. Curious about the relationship between Roussillon and his daughter, about the guests themselves. Claudia had said they were nice. Heck, maybe they were.

A handsome couple approached. The man was tall and strong, with black hair combed straight back, the confident smile of someone who knew that others wanted to meet him. His wife had once been beautiful but now wore the slightly stretched face that comes with cosmetic surgery. But the blue eyes were clear and the smile more genuine than that of her husband. Perhaps because of the sparkling rock on her wedding finger. Claudia made the introductions.

"This is Hugo Marston, head of security at that US Embassy. Hugo, meet Alain and Marie Mercier."

Hugo shook hands with them both. "*Enchanté.*"

Claudia turned to Hugo and spoke in French. "The Merciers are old friends of mine. Somewhere along the line Marie and I are cousins, but I'm not sure how far back."

"That's true of most Europeans, isn't it?" Hugo said.

The couple laughed gently. "*Alors*, Hugo," Alain Mercier said, "how do you know Claudia?"

Good question.

"The truth," Claudia said, and leaned in close to Alain. Both he and his wife cocked their heads expectantly. "The truth is, I caught him fucking your wife."

The French couple snorted delightedly and Marie put a hand on Hugo's arm, squeezing playfully as she looked at her husband. "If that were true, Alain, I would boast of it myself." Alain smiled indulgently, a man confident that his wife would never do such a thing. In these circles, that was his role. Despite his reservations, Hugo warmed to the couple, enjoying their easy banter.

A gong rang out from the other end of the room and the crowd started to shuffle through a pair of double doors to the dining room. As they were siphoned through, Hugo stood aside to let a portly couple pass, and he lost contact with Claudia and the Merciers.

Inside the dining room he saw that place cards had been set up, the guests floating around and bumping into each other as the discovery process began. He was looking for his own card when a hand took his. It belonged to a redhead, a young lady of no more than twenty-five. Large blue eyes met his look of surprise, but any innocence in them was undone by her smile, replete with intent.

"I believe we are seated together, Monsieur Marston," she said in English, her accent from somewhere south of Alabama. "My name is Jenny Reye."

"Nice to meet you," Hugo said, instinctively looking for Claudia. "Call me Hugo. And how do you know who I am?"

"I asked," she said, as if it were a stupid question.

"Of course." Hugo smiled. "I have no idea where we are, so I'll follow you." Following was a pleasure, even though her dress was less fitted than that worn by most of the women there. There was a subtlety about the way she moved her hips, not enough to draw attention from the men around them, but just enough to let Hugo know that she knew he was watching. They rounded the head of the table where Claudia stood by her chair, waiting for her father. Hugo was surprised to see a look of puzzlement on her face, a look she transferred from the girl to Hugo with a raised eyebrow. Hugo smiled and shrugged as he passed. *Don't ask me.*

He held Jenny's chair for her and they sat down, Hugo suddenly grateful for the tedious lessons in etiquette the ambassador forced all of his senior staff to take when they joined the embassy. Faced with a dozen forks, knives, and spoonlike devices, plus four different glasses, the Texas Hugo would have been at once confused, irritated, and amused. The head-of-security Hugo, however, knew which glass was for what, and why he had a fork shaped like a spoon nestled among the knives. His new neighbor seemed less sure. He could see her eyes flicking around the table as other guests settled in for the meal, watching to see who touched what. Napkin unrolled now or later? Pour my own water? He could empathize.

"It's nice to be speaking in English," he smiled. "Have you been here before?"

"No." Her big blue eyes flashed and she waved a hand over the place setting. "And I can't figure out whether I'm going to end up gorging myself or starving to death from choosing the wrong tools."

Hugo chuckled. "I know what you mean. I was always told to start on the outside and work my way in."

"That so?" Jenny looked at him and smiled *that way* again. "Sounds like a good lesson."

A young lady appeared behind them holding two bottles of wine, one red and one white. "*Mademoiselle?*" she said.

"Good," she whispered to Hugo, "I'll let her figure out which glass I should use." Jenny leaned into him, her bare arm brushing his jacket. She looked over her shoulder at the server. "*Blanc, s'il vous plaît.*"

Hugo breathed in her scent and tried to place it, but couldn't. Soft and flowery, quite unlike the way she was behaving. He wanted to splash his face with water, grab Claudia, and get out of there.

Hugo's eyes trailed over the rows of silverware. Only one, two, three . . . six courses to get through. He felt a hand grip the back of his chair and he twisted to see a man of about eighty, as round as he was tall and with a giant moustache, tugging at the chair next to him. Hugo stood, pulled out the chair, and helped him sit.

"*Merci*," the old man said. When Hugo told him he was welcome, the old man pointed to his ear, smiled sadly, and mouthed the word *sourd*. Deaf. Hugo smiled and nodded, then turned back to Jenny. "So what do you do for a living?" he asked.

"I work for the count," she said.

"Doing...?"

"Books. I have a Masters in European Literature and worked for two years at Sotheby's selling musty old books. The kinds of books that he," she thumbed toward the head of the table, "likes to pay way too much for."

"I see," said Hugo, noting another book connection. "That sounds interesting. Has he been buying lately? At auction?"

"Not that I know of, but sometimes he does his own buying without involving me. That's pretty rare, though. Why?"

"Just curious." But Hugo didn't want *her* to be. "Sorry, didn't mean to interrupt. You were saying that it's an interesting job."

"Mostly, yes. I get to travel a lot, that's fun. I get paid well, too, and meet interesting people. What do you do?"

"I work at the US Embassy." Hugo glanced down the table and saw Claudia watching them. "In the security section."

Jenny ran a finger around the top of her wine glass and cocked her head. "American Embassy, huh? You carrying a gun?"

"Here?" He laughed. "I think we're all pretty safe here, don't you?"

"How about handcuffs?"

He was saved from having to reply by a sudden hush that ran around the table, the diners quieting themselves to a signal that Hugo had missed. Roussillon was on his feet, a relaxed smile on his face.

"Ladies and gentlemen, my daughter, my chef, and I welcome you. We see you all so very rarely and I'm sorry I don't get to sit and chat with you individually. I've been wanting to say something and . . ." He paused and looked down, his fingers moving to a polished knife, which he turned over. His mouth opened and when he raised his head Hugo saw a look of surprise on his host's face. Roussillon looked at them all, studied them, then turned as his daughter took his hand. They smiled at each other and she half-stood to guide him back into his seat, pressing a glass of water into his hand. She stood and addressed the party with a smile. "My father usually likes to give thanks for his food. So please." Heads bowed around the table and she said a quick grace. Immediately after, the chatter resumed as though a dial had been turned and nothing out of the ordinary had just happened.

Throughout dinner Jenny continued to flirt with him, but the way a teenager would, full of innuendo and lingering looks, devoid of subtlety. Hugo didn't mind—after all, she was very pretty. And he was pleased, too, at the long looks Claudia was sending their way at increasingly frequent intervals, though she wasn't giving away much; her expression sat halfway between irritation and amusement.

The meal itself lasted two hours, and Hugo was experienced enough at the French table to pace himself and leave the bread well alone. Jenny fared less well, her sauciness diminishing as she filled herself with the quail, pastries, and cheese of the last three courses. At meal's end, via telepathy, it seemed, the men stood and excused themselves, moving back through the main room and into Roussillon's library, where three boxes of cigars lay on a table, flanked by decanters of port and brandy.

Hugo was wondering whether to indulge when Roussillon touched his elbow. "I'd suggest the port. It's a 1963 Croft; I'm not sure you'll find better." He reached out and picked up a glass, filled it with the ruby liquid, and handed it to Hugo. "Try it."

Hugo sipped obligingly and rolled it gently around his mouth, surprised at the difference between this and other ports he'd tasted. It felt like velvet, offering a perfect touch of sweetness and a fullness of fruit that kept opening up on his tongue. "I'm no expert," he said when he'd swallowed, "but I can honestly say that I've never had port this good."

Roussillon seemed genuinely pleased, clasping his hands together and flashing white teeth. "I shall have a glass myself," he said. "Not much of this stuff left, half a dozen cases maybe. Then it's on to the 1970s, of which we were sensible enough to lay down aplenty. Of course, it's the '77s and the '94s we're really looking forward to." He looked to the heavens, as if God himself were awaiting the ripening of those particular vintages. "Did you enjoy dinner?"

"I did, very much."

"You met Jenny. I trust you enjoyed her company, too?"

"Thank you, yes." Hugo took another sip. "I assume her . . . company will be waiting for me at the end of the evening?"

"Monsieur Marston, why would you ask me that?" Roussillon's look of shock was the same one that Hugo had seen on a thousand guilty faces.

"Oh, let me see," Hugo said, smiling to let his host know he was not offended. "First there was the seating arrangement. I suppose that putting me next to her could have been pure chance, two single guests. But the deaf gentleman on my other side meant no distractions, no way to avoid Jenny's charms."

"And charming she is," Roussillon said.

"Oh yes. Charming, pretty, and intelligent. And when she's actually attracted to someone she probably flirts quite well." Hugo waved away Roussillon's offer of a cigar. "But when she's told to do it, *paid* to do it perhaps, well, then she doesn't want her signals to be misinterpreted as mere friendliness, so she overdoes it. Which, ironically, makes her somewhat less appealing."

"Are you saying I should have hired a professional, Monsieur Marston?" Roussillon said, more amused than concerned that his ruse had been unearthed.

"Perhaps."

"But my other guests would have wanted an explanation for a stranger's presence." He leaned in to Hugo. "They do like to gossip, you know."

"Most people do." Hugo drank more of the port and wondered why he'd never bothered to seek it out before. "I assume it was done for your daughter's benefit more than mine," he said.

"Two birds with one stone. Although jealousy can be a powerful agent, don't you think?"

"No doubt." For all his money and his title, because of them perhaps, Roussillon was proving to be a manipulative and controlling man. "I guess I'm wondering what happens if I say no to young Jenny?"

"Then the next one I send will be younger."

"And if I still say no?"

"Then the one after that will be younger still. And if that doesn't work, I can always send boys. I have found that while one never knows the predilections of one's friends and acquaintances, one can be sure that they have them."

"Perhaps, monsieur," said Hugo, draining his port, "you should not judge others by your own standards." He set the glass down on the table and extended his hand. "Thank you for a delicious meal. I have an early start tomorrow so will excuse myself." Hugo didn't wait for the response, suddenly unsure of his ability to remain polite. And a senior member of the US Embassy didn't need to be throttling French nobility, no matter the provocation.

As he let himself out of the library he looked toward the main room. The flames from the fireplace cast flickering shadows on the white wall and he could see clusters of women standing and sitting, the conversation subdued after the large meal. Gossip still to be swapped, but the good stuff was out of the way. He thought about raiding the room for Claudia, but that might indicate a disagreement with the host, and it would stir up gossip for sure.

He walked into the reception hall and went straight to the closet to fetch his hat and coat. He stepped to the front door, willing no one to see him, but paused by the circular table when he realized that he didn't know how to contact his driver. No matter, that's what taxis were for; he'd find one sooner or later. If not, he could always call Emma and have her send one. Or Claudia. He opened the front door silently, closed it quickly behind him, and trotted down the steps, the cold night air surprising him with its bite, a pleasant contrast to the suppressed anger that warmed his face.

He walked down the gravel driveway to Boulevard D'Argenson and looked up. The moon was a thin sliver and the evening breeze had pushed the day's clouds out of sight. The homes around him sat in curtained darkness, blankets of trees softening their glow and allowing the stars their moment.

He started down the boulevard and had gone less than a hundred yards when a black Mercedes pulled up beside him. The window came down and Jean's face appeared. "Can I drive monsieur home?"

Hugo hesitated, but not for long. "*Oui*, Jean, *merci*."

Jean hopped out and opened the rear door. Hugo thanked him again and started to climb in, suddenly wondering whether it had been Claudia who'd sent Jean, whether she might be in the car herself. He plopped down into the seat and found the car empty. He wasn't sure whether the sharp twinge in his stomach was relief or disappointment.

CHAPTER FIFTEEN

Hugo awoke early on Friday to a Paris that twinkled after a long night's frost. The clouds that had sat over the city for two days had finally descended across the streets, buildings, and trees, clinging to them before disappearing with the dawn, leaving the city bright and glazed under a clear blue sky. He left Tom to sleep in and stepped out of his apartment, the crisp air and faint smell of wood smoke making the previous night's soiree seem like a fairy tale, a bizarre and unlikely fantasy wiped away by the stroke of midnight and made unreal by the bright light of morning.

His plan was to find the neighboring bouquiniste, and even though she'd not been there on previous occasions, he felt an urgency as if she was already in place, waiting for him. He was hungry but didn't want to spend time ordering in a café, so he stopped instead at a bakery to pick up a croissant and coffee to go. As he left the shop, he narrowly missed spilling the hot liquid on a man in a cloth cap who hurried past the store's entrance. He tried to apologize, but the man hunched his shoulders and kept going.

Hugo walked on, turning onto Rue Bonaparte, where he glanced into the window of a wine shop. Roussillon may have been an ass, but he sure had good port. *Another time*, thought Hugo. He continued walking north up Rue Bonaparte, and when he got within sight of the Seine he turned left, keeping the busy street between him and the stalls. He kept his head down, not wanting Chabot to spot him. When he did glance up, the little weasel was busy setting up for the day and not yet on the lookout for customers.

A hundred yards down the street, Hugo waited for a break in the traffic. When it came, he trotted across the road and turned right when

he got to the sidewalk. The woman he wanted to talk to, the bouquiniste who'd been harassed the day he'd bought the Rimbaud from Max,
was also setting out her wares.

He slowed as he approached her stall, not wanting to startle her,
and out of habit removed his hat when he greeted her. She was struggling with a stack of books, the slippery plastic covers making them
hard to hold with the woolen mittens that covered her hands. She
smiled and gave Hugo a friendly "Bonjour." Her wind-chapped face
glowed red in the cold and was the only part of her body not covered in
swathes of clothing. A nose crisscrossed with broken blood vessels and
watery red eyes suggested her affinity for strong drink. An unashamed
appraisal of his cashmere coat and obviously American boots suggested
an affinity for ways to obtain it.

"*Madame*," he said. He picked up and shuffled through a stack of
postcards, picking out two that were sepia photographs of well-dressed
couples, one holding hands in front of the Eiffel Tower, the other taken
alongside the Seine in roughly the spot they were standing now. She
asked for two Euros for the cards, but he gave her five and waved away
the change. A narrowing of her eyes told Hugo that the old woman
knew there was a reason for the tip. He pocketed the postcards and
decided to try a straightforward approach. "I am looking for a friend, a
bouquiniste. His name is Max Koche."

"Max?" A look crossed her face that fell between wariness and fear.
"He's a friend of yours, did you say?"

"Yes," said Hugo. "I've known him a long time. I work at the US
Embassy and have bought many books from him."

"Yes, I've seen you talking to him before." She turned her back
to him and straightened a few books. Hugo let her think about it. "I
haven't seen him for a week," she said, then looked over her shoulder.
"One day he was there, the next . . ." She shrugged.

"Were you working here last week?"

"*Oui*, all week."

"*Non*, your stall was closed for a while." Hugo stepped closer. "But
you were here to see what happened to him."

She stared for a moment, her watery eyes crisscrossing his face as she considered the question. She shook her head and turned to her stall.

"*Non.*"

"You told police that he got onto a boat with some people, voluntarily." It was a guess, he knew she'd been working that day and that if she'd returned to her stall she couldn't have missed the fracas. "But you saw what really happened, didn't you?"

"I saw nothing." She looked over her shoulder at him, and her tone softened. "I am old, monsieur, old and tired. And my memory is as bad as my eyesight, probably worse. I am sorry."

"Even an old woman would have seen that Max was kidnapped," Hugo urged. "Please, I need you to tell me what you saw."

All he got was a sad smile.

"*D'accord*, I understand," he said, softening his tone. "I'm Hugo Marston, by the way. What's your name?" Her eyes narrowed again. For some reason she was afraid. Hugo reached into his pocket and pulled out his credentials, and the shiny State Department badge seemed to reassure her.

"I thought perhaps you . . ." She pulled a glove off and offered a cracked hand, her grip surprisingly strong. "I am Francoise Benoit."

"Is there something going on with *les bouquinistes*, Madame Benoit?"

She looked up and down the street, but their only company was a family of frosted leaves that scuttled along the sidewalk, propelled by the wind. "I mind my own business. You might want to do the same."

"Max was my friend, which means his disappearance *is* my business."

"Your friend." She said it quietly, as if she finally believed it. She straightened and turned to him, glancing up and down the quai again. "It's supposed to be confidential, but we have been offered money for our stalls."

"Who has? All the bouquinistes?"

"*Oui.*"

"By whom?"

"I don't know. Not exactly." She went back to placing books on the metal shelves, talking to him with twitches of the head and side-long glances down the street. "About a month ago Bruno Gravois, the head of the SBP, called a meeting of all members. Most of us were there. Gravois told us that the *Chambre de Commerce et Industrie* in Paris, along with the *Office du Tourisme*, wanted to give the Seine *un ravalement*." A facelift. "You know how it is, Monsieur Marston. A year ago we got a new government, which means we got a new crop of bureaucrats with bright ideas. Monsieur Gravois said we would get severance packages for signing over our stalls to him."

"And what was he going to do with them?"

"He said he was working with the *Chambre* and the *Office du Tourisme* to update them and put in new bouquinistes."

"'He said,'" Hugo repeated. "You don't believe him."

Her laugh was more of a cackle and her breath hit him from fully six feet away. The mint she was sucking did little to hide the distinctive, sweet tang of alcohol. "Did you see that weasel Chabot? If that's his idea of attracting tourists, then Paris might as well fall into the Seine and float away. The man doesn't know which side of a postcard to write on, let alone anything about books." She looked up and down the sidewalk again. "I don't know what is happening, monsieur, but I know it's not being done for the good of Paris."

"But they can't force you out, can they?"

"No?" She snorted.

"If you're frightened and think they'll force you out, why not take the severance?"

She cackled again and reached under a folding wooden chair. She pulled an almost-empty bottle out of a brown paper bag and shook it. Vodka. "See this? You give me a lump of money and I'll stick it straight into my liver. At least when I work I am forced to drink myself to death slowly. If I am still alive when the money is gone, what then? What else can I do to make a living?"

Fair enough, Hugo thought. "Do you have any idea why he's replacing all the bouquinistes?"

"I assume he's putting his friends in place and taking a cut. Why else?"

Why indeed. Easy enough to make that kind of agreement with friends and acquaintances. Legal too, if you papered it right. Certainly a lot easier and more legit than extorting it from hundreds of unwilling sellers. But replacing all those bouquinistes was expensive and a lot of trouble, even assuming most were happy to take the money and get out of the cold. And what about the others, like Madame Benoit? And Max?

"That man you were arguing with last week," Hugo said, "who was he?"

"Him?" She spat. "That *salaud*. One of Gravois's *capitaines*."

"Capitaines?"

"That's what he calls them. He has three or four men who keep an eye on us to make sure we're not selling more postcards than books, telling us when our stalls are too untidy. They are men like Chabot who know nothing of the tradition of *les bouquinistes*, and they don't care. They are like Chabot, but with strong arms and angry faces."

"Why was he harassing you?"

"Why? Because I'm still here. I don't make trouble for them and I try to do what they say. But that isn't always enough, monsieur, because at the end of each working day, I am still here."

"I see." Hugo offered his hand again. "Is one of those capitaines called Nica?"

"I don't know their names."

"The one I'm thinking of, he's tall like me, with a face like it's carved out of rock."

"Maybe. I turn the other way when I see them coming monsieur, so 'maybe' is all I can say."

"OK. Thank you for your time, Madame Benoit." He turned to leave.

"Monsieur Mouton—"

"Marston," he corrected gently. "But please, call me Hugo."

"*Oui, oui*, Hugo. Have you thought—" she blew her nose into an enormous handkerchief, "have you talked to Ceci?"

"Who?"

"She was the last chief of the SBP."

"Before Gravois?"

"*Oui*. I think perhaps she was the first to be removed. She is a good woman and very wise. If something is going on, she might know."

"Might?" Good enough. "Where do I find her?"

She frowned and shook her head. "I think your badge might help you find her."

"Her last name at least?" The look on her face told Hugo that Ceci had never had a last name to her bouquinistes, that the idea of her with a last name was an oddity. He replaced his hat and smiled. "Never mind, I'll find her."

Hugo walked away from the stall, ambling slowly beside the river. He stopped occasionally to stare into its depths, but the surface slid beneath him, a lid of impenetrable steel protecting its secrets with no hope that it would hand out answers, or even comfort, today.

As he walked, he thought about coincidences. To him, life was too chaotic and random for them not to pop up now and again. Put differently, as he'd once explained to the church-going Christine, he did not believe in fate. Fate and religion, he'd said, were for those who didn't want to take control of their own lives—or weren't able to. Much easier to believe in fate or a slew of gods than to accept a universe of chaos. With a god or fate behind you, you could place your future in someone else's hands, let them be responsible, and when it went wrong you had a convenient patsy. Christine had argued with him, of course, blue eyes blazing at his heresy, but he always suspected her anger was to cover her own fear that she agreed with him. She certainly couldn't change his mind. No, those oddities that people ascribed to God and fate, the chance meetings with old friends or the car that swerved off the road and narrowly missed the little boy, they were nothing but coincidence and luck. Coincidence and luck were real, and if you didn't recognize their existence then you were looking for meaning where it didn't exist.

This meant that Max's disappearance immediately after selling him a book worth hundreds of thousands of dollars *could* be nothing more than chance.

And yet his mystical sixth sense, the one that conflicted with his views on God and the unknown, kept ticking away, nagging him to forget chance and happenstance and tie these random events together into a meaningful package.

Hugo shook his head, frustrated at twisting himself into unhelpful knots. He turned, crossed the street, and began to walk home the way he'd come, cutting south before hitting Max's stall—he still thought of it as Max's—and onto Rue Guénégaud. As he walked, he called Emma.

"Can I buy you lunch?" he asked.

"I brought mine."

"It'll keep 'til tomorrow."

"I don't eat leftovers on Saturdays. Are you planning to tell me what you're up to? If so, and you're paying for dessert, then I'm in."

"Yes," he said, "that's why I called." He hesitated, and she heard that, too.

"What do you need, Hugo?"

"Just a tiny favor. I need to know the name and whereabouts of a woman named Ceci. She used to be the head of the SBP before Gravois."

Emma snorted, delicately. "I told you her name once before. I'll look it up again and bring it to lunch. Where?"

Hugo wanted somewhere close to the embassy. "Brasserie Trudeau. It's been a week since I've eaten there. See you at one."

He checked his watch and saw he had plenty of time to go back to his apartment, shower, and grab Tom.

Hugo had always done his best thinking while walking. He decided that a meander through the Luxembourg gardens could only help.

As he passed down Rue de Sévres he noticed a new boutique directly across the street, the storefront wearing a fresh coat of dark red paint and the large window filled with hats. Another store that would last a few months, Hugo figured, as he slipped between two parked cars and trotted across the street. A blue Renault clattered toward him and honked feebly, its driver annoyed rather than at risk, but it startled Hugo enough to propel his final step into a leap for the safety of the pavement. As he landed, he pivoted as elegantly as he was able in order to avoid crashing into a man who'd been window shopping himself, a man alerted to Hugo's presence by the horn.

They locked eyes for just a second, and Hugo felt a hole open in the pit of his stomach. He stood still on the sidewalk as the man in his cloth cap lowered his head, muttered something in French, and walked quickly away. Hugo watched the man's back, testing his own instincts, knowing that if he were right, two things would happen. Both did; the man reached the end of the block and made a sharp right down a side street, and as he disappeared from view he pulled a cell phone from his pocket and began dialing.

This was no coincidence. He pulled out his own phone and dialed Claudia.

"Hugo!" Her voice was flooded with relief. "I'm so glad, I've been worried but didn't dare call. I thought you were furious with me."

"And I thought maybe my dinner companion had put you off me," he said.

She laughed, a gentle sound down the phone. "*Non*, Hugo. I know you went home alone. But can we meet? We should probably talk about all this."

"Sure, but not right now. Listen, something's going on, and I really do need some answers."

"OK. What is it?"

"I need to know if your father is having me followed."

"What?" Her surprise sounded genuine. "No, of course not. That's ridiculous, Hugo, why would he?"

"You tell me."

"Hugo, wait. Are you saying you're being followed? Right now?"

"Yes. Earlier this morning I almost bumped into a man. He wore a cloth cap and was keeping his face away from me. I didn't think anything of it at the time. But just now, I ran into him again."

"That doesn't mean—"

"I know, it wouldn't usually. Except, an hour ago he was in a hurry. I just ran into him a block away from where I first saw him. A man doesn't hurry like that and cover two blocks in an hour. And the way he scurried away from me, both times. I'm sure, Claudia."

"There could be other explanations. Coincidence? Maybe he was hurrying to an appointment nearby and is hurrying to another one now."

"As soon as he noticed me, he went to the end of the block and turned right. Before he made it, his phone was in his hand. He was letting someone know I'd spotted him. Oh, and just so you know, the street he turned down was Rue Récamier."

"I don't know it."

"It's a pedestrian street, no cars, and a dead end." *Which means he doesn't live around here*, Hugo thought, *else he'd know that*. And it also means that he'll be back this way any minute.

"Hugo, you're not going to confront him, are you?"

"What a good idea," he said lightly, "thanks for suggesting it."

"No, Hugo, it's not a suggestion. He may have a weapon."

"Then that'll make two of us."

"This is Paris, Hugo, not the Wild West. You can't have a shootout. *Merde*."

Hugo moved into the hat shop and ignored the irritated glance from its proprietor. He stationed himself behind a mannequin and watched through the window. He aimed his next words at both women, saying, "Don't worry, I won't make a mess." He tried to keep his tone light, but wasn't sure how it had come out.

"Look, can you meet me for lunch?" Claudia said.

"No, I have a date, sorry." That sounded petty, so he added, "with my secretary, Emma. She has some information for me."

"OK. Dinner?"

"A drink. Maybe dinner."

They agreed to meet at the intersection of three streets, Rues de Buci, Mazarine, and Dauphine, at seven o'clock. That would give them a choice of two cafés right there, and another nearby.

A moment after Hugo rang off, the man in the hat appeared at the corner and lit a cigarette, his eyes darting up and down the street. *OK, amateur, let's see where you're going.* Hugo moved further into the store and looked around. A gray Homburg sat atop the wire head of a two-headed mannequin. *Trendy mannequins for traditional hats*, thought Hugo, *very Paris*. He picked it up. His size. A lot like his own fedora, but different enough to change his outline. The middle-aged proprietor, whose wild, bleached blonde hair would defy any hat, moved toward him.

"This one is perfect." He pulled notes from his wallet and handed them over with a smile. "In a bit of a hurry, though."

"*D'accord. Un sac, monsieur?*"

"*Oui.*" He took the bag and put his own black hat into it. He stuck the new hat on his head and slipped off his coat, turned it inside out, and put it back on. It wasn't designed to be reversible but its muted wool lining would do the trick from a distance. "*Merci.*" He took one more look through the window and strode out of the store in the direction his follower had taken. At the corner he saw the man talking on the phone as he hurried along the sidewalk. Hugo followed him for two blocks with ease, staying directly behind him and using other pedestrians, mail boxes, and streetlamps as light cover. If the man turned around, all he'd see would be foot traffic and, maybe, occasional glimpses of a man wearing an unfamiliar coat and hat, his face invisible.

He trailed the man south as they continued along Rue de Sévres. If he didn't live in this area, Hugo figured he would probably take the metro. But the man marched right past the entrance to the station at Sévres–Babylon and then past the Vaneau stop. Hugo checked his pace when he realized that his interest in the man had brought him a little too close.

Hugo paused at the entrance to the Vaneau metro and studied the map, a hint of an idea in his mind. He found the street they were on and then picked out the next station along this road. He traced a finger north from it, his suspicion confirmed. *We have that in common*, Hugo thought, looking at the man's back. *You'd rather walk an extra two* blocks and get a direct train than have to wait ten or fifteen minutes underground to change trains. He was headed, Hugo was sure, to the next metro stop, Duroc, where he could take the train all the way to Place de Clichy. The stop closest to the offices of the SBP.

Hugo reached for his phone, intending to cancel his lunch, but it rang before he could pull it from his pocket. Emma. "Hey," he said, "you're not ditching me, are you?"

"Yes and no. Lunch is off, but blame Ambassador Taylor."

"Why?" Hugo started walking again, his eyes still on the man ahead. "Doesn't he know I'm on vacation?"

"He knows you're not in America, if that's what you mean."

"It's not. And you're supposed to run interference for me on this stuff."

"I did," she said. "And I'm very good at it, but it turns out that I'm just a secretary and he's some sort of ambassador."

"Ah, for a moment I thought missing lunch meant missing out on your sarcasm."

A gentle peal of laughter. "I wonder where I get it from?"

"Fine. Look, I'm in the middle of something, so what's going on?"

"He didn't say. Remember the whole secretary-versus-ambassador thing? But he wants to see you right away."

"Right away?"

"His words."

If it were anyone else, Hugo would make him wait. Especially under these circumstances. But Ambassador Taylor wasn't just his boss, he was a man Hugo respected. If he was calling Hugo in from his vacation there was a good reason, and Hugo wasn't going to ignore it. Even if he chose to, what would his explanation sound like? *Sorry, ambassador, I was following a man who I think had been following me for some unknown reason but possibly related to the bouquiniste whose apartment I broke into, the one you told me to stop investigating.*

"OK," he said, "it'll take me thirty minutes or so to get in, but tell him I'll be there."

"Will do."

"Thanks." Hugo slowed and watched the man in the hat trot down the steps to the Duroc metro station, allowing himself some satisfaction from an accurate deduction. He was about to hang up when a thought struck him. "Oh, Emma, did you manage to find Ceci for me?"

"Sure did. I'll print out everything I have, which isn't much, so stop by here first. And Hugo? Seeing as you're bailing on me for lunch, you can pick me up a pastry. Something nice for dessert."

She hung up before he could respond, and Hugo smiled. He turned around and started walking back the way he had come, dialing Tom to let him know where he was and keeping his eyes peeled for a patisserie.

CHAPTER SIXTEEN

Most of the murder scenes that Hugo had worked as an FBI agent involved children or people from the lower economic classes. Children, he'd realized, were easier targets and more fragile and, in Hugo's experience, rich people simply didn't kill each other in ways that attracted the attention of the FBI.

Once, though, while he was attending a conference in Philadelphia, he'd been asked to drive out to a grand house tucked away in the Pennsylvania countryside where the wealthy male owner had been killed in his study. On the way there, Hugo and a colleague had joked quietly about the butler using the lead piping, but when they walked into the room all humor fled.

The victim sat upright in his chair, and would have been staring at them if his head had still been attached to his shoulders. A crime scene tech had found it in a hollow globe normally used for storing drinks. It had been carefully positioned so when the lid was lifted, the elderly man's look of surprise would mirror the look on the face of the person who found him. Rather clever, Hugo had thought. His other thought was that the man's ornate study was forever ruined: blood had squirted from the dead man's neck, drenching the walls and ceiling. From the mess, Hugo estimated that the killer had tilted the body back and forth, spraying as much as he could. A waste of a life *and* a beautiful room.

Hugo thought of this case every time he met with Ambassador Taylor because the similarities between his office and the murder victim's study were inescapable. Both were lined with bookcases, a rolling staircase giving access to the higher tomes, both had stone fireplaces behind impressive mahogany desks, both had matching leather couches sitting *face-en-face*, and both sported heavy oil paintings of men on horseback carrying weapons as they chased down hares, foxes, and other men. Hugo had meant to find out whether, by chance, the same interior designer had constructed both but he'd never cared quite enough to ask, the similarities only seeming important when he was in the room.

Hugo arrived at the embassy an hour after talking to Emma, having stopped by her office to deliver her pastry and collect two sheets of paper. One contained the address and a description of Cecilia Josephine Roget and the other was a brief history of her tenure in charge of the SBP. As curious as he was, he could only glance over it as he hurried back down the hall to the elevator. He'd breezed past the ambassador's secretary with a wave and pushed the door open to the grand office and had started to greet the ambassador but stopped when he saw who else was in the room.

If this was another coincidence, he'd about had his fill.

"Hugo, come on in," Ambassador Taylor said, "I'm sorry to interrupt your vacation." He gestured to his guest. "You know Gérard de Roussillon."

Roussillon stood holding a cup and saucer, and Hugo didn't like the smile that was on his face. He tried not to let his own surprise show, instead shaking hands with the ambassador and then the Frenchman. "Yes, we met last night."

"So I gather," Ambassador Taylor said. "Sit down gentlemen, please." They followed the ambassador to the pair of couches. "Hugo, I know you're out of the office, so to speak, but Gérard had some concerns and I wanted to run them past you directly."

"Fine," Hugo said. "What's up?"

"Do you know what the SBP is?" the ambassador asked.

"I do, yes," said Hugo.

"The organization and the people it represents are kind of an institution in Paris," the ambassador said. "Gérard here has done a lot of work with them and sometimes acts as liaison between them and the government. You know, disputes about healthcare, working conditions, the limits that the government puts on what they sell."

"They need a liaison?" Hugo said. "Isn't that what the SBP does?"

"You'd think," the ambassador said grimly. "But depending on who heads it they sometimes need a tactful voice. Let's just say a mediator can work wonders. Gérard has filled that role for a long time."

"As you know, I collect books, Monsieur Marston," Roussillon said. "I get many from the bouquinistes, so if they are happy, I am happy. And I have a lot of contacts in the government, so I help when I can."

"I see."

"Anyway," the ambassador continued, "Gérard tells me that someone from our office, one of your agents, has been pestering Bruno Gravois, the head of the SBP, and starting rumors about disappearing bouquinistes."

"Rumors?" Hugo asked, cursing himself for giving Gravois his real name.

"There are no police reports and no reports from friends or family." Roussillon spread his hands wide. "No one has reported anyone missing, and these kinds of rumors . . ." He trailed off and looked at the ambassador for support.

"Just hang on a minute," Hugo said. "It's not one of my agents, it's me." He turned to address Taylor. "Mr. Ambassador, I was there when one bouquiniste was kidnapped."

"As I said," Roussillon repeated, "there is no police report, and no friends or family have reported him or anyone else missing."

"The man kidnapped was my friend, and I was there, I saw it. Whoever did it either paid off or threatened witnesses to say nothing happened. I'm just trying to find out what happened, that's all."

"Have you been to his home?" the ambassador asked.

"Yes. He wasn't there and his neighbor hadn't seen him."

"Well, maybe he was out buying books or groceries," Roussillon said. "I don't see my neighbors for weeks at a time."

"He lives in an apartment, not a mansion," Hugo snapped. "And last I checked, he didn't have servants to run out and fetch supplies for him."

"All right, that's enough Hugo," Ambassador Taylor said. "Even if you're right and this man is a missing person, unless he's an American citizen we have no interest in the case. And you have no jurisdiction. It's a matter for the Préfecture de Police, and them alone." The ambassador shifted in his seat, his tone softening. "Hugo, our job here, our mission at the embassy, is to foster and maintain good relations with our French allies. I don't need to tell you that. These bouquinistes, they are an icon for Americans coming here. We can't be stirring up trouble for them. We need to mind our own store and let them do the same."

"I understand," Hugo said, biting his tongue. This was not a conversation he wanted to have in front of Roussillon.

"OK, good." The ambassador turned to Roussillon. "Is there anything else, Gérard?"

"*Non, merci beaucoup.*" The Frenchman stood and offered a small bow to the ambassador, a nod to Hugo. "Thank you for your time."

When he'd left the room Hugo stood, but the ambassador closed the door and said, "Hold on a second, we're not quite done." Hugo lowered himself back onto the couch. "If I'd known it was you poking around," the ambassador said, "I would have handled it differently. Roussillon is a powerful man, though, so the lecture was necessary. And true. I thought we'd talked about this. Can I assume you have been disobeying my instructions?"

"Yes, sir," said Hugo.

"I figured. Then tell me what's really going on."

Hugo hesitated. "His name is Max. Max Koche. I've known him for years, ambassador. He's a grouchy old guy but loves what he does. Last week I bought a book from him that turned out to be worth a lot of money. Minutes later he was kidnapped, in front of my eyes. But the police won't make a report because some people nearby, who they won't identify, said Max went with these guys of his own accord. It's insane and a bunch of crap. Anyway, I went back to his stall and talked to the new guy running it. When I started asking him about Max, he clammed up after claiming that he didn't know him. So I went to Max's apartment—"

"Yes, you mentioned that. No one home."

"Right," Hugo smiled, "but I went to his apartment." He said the words slowly, making his meaning plain.

"Ah, I'm with you. And?"

"He'd not been there for days, but someone else had."

"You're sure."

Hugo nodded. "No one is that much of a slob, certainly not Max. I didn't see signs of a struggle or fight, but I did find his toothbrush. As well as empty suitcases and a closet full of clothes."

"Fridge?" Hugo remembered that Taylor had been a spook himself, many years ago.

"Full of perished perishables."

"Oh. That's not good. He have family close by? Or anywhere?"

"Not that I've found."

"Any ideas?"

"Other than it's something to do with the book, not really. He was once a Nazi hunter, though, so I guess it's possible that caught up with him somehow."

"Nazi hunter? Impressive."

"I know. The thing is, this isn't adding up, and no one seems to give a damn."

"So you say." The ambassador sat back on the couch and pondered. "Here's my position. I meant what I said before, we really can't go stirring up a hornet's nest for a missing Frenchman. On the other hand, you're on vacation, so forget what I said before. What you do on your own time is your business as long as it doesn't reflect badly on the embassy."

"Thank you, ambassador. I can be discreet."

"Really?" the ambassador said dryly. "I've never seen that side of you."

"It's not easy walking softly," Hugo said, "when you're wearing cowboy boots."

"I wouldn't know." The ambassador stood, signaling an end to the meeting. "And Hugo? Being discreet means you don't flash your badge."

"Understood."

"And no gun."

Hugo raised an eyebrow. "You want my pants, too?"

"No thanks," said Taylor. "But if you piss off Roussillon and his buddies, I'll have your hide. How's that?"

CHAPTER SEVENTEEN

It was dark by the time Hugo left the embassy, an afternoon killed off in his office doing some reading, some administration, and a lot of nothing. He'd wanted to spend a few hours with Tom at home or a café somewhere, but a short phone conversation with his friend had put paid to that idea.

"Sorry, got plans."

"Writing me a memo on your homework?"

"Nope, seeing a man about a horse."

"And I thought you'd come to Paris to see me."

"Don't be such a baby. Where do you think I'm getting your info?"

"No idea, Tom, you haven't given me any answers."

"Over dinner?"

"I'm seeing Claudia, but join us. I'd like you to meet her."

"Shit, she doesn't have any answers."

"True, but she has several things you don't. Can we talk later?"

"You mean if you don't get lucky and bring her home?"

"Funny. And I think we need to take a trip down to the Pyrénées tomorrow, see a woman about a horse. A horse's ass, to be precise."

"Hmm." There was a pause. "OK. Well, in that case I need to be done with this project tonight, which means I won't be home before bedtime. You kids have fun."

Hugo paused briefly on Pont Neuf, staring into the black ribbon of the Seine, then continued through the narrow streets of the Sixth for his rendezvous with Claudia. Another cold walk, somehow made colder by the stark glare of the Christmas lights that hung like icicles from the city's buildings and trees.

He arrived at the intersection before she did and chose the emptier of the two cafés. He found an outside table warmed by one of the nearby heating lamps. He'd noticed that this and other Parisian cafés had started putting up plastic walls at the sides and front to keep their clientele warm in the evenings. He wasn't in the mood to wait for Claudia before ordering, and was halfway through a scotch when he spotted her walking down Rue Mazarine toward him. He stood and waved, and she waved back.

She slid behind the little table, sitting next to him rather than across, giving him a peck on each cheek. "I like to watch the evening unfold, too," she said, nodding toward the street.

"I never met a journalist or a cop who liked having his, or her, back to the open," Hugo said. He caught the eye of a waiter and Claudia ordered wine. "I had the pleasure of your father's company this afternoon."

"Oh? How did that happen?" Her eyes twinkled with mischief for a second. "Was he the mysterious man following you?"

"No," Hugo smiled, "I'm sure he doesn't do that sort of thing himself. I saw him at the embassy. I didn't realize he was in thick with the SBP."

"The who?"

"Syndicat des Bouquinistes de Paris."

"Oh," she said, "I didn't know that either."

"Really?" Hugo sipped his drink.

She looked askance at him. "Really," she said. "So why was he at the embassy?"

"Apparently he doesn't like me poking around asking questions about Max. It upsets the bouquinistes, he says, and that's bad for business."

She sighed. "He has a lot of fingers in a lot of pies, so this doesn't surprise me. Are you going to back off? I assume that's what he wants."

"It is. And no, I'm not. Does he know you looked into this for me?"

"No, I don't usually talk about my work with him. He's happy when he sees my name in the paper, but that's usually all he knows about what I do."

They sat in silence for a moment, then the waiter swung past with a small bowl of olives. "So, tell me about your work. This new department or division you were trying to get a story about, how's that going?"

"Good, actually." She nodded thoughtfully. "They don't usually encourage journalists to get involved, or know too much, but I've been around for a while and I think they trust me. Plus, the fight against drugs usually involves a public relations campaign so I'm sure they plan to use me, too. In fact, I told a couple of people that I'd met an American cop, and they may even be needing your help at some point."

"Oh?"

"*Oui*," she said, "in an advisory capacity. In the last year or so we've seen a flood of drugs into Paris, two in particular: crack cocaine and meth."

"Drugs for the user on a lower budget," Hugo said.

"Yes. And no offense, but we think of them as American drugs."

He smiled. "Thank heavens for Hollywood."

"Right. The police know, or suspect, that the meth is being manufactured here. The crack, too, in that it comes into Paris as cocaine and then gets altered here. All of the shipments that they've intercepted so far, and there have been quite a few, have been pure cocaine. Too high in quality to go out on the streets."

"So what is this new task force supposed to do?"

"Well, in the past they've not had much luck stopping the stuff getting into the city. There are just too many access points. Roads, rail, even the river. For them to monitor or control all of those would bring commerce and tourism to a standstill, it's just not possible." Claudia sipped her wine. "Plus, they figure that if the bad guys are smart enough to get it across the borders, they can get it into Paris."

"And if it's getting manufactured here, closing down routes into the city wouldn't help anyway."

"Exactly." She nodded.

"So the cops are concentrating on finding out where the stuff is being made?"

"Indirectly, yes," she said. "The plan is to target drug distribution within the city."

"I don't know if that's a good idea." Hugo shook his head. "I'm guessing they'll just end up with a bunch of junkies and maybe some low-level dealers. We tried that approach in the United States, I worked on a few task forces myself, and all it did was fill up the jails. The big fish kept swimming."

"That's because it's all you did. And they're going to do things a little differently."

"How so?"

"They don't plan to take the users and small-time dealers off the street, they plan to use them to follow the flow of drugs upstream."

"I've been arguing for that approach for years," Hugo said. "It takes a lot of manpower and money though."

"I imagine that's where I come in. If the public cares enough, the police will have their money. For a while, anyway."

"Makes sense. And the other thing for this to work: the cops will have to make sure those street dealers are more scared of them than they are of the people they buy from."

"Now that could be a problem."

Hugo read something in her face. "What do you mean?"

"Have you heard of Anton Dobrescu? Is that name familiar?"

Hugo thought. "Maybe from the news, but I don't remember . . ."

"Romanian," she said. "Looked like Rasputin, all hair and wild eyes. He was one of the most dangerous drug dealers in Bucharest and Timisoara, where he made a fortune before moving his operation to France once the borders opened up. He set up in Paris and was the head of an especially violent organized crime group."

"He's running the drugs?"

"No, he's dead. Killed quite nastily by the other organized crime group in Paris, the North Africans. Algerians, mostly, they call themselves Les Pieds-Noirs."

"The Black Feet? Never heard of them."

"I'm not surprised, they're generally pretty quiet. The name refers to the French and other Europeans who settled in Algeria, I guess they all wore black shoes. Anyway, they were happy enough to divide up

Paris and share the proceeds for a while, but Dobrescu got greedy. He started putting his dealers in the French mob's territory. And he killed people he shouldn't have."

"North African mobsters?"

"No, cops. Like I said, his people had a kind of alliance with Les Pieds-Noirs, and mob violence was down for a while. But when he started encroaching on their turf and killing cops," she shook her head. "Everyone knows you don't do that. Ever. Except Dobrescu, who either didn't know or didn't care. Anyway, I think that once he started down that path, Les Pieds-Noirs figured he was threatening their entire way of life and they decided to hit him once, and hard."

"There was a fire, right?" He remembered the headlines now. "The papers never really said what happened. Not in any detail."

"Right, that's because the police and media weren't sure ourselves, not at first. We had to piece it all together afterwards, and that wasn't easy after a fire like that. Plus the authorities were pretty tight-lipped."

"So what do you think happened?" he asked.

"As best we could tell, Les Pieds-Noirs took a handful of Dobrescu's men hostage and somehow got Dobrescu himself. From the positions of the bodies, and their condition, it looked like the North Africans cut up the Romanians. Possibly while Dobrescu was made to watch, but we can't be sure about that. There were reports of a gun fight before the house went up in flames, and there were several Romanians who were shot and not cut up, so we think his men figured out where they were being held and launched a rescue mission."

"You keep saying cut up, do you mean . . . ?"

"Literally, chopped up. Years before, a member of Les Pieds-Noirs, an informer, turned up in a barrel floating down the Seine. Arms, hands, legs, and feet, all chopped off. We, and the police, wondered then whether it was a play on the name 'Pieds-Noirs.' Anyway, generally they were not violent, not on a day-to-day basis."

"Just don't piss them off, I guess." Hugo took a sip of his scotch. "You were saying, the rescue mission," he prompted.

"Yes. Big gunfight and someone started a fire. By the time the cops sorted through the evidence the place was a charnel house, bodies and bits of bodies scattered everywhere, almost all burnt beyond recognition."

"But the cops identified Dobrescu?"

"They did. They identified him and several of his top lieutenants through DNA and dental records, no doubt about it. Anyway, the Romanians disappeared entirely, which I'm sure was the point of that little exhibition."

"And with Dobrescu gone, no one to lead a comeback."

"Right. So, the bottom line is that the police have a good handle on who's running things in Paris now, but proving it is the problem. After that little massacre, and the previous instance of chopping hands and feet, people are afraid to cross them."

"I'm sure," said Hugo. "And if the cops have no rival gangsters to use, they will have to start from the bottom and build a case upwards, man by man. And you want to be in on the story from the beginning."

"*Exactement,*" Claudia said. She picked up a menu. "But enough about drugs and murder. I'm hungry. Share a pizza with me?"

"Is that your way of saying you want to stay a while and talk about us?"

"It's my way of saying I want to stay a while and eat."

"Then yes."

"Excellent, I'll choose." She hummed quietly as she picked out two pizzas for them to share, and when the waiter arrived, ordered them and a carafe of red wine. They sat in silence for a while, watching the evening parade. The café across the street filled and emptied rhythmically, just as theirs did, as office workers dodged traffic on the narrow but busy street, fresh baguettes sticking out of backpacks and shoulder bags. Many of those who passed the café peered into it with a look that said, *I'd be there, too, if I had time.*

"Oh, Hugo," Claudia said. "I completely forgot to tell you." She paused as the waiter arrived with their pizzas. It took some rearranging, but he managed to find space on the little table for them, and for the plates and wine. When he left she continued. "I can't believe I forgot."

"Forgot what?" he said.

"The river police pulled a body from the water today. A bouquiniste."

"Really?" A knot formed in his stomach, but if it was Max she wouldn't be telling him like this. "Who? What happened?"

"Right now they're treating it as an accident. They say she's pretty well known as a drinker, so she probably had a few too many trying to stay warm, took a turn by the water's edge, and fell in."

"She?" Hugo felt the knot tighten. "An alcoholic?"

"Yes," Claudia said. "And wearing a lot of very heavy wool clothing, so once she fell in it would have been hard for her to stay afloat, let alone climb out. Very sad."

Hugo sat back. "Do you know her name?" he asked quietly.

"No." She shook her head. "They told me but I can't remember, sorry."

"Was it Francoise Benoit?"

"Yes, that's it," Claudia said, surprised. "You know her?"

"Yes," said Hugo. "I sure did."

She was the first one to be honest with me, he wanted to say. She was the only one who cared enough about Max to speak up and send me in the right direction. He recalled Benoit's mottled face, watery eyes, and too-sweet breath. *She may not have been healthy, may not even have been long for the world, but this wasn't supposed to happen*, Hugo thought. And with a stab of regret he realized that if, somehow, Max was still alive, when he found out about Francoise Benoit's death the old man would be devastated.

CHAPTER EIGHTEEN

The next morning, Hugo woke early. He checked through his packed bag one last time and waited for his taxi to the Montparnasse rail station. He'd arranged the cab the previous night, after dinner, at the same time as he called one to take Claudia home.

They had, finally, talked about their situation, such as it was. She'd been surprised, and then curious, about Hugo's lack of resentment toward her father. He'd explained as best he could that a life chasing bad guys had taught him that there were, in reality, very few of them in this world. Mostly, he told her, good people did things that could be classed as good, bad, and everything in between. On the scale of possibilities, her father had done nothing but try to protect his daughter. And while she'd lied to him about her "humble origins," it was a harmless lie and one that lay in reason. The simple truth, one that he didn't articulate over coffee, was that he wasn't looking to get married and was keeping his expectations in check. She was surprised and pleased by his graciousness, or so she said, and he knew that when they parted the air was clear. She climbed into her cab just before eleven, but before she left they shared a hug of genuine warmth and, he sensed, a certain amount of relief. He knew they could have gone back to his apartment, but he also knew that tonight was a new beginning. And no need to hurry.

As promised, Tom wasn't home when he got in. Hugo called and told him about the morning's taxi, said not to worry if he couldn't make it in time. And when Hugo's taxi arrived, just after seven, there was no sign of, or word from, Tom.

On the ride to the station he studied the two pages Emma had prepared for him. Cecilia Josephine Roget lived in a small village called

Bielle, about twenty miles south of the city of Pau in the Pyrénées-Atlantiques department of France. It was Basque country, in the lea of the Pyrénées mountains and not far from the Spanish border.

Years ago, Hugo had spent two weeks in the region studying the antiterrorist techniques of the French and Spanish police, who had waged a quiet but bloody war with the Basque separatist group ETA since the late 1960s. He remembered it as some of the most beautiful countryside he'd ever seen, underdeveloped and with huge swathes of it protected by the French government as parkland. Few foreign tourists knew about it and fewer still took the time to visit. As a capitaine in the provincial police had told him, the British preferred the sun and sand of the Riviera, the Americans fell for the cultivated cuteness of Provence, and the Japanese rarely made it out of Paris.

A motorcycle raced past the cab window, startling him, and he put the papers down, unable to concentrate. The news about Francoise Benoit had shaken him more than he would have predicted. Death had simply been off his radar screen for too long and its reappearance like this had been a nasty reminder of the black side of his profession . . . and an even more unpleasant reminder of what may have happened to Max.

Claudia had been open to the idea that Benoit's death was more than an accident but told Hugo what he already knew: the detectives investigating the drowning had to follow the evidence, not supposition. Hugo himself tried to see both sides; he'd smelled her early morning breath, had seen the heavy clothing that she wore. And would someone really commit murder in broad daylight in the middle of Paris? Unfortunately, he knew they would. A quick shove while under another one of the bridges, the water low so she'd be invisible from the walkway alongside it. And how long for her to slip under? Seconds, Hugo knew. Just seconds.

The cab let him out in front of Montparnasse station and Hugo battled against the flow of traffic, making his way to the arrivals and departures board to find his platform. A taped, hollow-sounding security announcement echoed around him and every few seconds train numbers and destinations clicked on to and off of the board with a *tchk-tchk-tchk.* His train sat waiting at platform 3, giving him thirty minutes to get his ticket and board. But like most experienced travelers, he knew to buy his breakfast and lunch for the five-hour trip at one of the station's cafés—the coffee was decent enough in the dining car, but too many times Hugo had paid the railway premium for sandwiches that were rubbery in look, feel, and taste.

Hugo's first-class ticket gave him space in a compartment that turned out to be empty. As the train left the dense suburbs and picked up speed, the muffled chatter of the wheels beneath him blanketed the compartment in its own white noise, the occasional whump of a passing train and bleat of a whistle barely registering. Its gentle rock and the lure of a new novel—full of prewar subterfuge—quickly veiled the outside world. He sank deeper into his book and was transported to 1937 to witness the bravery of an English bookseller in Berlin as she foiled the Nazis by producing counterfeit passports for fleeing Jews. Time and the countryside passed by unnoticed.

The drive from the Pau train station to Bielle was, as Hugo knew it would be, a delight. He'd rented a car for two days but told the agent he might keep it longer. "It's winter," the man said, "keep it as long as you like."

Hugo drove out of the station with the windows down and the heater on full. Clumps of snow lined the roadway but the pavement itself was clear and dry. He'd not realized how stuffy the train had been until he'd stepped outside to get the car, and he'd not yet had his fill of the dry, cold air.

He drove slowly, but the curved roads soon brought him through Jurançon and into Gan. Once through the little town, he hit a straight stretch of road lined with plane trees and bordered by open land and the occasional farmhouse. Eventually his nose began to freeze, and he closed the window most of the way, leaving just an inch at the top for the air to stream in and ruffle the top of his head.

Twenty minutes later he slowed as he passed the village of Castet, looking for the turn to Bielle. The hedgerow fell away and he spotted a small road leading up toward the village where Cecilia Roget now lived, a gathering of stone houses that lay spread across the lower slopes of the mountain as if sprinkled by a giant as it strode to the peak.

Before entering the village, he pulled off the road to check his directions, parking in a lay-by next to a gate that led into an empty pasture, leaving just enough room in case someone wanted to get past on the narrow road. He looked at the second sheet of paper Emma had given him, listing the houses in Bielle that Ms. Roget owned. According to this, she had four.

Three of them were *gites*, houses that were rented out during the spring and summer to tourists but were usually empty in the winter. Hugo had rented several for weekend trips before and knew that *gites* were typically furnished with just the basics—an oven, a fridge, plenty of beds, and one or two bathrooms to share. Perfect for hiking or fishing vacations, and cheap to boot.

The fourth house was the one in which she lived, a five-bedroom farmhouse set behind stone walls. It was called *Le Nid*, the nest. *An odd choice of name for a place with two turrets*, he thought, *even if they were small ones*. For nine months of the year she ran it as a bed and breakfast, closing down in December for three months when mountain hiking became impossible, or at least unpleasant.

Four houses, and the question that had bugged Hugo all the way down here was simple: How did a bouquiniste get the cash to buy four houses all at once? Maybe Francoise Benoit was right, and the grim-faced chief of the SBP had greased Madame Roget's exit from the union with enough to get settled in Bielle. But that would be an awful lot of cash. Or perhaps she'd saved over the years and this had always been her plan.

He located the farmhouse on a more detailed local map he'd been given at the car rental office, then turned back onto the road, pulling over a moment later to let a tractor trundle past. He found the center of the village and parked in a small lot beside a World War II monument and within sight of the bed and breakfast. He shouldered his overnight bag and walked up to the open gate. A short driveway led him to the front of the house, and when he looked up Hugo saw smoke curling from a chimney. He didn't see a doorbell, so he knocked loudly and waited. A moment later he heard footsteps and the door swung open.

"*Bonjour*. Monsieur Marston?"

"*Oui, bonjour.*" He smiled and offered a hand. The woman was sixty years old at least, but had the strong jaw and fine features that told of beauty in earlier years. Her gray hair was hidden beneath a neatly knotted blue scarf, and she wore a faded Barbour jacket and tweed skirt. This one-time bouquiniste was a long way from the booze-soaked bundle of warmth that had been Francoise Benoit.

She shook his hand and then gestured for him to come in. He felt a rush of warm air the moment he entered the stone-flagged foyer, which opened straight into a large living area where a fire snapped and hissed in the grate. The furniture and drapes in the room were all designed for comfort, heavy velvet curtains, woolen throw rugs on the two formidable couches, and wing-backed armchairs positioned near the fireplace.

"I don't get too many guests here in November," she said. "In fact, we're pretty close to shutting down for the winter."

"I'm glad I made it in time," he said. "You have a beautiful home, Madame Roget."

"*Merci.* And please, call me Ceci. Everyone does." She led him into the main room and offered him a seat in one of the armchairs. "Your French is very good," she said, "but, maybe American?"

"Yes. And thank you. I've been in Paris a long time."

"I miss Paris." She smiled. "It can be very quiet out here; some days I see more cows than people. And don't bother trying to use your cell phone, if you have one, this village is a dead zone. Go to Louvie or Castet and it should work." She shrugged. "But I suppose that's why you are here, for some peace and quiet."

"And some hiking," said Hugo. *And some answers.*

"I hope the weather holds for you. Did you eat lunch? I have plenty in the kitchen if you're hungry."

"I ate on the train, but thank you."

"How about something to drink?"

"I don't suppose you have some tea?"

"I often have English guests," she said with a smile. "Black, green, chamomile even."

"Black tea. And with milk and sugar, like the English, please."

He hoped she would join him. The role of the formal hostess suited her, but Hugo didn't want that, he wanted someone who liked to talk, to answer questions rather than ask them. Timing and technique were everything in an interrogation. Forget the tough-guy act of the movies, that only worked on teenagers—and sometimes not even then.

In his last years at the bureau, Hugo had taught a class on interrogations and confessions at the academy in Quantico. He littered his class with anecdotes to keep it interesting and to show how the techniques from the course worked in the real world. He always began the first class with the story of his best confession, the one he was most proud of: child killer Charles Wilford. The portly little man had kidnapped a nine-year-old girl just outside of Houston, but the police didn't have enough evidence to go into his house and look for her inside. Hugo had seen cases like that before and knew she was dead, but he wasn't about to let Wilford get away with it, so he sat the man down just to talk. Like so many guilty men, he'd not called for a lawyer but had sat up all night talking to Hugo, getting closer and closer to giving straight answers but never quite doing so. Only when Hugo sat beside him, took his hand, and explained how it was going to go on forever, the urges and the killings, did Wilford break down and confess. After drying his eyes on Hugo's handkerchief, Wilford led police to his garage, where the little girl's body was wrapped in a sheet behind a stack of boxes.

Ceci Roget was no Wilford, of course, but if he wanted to find Max, then this, despite the blazing fire and the tea, needed to be just as effective an interrogation. The biggest dilemma he had was whether to try to obtain the information by subterfuge or just be open. His natural inclination was toward the latter, and he was fairly certain that honesty, even unwelcome honesty, would sit better with Madame Roget than subterfuge.

"I think it may snow tonight," she said, appearing with a steaming mug. "I hope not, it will make hiking difficult."

"Thank you." He took the drink and sipped. "If I can spend a day or two in the countryside I'm happy. Hiking or no hiking." He nodded toward her coat. "Were you on your way out? I don't want to keep you."

"Oh no. I have a Labrador, Sydney, who insists on being walked every afternoon." She walked to the fire and knocked a loose log back into place with her boot. "I have one more guest arriving today, any minute, actually, so I'll take Syd out when he gets here. If you don't mind being left alone."

"Not at all." Hugo cleared his throat. "Before he arrives, I have a confession, Madame Roget . . . Ceci."

"A confession?" She looked at him, suddenly unsure. "What do you mean?"

He lounged back in the chair, crossing his legs at the ankle to transmit through body language that it was no big deal and that he was no threat. "I'm not sure how to explain it best." He looked up. "Do you know Max Koche?"

She didn't move. "I know a Max Koche."

"The bouquiniste."

"*Oui.*" She nodded slowly. "Why?"

"I'm a friend of his. I've been buying from him for years." She waited for him to go on. "Madame, Max is missing."

"Missing? What do you mean?"

He told her the story. He told her about his kidnap from the walkway, about the Rimbaud book and his meeting with Gravois, and about Francoise Benoit. As he spoke, she moved from the fireplace to the armchair beside him, never taking her eyes from his face, but giving nothing away by her own expression. When he stopped talking, both his tea and the fire were low, but only Hugo noticed. She stared at her hands for a full minute then looked up. "I knew Max well."

"You did?"

"Many years ago, I helped him get his stall. He was a man with an obsession, did you know that?"

"What do you mean?"

"Well," she hesitated. "Do you know about his past?"

"I know he was a Nazi hunter, yes."

"He was." She nodded. "Although he got tired of that. Tired of the travel and the stress, not the idea of catching them. And I think he had one or two cases where he felt let down by the judicial system. Anyway, when he came to Paris, he changed his focus, I suppose. He became interested in, and then obsessed by, Nazi collaborators. He was a member of some group that did research to find them."

"I didn't know that," Hugo said. "What did they do when they found them?"

"Not much, I think. I mean, mostly they were very old men and women by the time they were discovered. About all they could suffer was the shame of their collaboration being made public."

"So that's what Max and his people did? They outed the collaborators?"

"Yes. Actually, I think his friends grew weary of it after a few years. As I said, these were old people, and sometimes their young relatives didn't take kindly to the information being revealed. But not Max. As I said, for him it became an obsession." She smiled sadly. "Do you know why he became a bouquiniste?"

"No," said Hugo, "he and I never talked about that."

"Well, you are too young to remember, but you may understand that during the war information was key. For both sides. Whether it was the location of munitions dumps, the routes being used to get Jews out of the country, or who was in the Resistance. But to be useful, the knowledge had to be shared, to be transported. The Gestapo were very good at extracting information, as I'm sure you know."

Hugo grimaced. "I know of their reputation."

"Yes. Because they were so good, the Resistance had to think of ways of protecting the information that it gathered. To protect it even as it was being transferred."

"How do you mean?"

"Well, information was smuggled in different ways, so the carrier didn't know what it said. One of the ways was in books."

"How exactly?"

"A variety of ways. Microdots, or notes pasted under the end-papers were common. Sometimes words or letters were highlighted in invisible ink. Those were probably the methods used most often by the Resistance."

"And the kinds of information they passed, you're not just talking about munitions dumps and German troop movements, but information about collaborators."

"Exactly. I think—no, I know, Max believed he could locate more collaborators if he could just search enough books. That's why he became a bouquiniste; he thought it was the best way to search as many old books as possible."

Hugo pictured Max clinging to the copy of *On War* by Carl von Clausewitz on that cold, cloudy afternoon. Now he knew why. "Poor Max," Hugo said. "I had no idea." He sat back and shook his head. No idea at all.

"Don't feel bad, it did not make him an unhappy man. You know him, so you know that's true. It's almost as if it gives him purpose."

They sat in silence for a minute, then Hugo looked up. "And you knew Francoise? They are calling her death an accident."

"Yes, I knew poor Francoise. Frankly, her death could have been an accident. She used to leave her stall and go down by the river to drink. She thought no one would know that way. Perhaps it was inevitable that one day she would fall in." She smiled sadly. "*C'est dommage.*" A great shame.

A knock at the door interrupted them and she excused herself. Hugo turned to stare into the fire. He'd not asked about Gravois yet, she needed to process this shock first. And so far she didn't look like being much help. But then why would she? A nice house, a safe business, and hundreds of miles from Paris. No reason in the world to get involved in whatever nasty stuff was happening in and around the Seine.

A man's voice spoke beside him. "Mind if I join you?"

Hugo twisted in his seat, looked up at Tom, and grinned. "Be my guest."

"Thanks." Tom flopped into the vacant armchair. "I got your message and was in the neighborhood."

"Marseille is in the neighborhood?"

Tom grinned. "What a good memory you have."

Madame Roget arrived with a large glass of water, which she handed to Tom. "I'm going to take Sydney out, I'll be back in an hour. Please, make yourselves at home. Would you care to eat here tonight, or will you be going out? I'm happy to cook, if you don't mind peasant cuisine."

"Let's eat here, if you don't mind," said Tom. "Just be sure and add it to his bill."

"*Bien*. You like pork?"

They told her they did and watched her leave. Tom looked around the room, then back at Hugo. "So did I miss the interrogation?"

"Most of it. She doesn't seem to know much, I'm afraid."

"The picture's the same, then?"

"Sadly, no. One other bouquiniste is dead for sure." Hugo filled him in on his encounter with Benoit on the Seine's walkway and on the details of her death. He also told Tom about his being followed and about Roussillon's interference. Then he asked. "Tell me you have good news."

"I have news." Tom watched him for a moment, in a way that made Hugo uncomfortable.

"Spit it out."

"I looked into your unhelpful cop, David Durand. Word I got, he was passing the scene and offered to check it out."

"OK. And?"

"And, sheesh." Tom sighed and rubbed a hand over his face. "Here comes the real news. Your new girlfriend has been hanging out with him."

"What?" Hugo sat forward, his eyes fixed on Tom.

"They met at a café, played kissy-face like the French do, and were still there when I strolled past twenty minutes later."

"Doing what?"

"It was a café, what do you think?"

"I don't understand. Were you following Durand or Claudia?"

"Does it matter?"

"Hell yes."

"Fine. Claudia."

"Tom, what the hell?"

"You're welcome." He threw up a sheepish smile. "You have to admit, it's interesting information."

It was, though Hugo wasn't happy about admitting it. "So they were having coffee. No idea why?"

"Nope."

"Did you find out who bought the book?"

"I did, actually. Can you guess?"

They locked eyes for a moment, then Hugo spoke. "Roussillon bought it, didn't he?"

"He sure did. Well, not him, but a little girl he has working for him, I forget her name."

So did Hugo, but no matter. Roussillon again. Did Claudia know about this? "I assume you didn't approach him yet?" Hugo asked.

"Not yet. Did a little digging and saw he was a big shot and figured you might want to handle with care. Glad I did, sounds like he's a thorn."

"Good assessment."

"So what's the plan?"

Hugo stretched his feet toward the fire, pushing away thoughts of Claudia meeting with a detective he didn't trust. "Let's ask madame about Gravois when she gets back," he said. "We'll see if she has any more insight into that guy. And then we'll have a nice peasant dinner."

CHAPTER NINETEEN

She cooked supper in the pot, a shank and several thick cuts of roast boar that had baked in its own juices and red wine for a good two hours—time that Hugo and Tom spent by the fire. They talked about Max and the book, but found themselves coming up with more questions than answers so they turned to old times and frequently just stared into the flames. Ceci moved back and forth from the kitchen, bringing fresh drinks and slices of local brebis cheese, and dropping new logs on the fire when the two men forgot to do it themselves.

Once, as she was cooking at around six o'clock, Hugo wandered back to the kitchen to see if he could help, and when she declined with thanks, he stood and watched approvingly as she added onions, potatoes, and handfuls of whole garlic to the pot. When he went back to his chair by the fire, he carried the rich aroma with him.

The meal was served at a battered oak table in the kitchen and Ceci ate with them, a small wood stove pumping heat into the room. She'd put a bottle of wine and three glass tumblers on the table, and the men decided it would be impolite not to partake. A second bottle, with Ceci keeping pace, saw them through to a circle of pastry covered in crème patisserie and layered with strawberries. Night closed in around them but they didn't notice, and if they had, they would have welcomed it. No reason to go out and every reason in the world to stay in.

After they'd eaten, they moved back into the living room. Ceci offered to open another bottle of wine, but Hugo had turned pensive and his mood seemed to color theirs. He knew they had more talking to do. Or, he hoped, Ceci did. He asked what she knew about Gravois.

She frowned and thought for a moment, then told them that the man had come out of nowhere. After twelve years heading the SBP, she'd thought about retiring but didn't have enough saved and so settled in for an unopposed election and another four-year term as the union's leader. But as the election drew near, she began to hear rumblings. Not so much of discontent, she said, but of concern. And then Bruno Gravois paid her a visit.

"He was nice enough," she said. "Polite but in that way some people have, the way that lets you know they are not always so gentlemanly. He told me that some of the bouquinistes had asked him to throw his hat into the ring."

"Wait, was he a bouquiniste himself?" Hugo asked.

"No. That's what was odd. That was always the tradition. I'd only run a stall for a few years, then gotten myself a part interest in a bookshop in the Third Arrondissement. But I had been a bouquiniste."

"Interesting," said Tom. "Did you ask him about his background? Why he of all people should be any good at the job? Or want it?"

"Of course. He told me that he was well-connected, that he could give the bouquinistes a louder voice. No, wait. 'A bigger stick to wield,' that's the way he put it."

"Nice image," Hugo muttered. "Go on."

"I remember after that he did something odd. We'd been talking with my office door open, but he got up and closed it. He came to my desk and half-leaned over it. Have you seen him? Then you'll know what he looks like. To a woman, *messieurs*, he can be quite frightening."

"I can see that," Hugo said. "Did he threaten you?"

"No, I don't suppose I can say that he did." She laughed gently. "That face, the look he had, that was threat enough. He didn't use any words that, when I repeat them now, sound threatening, but after he'd closed the door like that, walked so slowly to my desk . . ." She looked at Hugo and shuddered. "You've seen the limp? Then you know. Anyway, he offered me money. I remember his voice, so clear and cold. It's almost funny, he offered me money the way a robber demands it. You feel like you have no choice but to go along." She waved a hand at the living room. "And this is what I did with it."

"And some *gites*," said Hugo.

"Yes. It was a lot of money."

"Didn't you wonder, though? Wonder why?" asked Tom. "Or go to the police, even?"

"And say what? That a scary man had offered me lots of money? 'Take it!' they would have said, 'take it, you foolish woman!' So that's what I did."

They sat in silence for a moment, then Hugo spoke. "Did you know he offered other bouquinistes money to quit?"

"No." She looked up. "Why would he do that?"

"I don't know," Hugo said. "For the same reason he offered you money, whatever that is."

"You know, I have some files here," she said. "They may be out of date, but you are welcome to them. They'd tell you who had stalls when I left Paris, maybe you could see who has left and find out why."

"I think that's exactly what we should do," said Hugo.

"I can take care of that pretty easily," said Tom. "I'll get the names, find contact info, and start calling."

"I'll go get them," Ceci said. She stood and went to a heavy desk at the far side of the living room. She opened a file drawer and spent a few minutes looking through it. She returned with a manila folder containing half a dozen sheets of paper and handed it to Tom. "Not much more than a list of the bouquinistes, but it's something."

"*Merci*," Tom said. "I'll get started first thing tomorrow. Now, what do you say about just one more little bottle of *vin de table*?"

Ceci smiled and headed into the kitchen. Hugo looked at his friend, sprawled out in his chair, disheveled and bleary-eyed. *Good to be working with you again, Tom.*

When Ceci returned, Hugo was glad to see she carried a jug of water along with the bottle, and all three of them paid more attention to it than they did the wine. Somewhere in the house a grandfather clock chimed ten times. As Hugo stood to excuse himself for the night, the house phone rang. Ceci answered it, her eyes on Hugo. "*Oui. Il est la.*" Yes, he's here. "It's for you. A woman."

Tom stirred in his chair and mumbled, "At this time of night? Don't bother ordering one for me, I'm turning in."

Hugo took the phone. "Hello?"

"Hugo, it's me, Claudia." Her voice was strained.

"Claudia, are you OK?"

"Yes, I'm fine. Been trying to get hold of you for hours."

"Sorry, no cell phone coverage here."

"So I gather. You didn't tell me where you were staying so I had to call the embassy, get your secretary's home number, and have her tell me where you were."

Poor Emma. "So what's going on?"

"Hugo, I'm really sorry." He could hear her take a breath, steadying herself. "I got a call from one of my contacts at the prefecture, they found another bouquiniste in the river. I'm so sorry, Hugo. It's Max—he's dead."

CHAPTER TWENTY

Hugo pressed his head against the cool stone of the wall and closed his eyes. "Where exactly, Claudia?"

"Some tourists found him at the tip of Ile Saint-Germain this afternoon. He'd been in the water for some time. The cops are not sure how long, or how far he was carried downstream, so they can't say where he went in. Or how. I'm sorry."

"It's definitely him?" A question other people used to ask him, and he heard the same desperation in his own voice.

"Yes. There's no doubt."

"OK. Thanks for finding me." He shouldn't have been surprised, and really he wasn't. A man isn't taken like that only to pop back up, all happy and well. But, dammit, he'd hoped. Really hoped. "Tell me they're not treating this as an accident," he said.

"No. They have the tip of the island cordoned off, but no one expects to find anything there, as it almost certainly wasn't the murder scene. If it was murder. They'll do an autopsy in the morning, we'll know more after that."

"Of course. Do you know who's going to handle the case?"

"No, but I can find out and let you know. Want me to call you there tomorrow?"

"No. I'm coming back." He glanced at Tom, who stood watching him, trying to read his face. "I have someone to help me here, my friend Tom, so I'll just head back to Paris tomorrow."

"OK. Call me when you get in, will you?"

"Sure." Hugo hesitated. He had two questions he wanted to ask her, but the one about Durand could wait. "Claudia, did you know your father bought Max's book? The Rimbaud he sold to me?"

A sharp intake of breath told him she didn't know. Or was an exceptional liar, which was possible. "No. He didn't tell me."

"Is there any reason why he would?"

"No, I suppose not. He buys and sells books all the time and doesn't usually mention it unless he's found something he's wanted for a long time. But he didn't say anything about this."

"OK."

"Hugo, you don't still think this is about the book, do you? This may be a murder investigation now and I need to know what you know, what you are thinking." They were both thinking the same thing, but she said it first. "Do you think my father could be involved?"

"I honestly don't know, Claudia. There are a lot of coincidences, an awful lot, but some of them have explanations." He thought of Roussillon buying the Rimbaud. A gay book collector had every reason in the world to cherish an almost priceless copy of *Une Saison En Enfer*, especially one inscribed by the author. "Look, I'll call you tomorrow. And Claudia?"

"Yes?"

"Again, I appreciate you getting this news to me, I really do."

"But of course I would, Hugo." She sounded almost taken aback, but her voice softened. "I am sorry he's gone, truly."

"Thank you. Now, get some sleep, and we'll talk when I get to Paris."

He rang off and handed the phone back to Ceci. Like Tom, she'd been listening to his every word and her eyes were glistening.

"Max is dead, *oui*?" she whispered.

"*Oui*," Hugo said, "*il est mort.*"

She clutched the phone to her chest and closed her eyes. "What is happening up there? Is it Gravois?"

"I don't know," said Hugo, "I really don't."

"Let me at him," Tom growled, "we'll find out soon enough."

Ceci gave him a sad smile and shook her head. "If I understand you, I think we've had enough violence." She walked to the desk and put the phone down, then turned to her guests. "Good night, *mes amis*. Sleep as late or early as you want. I always wake before dawn to let Sydney out, so I'll make breakfast whenever you get up."

The two men bade her good night then stayed for a moment, standing on either side of the fireplace.

"I'm sorry about your friend, Hugo."

"Thanks. At least they aren't assuming it was an accident."

"That's a start," Tom nodded. "Of course, you've got a whole new set of problems now, you know that, right?"

"What do you mean?"

"Well, your boss already told you to keep a low profile. If you keep poking around and asking questions while there's an official police investigation, word'll get back to him pretty damn quick."

"Good point," said Hugo. He looked up at Tom and smiled. "If only I knew someone who was used to operating without anyone knowing."

"Well shit," Tom said, "if you're really expecting me to do my thing, I need to hit the sack. Wake me when you get up. And be sure the coffee's made, else I'll kick your ass."

The next morning, Hugo called the train station in Pau. He'd forgotten it was Sunday, and when he asked about train times he was told that the first one left for Bordeaux at two that afternoon. He wouldn't be back in Paris until the evening.

He used the morning to sketch out a plan of action with Tom. Ceci wanted to help, but they explained that it was best, safest, that she stay out of it. When that didn't work, they promised her that if they could use her help, they would. That didn't wash either, so they put her on the phone, making calls to as many bouquinistes as possible to find out where they were now. "I'm not sure I understand why," she said, even while agreeing to do it.

"And Tom, when we get back to Paris I'm thinking we make a visit to Roussillon's place and look at that book."

"Sounds good," Tom said. "Assuming he lets you see it."

"He's got no reason to deny me. And if he does, well, you can put on your ninja suit and fly down the chimney."

"Not sure I'd fit into the suit, let alone the chimney."

Hugo smiled. "And there's this other book I should tell you about, it may have something to do with all this."

"Oh, great, another mysterious book. Who's it by, Agatha fucking Christie?"

"Good guess, but no," Hugo said. "It's by a guy called Clausewitz."

"The military man? So did you sell this one, too?"

"That's the thing. I have no idea where it is." But he couldn't help thinking that Max's copy of *On War*, wherever it was, might just give them some answers.

CHAPTER TWENTY-ONE

The train drew into the station at Montparnasse just before eight o'clock that evening. The journey had been frustrating, Hugo unable to reach Claudia or get any news about Max's autopsy, and Tom complaining about the food from the dining car.

They did talk seriously about *On War* but came to no conclusions. Assuming it was of value, Hugo wondered whether whoever took Max also had the book. Hugo cast his mind back to the kidnapping, trying to picture the book at the stall or even in Max's hand in those final moments, but he couldn't see it in that much detail, couldn't resolve the question one way or the other. Even if he could have, though, neither he nor Tom were able to come up with a reason the book had warranted kidnapping or killing Francois and maybe Max, let alone parting bouquinistes from their stalls. And that meant whoever searched Max's place was probably looking for something else.

"So *On War* is irrelevant?" Tom had asked.

"Could be. Seems like it, don't you think?"

"I do. But let me know if you change your mind on that."

"I will." They sat quietly for a moment, and Hugo let himself think about a conversation they'd started earlier, one they needed to finish. "About Durand."

"You mean about Claudia."

"Fine. What else can you tell me?"

Tom frowned. "How about you do the telling."

"What does that mean?"

"It means there's some shit that looked linked, but I don't get how." When Hugo didn't respond, Tom continued. "You've got books that

163

turn out to be extra pricey, a bookseller who gets kidnapped, an old geezer who collects books, and now you're banging the old geezer's daughter."

"You don't like the coincidences."

"I got no problem with them as long as you're not so blinded by finally getting laid that you chalk stuff up to coincidence when it isn't."

"You think maybe Claudia followed me into the café and put her hooks into me?"

Tom grinned. "No fucking idea. But the mere fact the thought has occurred to you makes me happy."

"Don't worry, I'm rethinking everything that's happened. Now tell me more about her meeting with Durand."

"Nothing more to it, man, I told you everything. They had coffee, she was making goo-goo eyes. Look, she may be clean or she may be dirty but what I saw her doing is what reporters do, so don't sweat it. I didn't see them passing money or dope or hand grenades under the table. Not even playing footsie. I'm sure she's fine."

"So am I. But let me know if you change your mind on that."

"I will, trust me."

Hugo sat back and watched as Tom squeezed his bulk out of the compartment and plodded off toward the dining car in search of beer and more rubbery sandwiches.

The taxi pulled up in front of Hugo's building, gliding into a space between a motorcycle and a poorly parked Renault, half of which hung out into the street. This fell under Tom's bad-driving rubric, one of his pet hates, and Hugo talked him out of exacting street justice. He pointed out the two men smoking nearby and how they'd probably call the cops. Tom snorted, insulted at the suggestion he was incapable of slashing tires without anyone noticing, but he followed Hugo into the black-and-white tiled foyer without protest. Dimitrios was missing from behind his desk—no great surprise on a Sunday evening.

They trudged slowly up the stairs, Tom laden with his overnight bag and Hugo carrying his full duffel bag.

"Get a fucking elevator put in, will you?" Tom panted. He stopped to catch his breath on the first landing. "Stairs, Jesus, it's like the fucking Stone Age."

Hugo smiled and kept going. By the time he reached his apartment on the fifth floor, Tom was sitting on a suitcase on the third-floor landing, huffing and swearing. Hugo put his hand on the door knob and stopped as a shot of adrenaline fizzed through him.

It was unlocked.

Did I forget? No chance. He put his ear to the door and held his breath, then moved to the banister and waved at Tom. He held a finger to his lips and pointed at his door.

Tom stood and mouthed the question: *Gun?* Hugo shook his head. He'd followed the ambassador's request and locked it away before heading to Bielle. Tom, it turned out, did have one. He gestured for Hugo to stay put as he slipped off his shoes. Abandoning his bag on the landing, Tom lumbered silently up the stairs. Hugo gave him a moment to catch his breath, and when Tom nodded that he was ready, Hugo counted them down in a whisper.

Hugo turned the handle and Tom slipped into the apartment first, his gun sweeping the short hallway and what they could see of the living room. They inched forward until they could see the whole room. Empty. A thud from Hugo's study, off to the right. They edged through the living room, backs to the wall, Hugo walking sideways so he'd see if someone appeared from his bedroom behind them.

They paused either side of the study door and Hugo peered through the inch-wide opening. He shook his head and pointed to his ear. *I can't see anyone, but I can hear them.* Tom nodded and moved first. He kicked the door open, spinning to locate the intruder. Hugo stepped in behind him, feeling naked without a weapon.

The moment he was through the door he saw Tom fall. Hugo moved toward him but felt a sudden, searing pain across his shoulders, knocking him to his knees. Tom lay on his back by the bed, clutching his shin. A foot swept past his head, kicking his gun to the far side of the room. Hugo tried to recover, to push himself up, but pain slashed across his back again. *What the hell was that?* He collapsed beside Tom and looked up.

Two men stood over them, one carrying a short length of wood, a club, the other holding a longer, thinner rod. The man with the club stepped away and picked up Tom's gun.

"Who are you?" Hugo demanded. An image of the man who'd harassed Francoise Benoit flitted across his mind. *Could be him*, Hugo thought. *Could be.*

"Shut up." The man was built like a rugby player, a solid mass of muscle under a layer of fat that gave him an extra forty pounds of fighting weight. His jaw was covered with stubble and he had the close, round eyes of a man with a temper. "Which one of you is Hugo Marston?"

"Fucking amateurs," Tom gasped, "cocksucker hit me in the shin, he must have been kneeling on the fucking floor waiting for us. Jesus." He rubbed at his leg but Hugo knew Tom's tibia was intact. If the man had broken it, even Tom would still be screaming.

"I said shut up." The burly man turned the gun on Tom. "You're Marston?"

The second man moved to the bedroom doorway, presumably checking to see if anyone else had come in. He was shorter, stocky, and very black, with a wide, flat nose that had dented many a fist. Wary eyes held a cunning that was absent from the raw anger of the rugby player. Hugo looked at his weapon. No more than two feet long, it had a pair of small, blunt prongs at the end of it. A cattle prod.

"This one is," the black man said, pointing to Hugo.

"How do you know?"

"The photos in the other room."

As the man moved closer to Hugo, Tom rolled onto his side. "I think I'm going to throw up," he said. He pushed himself onto all fours and started retching, causing the man with the gun to back away. *He should be getting him closer*, Hugo thought, *not further away. What the hell? Fine, then I'll start it.*

Hugo shifted his weight onto his arms, waiting for the black man to look at Tom. As soon as he did, Hugo slid forward and slammed his heel into the inside of the black man's knee, making him cry out as his leg crumpled. The man crashed to the floor and Hugo drove his boot into his face, then twisted to see how Tom was faring.

And froze.

The rugby player stood with the gun pointed at Tom's chest. Five feet separated them, as good as a mile. Yet Tom just stood there, a smile on his face. He looked over his shoulder at Hugo. "I told you they were fucking amateurs." He started toward the man.

"Stop, asshole. One more step and you die."

Tom paused. "Or maybe I take four more steps and you die."

"Try it," the man smiled, "if you think you can walk faster than I can shoot."

"Tom," Hugo spoke in English. "Just wait. We don't know what they want. Maybe we can talk to them."

"Fuck that," Tom said. He turned back to the man with the gun and spoke in French. "You gonna hand that over now, ugly motherfucker?"

Tom took a step forward and Hugo's heart sank. He watched as the man's finger crept tighter around the trigger.

"Tom. No!"

Tom ignored him. He took another step toward the thug, the barrel of his own gun two feet away from his chest. Hugo watched in slow motion as Tom took the final steps toward the intruder, who hesitated barely a second before he squeezed the trigger, once, twice.

No sound.

Tom reached out and wrapped his hand around the gun, twisting it up and out, wrenching it from the man's grasp. In less than a second, Tom had the barrel pressed to the stubble of the man's chin.

"You just met the latest in CIA smart technology, fuckhead," Tom said. He kneed the man between the legs. "Don't you just love having your own set of fingerprints?" He kicked the groaning man once more for good measure, then looked at Hugo. "Told you they were fucking amateurs."

But the black man wasn't. Hugo had expected his friend to be shot in the chest at point blank, more than enough to distract him from his own assailant, who had retrieved his weapon. As Hugo looked back to check on him, the man jabbed it into Hugo's thigh. His leg contracted of its own accord and he collapsed backward into Tom, knocking them both off balance. The black man swiped at them once more, then turned and headed for the door.

"Shit," Tom said.

Hugo tried to push off, to chase him, but his leg wouldn't move and he fell sideways onto the desk. Tom hesitated, Hugo could see he didn't want to leave him alone with the doubled-over man. "I'm fine," Hugo said. "Go get him."

Tom kicked the burly man once and then leapt over him. He winced from his bruised shin as he landed but kept going. Hugo could hear him cursing as he moved as fast as he could through the apartment. Hugo tested his own leg, flexing it as he leaned against the desk. Feeling returned and he pushed himself up slowly, able to put weight on it.

"Fuck." Tom appeared in the doorway. "He got away. Sorry man, I'm not much for chasing these days."

"That's OK, we have this one."

The burly man looked up at them, hate written all over his face. *The guy would charge a cattle prod or a wooden club*, Hugo thought. Probably both. Not so happy, though, to charge Tom's gun.

"What do you want to do?" Tom asked.

"Call the police."

"Dammit, Hugo." Tom never took his eyes from the man on the floor. "Let's just ask him a few questions."

"No."

"I promise it won't take long."

"That's what I'm afraid of," Hugo said. "I can't do things that way, Tom, I'm sorry."

"Why don't you just run out and buy some bread or something?"

"I'm not hungry." Hugo shook his head. "Sorry Tom, we've gotta do this by the book. You call the cops, tell them to look for the other guy on their way over." He opened the window and looked up and down the street. "That Renault is gone." He looked at their captive. "You get here in a blue Renault?"

The man spat on the floor and growled.

Tom walked to the desk and dialed 17, the emergency number. As he spoke to the dispatcher, he perched on the edge of the desk, his gun angled toward the man's groin. Hugo went into the living room and dialed Claudia on his cell phone. When she answered, he told her what had happened. She listened without interrupting, and he noticed she quickly switched into journalist mode, dispensing with the "Are you OK?" formalities in favor of learning what had happened.

"Did they take anything?" she asked.

"I haven't checked yet, but I don't think so."

"And no idea what they were after?"

"No. I'm guessing they were just nosing around and then were going to smash the place up. Warn me off."

"What makes you say that?"

"First of all, they weren't armed to kill. Second, for the five seconds they were in charge, one of them wanted to know which one was me. I'm guessing to deliver a message."

"Be interesting to know who from."

"Yeah." Hugo chuckled. "Tom's dying to ask him."

"You should let him." She sounded angry.

"No, I told him not to. Your cop buddies can interrogate him all they like. Hell, they can borrow Tom, if they want."

"Maybe I'll tell them to," she laughed. "*Merde*, Hugo. I'm sorry about all this. I just don't understand what's happening. And I'm glad you're OK."

"That makes two of us." Thank god for Tom and his visit. "Do you have any news on Max?"

"You want to talk about this now?" she asked. "I'd rather come over to tell you in person."

"Honestly, Claudia, once the police take this sack of crap away, I'm getting drunk with Tom. You better tell me now."

"Fine, yes, OK." She paused. "They did the autopsy this morning. You're not going to believe this, but they are telling me that Max died of an overdose."

"An overdose? Of what?"

"Cocaine."

"That's ridiculous, Claudia. Max didn't use cocaine."

"How do you know that, Hugo?" It was a sensible question. He didn't know it, not for sure, but it irritated him all the same.

"Look," he said, "I've been around drug addicts all my working life. You've seen your share, I bet. We both recognize junkies quicker than we recognize our friends, and Max was no junkie." He had a thought. "Do you know if the cops searched his flat today?"

"Yes, they must have."

"Did they find any cocaine?"

"I don't know, Hugo. I have good contacts, but I'm still just a reporter."

"But they would have told you if they'd found drugs there, no? They would have mentioned it, surely."

"Maybe. Maybe not. Probably only if they'd found a lot."

"But you could ask some questions for me, right?"

"Yes, I suppose so."

"OK." Hugo could hear sirens coming down Rue Jacob. "I have to go, the cops are here."

"You sure you don't want me to come over?"

"No, really Claudia, thanks. By the time we're done giving statements the only thing we'll be in the mood for is scotch."

"*Bien*," she said. "If you have any trouble with the cops, let me know straight away. In fact, I'll make a call, let them know who you are."

"Thanks, I'd appreciate that." His phone beeped. He didn't have call waiting, so it went straight to voicemail. He rang off and dialed his messages.

"*Salut*, Hugo, this is Ceci. I called thirty people today. Or tried, it's like they don't answer the phone on Sundays. I talked to a few bouquinistes I know, three. They all took money from Gravois and the SBP to give up their stalls. But they don't know why he was paying them. They took the money without asking questions. And Hugo, I talked to the brother of another bouquiniste. Pierre is one of the old-timers, I've known him forever. This man said that Pierre has been missing for five days. He said that someone else is working Pierre's stall now. He reported him missing straight away, but the police weren't interested, he said. Then he saw the news about Max and he's terrified.

"Hugo, he wants to know if his brother is floating in the Seine, too."

CHAPTER TWENTY-TWO

The police were at the apartment for an hour, taking photographs and statements, and drinking coffee. Hugo had left his front door open, waiting for them, but had been disappointed when he saw which detective was assigned to the incident. For his part, Capitaine Raul Garcia shook hands with Hugo and acted as if they'd never met. A different bow tie, Hugo noted. Red polka dots this time.

Garcia moved about the apartment taking in everything, not letting his crime scene technicians touch anything until he'd taken a mental photo. When he was done looking, he stepped out of their way and watched from a corner of the room with Hugo and Tom as his men dusted and snapped the evidence into place. He declined the scotch that the Americans were drinking but took a cup of coffee, black, one sugar.

Hugo watched a man in green scrubs dust the front door. Everything had happened so fast after Hugo had discovered it unlocked, he'd not had time to wonder how the men had got in.

"Tom, come with me." He put his drink down and Tom followed suit. "Excuse us, capitaine."

Garcia raised an eyebrow.

"I need to check on someone," Hugo said.

"You need one of my men to come with you?" Garcia asked. It was very close to not being a question.

"No, thanks," Hugo smiled, "they are all busy. This won't take a moment."

They headed down the hallway and past the tech, careful not to touch anything.

"What's up?" asked Tom.

"I'm wondering how they got in."

Tom stopped at the top of the stairs and looked down mournfully. "You gonna make me climbs stairs, after all I've been through?"

"Think about it." Hugo was halfway down the first flight, but he stopped and turned. "They didn't kick it in and I didn't leave it unlocked."

"You sure about that?"

They both knew the answer. Neither of them would leave an apartment unlocked when they were inside, let alone away for a few days. It was second nature. "They had to have used a key."

Hugo watched as Tom understood. "You wouldn't have left one lying around, so they must have gotten it from someone else. The concierge."

"Exactly. He wasn't here when we got in, so let's go find him."

"The cops are pretty good at finding people, you know," Tom grumbled as he started down the stairs.

"Good but slow," Hugo said. He trotted down the four flights and paused in the foyer. It was almost eleven, so Hugo wouldn't have expected Dimitrios, or anyone else, to be there. He checked behind the concierge's desk and saw nothing out of place.

Behind the desk a door led to a storage room and the water heaters. Hugo rounded the desk and tried the handle. Unlocked. He waited as Tom caught up and then pushed the door open. They walked into the room together, Hugo feeling for the light switch. He clicked it on and they moved further in, shoes crunching lightly on the concrete floor. Around them were stacks of old furniture, broken armchairs and tables upside down, waiting to be fixed. A row of paint cans lined the wall to the right and a twelve-foot work bench laden with tools lay to their left. The room smelled of oil and dust and not enough ventilation.

No sign of Dimitrios.

Ahead of them was a second door, leading to the boilers. Hugo reached it first and went straight through, finding the light already on. Dimitrios lay bound and gagged on the floor between two boilers, his eyes at first terrified and then flooded with relief as the two men walked in. His cheeks were wet with tears.

They knelt by him, helping him sit up. Hugo pulled off the tape that covered his mouth and Dimitrios spat out a piece of cloth that had been sealed in to prevent him screaming. He rolled his head and breathed deeply. Tom reached for his boot, drew out a knife and flicked it open. He sliced through the rope that pinned the old man's hands behind his back and wound around his legs. Dimitrios sat there for a moment, rubbing his wrists and arms, sobbing quietly.

"*Ça va*, Dimitrios?" Hugo asked gently.

"*Oui*." The old man turned his wide and tear-filled eyes to Hugo. "I am sorry, Monsieur Marston, so very sorry. They made me give them the key, they made me. I am so glad they didn't hurt you. And so ashamed."

"Don't be, Dimitrios, please. Everything is fine," Hugo said. He and Tom helped the old man to his feet, draping his arms around their shoulders. "Let's get you to the hospital."

"That's not necessary, monsieur."

"I think it is," said Hugo. "Do you remember what time those men arrived?"

"I think about eight; I was about to leave."

They helped him to a sofa in the foyer where they found Capitaine Garcia, whose suspicious nature had caused him to follow the Americans downstairs. He radioed for an ambulance and pulled out a pen and notebook and began taking a statement from the concierge.

"Well, this appears to answer one question," Hugo said.

"What do you mean?"

"We surprised them, right? Which means they weren't expecting us."

"Right," said Tom. "And that means they didn't follow us to Bielle and back."

"No," said Hugo, "it just means they didn't follow us back."

"Good point. No great surprise, they've already shown how good they are at tailing you." Tom grinned. "Nice work getting followed to the train station yesterday, though. Dumbass."

"Yeah," Hugo shook his head. "I'm out of practice."

"Pretty good kick to the knee, though."

"Thanks." He looked at Tom, then steered him out of Garcia's earshot.

"About your gun. You know you're not supposed to have one, right?"

"Gun?" Tom raised his eyebrows dramatically, his face the picture of innocence. "What gun? No idea what you're talking about."

"Excellent," Hugo said, "thanks. I've got a feeling the ambassador is going to have enough to say without that added complication."

"You may be out of practice, Hugo, but I'm not."

"Yeah," Hugo nodded. "You love this shit, don't you?"

"As I said, it's just like old times. Now, can we go up and finish those drinks?"

Capitaine Garcia joined them upstairs after Dimitrios had left for the hospital and as the crime scene techs were finishing up.

"No word on the other intruder," he said. "We've got men looking but I don't expect to find him. Not tonight, anyway."

"Is the guy talking?" Tom asked.

"No, he's still sitting in the car downstairs. I'll take him to the station when we're done. I like to process them myself, watch them every step of the way. Makes them feel important, which in turn makes them think they are in more trouble than they are."

"I'd think this guy is already neck deep in the shit," Tom said.

"He is. But by the time I sit down and talk to him, he'll think he's being charged with trying to assassinate our president. And yours."

"Thanks, capitaine." They moved toward the door but Hugo stopped. "We talked before about my friend Max, the bouquiniste who was kidnapped."

"Of course, your suspicions about Monsieur Gravois."

Hugo nodded. "What are the police doing?"

Garcia appraised him for a moment. "Everything we need to do, everything that we should be doing. That is all I can say right now."

Unsatisfied, but recognizing a brick wall when he saw one, Hugo steered Garcia toward the door, double locking it behind him, then walked to his leather armchair in front of the fireplace and leaned on the back of it. He was exhausted but somehow not ready for bed. For all the crimes he'd investigated, crimes much worse than burglary, he'd never been a victim before. As Tom recharged their whisky glasses, he walked through his apartment touching his furniture, checking the windows. When he went back into the living room he clicked the gas fire on and the men sank into their chairs.

"Helluva day," Tom said.

"I'm too old for this."

"Come on, this is the stuff that makes you feel young."

"Speak for yourself."

"Hey." Tom cleared his throat. "Can I ask you something?"

"Sure."

"I was just thinking about your Claudia again," Tom began.

"Yeah, me too."

"I figured. I'm not saying she's in on anything, I just don't feel like I'm sure she's not."

"I don't think so, Tom, I really don't. But my mind is open, if only a little."

"OK. Did she know you were going to the Pyrénées?"

"Yes."

"Then it's possible those mugs didn't follow you."

"She told them?" Hugo shook his head, unable, or unwilling, to believe that. "She also knew we were coming back early. If she was in on this somehow, she'd have told them and we'd never have caught them here."

"That's true, too. So tell me what the plan is for tomorrow."

Hugo wiped a hand over his face. "Sleep late, for one thing. I'll have to call Ceci. And I'll have to talk to the embassy and play the victim."

"How about a visit to Gravois?"

"Are you serious?" Hugo sat up. "No way, Tom. If that guy squeals to Roussillon, I'll get chewed out for real this time." Hugo looked at Tom and recognized the amused glint in his eye. "No, Tom, I don't want you going all black ops on me. Not yet."

"You'll be going into the embassy to report to the ambassador?"

"Yes, and you're coming with me."

"I'll probably just hang out here."

"The hell you will."

Tom stood and walked his glass into the kitchen, then headed for the study. "Sleep well, gorgeous."

Hugo couldn't help smiling. "Good night, Tom."

Tom waved and went into the study, closing the door behind him. Hugo stared at the fire for another five minutes, then pulled himself upright and went to his bed and lay down. *I'll undress in a minute*, was his last thought before sleep rolled over him like a bank of fog.

When Hugo woke at eight the next morning, Tom was gone. He'd left a note on the coffee maker.

Souvenir shopping. I'll bring you back something. —T.

Something.

Looking at the scribbled note, Hugo had the sense that what he wanted most of all was a stronger connection with his mercurial friend. He thought back to their days at Quantico and then in LA. They'd had no secrets back then, Hugo was sure of that. It was Tom's tour with the CIA that had closed him off, not just from Hugo but from everyone else. From the carefree Tom of old. The way he was now, the jokes, the drinking, the attempts at womanizing, they felt forced, as if Tom was looking for his former self, hunting around for the personality that used to be as natural and fitting as his own skin. He was like a man whose memory had been wiped, a man who had to try on different coats to find the one that fits, the one that's his.

Hugo had no idea if his friend needed help or if he needed space. Hugo's expertise with the human mind lay in diagnosing the behaviors of strangers, not friends, and he felt guilty for that. He wanted to be there for Tom but, in truth, he wasn't sure where it was he needed to be. Right now, for example, Hugo had no idea whether Tom was working on finding Max's killer, doing something unspeakable for the CIA, or maybe, just perhaps, really and truly shopping in Paris for souvenirs.

CHAPTER TWENTY-THREE

Into his second cup of coffee and gathering the energy to walk to the embassy, Hugo tried Ceci's number. It rang and rang. *Maybe out walking Sydney*, he thought. He called Emma and was at least able to leave a message. He told her the basics, said he was fine, and asked her to warn the ambassador that he would be in to talk to him. Ten minutes later he was about to try Ceci again when his cell phone rang.

"Capitaine Garcia here, Monsieur Marston."

"Good morning, capitaine. Any news?"

"A little. Your ugly friend didn't want to talk to us, and he has that right. But we found out who he is. Or, more precisely, what he is. A small time drug dealer. He has spent some time in our jails, and will be going back there, of course."

"Do you know who he works for?"

"Not exactly. We know who his associates are, who he's done work for in the past, but we have no idea who he's working for at the moment. If anyone, of course."

"You think it might have been just a burglary?"

"Not really, no. I assume you don't either."

"No."

"That poetry book you told me about, do you think they might have been looking for it?"

"It's possible," said Hugo. If so, Roussillon hadn't sent them: he already had it. But maybe it wasn't that simple. There was still some question in his mind about the Clausewitz book. He'd already told himself that whoever took Max had taken the book, either from his person or from his flat. But maybe not.

"By the way, the only thing he would tell us was that your friend had a gun. I've checked the manifests kept by the airlines and I see no record of him declaring a gun on the way in. Care to comment?"

"Capitaine, that would be a very serious matter."

"Precisely. And, of course, I place very little stock in what a violent drug dealer tells me. I just thought I'd mention it."

"I'll speak to my friend, make sure we're all on the same page."

"I'd appreciate that."

Hugo remembered Ceci's call. "I may have another missing person for you, capitaine."

"What do you mean?"

"I got a call late last night, a message left on my phone from Cecilia Roget, the former head of the SBP. Apparently another bouquiniste is missing."

"Do you have a name?"

"Just a first name. I'll find out more and get it to you as soon as I can."

"*Merci*. Tell me again, the name of the lady who gave you this information?"

"Cecilia Roget."

"I see. Please, no offense Monsieur Marston, but tell her to call me next time she has something important to report."

"Of course." *Let the turf wars begin*, Hugo thought. "As soon as I get hold of her, I'll tell her. Are you planning to talk to Monsieur Gravois, capitaine?"

"*Non*, I don't think so. We have no reason to believe he's involved, no obvious connection between the deaths or to your burglary."

"Two bouquinistes in one week isn't a connection?"

"Maybe they both used Microsoft computers, monsieur—should I go interview Bill Gates?"

"That's your analogy? Come on, capitaine."

"Until you or someone else can show me how their deaths are related, I have no reason to think they are anything but very unfortunate coincidences."

"Coincidences?" Hugo bit his tongue. He knew they were more

than that, and he knew that sooner or later he'd find something to convince this cop. "Fine, you're in charge, capitaine."

"Thank you. I need to make an appointment for you to come to the station with your friend to look at photos, to try and recognize the intruder. When are you available?"

"How does this afternoon sound?"

"Fine. The sooner the better, of course. If I'm not here, just tell them who you are. Everything will be ready."

Hugo tried Ceci one more time, the specter of worry moving across his mind when she didn't answer. Nothing he could do from Paris, though, so he set off for the embassy, keeping his head down despite the beauty of the day. He didn't want to see Chabot or whoever had taken Francoise Benoit's place. He paused only briefly on the narrow pedestrian bridge, Pont des Arts. The heavy roll of the murky water beneath his feet carried a new and unwelcome menace.

"Hugo, come in," Ambassador Taylor said. "I got your message, are you OK?"

"I'm fine, thank you ambassador."

"So what the hell happened?"

Hugo told him, leaving out any reference to Tom's gun. The ambassador sat there shaking his head.

"You think it has to do with this Max Koche?"

"I do. Even the capitaine doesn't think it was a random burglary, though he doesn't seem inclined to bother Bruno Gravois."

"Why not? I don't want you bugging him, but I sure as hell don't care if the cops do."

"I think it's for the same reason your friend Roussillon didn't want him bothered. Political reasons."

The ambassador stroked his chin. "This still isn't our jurisdiction, you know. I wish I could help, Hugo, suggest something to get you involved formally, but I just don't see how."

"There is one way," Hugo said. "Most homicides in the United States are local matters, right? For the state or county police to deal with."

"Go on."

"But these days, when they need help they often call in the FBI."

Understanding dawned on the ambassador's face. "You mean when they have a serial killer and think a profile might help."

"Exactly. Now, the prefecture may have its own profilers, I don't know."

"They may, but you taught at the FBI academy and have a ton of experience. I like it, nice idea. You want me to pitch it as an offer of help, nothing more?"

"If you would, ambassador, I'd be grateful."

"I'll do it. No promises, of course, and if they say no then you'll have to stay out of it. Agreed?"

"Agreed. Although if they come after me again, I won't be a passive victim."

"Understood." The ambassador's eyes twinkled for a moment. "By the way, my sources tell me that although your robber didn't make any statement, he did ask for medical treatment for his, umm, manhood."

"It's called the castle doctrine," Hugo grinned. "Break into my house and my soldiers get to crush yours."

On his way out, Hugo stopped in to see Emma. The relief in her face was evident, although she tried to mask all signs of worry. "Hugo, can you not stay out of trouble while you're on vacation?"

"Not my fault," he said. "People keep forgetting that those guys broke into my place, not the other way around."

"Even so, did you consider backing away and calling the cops?"

"As a matter of fact," he said truthfully, "the thought never entered my mind."

"Figures."

Hugo's cell phone buzzed in his pocket.

"Claudia," he said, flipping his phone open. "What's up?"

"Can you meet for a quick cup of coffee?"

"Sure. Where are you?"

"If you're at work, three blocks away. You know Café Bleu? On Saint-Honoré?"

"The new place, sure."

"Meet me there."

"Claudia, is everything OK? You sound upset."

"I'm fine. Just tired."

"Give me ten minutes, I'll be there."

The Rue du Faubourg Saint-Honoré, Hugo had often thought, would be the only street to get Christine to Paris and, maybe, keep her there. Narrow and nondescript by Paris's architectural standards, it was nevertheless one of the most famous shopping boulevards in the world. All of the famous fashion houses kept stores on the street, as did dozens more designers that Hugo had never heard of. The boutiques sold only the finest art, the jewelry stores were almost too intimidating to enter, and the few hotels on the road were subtle affairs of supreme elegance, small and intimate, with better service than you'd get at some of the more palatial hotels in Paris.

Café Bleu fit right in. With just a single row of tables along the sidewalk, Hugo had walked past often and never seen one remain empty for more than thirty seconds. The waiters here were fast and efficient, they knew they were dealing with exacting customers who wouldn't hesitate to drop large amounts of cash at the boutiques nearby . . . or make a polite fuss if their coffee was cold or slow to arrive.

Claudia had managed to snag a table and two chairs beside the entrance. He kissed her on the cheek and slid into the vacant seat, momentarily battling the outer limits of a puffy Italian woman who'd overflowed into it.

"Nothing like privacy," Hugo grimaced.

Claudia smiled, but she looked tired. "Sorry to drag you away like that."

"No problem. What's up?"

A waiter appeared and Hugo ordered a café crème. Claudia asked for the same.

"I wanted to let you know a little of what is going on, but you have to promise to keep it to yourself."

"Tom?"

"No, Hugo, not even him. Not yet." She held his eye. "Promise?"

"OK. What's going on?"

"You remember we talked about Dobrescu and Les Pieds-Noirs sharing power in the city?"

"I do."

"We think Les Pieds-Noirs may have a new partnership."

"We?"

"OK, the cops. They really are trusting me with a lot of this information, which is why you have to keep it quiet."

"Sure, I get it. You said a partnership—between whom?"

"They are not sure. Not exactly. But possibly another Romanian group. Or Bulgarian, those two seem to work together a lot in Europe. London and Madrid have had problems with criminal alliances with people from those countries."

"I didn't know that," Hugo said truthfully.

"And talking of Madrid, there's even speculation that ETA might be behind this."

"The Spanish separatists? I thought they'd gone away."

"They're back," said Claudia. "It's just a question of whether they are back and in Paris."

"It seems unlikely but then again, it's a model that worked for some terrorist groups, the FARC and ELN in Colombia, selling drugs to make money for their other activities."

"Precisely. So many to choose from." She took two coffee cups from the waiter and put one in front of Hugo, then unwrapped a cube of sugar and stirred it into hers. "As I said before, a border-free Europe has done wonders for business, tourism, and criminals. New markets for everyone to enjoy."

"You think all this has something to do with Max and the other bouquinistes?"

"Actually, no."

"Then I don't understand why you're telling me this."

"Hugo, I'm worried about you." She picked up her spoon and stirred her coffee again. "I have no right to be, but I am. What happened last night...I don't know. I've just seen too much death and destruction lately."

"I still don't understand, I'm sorry."

"I'm asking you to let the police find out what happened to Max. Leave it alone, Hugo. I know you are good at what you do, or were, but so are they."

"What do you mean, 'were'?"

"You're not a cop anymore. Why do you want to be?" She put the spoon down and cupped her hands around her coffee. "It's not a game, you know that. If those Romanians or Bulgarians, or whoever the hell they are, think you're poking around, they won't send a couple of idiots with sticks to your apartment, Hugo."

"Which reminds me, did I tell you I spoke to Garcia earlier? One of those goons was a drug dealer."

"All the more reason to leave it alone. Those people mean business, they are vicious and ruthless."

"I know." He put a hand on her arm and squeezed. "Your father told me about your husband, what happened. I'm really sorry, Claudia, I wish you'd told me."

She gave him a weak smile. "I try not to think about it." The smile faded. "And I don't want it to happen again."

"Me neither. But why would they think I am poking around in their business?"

"Because that's what Americans do. You want to save the world, to make it look the way you think it should be, so you stick your nose into other people's business. And the drugs business is the best possible example. The underworld exists, Hugo, but it's not like in the movies. You can't be the American action hero, kicking in doors and roughing up the bad guys. Just asking questions will make you stick out, *non*? Someone from the US Embassy who is a former FBI agent? Of course you will. They will think you are using the bouquiniste thing as an excuse to investigate the drug business."

Hugo sat back. He hadn't thought about it that way, and some of what she said was true. "People keep telling me to back off, Claudia. The ambassador, your father, Capitaine Garcia. And now you. And I still don't see Max's killer behind bars. I don't care about your drug war. I really don't. But a friend of mine is dead. Dumped in the Seine. And as far as I can tell, the cops are more worried about what I'm doing than who his killer is."

"That's not true."

"No? Tell me, what do you know about a detective called Durand?"

Her eyebrows lifted. "David Durand?"

"Yes."

"Why do you ask?" Her eyes slid over his face as if she were having trouble looking at him.

"Claudia. He was the cop who shut down the initial investigation. And you've been meeting with him."

"How do you know that?"

"It doesn't matter how I know."

"Have you been following me?"

"No," he said. "And stop avoiding the question. I just want to know who he is."

"And why I'm meeting with him, I'm sure."

"Can you blame me?" He wasn't happy about the outrage in her voice, but he needed to know.

"I'm a reporter. I talk to a lot of cops. That's all Hugo, nothing to do with," she waved a hand, "any of this." Her phone rang and she picked it up to look at the display. "*Excusez moi un moment*, I have to take this." She stood and walked along the row of tables, talking into the phone. She reached the end of the row and nodded twice, then hung up. She put the phone in her pocket and started back toward him.

Behind her, a motorcycle carrying two people came down the street toward them. Rider and passenger both wore black leather jackets and chaps and helmets that hid their faces behind mirrored visors. Hugo saw them slow fifty yards away from the café. Hoping for an empty table, he first thought.

"I have to go," Claudia said as she reached him. "They called a task force meeting and they said I could be there. Duty calls."

He stood and dipped into his pocket for money to pay for their drinks. As he counted out change on the table the motorcycle drifted closer, out of the center of the road toward them. The passenger had his hand inside his leather coat and seemed to be adjusting his position.

Hugo realized too late what was happening.

Claudia had moved close to the curb to let him out, and was wrestling with the zipper on her bag as she tried to put her phone away. Hugo shouted her name and she looked up, eyes wide, at the sound of his voice.

He sprang forward as the motorcycle passenger pulled a small, dark object from inside his coat. He flung himself at Claudia and wrapped his arms around her shoulders, using the weight of his body to pull her to the pavement. People behind him screamed and he heard the crash of cups and plates as the café's patrons scattered. As he hit the sidewalk, Hugo heard the distinctive crack of a pistol and he felt Claudia's body lurch. He tried to roll on top of her but she cried out, pushing herself up as if trying to run.

Two more shots split the air. Claudia cried out again and fell.

Hugo looked up as the driver twisted the throttle, and he saw the rear wheel smoke as it fought for traction. He reached for his own gun, but with a roar of exhaust and squeal of rubber, the tire gripped the road and the bike leapt away from the curb. The passenger clung on as the machine fish-tailed past two parked cars and into traffic, and Hugo dared not shoot.

He tucked his gun away and crawled toward Claudia. His knees and one elbow throbbed from the fall, but he felt no other surges of pain. Claudia lay face down on the sidewalk, a ribbon of blood spreading from her body to the curb.

He slipped her scarf from around her neck and rolled her gently onto her back to see how badly she was hit. He saw two wounds, a graze to the outside of her left shoulder and a more severe wound to her left forearm. He ran a hand over her scalp and felt a significant bump, which explained her unconsciousness. He pressed the scarf against the gash in her lower arm to stem the flow of blood.

"Claudia, can you hear me?" His voice was urgent.

She groaned and tried to move, her mouth twisting in pain, her voice a whisper. "Hugo . . ."

"Hang in there, you're going to be fine, OK?" He meant it, the wounds did seem relatively superficial, but inside he was boiling with anger at whoever had done this. He put his head by hers. "I promise, Claudia, you'll be just fine."

He heard the wail of sirens in the distance, and behind him several people started to edge out of the café, moving fearfully toward them.

A woman pushed her way through and knelt beside Hugo. She said something he couldn't understand and when he just stared, she pointed to herself and said in English, "Doctor."

Hugo nodded and held still as the woman checked Claudia's vital signs. She took off her own white scarf and pressed it onto the bleeding shoulder, and it turned red almost instantly. Hugo looked at Claudia's face. Where she'd seemed pale to him before, she now looked like a ghost, her skin translucent and her lips gray. The doctor held her pulse at the wrist, and she caught Hugo looking at her. She frowned.

The sirens were louder now and Hugo looked down the street. Car by car, the traffic on the Rue du Faubourg Saint-Honoré nosed into the curb to make way for a police car and, right behind it, an ambulance.

The emergency vehicles pulled up where the motorcycle had been just minutes before and a baby-faced medic leapt out of the ambulance and ran to them. Hugo moved out of the way as the medic began to cut Claudia's shirt sleeve off. That done, he swiftly taped a large gauze pad onto her shoulder wound.

The bleeding seemed to have slowed, but Hugo knew that if he was wrong about it being a graze, and the bullet was still in there, an artery could rupture and kill her in minutes. The young man double-checked her dressings and, satisfied, nodded to his colleague, who had inserted an IV line and was finishing up with a neck brace. Claudia moaned when, on a silent count, they eased her onto a stretcher, raised it up, and rolled her swiftly to the back of their vehicle. Hugo moved to climb in with her but a uniformed gendarme stepped away from a bystander and stopped him.

"You are family, monsieur?"

"No, a friend."

"And are you hurt?"

"No."

"I'm sorry, we need you to stay here and tell us what happened."

Hugo gestured vaguely to the crowd. "Let them tell you, they saw everything."

"We will take all their statements, monsieur," the gendarme said.

"And I'll give you mine later."

"*Non.* That is not how it works."

Hugo briefly contemplated pulling out his embassy credentials but resisted. Every police contact like this had to be logged and explained, and the ambassador wouldn't want too many more explanations from him. "Look," said Hugo, pointing to the café. "They know as much as I do."

"I don't think so, monsieur. From what I have heard so far, you were the intended target."

CHAPTER TWENTY-FOUR

Tom laid a hand on his friend's shoulder, then stooped and put a steaming mug on the low coffee table in front of Hugo. "Here, this always works."

"Is that tea?"

"I know, the Brits can't cook for shit, but they do know their magic potions. Trust me, tea is a magic potion." He sat down in the chair beside Hugo and grimaced. "Just promise me we won't be watching any of that cricket crap."

"You could learn from that game, you know. Politeness, civility, that kind of thing."

"I do just fine without." He looked at Hugo for a moment. "You sure you're OK?"

"I am, yes." Hugo sat back and stared into the fireplace. "I just hope she is."

"Not every day you get shot at and save someone's life, so you worry about her and I'll worry about you."

"Thanks." Hugo smiled. "But don't, I'm fine. What the hell were you doing all day?"

"Souvenir shopping," Tom said.

"All day?"

"No, not all day," said Tom. "I'll admit that I did go nose around the offices of the SBP, but I didn't talk to anyone."

"Or upset anyone?"

"No, nothing like that." Tom sipped his tea and looked at his friend over the rim. "Unlike you, apparently."

"Apparently." Hugo's phone rang. "Ah, Monsieur de Roussillon. How is she?"

"Tired. But doing well." Roussillon sounded rattled, the first time Hugo had witnessed a dent in the façade. "She's lost some blood but she wasn't too badly hurt. The police told me what happened, that you saved her life."

"I'm sorry I didn't do a better job. They told me I was the target."

"I don't understand. Why would someone want to kill you?"

"It's complicated."

"Well, it makes no sense to me."

"None of it makes sense, Monsieur de Roussillon. Don't worry about that end of things, just take care of Claudia."

"I just wanted to thank you for trying to help her. After her husband was killed by those people . . ." The old man sighed. "And please, you saved my daughter's life, you should call me Gérard."

"Very well." Hugo looked up and saw Tom scribbling a note. It read: *the book.* "Can I ask a favor of you, Gérard? Two of them, actually."

"*Mais oui.* Anything."

"First, call the hospital and tell them I can visit Claudia. I tried and they wouldn't let me in, I guess she's under police guard."

"Consider it done."

"Thanks. Also, you recently bought a copy of *Une Saison En Enfer.*"

Silence. Then, "How did you know that?"

"I can't tell you right now. But I need to see the book." Hugo decided to take a chance. "I'm the one who sold it."

"*Non,* you are mistaken. I bought it from an English dealer."

"Yes, I know. I bought it from a bouquiniste and took it to a dealer to sell it for me. Peter Kendall."

"Yes, that's him. But if you sold it, why do you need to see it?"

"I wish I knew exactly. Look, there's a chance that the book has something to do with your daughter's shooting."

"What? How?"

"Again, I'm not sure. That's why I want to see the book." He looked at Tom. "To be more specific, I want a friend of mine to look at it."

"As you know, the book cost a lot of money," de Roussillon said, "but as long as it stays here, your friend is welcome. It's the least I can do. I'm here tomorrow morning, if that suits your friend."

Hugo thanked him and rang off.

"How is Claudia?" Tom asked.

"Resting. She lost some blood but I don't think any major harm was done."

"Well that's good news." But Tom was biting his bottom lip and staring intently at Hugo.

"What?"

"So you randomly decided Roussillon is on the side of right and justice?"

"You told me to ask him about the book."

"Yeah, that's all I said, you fucking dolt. You didn't need to open your heart and confess everything."

"Come on, Tom, I can't imagine he had anything to do with that shooting."

"Bullshit. Yesterday men with clubs and a cow poker do a shitty job, so today he sends someone with a gun. He doesn't know you're meeting with his daughter at the café, so yeah, he's upset when she gets shot." He stood and went to the drinks cabinet. "If he is behind this, I wouldn't want to be the clown on the bike who pulled the trigger."

"If he is behind this, maybe you shouldn't go look at the book."

"No shit. But now you've opened the door, I'd be an idiot not to go take a look around, wouldn't I?"

"I don't know, Tom." He rubbed a hand over his face. "Now you've got me second guessing myself."

"Maybe a drink will help. Tea is only good for holding you together until five o'clock. Whisky is better for you after a shock like that."

"If people keep trying to kill me, I'm going to turn into an alcoholic."

"Way ahead of you," said Tom. "Come join the party."

"Fine. A small one. And tell me about your visit to the SBP."

"Good man." Tom poured a large scotch and handed it to Hugo. "You know, they were closed for lunch by the time I got there."

"Nice timing."

"Very. You've been inside Gravois's office, right? Obsessive-compulsive, if you ask me."

"I noticed that. But he told me he had cancer, so maybe it's something to do with keeping germs out. Lots of cleaning." Hugo held up his drink. "Thanks for this, but if you keep me in suspense much longer, I'm going to fall asleep."

"Then go ahead and fall asleep. The only interesting thing about him is that he has no personal mementos or information stored anywhere on that premises."

"That's interesting?"

"Of course. Think about it, Hugo. You go to anyone's office in the world and you'll find a pic of their wife, kid, dog, or favorite centerfold."

"That's not allowed anymore."

"It just seemed too sterile, and I don't mean in the medical sense."

"You think he's hiding something?"

Tom frowned. "You know, it could be the opposite."

"Tom, for crying out loud." Hugo pointed to his glass and then himself. "Large whisky. Shot at. Tired. Now, stop being cryptic."

"Fine. Maybe it's nothing, maybe he's a friendless, petless, family-free freak. But it reminds me of something I saw once before. This guy, it wasn't that he was hiding anything, it's that he didn't exist. Not as the person he made himself out to be. What I'm saying is, if this is the same kind of thing, Bruno Gravois isn't real. He's an invention, a character created for a reason. Did you check into his background?"

"Yes. On the DCRI database. Nothing."

"At all?"

"At all. Shit, you may be right." Hugo swallowed the rest of his scotch. "No criminal history, no driver's license, no applications for government permits. Just a birth certificate and nothing since."

"Everyone has a history, Hugo. Everyone leaves a footprint for the government to follow."

"Except people who don't exist," nodded Hugo. "And CIA operatives."

"Well he ain't one of them, I can tell you that."

"Interesting. Our Bruno Gravois appears to be a ghost."

CHAPTER TWENTY-FIVE

The nurse told Hugo when he called the next morning that he wouldn't be allowed in until eight. But he'd woken early and didn't want to spend an hour pacing his apartment, so he set off toward the hospital soon after seven.

He walked with his collar turned up against the sharp morning breeze, enjoying the emptiness of Paris's side streets at that time of day. Occasionally a student would scurry past, winding a long scarf around her neck or balancing books on the handlebars of a bicycle, woolly hats pulled over chilly ears. Puffs of coffee and warm air punctuated his walk, a meandering wander toward the hospital Hôtel-Dieu. After half an hour he stopped and bought a croissant and coffee, eating and drinking as he strolled along the Boulevard Saint-Germain, window shopping to kill time, watching Paris come alive minute by minute.

He dropped his cup into a trash can as he started across the bridge to the Isle de la Cité, the tiny island that was the foundation of Paris and sat in its geographical center, roughly a one-mile walk from Hugo's apartment. One of two natural islands in the River Seine, Hugo knew it to be perhaps the most expensive patch of real estate in the city. Half a dozen bridges spanned the island, bringing in tourists and Parisians alike to one of the greatest of Paris's attractions, the Cathédrale de Notre Dame.

Behind Notre Dame sat the Hôtel-Dieu Hospital, founded by Saint Landry in 651 CE. And behind the hospital was Hugo's second stop, the Prefecture de Police, where Capitaine Garcia would be waiting with a stack of photos and a skeptical frown, Hugo knew.

Claudia was sitting in bed reading *Paris Match* when the policeman stepped aside to let him in. She looked up when Hugo entered and he was pleased to see color in her cheeks and a smile on her face. Her left arm was bandaged and resting in a sling.

"My hero," she said. "Come for your reward?"

"I don't think they allow that here."

"Good, I'm exhausted." He leaned over and kissed her cheek, but she turned her head so their lips brushed. "Seriously, Hugo. You saved my life."

"Actually, I'm not so sure," he said. "If they were trying to hit me, then I'm the one who put you in danger."

"Semantics." She put a hand on his as he sat beside the bed. "Are you OK?"

"Oh yes. On my way to give a statement at the prefecture."

"Good. My father is coming by later. I think he likes you now."

"Well if I saved your life, he has to." He smiled and squeezed her hand. "So are you getting out of here anytime soon?"

"Today. I lost some blood but they put some back in. No harm done."

"Makes for a good news story."

"Yeah." She grimaced. "Only when you're the one who gets shot, you don't get to write it."

"That doesn't seem fair."

They talked for an hour, about the shooting some, but mostly not. When her head started to nod and her eyes droop, Hugo kissed her forehead and took the magazine from her lap, putting it on the side table. He watched her for a few seconds, sleep taking over a tired body, then let himself out of the room as quietly as possible.

The walk to the prefecture was quick but pleasant, the air warmer than it had been earlier, and the breeze carried a teasing reminder of autumn, or maybe a false hint of spring.

He had telephoned ahead to let Capitaine Garcia know he was coming, but he nevertheless had every expectation that he'd be made to wait. In Hugo's experience, French concepts of time were like those in South America: malleable, so that a rendezvous scheduled for ten o'clock usually meant that just one of the parties concerned would be there close to the appointed hour.

Hugo was surprised, then, when he walked into the prefecture to be welcomed as if he were late. A young assistant took him straight into the offices of the directorate of judicial police, the section of the building that houses the national police force's plainclothes division. After a brief wait on a hard bench, a door opened down the hall. Capitaine Garcia came out and the men shook hands.

"Thank you for coming, Monsieur Marston. This way."

Garcia led him into a large carpeted room where secretaries typed quietly at their stations and several disconsolate individuals sat waiting for attention. They wound their way through the rows of paper-filled desks to a row of offices at the back of the room. Garcia held open a frosted glass door and bade Hugo enter.

"Please. Take a seat."

Hugo walked in and sat on the only chair in front of Garcia's desk. Out of the capitaine's window he could see across the tree tops and over the Seine to the Right Bank. "Nice view," he said.

"*Oui.*" Garcia rounded his desk and turned his computer monitor so that Hugo could see the screen. "Monsieur, I heard about the shooting and am pleased that you were not hurt, and that your friend will be fine. You may be accustomed to such things in Texas, but shootings like that are very rare here and we are looking hard for those responsible."

"*Merci*, capitaine, I appreciate that. And I promise, the rumors of frequent gunplay on the streets of our towns is greatly exaggerated. At least in modern times."

"I am pleased to hear that. Now, monsieur, I have pulled together the mug shots of as many black men as I could find matching the description you gave who have some connection to the other intruder, or some history of drugs."

"You think this is about drugs?"

"I still don't know what this is about, but I do know that criminals tend to stick with their own type. If one is a petty criminal, his friends will be. Your burglar, or whatever he was, is a drug dealer, so I have to assume his friend is." Garcia shrugged and turned to a stack of unopened mail. "If you don't see him, we'll find more photos for you to look at." He slid his computer mouse to Hugo, who began scrolling through the faces, twenty-five to a page. Ten minutes later, on the tenth page, Hugo saw him, the familiar cunning scowl worn by a man in custody.

"Here you go. This is him."

Garcia came around the desk to stand behind Hugo. "Click on the picture, let's see who he is."

Hugo did, and the men looked over their suspect's profile. Alex Vacher, a Frenchman. Forty-one years old, with multiple arrests and convictions for theft, fraud, and drug dealing. His most recent conviction had been three years earlier.

"Good," said Garcia, "I'll print this out, give it to some of our people, and they'll pick him up."

"That was easy."

"We're not done, monsieur." Garcia walked back behind his desk and sat. He began to stroke his mustache. "My superiors received a call from your embassy. It seems you have offered assistance and I am to accept your offer."

"Ah, yes. Look, capitaine," Hugo began, "I don't mean to—"

"No need, monsieur," he held up a hand. "I have been ordered to open our files to you on the bouquiniste deaths and give you other assistance as requested. I am told you are a gifted behavioral profiler."

His tone and expression would have been the same had he been accepting assistance from a crystal-ball-holding gypsy psychic, Hugo thought. But he just smiled and said, "I promise not to get in your way, capitaine, and you can do what you want with my findings and opinions."

"Very kind of you. I should make it clear that I do not approve of guesswork masquerading as science, I do not approve of potential witnesses, or actual victims, involving themselves in investigations, and I have already expressed to you my opinion that the deaths of the three bouquinistes are unrelated."

"You mean two. Max Koche and Francoise Benoit."

"Three." He opened a notebook in front of him. "A Pierre Desmarais was pulled out of the river this morning. The autopsy is going on right now, but it looks like he drowned." Garcia looked up. "*Attendez*, is that the name of the bouquiniste that Madame . . ."

"Roget. And yes, that's him."

"I see. She is not officially involved, so I would appreciate it if you would wait until his family is told before passing on the news. At least tell her to keep it to herself."

"Of course." Hugo hesitated. "Capitaine, you have two accidental drownings and an overdose in less than a week. All three bodies popping up in the same stretch of the Seine. Do you really think this is all just a coincidence?"

"My mind is not closed to any possibility." Garcia rested a finger on the tip of his mustache and leaned forward. "But the word *coincidence* exists for a reason. This is not America, monsieur. We don't have guns or serial killers like you do, which means that people have to die in other ways. And when you have a major river running through your city, dead people tend to pop up in it." He waved a hand at a long table pushed up against the wall behind Hugo. "There you have copies of autopsy reports, photographs from each place where the bodies were found, and relevant investigation reports and witness statements. If you can find a serial killer among them, Monsieur Marston, I will be genuinely interested to see how."

Hugo decided not to argue the matter. He now had access to the files, which was all he'd wanted. And he planned to take his time; if the police didn't want him there and weren't bothering to look for a connection, this might be his only chance to spot it. He looked at Garcia, who'd returned to his stack of mail.

"So, do you plan to sit there and watch me?"

"*Non, monsieur.*" Garcia put down his letter opener and picked up the printout of the black assailant, Alex Vacher. "Now that I can say I've been through my mail, I have real police work to do." He got up and walked out of his office, closing the door gently behind him.

Hugo began with the photos. *Human nature*, he thought to himself, *to look at the pictures before reading the words*. He learned little from them, but hadn't expected to. Soggy and bedraggled, the three corpses in the color pictures were hard to imagine as people, alive and vital.

And yet one of them was Max. Hugo looked at his picture for a long time. *You're gone, old friend. This isn't you.* Hugo shook his head and tried to concentrate. Reminiscing wouldn't help find the truth. He finished with the photos and put them away. He turned to the two autopsy reports. Each consisted of a series of diagrams of the body, the skeleton, and the organs, standard forms that the medical examiner used as he went through the exam. Hugo knew that the medical examiner would either dictate into a voice recorder as he went and make the notations afterward, or have an assistant make notes as he went along.

He started with Francoise Benoit.

The medical examiner had seen no bruising, cuts, or other signs of violence, either intentional or accidental. His comments did indicate, unsurprisingly, extensive damage to her liver. Her other vital organs had been weighed and each was compared with a range of expected weights. All seemed normal enough, for an overweight alcoholic. Hugo read through her other materials but found no obvious indicators of homicide.

Except . . . Hugo sat back and looked again at the list of her possessions. It was divided into two groups, those found on her body, which included her clothing, and those items retrieved from her stall by police after she was found. It was the latter that interested him. According to the list, there had been a receipt in a canvas bag showing that she'd bought two bottles of vodka at about noon. One was the regular, 750 cl bottle, the other much smaller, just a pint. In the canvas bag, buried at the bottom according to the notes, was the small bottle, three-quarters full. The larger one hadn't been found.

Hugo went to Garcia's desk, tore a piece of paper from a notepad, and borrowed a pen. He made a note of this finding and then turned to the information about Max. He knew that whatever he found would have to stand up to Capitaine Garcia's skepticism.

He found it quickly. The autopsy report noted severe bruising to his chest and back. He might have been hit by boats or driftwood, Hugo knew, assuming he'd fallen into the river alive. But he found what he was looking for in the toxicology report.

Hugo knew that the capitaine, like many cops, might skip over the numbers in the report, the micrograms of whichever substance was found in the blood, the digits showing oxygen levels and concentrations of the drug. But Hugo had done a stint in the lab. He was uncomfortable with relying on the technician's conclusions when he didn't understand the numbers themselves. What this report told him was that Max had ingested not only a large amount of cocaine, but cocaine of an extremely high grade. Not the kind you get on the street, even if you're a lawyer or stockbroker paying the big bucks. No, this was what you found at the wholesale end, not the retail end. And certainly not what you'd find in the hands of a hard-up bouquiniste.

Someone with access to pure cocaine, Hugo was sure, had held a gun to Max's head and made him ingest enough of the drug to kill him. Kill him unpleasantly, too. Such purity would have given him the briefest of highs before torturing his old body to death. First his muscles would be set on fire with tremors that quickly turned into convulsions, then his whole body would have started seizing, the old man wracked with pain before his system gave out entirely, the drug killing him suddenly with a massive heart attack or, if his heart was somehow strong enough to cope with the drug, shutting down his lungs, suffocating him to death.

Hugo calmed the anger rising inside him and turned to the third file. He had less to work with in the case of Pierre Desmarais. Another drowning, supposedly, but a quick look at the photographs made Hugo frown.

Did Garcia even look at these?

A large bruise was evident on the man's forehead and his chin was bloodied. It was hard to tell from the angle of the picture, but his jaw may even have been dislocated. The autopsy report, when it came in, would confirm that.

Hugo picked up the crime scene report and walked out of Garcia's office. He looked around until he found a secretary willing to meet his eye. "Is Capitaine Garcia returning, do you know?"

"*Oui, monsieur*, he said he was getting himself a sandwich and would be back."

Right, thought Hugo, *a sandwich*. There's real police business for you. "Thanks," he said, "I'll wait."

He went back into Garcia's office, sat down, and dialed Ceci Roget. She picked up just as he was about to give up. They exchanged pleasantries, then Hugo took a deep breath. "Ceci, I have some bad news."

"Oh no, is it Pierre?"

"*Oui.* I'm sorry, Ceci, he's dead."

"Dead? You're sure?"

Hugo pictured the old man's bedraggled hair, his lifeless but open eyes. "I'm sure."

"How?"

"That I don't know. The police are taking the position that he drowned but I'm hoping I can persuade them to look again, more closely."

"Do you think it's Gravois?"

"I still don't know, Ceci, I wish I could answer that. The trouble is, other than their jobs, there's nothing tying him to these people, not directly."

"I know. I know." He heard the deep sigh. Then, "Oh, I talked to several more bouquinistes."

"And?"

"More of the same. Offered money to give up their stalls. They got the same feeling I did, too, though none of them were threatened or hurt."

"OK, thanks Ceci. Listen, you probably shouldn't call any more people. We don't want word to get back to Gravois."

"Do you think I am in any danger?"

"Even if he is behind this," Hugo said, "I wouldn't think so. You don't know anything and you did exactly what he wanted you to do. Keep your eyes open, though, and call the police if anything happens. But I think you should be safe if you stay in Bielle."

They rang off, and fifteen minutes later Garcia arrived. He had two sandwiches, one of which he was most of the way through. The other he offered to Hugo. "*Je m'excuse*, Monsieur Marston. I was a little rude earlier. Too much to do and not enough help to do it. It's ham and brie. I hope you're not one of those vegetarian Americans."

"No," Hugo said. "I'm from Texas."

Garcia grunted and sat behind his desk. He began to unwrap the remainder of his sandwich, and as he did so, he looked up at Hugo. "I should perhaps clarify my position on these deaths. I am far from convinced they were accidental, but I am equally unconvinced they are related. You must understand that to present a claim like that to my superiors would require a significant amount of proof, because they would then be obliged to devote many resources to solving the killings." He looked at his sandwich, then back at Hugo. "So did you find anything?"

He's being careful to keep his voice neutral, Hugo thought. *And he's not expecting me to find a damn thing.*

"Actually, yes." Hugo turned to the file on Francoise Benoit and picked up the possessions log. He passed it to Garcia and explained about the small bottle being found in the bag, while the larger one was missing.

"*Oui.*" Garcia nodded. "She was drinking down by the river, we assumed that. She could have dropped the large bottle in the water, we'd never find it." He took a bite of sandwich and sat back to listen.

"*Oui, c'est possible*," Hugo said. "But think about it this way. She has two bottles, one large and one small. Why? I think it was because she doesn't want people to know she's an alcoholic, capitaine. That's why she bought a small bottle, so she could drink without people noticing. It's a pretty classic ploy for alcoholics, and when I talked to her, she was chewing breath mints."

"To hide the smell of alcohol."

"*Exactement*." Hugo had to be careful not to oversell the theory. After all, she'd admitted being an alcoholic to him, maybe she had to others. And yet the way she told him seemed like a confidence being shared. "It's entirely reasonable that she'd try to hide her drinking, particularly from her customers."

Garcia grunted again and kept chewing.

"My point," Hugo went on, "is that if she'd been down by the river's edge for a drink, she would have taken the little bottle. That's why, I think, she bought it. You can see from the report that she'd been drinking from it. I'm guessing she was planning to take the big bottle home."

Garcia swallowed. "So where is the big one?"

"I don't know. Maybe someone walking past the stall saw it and took it. I don't know, but I don't think it matters. What matters is that she was by the Seine for some reason, but that reason wasn't to drink."

"OK," Garcia nodded slowly. "Anything else?"

"On her, no. But Max Koche, yes." He went through what he'd found, starting with the bruising. "That must have come right before he died, not after. Possibly boats, I grant you, but probably not. Look how it's just his chest and back, not his legs or his face."

"You think he was beaten?"

"Sure looks that way to me."

"Go on."

Hugo pointed to the drug reports and explained that the high concentration of cocaine meant the substance had been pure, very pure. "And if you look at the rest of the autopsy report, you'll see it's consistent with him not being a drug user. No signs of damage to his nasal cavities or any internal organs, including his brain. And," he held up a finger, "you'll see that no cocaine was found at his home or at his stall. There's just no reason to think he was a user."

"After I talked to you last time I looked at his file again," Garcia said, wiping his mouth. "I also noted that no evidence of prior drug use was found. I did not appreciate those toxicology figures, though. How about Desmarais?"

"Harder to tell with him, but I think these photographs are enough to at least cast doubt on his death being an accident." He laid three of them on Garcia's desk. "See these bruises?"

"From when he fell in?"

"Well, water doesn't bruise, obviously. So the theory must be that he fell on the ground, then into the water. Right?"

"*Oui.*"

"But think about how that works, practically." Hugo stood and moved the two chairs out of his way. He stepped back by the wall and then let himself fall forward, arms extended. He caught himself in the push-up position on the floor. Garcia stood and leaned over the desk to watch. "If I fall on my front, onto something hard, how do I end up in the water? With difficulty. Now, if I'd fallen on my side, then maybe I would roll. Maybe. But not my front."

"I see. Not definitive, but interesting."

Hugo jumped up. "And look at the photos again. See how his forehead is bruised, and his chin messed up?"

"Yes, I see that," Garcia said. He picked up the photos and looked closely at them. "I know what you are thinking. If he'd fallen, he'd have hit either his chin or his forehead. Not both." As if to convince himself, he put his face on the top of his desk. "You can't do both at the same time."

"Exactly. And if he'd hit one then the other, which is theoretically possible, then only one would be badly damaged. Here he has a major contusion on his head and I bet the autopsy report will show his jaw was broken, too."

Capitaine Garcia spread his hands. "I am impressed. And, more importantly, I think you may be right." He held up a warning finger. "And I mean, you *may* be right." He smiled. "I'm guessing it's not a serial killer, though."

"No," said Hugo. He returned the smile. "Not in the traditional sense, I don't think so."

"Then who?"

"The only thing that makes sense to me is Gravois. He is replacing bouquinistes with his own people."

"For kickbacks?"

"Maybe. But I can't help feel like there's more to it than that. Murder is just too extreme." Hugo picked up the toxicology report on Max. "And why go to all the trouble of making Max's death look like an overdose?"

"Because three accidental drownings is more suspicious than just two?" Garcia shrugged and looked at Hugo, as if for an answer.

"Three drowned bouquinistes so close in time would be pretty odd, that's true," said Hugo. "And if it is Gravois, how does he have access to such pure cocaine?"

"I don't know that either, but I intend to find him and ask," said Garcia. He rounded his desk and reached for his coat, then stopped and looked at Hugo. "Are you coming?"

CHAPTER TWENTY-SIX

"**W**hat do you mean he wasn't there?" Hugo asked. He'd called Tom when Capitaine Garcia stopped at the front desk to speak to one of his junior officers.

His friend had answered from the sidewalk in front of Roussillon's house. "Look," said Tom, "he told you he's happy for us to look at the book, no big deal. I'll just come back another time."

"Did he call you?"

"No, man, I showed up at his fucking palace. The beefeater said he'd left earlier and hadn't come back."

"It's a butler, not a beefeater."

"Whatever. He wasn't there so I didn't look at the book."

"OK. I'll call him."

"Where are you?"

"At the prefecture. I identified our intruder, so it's just a matter of time before they pick him up. Hopefully."

"Yeah, hopefully. The frog police haven't been too impressive up until now."

Hugo glanced up as Garcia came down the front steps and reminded himself to keep the two men apart. "They're working with me now. Garcia and I are off to find Gravois."

"Awesome, where do I meet you?"

"No."

"Bullshit. Why not?"

"Because I'm going to have to deal with Gravois and Garcia. I don't want you needling one or both of them while I'm doing it."

"Fuck off, then. Call me when you're done."

"What are you going to do?"

"More sightseeing. You prefer the Louvre or the Musee d'Orsay?"

"Go to the d'Orsay. I'll take you to the Louvre myself; I haven't been there in a while."

He hung up and turned to Garcia. "Sorry. How do we get there?"

"I have a car in the garage," Garcia said, "let's go. But let me say something first."

"I won't shoot him," Hugo said, with a half-smile.

"No, it's not that." Garcia was serious, troubled even. "I owe you an apology, a very sincere one."

"It's OK, I know what you're going to say."

"Then let me say it." He put a hand on Hugo's shoulder. "I wish I had listened to you, believed you. I wish I had acted on what you saw. I think it's possible we could have saved your friend."

"I appreciate that. But I suppose you had to go with what your detective told you."

"Ah, yes. Durand. I would like to tell you the full story, but I can say that I've had my eye on him. Believe me when I say that he won't be getting promoted any time soon."

Hugo waited for more but Garcia looked away, ending the conversation. If it was that confidential, Hugo thought, it must be serious. Was Durand just lazy or incompetent, or was he on the wrong side of the law? He couldn't help but wonder about Claudia and her connection to the man. Was she charming a story out of the detective that he'd later regret? Hugo could only hope she knew what she was doing and exactly who she was dealing with.

The drive to Rue Nollet took fifteen minutes. On the way, Hugo told Garcia about his previous visit, a little embarrassed at his role play as a journalist. Garcia just smiled and nodded that he understood. Hugo told him more about the book he'd bought from Max, its progression from the Pont Neuf to Kendall and into the hands of Roussillon. Garcia's face tightened when he heard Roussillon's name, but he didn't say anything.

At Hugo's suggestion, they parked away from the entrance of the SBP building, wanting to ensure a surprise visit.

The street outside the office was empty and the note about the broken bell was still attached below the SBP sign. They climbed the stairs quickly, and when they reached the top the beehive secretary looked up at them, eyes wide.

"*Bonjour,*" said Garcia. "Capitaine Garcia for Monsieur Gravois."

"Capitaine . . . He is expecting you?" Her eyes rested on Hugo, and he knew she was wondering why a journalist accompanied this policeman.

"*Non.*"

"*Un moment, s'il vous plait.*" She got up, walked to Gravois's office, and knocked lightly, a definite request for permission rather than a formality. A muffled "*Oui*" from inside and she disappeared, closing the door behind her. She was in there for a full minute, and when she reappeared she just nodded and held the door for them to enter.

Gravois was, as before, presiding over an office devoid of clutter. His gloved hands were folded on the desk top, his gaunt face a blank. He did not rise when they came in, and he looked directly at Hugo. "You brought *un flic* to make me answer your questions, monsieur?" If it was a joke, there was no humor in the man's eyes.

"He is not a journalist," Garcia said, "Monsieur Marston is working with the police on a matter of extreme importance."

Gravois's black eyes bored into Garcia and then Hugo, as his right hand clenched and unclenched. "And what matter is that?"

"Murder," said Garcia. "Three bouquinistes have turned up dead in a week, and we don't think they were all accidents."

"Three?"

"Yes."

"I don't know anything about this."

"I am glad to hear that," Garcia said. "But you are the head of the SBP and, I am told, took some extreme measures to remove each of these people from their stalls."

"I would hardly call a severance package an extreme measure, capitaine."

"Severance package or bribe, monsieur?" asked Hugo.

"You chose your words, American, I will choose mine."

Capitaine Garcia sat down unasked. "Do you have records of those you offered severance packages to?"

"I offered them to all bouquinistes."

"Why?"

"Because the current system is not a good one. We have a group of ancient alcoholics selling trashy books to tourists. I would like to see the old bouquinistes replaced by a younger and more vibrant group. Return the banks of the Seine to its former glory and attract more tourists, sell more quality merchandise."

"And you get a cut from the new bouquinistes?" Garcia asked.

"Not at all. Ask any of them. Not one Euro."

Hugo walked to the man's bookcase then turned. "Do you have a current list of bouquinistes?"

Gravois stared at him. *As much as he doesn't like Garcia asking him questions*, Hugo thought, *he sure as hell hates me doing it*. Gravois rubbed his left wrist and answered slowly. "Yes. I assume you would like to see it."

His cancer must be bothering him, thought Hugo, as he watched Gravois reach over and open a draw on the left side of the desk with his right hand. Gravois pulled out a leather binder and opened it. He looked over the rows of neatly typed names and placed it on the desk for Garcia to see. "I can't think what you are trying to learn, gentlemen. Do you have any specific questions for me, or just veiled accusations?"

"We can unveil them if you like," Hugo said mildly. He ignored a look from Garcia. "Actually, I do have a question. Have you heard of a book called *Une Saison En Enfer*?"

"No. Who is it by? Perhaps I know the author."

"Arthur Rimbaud," Hugo said. "Mean anything to you?"

Gravois looked back and forth between Hugo and the capitaine. "No, it means nothing. What does this have to do with me? With those bouquinistes?"

"You have never heard of the book, monsieur?" Garcia repeated.

"No. Not the book, not the author. I am not a bouquiniste, gentlemen, you probably know that already. Instead, I am their voice, a resource for them."

"What about Gérard de Roussillon?" Hugo asked. "How do you know him?"

"Roussillon?" The eyes blinked once. "I am not a policeman. I think that if I were," he said, "I would try and ascertain the truth. I would not go barging into the offices of public servants. I see your smirk, capitaine, but yes, I regard myself as a public servant. As I was saying, I would not go barging in and asking cryptic questions and making such unpleasant allegations. In fact, let me ask you a question, capitaine. Do you have any evidence, any evidence at all, that connects me to the deaths of any one of those bouquinistes?"

"If you were a policeman, Monsieur Gravois," Garcia paused as he stood, "you'd know that my suspects find out about the evidence *after* I put on the handcuffs."

"Ah, is that so?" Gravois smiled and held up his wrists. "I don't see handcuffs, capitaine, so I am assuming you have no evidence." He put his right hand on the desk and pushed himself up. "You may see yourselves out. And please do not trouble to come back. If you do, I may have to call a real policeman."

Hugo turned and walked out of the office and Garcia followed. They nodded to the secretary, who got up as soon as they passed her desk. As they descended the stairs, Hugo heard the click of Gravois's door shutting.

Outside, Hugo turned to Garcia. "Did you notice his accent?"

"Yes. Not much of one, but he wasn't born and bred here."

"I hadn't noticed it before. Spanish maybe?"

"I don't know," Garcia said. "But I think you're right, it's one of the Romance languages." They walked down the street toward the police car in silence. When they got to the car, Garcia stopped and looked at Hugo. "Do you really think the book has something to do with this?"

"I don't know, capitaine. I really don't."

"We have no motive for these bouquinistes to be murdered. We have suspicions, yes, but no real evidence or motive, especially for Max Koche, assuming that what you told me is true. As Gravois seems to know. We need to be careful, Monsieur Marston, both of us need to be careful. I did not know about the involvement of le Comte d'Auvergne. That makes me both curious and also very concerned. He is well-connected in this city, as I'm sure you know. Not just to Claudia Roux, but to some very powerful and influential people. I am happy to lean on a thug like Gravois, but less happy to dirty the rug of someone like Gérard de Roussillon."

"I understand." Hugo grimaced as he thought of the ambassador. "I am in much the same position."

"Did you believe Gravois when he said he didn't know about the book?"

"Yes," said Hugo, "as a matter of fact I did. Did you see the way he looked back and forth between us? He was unsure of himself. Specifically, he was unsure what the answer should be. I think he was telling the truth."

"A wasted trip, then?"

"Not necessarily. I think we found out something quite important."

"And what is that?"

"It seems to me that one of two things is true. Either the Rimbaud book is somehow connected to the murders and Gravois is not, or—"

"Or," Garcia interrupted, "the book has nothing to do with their deaths, and Gravois does."

"I hope to look at the book this afternoon, capitaine. After that, maybe we'll know more. Gravois, though," Hugo grimaced. "He is a little harder to read."

As they climbed into the car, Garcia's phone rang. He put the key in the ignition and answered with his other hand. "*Oui*?" He looked at Hugo as he listened. "Address?" He nodded. "Got it. I'll be there in ten minutes." He hung up and looked out of the windshield, shaking his head. "*Merde*. They think they found your intruder."

"They think?"

"Hard to tell. Half of his head is blown off."

"Where is he?"

"My colleagues went to his apartment and saw him leaving. They followed him to a restaurant in the Nineteenth Arrondissement. As soon as he got there, he pulled a submachine gun from his bag and opened fire on a table of patrons. He killed all of them but one. The survivor removed the top of his head with a bullet."

"He was shooting at people who carried guns?"

"Oh yes," said Garcia. "He killed two organized crime bosses and their bodyguards."

"Organized crime?"

"Les Pieds-Noirs. Which means we definitely have a new player in town." He looked at Hugo. "We may even have a war on our hands."

CHAPTER TWENTY-SEVEN

Garcia offered to drop Hugo at the metro station at Place de Clichy. He wouldn't be needed at the restaurant, the policeman told him, as they'd have to identify Alex Vacher's body through fingerprints.

Outside the station, Hugo shook hands with Garcia and promised to call later if he found any new information about the book. Hugo thought that the capitaine was a little embarrassed, or uncomfortable, at leaving that line of questioning to an outsider. But with no evidence to suggest a link to the book, and given Roussillon's privileged position, they both knew that even the suggestion of a police investigation would be unwelcome.

Hugo also felt that by leaving Roussillon to him, Garcia was intentionally showing his trust, perhaps even an apology for the way Hugo had been treated early on in the investigation, for Garcia's own brusque tone at the prefecture. For his part, Hugo had never really minded Garcia's suspicious nature and he appreciated that the capitaine had been willing to revise his opinions. Not many senior cops were so open minded, Hugo thought, and such flexibility of mind showed Garcia's confidence and intelligence. And having spent a few hours with Garcia, there was an honest charm to the man that Hugo liked.

From the street, Hugo called Roussillon's house. One of the servants answered and politely asked him to wait. After a minute, Roussillon came on the line.

"Monsieur Marston, how are you?"

"I'm fine. I went by to see Claudia this morning, she looked good."

"She does, doesn't she? The doctor said that just being shot is enough to make the body shut down, even a minor flesh wound like hers." He sighed. "I can't help but feel very lucky. And grateful. I just got back from the hospital myself, they are releasing her today. I have arranged for an ambulance to bring her home."

"Good. She's a tough one, I'll say that much. And I guess we both got lucky." He cleared his throat. "Gérard, the other reason I'm calling is to come by and see the book." *And to ask how you know Gravois*, he thought. "My friend Tom came by earlier but you were out."

"Yes, I'm sorry. I went to the hospital and then had a sudden business matter, nothing important to me, but it was to my colleague. You know how people can be."

"I do," said Hugo. "May I come by now?"

"If you want." He wasn't sure, but Hugo thought he detected a note of hesitancy in Roussillon's voice.

"I don't want to impose, but it's important."

"To you, I see that."

"Thank you."

A few minutes later Hugo tried calling Tom from the platform at Place de Clichy, but got no answer. With any luck he had his nose in a Monet. Hugo smiled at himself; he felt like a parent now that Tom was around. When they were together his old friend was fun, interesting, and excellent company, but when he had the run of the city, Hugo could never quite shake the feeling that Tom was up to something.

Hugo smiled at the thought, especially because he planned to do some snooping of his own before visiting Roussillon. Snooping from the comfort of his office at the embassy.

He began with the databases of France's foreign intelligence agency, the DGSE, and got no hits. He then tried the domestic intelligence network, the DCRI. A new screen came up, one he'd not seen before. It contained the name "Alain de Roussillon," several addresses including the house Gérard lived in now, and his dates of birth and death. After the general information page, the *Notes* tab was the only one Hugo was able to see, which puzzled him. He clicked on it and all that came up was what looked like a reference number: OIM-67892-01946. Hugo sat back and wondered.

He turned to his computer again and cleared the screen. He tried a general Internet search on the Roussillon family, but after half an hour was coming across the same information over and over again, none of it useful.

He then went to the website of *Le Monde* and typed in "Anton Dobrescu." He paged through the articles but didn't learn anything new. He was interested to see a picture of the man, though. It looked like a surveillance photo, a good one. He stood taller than the man he was with, unidentified in the caption, and he had a full head of black hair. Thick, dark eyebrows sat over a heavy nose and his cheeks were pale but looked like slabs of meat. *A strong, healthy Romanian*, Hugo thought, *who might have been a farm laborer or dock worker*.

As he looked at the picture, a thought tugged at him, a question, and he called Garcia to try and get it answered.

"*Merde*, are you serious?" Garcia hesitated. "You really need that?"

"Yes. And he won't know."

"I suppose it's not like we're actually bugging his phone, right?"

"Right," Hugo said, giving the capitaine the reassurance he was seeking. "And all I want are the records from one day, just one day. I promise."

"*D'accord*. I'll get my lieutenant to e-mail instructions. If you're in a hurry he can call you, he's good at this stuff, gets all kinds of records for me."

"I'm in a hurry. You sure we don't need a subpoena or court order?"

Garcia snickered. "I don't know. But my lieutenant does, and he also knows if he doesn't do it by the book he'll feel my boot up his behind."

Hugo grinned. He liked a by-the-book policeman. Especially because, every now and again, he had a tendency to push the bounds of what one former boss had called "procedural acceptability." Working

with a straight-shooter like Garcia was a healthy reminder of the rules
and what might happen if he pushed too hard. They rang off and Hugo
wondered if that was how Tom saw him, the rock of propriety in his
ever-shifting world.

Hugo brought himself back to the present as he closed his office
door behind him, an idea growing in his mind. His immediate need,
though, was a taxi.

Traffic clogged the main arteries leading out of the city center, forcing
the taxi driver to duck down smaller streets where they were at the
mercy of stop lights and pedestrians lingering in the crosswalks. At
each turn Hugo checked his cell phone, willing it to ring, checking the
signal and battery strength. It took almost an hour to reach Roussillon's
house from the embassy, and the lieutenant finally called just as they
were pulling into Roussillon's tree-lined street, as tranquil in the day as
it was at night. Hugo sat in the idling taxi while he got the information
he needed, then got out and tipped its driver more handsomely than
was customary in Paris.

"*Merci*," said the cabbie, eyeing the bills. "You would like me to
wait?"

"*Non*," Hugo said. "I'll manage."

As Hugo walked up the front steps the door opened and Hugo
recognized Jean, his driver from the night of the party. "Monsieur
Marston, *bienvenue*. Please, come in, le Comte asked me to show you
to the library."

Jean led him past the large table in the reception hall, its oversized
vase brimming with a new crop of fresh flowers, and Hugo nodded his
thanks as the driver held open the door to the library.

The room still smelled of wood smoke and cigars, but Hugo could
smell the books now, too, that familiar and comforting mustiness. *If
peace had a smell*, he thought, *it would be the smell of a library full of old,
leather-bound books*. He looked around but didn't see Roussillon, so he

walked over to one of the shelves and began to look for familiar titles. He spotted a row devoted to the history and practice of hand-to-hand combat, judo, and the other grappling arts. Not Hugo's area of interest, but above it were two shelves filled with the works of Arthur Conan Doyle and his finest creation, Sherlock Holmes. Hugo paid particular attention to a three-volume set of books covered in gray cloth, with black and gilt lettering on their spines.

He pulled the first volume out, *A Study in Scarlet*, and admired the gilt embellished pictorial cover plate depicting Sherlock Holmes smoking a pipe.

"First edition, published in 1903," said a voice behind him. Roussillon. Hugo hadn't seen him slip into the room. He wore dark blue jeans and a white collared shirt. A pale blue sweater was draped around his shoulders.

"You are a fan?" Hugo said, indicating the many Holmes books.

"Oh yes, the finest detective ever created. By far. Brilliant but flawed, a nuanced character that you so rarely see these days. Can you imagine a heroin addict as the hero in a modern novel? Of course not, it would never happen. They are all tall and strong and handsome and shoot like Wild Bill Hickock." Roussillon ran his fingertips over the spines. "I can say I have read every single one of his adventures, several times, and they still delight me."

"I agree completely. You have a fine collection."

"Thank you." Roussillon straightened a book and then offered a manicured hand to Hugo. They shook and Roussillon thanked him again for saving Claudia's life.

"Come," Roussillon said. He moved away from the fireplace toward the back of the library, and Hugo followed. A glass cabinet had been built into the wall, rows of shelves from floor to ceiling protected by thick glass. De Roussillon rapped on the glass with his knuckles. "Bulletproof," he said. "For the stars of my collection."

Hugo studied the books behind the glass. "*L'Étranger*, by Camus. Very nice. Softcover?"

"Yes. So only valued at about fifteen thousand of your dollars."

"Only?" Hugo shook his head. "*Paradise Lost*, too."

"I got that for twenty-five thousand. A steal. It's first edition, from 1668. Print run of just thirteen hundred copies. And did you know, Milton himself was paid just ten pounds? Amazing."

"It is. Clearly the Rimbaud fits into such esteemed company."

"Oh yes." Two armchairs had been placed near the cabinet, their backs to it and a low table between them. Hugo now noticed that two glasses of water sat on the table. "Please sit. I will show you the Rimbaud."

"Wait. Let's talk first, if you don't mind."

Hugo moved around to the chairs and played host, gesturing for Roussillon to sit. The Frenchman hesitated for a moment, then went to the empty chair and lowered himself into it, eyes on Hugo. "Is this about Claudia?"

"No," said Hugo. "It's about your father."

"My father?"

"Yes." Hugo had thought he'd seen a shadow pass across Roussillon's face, but now the eyes and mouth were smiling.

"What about him?"

It was Hugo's turn to smile. "I think you know, Gérard."

Roussillon spread his hands. "*Non*, I'm sorry I don't."

"Then let me ask you about another book, before we talk about the Rimbaud. It's called *On War*, and it's by . . . well, you know who wrote it, don't you?"

"Yes." There was the shadow again, there and gone in a moment. "Carl von Clausewitz. But then, any respectable book collector can tell you that."

"I suppose so. Do you own a copy, by any chance?"

"No, I don't. What exactly is this about?" Roussillon's tone was harder now.

"I'm curious about a copy of the book, an early translation, owned by a friend of mine."

"What friend?"

"A man called Max Koche."

"I don't know him. Is he German?"

Hugo smiled. "Sort of. You're sure you don't know him?"

"I said I didn't. And what does this have to do with my father?"

"To be honest, Gérard, I don't have all the answers. I'm here to get some of those. But you told me before that you prefer plain speaking, so I hope you will excuse me if I am blunt."

"I do prefer it, yes."

"Then I'll tell you what I think. I think that your father was a collaborator. I can't prove it, not right now, but I have several reasons to think this. First, your government's research tools have closed up his file, a file that once existed but has since been erased, moved, or hidden. All I know is that it was closed in 1946. That's just one year after the end of the Second World War, a time when scores were being settled, people were being held accountable. If I remember my history, young women who collaborated with the Germans had their heads shaved in public, am I right?"

"Yes," said Roussillon, his face impassive.

"I suspect the penalty increased the higher up the social ladder you were. Or maybe not—public damnation is more ruinous to the aristocracy than to the common man. Or woman. Anyway, what I know for sure is that your father's file existed and was shuttered up in 1946. I also know that you received a call from my friend Max two weeks ago, the same day he got his hands on a book called *On War*. I know, too, that Max was a Nazi hunter at one time, but had moved on to looking for collaborators. And he looked for them in the books that came to his stall. I think, Gérard, that he found such a book and that when he looked through it he found your name, your father's name. I think he found it, called you, and then . . ." Hugo's voice was soft now, and he shrugged his shoulders. "And then what, Gérard? That's the bit that needs filling in."

Roussillon was staring at him, eyes unblinking. His face had paled noticeably and he reached slowly for his water glass. He began to raise it to his lips, but his hand shook and he put it down, a rattle of glass on glass.

"Can you prove any of this?" Roussillon's voice cracked. "Can you?"

"Just the phone call. But if I get my hands on the book, and if I can access that closed file . . ." He smiled. "And I know all sort of tricks to get through red tape."

"I'm sure you do," Roussillon said, surprising Hugo with a smile of his own. "In any case, I don't intend to lie to you, Monsieur Marston. The truth is that you are right about my father. Everything you said, it's true."

"OK," said Hugo. "Tell me."

"First, let me ask you this. Do you believe in God? No, wait, let me be more specific. Do you believe in the Christian God and his Bible?"

"No, I don't. I don't believe in any God. Or any collection of them, for that matter."

"I see. Well, many do, as you know, and I have come around to their way of thinking in recent years. Anyway, the Bible speaks of the sins of the father being visited on the son. Are you familiar with the concept?"

"Only as a cliché."

"You know, even the Bible isn't sure about the answer. Exodus says, 'I, the Lord your God, am a jealous God, visiting the iniquity of the fathers on the children.' Deuteronomy I like, it's very cheerful, listen: 'Fathers shall not be put to death for their sons, nor shall sons be put to death for their fathers; everyone shall be put to death for his own sin.' Much better, but then one is left wondering, which is it?"

"No clue." Hugo shook his head. "And I'm not sure I care all that much."

"I do." Roussillon stood. "And I'll tell you in a moment, but first you wished to see this Rimbaud book, so you will see it." He pulled a key from his pocket and Hugo twisted in his chair to watch as the Frenchman unlocked the cabinet, reached in, and retrieved the Rimbaud. He stood there for a moment staring at the cover. "It's not an irony, I suppose, that I would go to such lengths to get this book."

"You mean the content?"

"The content, the author, yes. In some ways, being homosexual back then was more acceptable than it is now." He frowned. "Especially for those who worship a Christian God."

"There are gay ministers," Hugo said. "And it's not just Christians who judge homosexuality a sin."

"Oh, I know that, of course." He looked up and his eyes twinkled for a second. "But it's amusing to hear you, the atheist, defend them."

"Defend? No. I've just found bigots in every walk of life, no more and no fewer in churches than anywhere else."

"As you say." Roussillon walked around his chair and sat down. "There are other sins of the flesh, Monsieur Marston, I alluded to them earlier."

"The sins of the father."

"Yes." He looked up from the book. "You seem to know your history, Monsieur Marston, I mean your Second World War history. For Americans, I suspect that war takes up only a few pages in your schoolbooks, but maybe you know that here in France, and also in Germany and England, the war is very much alive in the memories of the people. To deny the Holocaust is a crime in some places. In Germany, you may not name your son Adolf. And we, the French, endure jokes about surrender from the British and Americans, even sixty years later."

They shared a smile and Hugo said, "I've told a few of those myself."

"Ah yes, how quickly you Americans forget that without the French, you would still be a British colony. History isn't just written by the victorious, you see. Sometimes it's rewritten by them. You already know where I am going, and that it's somewhere painful, which is why I am talking around the subject." He cleared his throat. "You are right that my father was a collaborator. There, now the truth is out. He confessed it to me before he died. And as deathbed confessions go, it was a difficult one for both of us, as you might imagine." Roussillon smiled sadly and looked at Hugo. "I had of course suspected something like that; it's hard to keep such an enormous secret even in so large a house. But it was easy to look the other way, to ignore my suspicions."

"I'm sure," said Hugo.

"He was not a bad man, you understand, but he was far from a brave man. He couldn't stand the idea of losing this house, our other homes, his fortune." Another sad smile. "Perhaps he and I are not so different. Anyway, as the war began and then progressed, like so many Frenchmen he was forced to choose sides. He chose the losing one. He sided with the Germans to save our lands and property, and save them he did. He also managed to save our name, but only by keeping his collaboration a secret."

Hugo said nothing, but nodded for him to continue.

"His collaboration could be excused as bad luck," Roussillon said, "or so I have often thought. You have to bet on a game when you don't know much about the teams." He shrugged. "Maybe the one you pick wins, maybe it loses. There's no shame in bad luck. No, the shame doesn't lie in the side you choose, but what you do for that side, how far you go. Do you provide food? Shelter? Money? Or do you do more than that?" Roussillon shook his head, and his shoulders sagged. "The saddest truth is that my dear father was worse than a mere collaborator, much worse than a café waitress who served coffee to, or even slept with, some grubby soldier. My father was a spy. Every month or two the Wehrmacht, or sometimes the SS, would come in and smash a few worthless pieces of furniture so that he could protest his treatment in public, protect his name. But when they left, those soldiers would have a list of names or safe houses or whatever else they could use against the Resistance." He looked up at Hugo. "It is my lifelong shame that my father sacrificed others so that he might live in comfort. He was a traitor."

"Maybe he did it to protect you," Hugo said.

"I'm sure he would say so, yes. But from what? Living in a smaller house? Being called Gérard by my teachers instead of *Monsieur le Comte*? I think I could have survived that better than the shame of knowing what he did." Roussillon looked down at the book, his fingers caressing the cover.

"Forgive me, but this has something to do with the Rimbaud?"

"No, actually. It is you who asked to see it, and I am showing it to you." He passed the book to Hugo. "Look through it if you wish, you will see only a valuable book, prized by a gay man as old as the author." Roussillon's eyes twinkled for a moment. "Or almost as old."

"The story of your father's collaboration was written in the Clausewitz."

"Yes. You see, the Nazis and the collaborators were not the only ones passing notes. The Resistance did, too."

Hugo thought again about the conversation he'd had with Ceci and silently thanked her for solving this part of the puzzle. "So I understand."

"*Bien*. After the war my father spent all his time looking for the book, but never found it. He said it would be our undoing. I don't know how he knew, I never questioned him on these matters. All I knew was that as long as the book remained hidden away on someone's shelf, I was safe, my family name was safe. But I also knew that if it ever came onto the market, I would have to buy it, no matter the cost."

"What does it say?"

Roussillon smiled sadly and shook his head. "Not much, but more than enough. The words, at least as my father relayed them to me, are not easy to forget. For a Roussillon, anyway."

"Tell me."

"The message is contained in a microdot in the lower right corner of the endpaper, and it is short and to the point. Here." He reached into the coffee table drawer and pulled out a pen and notepad. He scratched a line on the paper and handed it to Hugo.

C. de Auvergne—collab. avec Nazis. Traître. Tuez-le."

"Kill him," Hugo translated the last phrase aloud. "Short and to the point."

"Actually, there was more." Roussillon wrote on a fresh sheet. "The most sinister part was this." He handed it to Hugo: *A l'air de suicide.* A list of six names followed.

"Make it look like suicide," Hugo read. "You'd think they would want to make an example of him."

"Not someone so powerful, so connected. The Nazis would have wiped out dozens, maybe hundreds, of innocent people in revenge."

"Yes, I'd forgotten that tactic. And this list of names, they are the people ordered to kill your father?"

"No," Roussillon said, his voice almost a whisper. "No, those are the names of men who died because of my father. And as much as those names tortured me, imagine how they tormented him."

Hugo nodded, then glanced up and found Roussillon looking at him. "I'm curious, would you have destroyed the book?" Hugo asked.

"No, I don't think so. It holds too much history, it is too valuable to disappear in flames. Do you know, neither my father nor I ever even saw the book, never laid eyes on the pages that contain secrets powerful enough to destroy us."

"You are sure it even contains those secrets, those names?"

"My father was, and the information he passed on to me was very specific. I am sure it is true, as sure as he was. And so you see that quite apart from the monetary value of such an old book, the secret it holds is itself historically significant, of course."

"True, but that secret only makes the book more valuable, histori-cally speaking, if someone discovers it."

"Of course," said Roussillon. "And perhaps you misunderstand. I said before that the victorious get to rewrite history. That's never been my intention, and it's precisely what I would be doing if I buried this secret forever. No." He shook his head and took another sip of his water. "In all honesty, I am not entirely sure what I would do with it. On the one hand I feel obliged to let Claudia know her family history, to tell her myself in case she first hears it from someone else and wastes time and effort in a futile defense of the Roussillon name." He shrugged. "But on the other hand, I still want to protect her. Not only from the secret itself, but from having to carry it around for the rest of her life."

"Your daughter is a strong, intelligent woman. She can cope with the truth," Hugo said. "Look at her career—she hasn't relied on the Roussillon name to get where she is. Of course you should tell her."

"Maybe. You know, I had thought that I might like to sit down with a writer and explain it all. It would make a fascinating story, don't you think? And sooner rather than later."

"Why do you say that?"

"Several reasons. Like an alcoholic repenting his ways to those he sinned against, I must in my pursuit of spiritual and religious sobriety repent the sins of my father."

"So you think that's what the Bible is saying?"

"I have no idea. But it doesn't matter because it's my sin, too. I have been hiding the truth from the world, from my own family even. And the Bible is clear about one thing: I may not continue to sin and also find salvation."

"That's the why," Hugo said. "Even if it's not a great one from the atheist's perspective. But why now?"

"It's not only cowardice I inherited from my father," Roussillon said. "He also blessed me with the genes for early onset dementia. My daughter tells me I have blank moments, that you witnessed one at dinner. I don't notice those so much, but I do know," he spread his hands, "that I have been forgetting things lately. Small and unimportant things, but my doctor tells me this is how it starts. I need to tell Claudia, and maybe the world, this story before I forget it." He offered a weak smile. "And after that, well, you know we Europeans are embracing the idea of euthanasia. It does seem like a dignified option, don't you think?"

"I can't say I've thought about it much."

"Well, I suppose you've had no reason to."

Hugo let that part of the conversation trail away before asking, "And Max?"

"Ah, yes. I didn't realize that he was your friend. But yes, I spoke to a man called Max. I didn't get his last name and I didn't even know he was a bouquiniste. I don't know why, I thought he had a book store somewhere though, as I think about it now, he never said so explicitly."

"He called you?"

"Yes. He said he knew I was looking for the book, *On War*. That was no great secret, collectors like me make it known when they want certain books. I myself have put word out for dozens over the years, *On War* was just one. The secret, of course, was *why* I was looking for it."

"What did Max say?"

"We didn't talk for long. He said he had the book and wanted to meet with me." Roussillon shrugged. "To try and sell it, negotiate a price I suppose."

"Where did you meet?"

"We didn't. I didn't have time. I was on my way out of the country for a couple of days, literally on the way to the airport."

"So what did you do?"

"I asked someone to handle the purchase for me. I authorized him to offer up to two hundred thousand Euros."

"That's a lot of money," Hugo said, an uneasy feeling rising. "Who did you ask to handle the purchase?"

"I wanted someone with natural authority, someone I knew would bargain hard. I wanted the book badly, of course, and would have paid a lot more, as I'm sure you can guess. But why pay more if you don't have to?"

"Gravois." Hugo held Roussillon's eye. "You asked Bruno Gravois to get that book for you."

They sat for a moment, watching each other. Then Roussillon nodded his head slowly, a frown forming.

"You are right, yes. But now I feel like you are hiding something from me."

Hugo leaned forward. "What happened after you spoke to Gravois?"

"With the book?" Roussillon shrugged. "Nothing."

"What do you mean, nothing?"

"Gravois said that he called the number your friend gave but that your friend didn't answer and never called back."

Hugo processed this for a moment. "So you really don't have the book?"

"No. I never even saw it. And I didn't hear from Max again."

"You wouldn't have," Hugo said, watching de Roussillon closely. "Max was killed very soon after you spoke to him."

The Frenchman's head snapped up and Hugo saw the color draining from his cheeks. "Killed? How do you mean?"

"I mean he was murdered."

"What?" Roussillon's mouth hung open in shock and the hand holding his water began to shake. He put the glass on the table, spilling some in the process. His voice trembled. "What happened? Why would someone murder him?"

"I'm not entirely sure." Hugo shook his head. "I've been trying to figure that out for a couple of weeks now."

"You think it has something to do with the book, *On War*?" Roussillon shook his head. "Please, God no." He lifted his eyes and looked directly at Hugo. "Hugo, this cannot be. Too many men, good men, patriots and heroes have died because of the cowardly blood that runs in my veins. Please, don't tell me that I, too, have killed an innocent man somehow. That would go against everything I have believed, everything I wanted to do."

"I don't know, Gérard. But every time Gravois's name comes up, I'm seeing bodies."

Roussillon started to rise but his legs shook and he sank back into his seat. "Tell me the truth," he said. "What has Gravois done? What have I done?"

"To be blunt again, I think that by asking Gravois to negotiate your deal, you may have unintentionally sent Max to the bottom of the Seine." Hugo immediately regretted his choice of words because Roussillon's body seemed to crumple with despair.

When Roussillon looked up, his eyes were wet but his voice was strong. "What can I do to help you? Whatever it is, I will do it."

"I'm not sure. I am not even sure I'm right about Gravois. But tell me this: What's your connection to him?"

Roussillon shook his head again. "I always thought him an atrocious man, really I did. He reminds me of a zombie, limping around like a corpse. Something about him has always frightened me."

"So why did you intercede on his behalf?"

"You mean to the ambassador?" Roussillon shrugged. "I owed Gravois a favor and I didn't think, honestly, that it would do anyone any harm."

"What favor?"

"When he took over from Ceci Roget, I went to him. I told him that I was looking for a few prewar books. I didn't tell him why, but I figured that as the head of the SBP he was in the best position to help me keep an eye out for books moving though the stalls. He agreed to help, not just with the Clausewitz, but he helped me acquire a number of valuable books."

"And so talking to Ambassador Taylor was just a favor."

"Yes. And despite my personal feelings about the man, I had no reason to think that his motives were impure."

"I believe you, Gérard. And it may be that he is entirely innocent."

"The police will look into him, I assume."

"There has been some hesitancy, to be honest. As you yourself pointed out, he has political clout."

"He does." Roussillon stared at him for a moment. "And you know the ways of law enforcement better than I do, but it seems like an investigation into the man would go a long way into answering some questions."

"Oh, I agree. But no police agency will just investigate someone unless they are pretty sure it'll lead somewhere, or if they simply have no choice but to do so. Searching someone's home or office, even digging into their background too obviously . . ." Hugo shrugged. "Policemen are busy people, sometimes when the bit is not yet between their teeth, someone needs to put it there."

"So do you think I should talk to him, to Gravois? Confront him?"

"I don't think that would be a good idea, no."

Roussillon grimaced. "I am not scared of him. Not now, not anymore." He looked at Hugo. "Now I am just angry."

"I know," Hugo said. "I feel the same way. But if I'm right, then he's dangerous and you are not equipped to tangle with him. And if I'm wrong, you certainly don't want to be accusing him of murder."

"Perhaps. *Mon dieu*, I don't understand all this. I couldn't bear it if I thought I'd caused your friend's death."

"Even if I'm right, this isn't your fault. It isn't."

"I hear what you say, but mark my words. If he is responsible for this, and I believe you when you say he is, I will see that he does not escape justice. Whatever it costs me."

They both looked up as, from the other end of the library, someone knocked twice. The door opened and Jean stepped in.

"Monsieur, the ambulance is here. Your daughter is home."

CHAPTER TWENTY-EIGHT

Hugo spent a few minutes with Claudia before leaving her in the care of her father. The Frenchman seemed suddenly old and frail, perhaps rattled by their discussion, or maybe distressed at seeing his daughter in bandages. As Hugo bade them farewell, Roussillon was fussing around her like an overprotective hen, fetching water and cushions, brushing her hair and forehead with his fingers as if to reassure himself she was really there. Every now and then he would turn sad eyes on Hugo, who felt like he'd said too much, burdening Roussillon more than he should have.

Jean drove him back to Rue Jacob, and Hugo spent the afternoon wandering around his apartment completing small but meaningless tasks. Tom was missing in action again but this time had left no note. Real sightseeing, Hugo hoped. He tried calling and bit back his impatience, wanting to share what he knew with his best friend, with the mind that was considerably sharper than its owner ever let on. But he got no answer. At five o'clock his phone rang and he snatched it up without checking to see who was calling. He smiled when he heard the voice on the other end.

"I'm downstairs," Claudia said. "I need a drink and some company, but I'm not walking up four flights of steps. You busy?"

He found her sitting on the bottom step, her handbag resting beside her. As he helped her up Tom walked through the door, whistling softly and clapping his hands in delight when he saw them. Claudia put her good arm around Tom's shoulders and laughed, "So this must be Tom. *Bien*, now I have two men to buy me drinks."

They headed to a café nearby where Tom shooed away the wine list and started ordering vodka. This pleased Claudia who, Hugo guessed, had some pain and a few bad memories to chase away. He didn't feel like keeping pace with them, but he was glad to have his old friend there to keep Claudia company amid the shot glasses.

For much of the evening, in fact, Hugo stared out of the café at the bundled up passersby and tried to pick through the confusing mass of coincidences and dead-end facts that he'd turned up in the hunt for Max's killer. The wraiths of cigarette smoke and rising aromas of alcohol and garlic filled the air around him, closing in and heightening the already strong sensation of being trapped in a maze. He knew full well there was a way out, an answer, and he was certain Gravois was it. But he had no idea which way to go, how to get to him. And, while he sat there scratching his head like a dumb cartoon detective, it seemed like someone was out there trying to kill him. Garcia had suggested that it was Claudia they were after, perhaps because of her growing connection to the police, or maybe because of unfinished business from her husband's death—and maybe that was right. Either way, Hugo was under no illusions that the shooter was finished.

As the laughter and chatter went on around him, Hugo sipped his watered-down scotch, aiming for the peaceful patch of consciousness that lay between relaxation and intoxication. If he made it there, he hoped, some of the loose ends would tie themselves together and give him a rope to hang Gravois.

But for what? Being creepy? Hugo was sure the SBP leader was at, or close to, the center of the mystery, but the man had insulated himself from questions, from answers.

Hugo looked at Tom, red-eyed and laughing so hard his belly shook. A washed-up CIA spook and an out-of-practice FBI agent. Even they should be able to do better than this.

In the end, Hugo decided that the one decision he'd got right was spending the evening at a neighborhood café. By the end of the night, Tom was too drunk to walk by himself and Claudia, who'd sensibly swapped her vodka for Perrier an hour before they headed home, was too tipsy, talkative, and wounded to be of any help dragging Tom

home. After Hugo had hauled them both to the top of the stairs and
into the study, he propped Tom in a corner. Hugo opened up the sofa
bed and then put an arm around his friend's shoulders, making sure he
fell in the right direction.

"Should you undress him?" Claudia said. "Cover him up?"

"Probably," Hugo said, heading for the door.

They went to the bedroom, and the light from his bedside lamp
guided them as they undressed each other—she insisted on doing her
share. Hugo was tender, afraid to hurt her, but saw fire in her eyes and
gave in to an urge to run his hands through her hair.

"Pull it and see what happens," she whispered.

He tightened his grip and tugged her head back, exposing her
pale throat to his kiss. Claudia gasped and her breath quickened. She
cupped the back of Hugo's head with her good hand, then trailed her
fingers to his chest and tore off the last of his shirt buttons.

They awoke just before nine, the room stuffy and tainted with the
sweet smell of sex, stale alcohol, and sweat. Hugo slipped out of bed,
promising coffee to a mumbling and bedraggled Claudia. He pulled on
pants and a T-shirt and walked into the living room. Even from there
he could hear Tom snoring. He set about the coffee maker, erring on
the side of stronger rather than weaker, for Claudia's sake and his own.

He walked through the living room, straightening and picking up
as he made his way to the window overlooking Rue Jacob. The blast of
fresh air made him shiver, but he left the window wide open as he went
back to the kitchen. He heard the shuffle of feet behind him and Claudia
appeared, her healthy arm held high, covering her eyes, shielding them
from the morning light. He looked at her other arm and was relieved not
to see any red stains on the bandages. She wore a blue T-shirt of his and,
he saw when she leaned on the counter, nothing else except a few goose
bumps on her bottom. Her whole body suddenly shivered.

"I was going to bring it to you in bed," Hugo said.

"I needed to pee." Her voice was hoarse and cracked. "If I go back to bed I won't get up for a week. Mmm, bed for a week sounds good."

Hugo put a cup of coffee under her nose. "Milk and sugar?"

"Just sugar. Lots."

He dropped in three teaspoonfuls and stirred for her. "Food?"

"Later. Maybe." She looked at him and rubbed a hand across her forehead. "God, I haven't done that in a while."

"Which?" Hugo asked with a wink.

"Funny." She sipped at the coffee then licked her lips. "Mind if I finish this in the bathtub? The shower's out for a while."

"Help yourself."

She reappeared thirty minutes later in the jeans and blue cashmere sweater she'd worn the previous night. She was still pale, but she'd brushed her hair and put on some makeup. She went straight to the coffee pot and refilled her cup. Stirring in sugar, she lowered herself gingerly onto the couch beside him then nodded to the window. Hugo had closed it in anticipation of more nakedness. "Looks like a pretty day. Can I see you later?"

"Are you going somewhere now?"

"I should check in with my father. He told me about the conversation you had with him yesterday."

"He did?"

"Yes. And it's funny, I've always known something was up, something kept hidden from me. But I'm glad he told me, he seemed to need that, to talk about it after discussing it with you like that. He seemed very sad about the whole thing. I've never seen him like that."

"Understandable," Hugo said. He squeezed her hand. "It's been quite a week for you. Are you OK with everything?"

"Still processing, I think. I keep telling myself that nothing changes who I am, and that nothing should change how I see my father. But this, it's not something I could ever have imagined."

"He didn't do anything wrong." Hugo didn't mention Max, unsure whether Roussillon had shared with his daughter the possibility of having played an unwitting role in the bouquiniste's death.

"I know. But his father did, so I want to check on my father, have lunch, and talk it over some more. Maybe see you later?"

"I hope so. You want me to call Jean to come get you?"

She pulled a face. "I'll take a taxi. Jean's sweet, but I don't need his disapproving looks in the mirror. One overprotective father is enough. By the way," she said, jerking her thumb toward the study. "He's fun."

"He is that," Hugo said. "And I expect he'll want to head out for another bender tonight."

"Really? So what does he do for a living? I'm sure he told me last night but . . ."

I'm pretty sure he didn't, Hugo thought. "He used to work for the State Department. Shuffled papers on seven continents, is how he puts it."

"Sounds wonderful. What are you going to do with him while I'm away?"

Hugo pursed his lips. "I had an idea that we'd go boating."

The phone call came less than an hour later, and as soon as it rang Hugo knew it was her. Claudia's number flashed on the little screen and he flipped it open.

Three seconds of silence followed by her sob made the hair on the back of his neck stand on end.

"Claudia, what is it?" He was already moving toward the kitchen counter, looking for his keys.

"Papa, it's Papa." Her voice caught and he could almost feel a tremble run through her body.

"Claudia, are you OK? Is someone there?"

"No, just me. Oh Hugo . . ."

Hugo's mind kicked down a gear, slowing time and assessing her words. "If someone is there with you," he said slowly and clearly, "and if you're not allowed to say so, repeat the words 'I'm fine.'"

"Hugo, it's not that. It's my father. Oh my God, please come quickly. He's . . . he's dead."

"Dead? What happened, Claudia? Where is he?"

"In the library. He's been shot. Please come."

"I'm on my way, I'll bring Tom. And I'll call the police, please make sure you don't touch anything."

Five minutes later they were in a taxi, Tom miraculously alert and asking questions Hugo couldn't answer, the driver confused but cooperative after seeing Hugo's badge, gun, and a large wad of cash. Hugo tried calling Claudia from the car but it went straight to voicemail, and he was suddenly afraid for her. He left her a message to call back, and then left one for Capitaine Garcia, telling him what little he knew and asking him to meet them at Roussillon's, if at all possible.

Outside the car's window Paris flashed by, the sluggish river Seine appearing and disappearing beside them, seeming to slow their progress with her magnetic pull, a seductress winking through the plane trees, teasing them with glimpses of her silvery skirts, and with the threat of more death, more bodies hidden within their deadly folds.

He delayed calling the police, worried about Claudia being there alone but knowing enough about crime scenes to be sure she was safe, that if she'd been the intended target she'd never have been able to call him. Knowing enough, too, to be confident that once the French police arrived he wouldn't get a look at the crime scene unless, or until, Garcia showed up. And this was one crime scene he didn't want to wait to see.

When they got to Boulevard D'Argenson Hugo was out of the door before the taxi had stopped. Claudia must have been waiting by the window downstairs because the door opened immediately, her thin silhouette leaning against the wide door jamb. Hugo leapt up the stone steps and held her.

"Claudia, what's going on?"

She clung to him for a few seconds, her body shaking, the fingers of her good arm working his shoulders and back, getting as close as she could. Then she stiffened, strong Claudia returning, and Hugo felt a squeeze that was more controlled, assertive.

"In the library," she whispered. "He's in there." She looked up and her eyes were red rimmed. "I don't know what's happening."

Hugo looked at Tom and both men moved toward the library. The room was bright, brighter than Hugo had seen it before. And at first it seemed like nothing was amiss, but when they walked toward the glass cabinet at the back, Hugo noticed an open window and, lying on the parquet floor beneath it, the still form of Gérard de Roussillon.

He lay on his back, arms and legs splayed out wide, the way he'd have lain to make a snow angel as a child. He was dressed in dark pants and a velvet jacket that had fallen open to reveal a plain white T-shit. He'd been shot in the forehead, once, a clean, tidy, and instantly fatal shot.

Tom knelt over the body, and Hugo didn't need to tell him not to touch anything.

"Small caliber," Tom said. "Twenty-two probably, or his brains would be all over the place."

A noise from the doorway made them both swing around. Claudia hovered there, and Hugo knew she wanted to be with them yet was terrified to see what she'd already seen, what no daughter should ever see. He held up a hand, *I'll be right there.* He looked up at the open window and stood.

"They come through there?" Tom asked.

Hugo stepped over the body and looked out, looked down. "No, I doubt it. There's a pond right beneath the window. No way to avoid getting wet, so not the best way in, and I don't see track marks anywhere." He moved away from Roussillon, toward Claudia. His voice was gentle but urgent. "Tell me how you found him. Was the front door open?"

"No. I mean, yes," she said. "It was closed but it wasn't locked. I didn't think anything of it because when Papa and Jean are home they often leave it that way. This area, it's safe."

"Where is Jean?"

"I . . . I don't know. It's his day off, I don't think he's here."

"OK, we'll find him. Tom," Hugo called, drawing his weapon as Tom left Roussillon and hurried over. "We need to clear the house."

Tom nodded and they worked in tandem like they used to, eye

contact and nods their way of communicating who would open a door, who would go in first, and when. They moved quickly through the downstairs, Claudia hugging the walls ten feet behind them, Hugo not wanting her out of sight. They left her on the stairs as they moved to the second floor, listening at each door, the sweat beginning to dampen their shirts and loosen the grip on their guns.

But in two minutes they knew that the house was empty.

As they sat on the stairs, Hugo and Claudia side by side, Tom behind them, they heard the sirens. They had left the front door open and the familiar figure of Capitaine Garcia was the first to enter. Behind him, four gendarmes in uniform stood looking around, awaiting orders.

Hugo left Claudia with Tom and took Garcia into the library, telling him about the unlocked door and the small but precise bullet hole in Roussillon's head.

"You think he did this too?" Garcia asked as they looked down on the gray, waxy face of the Comte d'Auvergne.

"Gravois? Your guess is as good as mine."

"But why? Did he have any reason?"

"He might." Hugo told him, sparingly and quickly, about Roussillon's father the collaborator, the book, and his desire to confront Gravois over Max's death. "If he did, and if he threatened Gravois, then maybe." Hugo shrugged, and Garcia said what he was thinking.

"But we have no proof, right?"

"Right."

Garcia looked around the library. "I'll get my crime scene people in here, see if they can find anything at all. And Claudia can help us figure out if anything was taken."

"There should be surveillance cameras," Claudia said from the doorway. Tom hovered behind her. "He had some high-tech ones installed a couple of years ago after some kids started throwing rocks at the houses on this street. He was afraid they'd escalate to burgling. They never did, but he kept the cameras."

"We'll check it out, thanks," said Garcia. He turned to Hugo. "You want to stay?"

"I can, of course." But he didn't want to; he wanted some time and some space to think this insanity through. He looked at Claudia, who smiled thinly and shook her head.

"I have a friend on the way," she said. "You don't have to." She walked to him, her eyes holding his, not looking down at her father. "As long as you come back."

"Deal," said Hugo. "Tom and I will go somewhere and figure this out, talk it through."

"Talk what through, exactly?" asked Garcia. "Do you know what's going on?"

"Fuck no," said Tom. "He's got no idea what's going on. That's why he wants to talk."

CHAPTER TWENTY-NINE

Just before two o'clock, Hugo and Tom trotted down the stone steps that led from the Quai de Conti to the walkway by the river. The wind had dropped but so had the temperature, again, and Tom cursed as a band of cold air rose from the water to greet them. Frigid weather usually killed the fetid aromas that came up from the Seine, but not today. Somewhere nearby a fish had died, caught in a piece of stray netting perhaps, out of reach of the river rats that scoured the walkway sniffing for such delights.

"Hors d'oeuvres?" Tom asked, wrinkling his nose.

Hugo smiled but didn't respond. He'd stuck to his original plan for the day, and he'd been right that the only way Tom would agree to go on a boat was if lunch was included. And if Hugo paid.

Down on the walkway, Hugo swapped Euros for tickets to the only lunch cruise he'd been on, departing from the Left Bank in front of the Institut de France. A rosy-cheeked waiter showed them to a table on the starboard side of the boat, protected from the icy air by a glass wall. Ventilation ducts let warm air from the engine compartment drift around their feet and a blanket had been laid on each seat. Tom tucked one around his legs and asked for another.

"Why don't you have heating lamps like the cafés?" he grumbled to the waiter.

"It's not allowed, monsieur. Fire on board boats is a bad idea."

A coffee laced with brandy improved things a little, but Hugo couldn't shake the feeling that there was more to Tom's mood than the hangover and Roussillon's death.

"What's up with you, are you sick?" Hugo asked as the boat chugged away from the dock.

"Something like that."

"Come on, spill it."

"Oh, Jesus, the usual shit. Lonely old man who drinks too much because he's bored and then sees his best friend banging the hottest chick on the block."

"Really? I didn't think self-pity was your style."

"It's not, but I ran out of other people to pity."

"Are you really that bored back home? If so, I can give you a job here, working with me. Seriously."

Tom smirked. "Work for you? I don't know, I'm a pretty disrespectful employee."

"I said with me, not for me. And you're a pretty disrespectful human being. I wouldn't expect you to be any different in the workplace."

"Fucking right."

The waiter reappeared and took their order. The hottest food on the menu for them both: onion soup, followed by risotto, and then bananas flambé. Tom tore a piece of bread and tossed half over the glass wall and into the water. They watched as two screeching gulls dove for the morsel.

"So what are we doing, Hugo? Are we gonna catch a killer or just fuck around?"

"Good question." Hugo shook his head. "I don't know, I feel like I've hit a wall."

"Tell me."

This is what Hugo wanted. A sounding board—Tom's suspicious, aggressive, and determined mind working on the problem. Perspective too, though he knew Tom would suggest a few options he wouldn't be able to follow up on.

"OK. Let's start with Gravois . . ."

"Slimy fucker."

"Yes. Definitely up to something . . ."

"Or maybe he just hates cops."

"Or maybe you should shut up and listen," Hugo said, grinning. "Whether he's naturally slimy or hates cops, he's hiding something. Wouldn't talk to me as a journalist or when I went with Garcia. You just have to look at him to know something is going on. But what? That's the impasse. I can't make him talk, and he knows we don't know enough to force the issue." Hugo sat back. "So what the hell am I supposed to do?"

"No hard connection to any of the corpses?"

"Nothing more than being their union leader."

"And any link to shooting Claudia?"

"No idea. As far as I know, they haven't caught anyone for that."

"And no connection to the clowns that busted into your apartment?"

"Nope. Well, maybe. It's possible that the one you castrated is one of Gravois's capitaines."

"Capitaines? What the fuck is that?"

"He has guys who go around and check up on the bouquinistes. It's really just harassment, to get them to leave. Anyway, it's possible I saw that guy picking on Francois Benoit but I can't be sure they are one and the same, I wasn't paying that much attention."

"I see." Tom nodded. "Well, I can see the impasse thing. You need to find another way to get to him."

"Such as?"

"Such as real evidence."

"I don't have any, Tom, that's what I'm telling you."

"Then why the fuck do you think this guy is guilty of anything? Jesus, Hugo, you're an FBI agent, not Miss-fucking-Marple. You don't assume people are guilty because they make your tea curdle."

"Tea doesn't curdle."

"Shut up, you know what I mean."

"Fine, we'll do it your way," Hugo said. "Why would he want those bouquinistes dead?"

"So he can replace them with his men."

"And women."

"Fuck off. Question is, why does he want to do that?"

"Because he's taking a cut from them? He denied it when I asked him."

"Oh, well, that's that then," Tom said, waving a hand. "If he said he wasn't, then I'm sure he wouldn't lie."

They sat quietly as the soup arrived, still bubbling. Hugo picked up his spoon. "Those guys don't make enough to kick much back to him, do they?" he said.

"No idea. What's your point?"

"My point is this: would he really pay off Cecilia Roget and a bunch of others, and commit three murders, just to get a few extra Euros each week?"

"Yeah," Tom slurped his soup. "Does seem like a hell of an investment for not such a great return. And don't forget, he's a cripple."

"Cripples don't kill people?"

"Sure they do. But they don't push them into rivers. They shoot them, maybe stab them."

"OK, so we can agree he didn't kill all three himself." Hugo spooned the steaming soup into his mouth, savoring the rich flavor and the warmth.

"Which means he's got people working for him," said Tom. "We know that already, seems likely we met two at your place the other night."

"But they weren't there to kill."

"Why were they there?"

"I'm not sure," Hugo said slowly. He looked out at the water for a second. "But I assume they were looking for a book."

"They don't have libraries in Paris?"

"Funny. But listen, I have an interesting story for you. I didn't get a chance to tell you yet."

He started with Roussillon's past, his family history, and the collaboration. He recited the secret code from *On War* and enjoyed the surprised look on Tom's face. Then he told him about Roussillon's conversation with Max and his attempt to have Gravois buy the book. When he'd finished with every detail he could remember, Tom spoke.

"Roussillon called Gravois, didn't he? He called him and got upset, maybe threatened him. And Gravois put a bullet between his eyes for it."

"Or one of his men."

"Right. And of course, still, we have no proof."

"We can check phone records, see if Roussillon made that call. But even if so, you may be right."

"Another ghost killing."

It was Tom's turn to stare out at the water. Hugo watched him, saw his eyes working left to right like a typewriter as his mind churned. "Hang on," said Tom. "If those thugs were at your apartment for the reason you say, and Roussillon was telling the truth—"

"Then where is the book?"

"You already thought of that." Tom shook his head then slurped his soup noisily.

"I did."

"And you know the answer."

"Actually no, I don't. I have no idea."

"Jesus, we're going around in circles, Hugo. Although this soup is fucking awesome." He put his spoon down. "Look, forget Gravois for a moment. Imagine he's our Barney."

Hugo nodded. A "Barney" was the grim nickname Tom and Hugo had for a distraction, a red herring that could screw up an investigation. They'd worked a case together in LA, two girls stabbed to death in the bedroom of one of them. The killer had covered their heads with towels and left them face down on the bed. When police found them, a Barney toy was nestled between their heads. Hugo had been called in to give a profile, easy enough with the towels and the face-down positioning. But he could never figure out what the placement of Barney meant. The local cops suggested it was a decoy, but Hugo didn't think so. If the perpetrator wanted to avoid being profiled, Hugo told them, he simply would have left the bodies in different positions or not covered them up.

Eight months later, the man struck again. James L. Wright was a neighbor to the two girls who'd died in February of that year. In October,

Wright broke into another neighbor's home and stabbed a little girl in her room, but didn't realize that her teenage brother was in the house. The boy ran for his father's gun, shot Wright, and saved his sister from bleeding to death. Wright survived and together Hugo and Tom got him to talk. One of their first questions was about the Barney toy. At first, Wright just stared back, a blank look on his face. But as Hugo took him step by step through the crime scene, Wright remembered. As he'd left the bedroom, the toy had been on the floor, in his way. He'd turned to kick it back into the room and by pure chance it had landed between the girls. It was a decoy, alright, but entirely unintentional. Since then, Hugo and Tom had been vigilant for such distractions.

"OK," Hugo said, "I don't think Gravois is another Barney, but I'll pretend he is. What then?"

"Right, just leave him out for now. So then let's talk about the other important things. What about the Rimbaud?"

"Let's rule that out, too. No connection to anyone but Max, and it had left his hands by the time he died. And no reason to think Roussillon lied about his buying it being purely a personal matter."

"OK." Tom flipped another scrap of bread over the glass partition and more gulls joined the diving chorus. They'd passed the Grande Bibliotheque and were executing a slow U-turn, preparing to head west along the Right Bank, back past Notre Dame and toward the Eiffel Tower. "Which leaves us with what?"

"A missing copy of *On War*."

"Right. What else?"

"Three dead bouquinistes."

"One of whom was Max. But didn't you tell me he was willing to give up his stall?"

"That's what he said to me, yes. I believed him, too."

Tom went back to his soup, his head low over his bowl as he spoke. "Which destroys our theory that Gravois killed him to get his stall. Maybe he killed him to get the book."

"No," Hugo said. "I don't think he has it."

"Gravois? Why not?"

"Because if he did, he wouldn't kill the one man who'd pay a shit load of money for it. A man he could either sell it to, or a man he could blackmail."

"Assuming Gravois is the killer again."

"All roads lead in his direction, don't they?"

"No shit." Tom ran a piece of bread around the inside of his bowl. "So what else?"

"The attack on me and Claudia and the raid on my apartment."

"Maybe we should be looking for a link between Claudia and those bouquinistes." Tom sat back. "Did you ask her about Durand?"

"Yes. She didn't like that I was snooping."

Tom grinned. "You weren't."

"Yeah, that helps. Anyway, she just pointed out that she's a police reporter and he's a cop." Hugo shrugged. "She has a point. I know that she's currently covering a new antidrug task force, maybe he has something to do with that. And she's not writing about the bouquiniste murders, she's writing about drugs."

"See, that's good information right there." Tom scratched his head. "I'm just not sure what. Let's talk about a drugs connection."

The men looked up and sat quietly as the waiter arrived with their risotto. "Wine, *messieurs*?" he asked.

"No, thank you," Hugo said quickly. Tom frowned.

"So drugs, eh? Nasty work sometimes. I did a spell in Colombia. Did I ever tell you about that?"

"No."

"Ah well, I don't suppose it's the same as in Paris. What exactly was she writing about?"

"She told me that there used to be two organized crime groups who'd split the city and were sharing power." Hugo told Tom about Paris's recent drugs history, about the way the police had changed tactics, targeting distribution points instead of the channels into Paris. He told him about Dobrescu and the North Africans, and about Claudia's suspicions that the African monopoly was now being challenged.

"Which is why," Tom mused, "Garcia was afraid of a war after the restaurant shooting. But shootings in restaurants, killing cops. That's pretty drastic."

"It is." Hugo toyed with his fork for a moment. That was the one constant with criminals: they knew better than to shoot cops or take out innocent civilians. Not out of respect, of course, but because there was no surer way of raining hell on you and your accomplices than to spill the blood of a man with a badge or, God forbid, a small child. Those who ignored that rule were few and far between, and in their own minds such renegades always had very good reason to do so. "What if it's not just the police who are changing tactics? I don't mean the shootings, I mean the dead bouquinistes."

"Explain," Tom said, his mouth full.

"Think about it. They make for perfect drug distribution points. Cash and merchandise change hands every hour of every day. Anyone watching would see nothing more than a book or a plastic Eiffel Tower being passed. That's usually a giveaway for drug dealers, they always have loads of cash on them, and in small denominations. But so do bouquinistes, so it's perfect for not only collecting money but laundering it."

"Fuck me, you're right." Tom nodded, eyes alive with excitement. "Go on, don't fucking stop now."

Hugo felt a surge of excitement as the jigsaw pieces floated toward each other in his mind, rotating, lining up. "And what if there is a raid by the cops?" he said. "At the first hint of a siren the dealer who is also a bouquiniste can just drop his gear down to the causeway below, or if he's got a good arm, throw it straight into the Seine."

Tom banged his fist on the table. "It's like have a huge fucking toilet to flush the junk down, right there."

"Exactly." Hugo held his eye, felt his thought process slow as the jigsaw pieces hovered in place, leaving the picture still incomplete. "But of course, that's the tail end of the setup. You have to have everything else in place before you can start selling."

"Ah, you mean the supply of drugs, the people to ship it, all that crap. Yeah, how does someone do that under the noses of the unfriendly Pieds-Noirs?"

"Not just how. Who would be able to do that?"

Tom put on his smart-aleck face. "How about someone with an existing drug supply and people working for him?"

"Very funny." Hugo frowned. "But you're right. And it would have to be someone who is, for all intents and purposes, invisible to the North Africans. And the police."

"Invisible? What do you mean?"

"Well, back in the 1920s Al Capone couldn't just swagger into Austin, Texas, and start peddling coke. Same thing here. None of the Italian mobsters could slide into town and bring their dope factories and soldiers with them, they'd stick out like sore thumbs. To succeed, someone setting up in Paris would have to develop their routes and supply lines without anyone suspecting what they're doing. Which means that, in some form or other, whoever is doing this has been oper- ating for a while. Right?" Hugo talked faster now, realization dawning. "Tom, who is the only person that organized crime won't go after? The only person the police will leave alone?"

"Shit, I don't know." He rubbed his chin. "The police can fuck up anything, they'd probably confuse Al Capone with Al Pacino and roll out the red carpet. But organized crime? Hell, the only person they won't try to kill is a dead man."

"That's exactly right." A smile spread across Hugo's face. "We called him a ghost before, but he's not. He's a phoenix, rising from the ashes."

CHAPTER THIRTY

Tom wanted to eat dessert inside at the boat's small bar, where they had access to brandy. For medicinal purposes, he assured Hugo. Tom went in first, to order for them both, while Hugo lingered outside to call Emma.

"Another research project. Quick as you can."

"Yes *sir*."

"That's better." Hugo grinned. "I need to know everything about the identification of the bodies at a crime scene." He gave her the general date and as many other details as he could, and added, "Try the DCRI, the DGSE, Interpol, Europol. And if you don't get anywhere, call me back, I can get Capitaine Garcia to find out."

"You sound like a little boy at Christmas, Hugo. What's going on?"

"Can't tell you just yet, I need to make sure I'm right."

He left her to the task and went into the boat's small cabin. Tom was at the bar, two brandies in front of him. "What am I missing that you figured this out first?" Tom asked.

"For one thing, you never had the pleasure of his company."

"So help me out."

"OK. And tell me if you think I'm insane. Really."

"With pleasure," Tom said. He swirled his drink and nodded for Hugo to continue.

"Start with the assumption that no one lies unless they have to. Or, put another way, if you lie, you have a reason to do so."

"Liars have something to hide. You're a genius."

"Bear with me," Hugo said. "My experience has always been that the lies about small stuff, why you wear a watch or got a parking ticket, those are the ones that trip you up. Trouble is, people don't spot them because no one expects you to lie about those things. Now, go back to what Claudia told me."

"About what?"

"About Paris. The drug problem. She said that before Dobrescu and his crew were killed, they'd started shooting at police, trying to expand their turf."

"Never a good idea, killing cops."

"Which the North Africans already knew. And when Dobrescu started, it pissed them off. Which tells us two things. One, the North Africans probably wouldn't try to kill a reporter working with the cops. And two, that even drug dealers and mobsters know better than to target cops."

"So Dobrescu was a dumbass and got hacked to pieces for it."

"Right." Hugo tried to remember Claudia's exact words. *They identified him and several of his top lieutenants through DNA and dental records.* "Except not necessarily."

"We all know you're smarter than me, so stop being so fucking cryptic."

"Sorry," Hugo smiled, "but I have to get there logically, step by step, in my own mind." His phone rang. "Emma. That was quick."

"I'm good," she said, "plus the full report is on all those databases you mentioned. Easy pickings."

"And the answer?"

Emma read the section of the report he'd asked about as Tom scrutinized his face. When she finished reading, Emma said, "Does that satisfy?"

"Sure does, thanks. Oh, and can you send a car for Claudia, to her place on Boulevard D'Argenson?"

"Right now?" She listened quietly as Hugo told her about Roussillon's murder and how he wanted Claudia close to him, whether she brought a friend with her or not. "Poor thing," Emma said quietly when he'd finished. "You keep doing what you're doing, catch these people, and I'll call and let her know someone's on the way. I'll take care of her until you get here."

"Thanks Emma," Hugo said. He rang off and picked up his brandy.

"Well?" said Tom.

"He's insane. He must be."

"I will be if you don't tell me what the fuck just happened."

"Right. So. Now that I think about it, those small things seem so obvious, make sense. I guess I'm just out of practice." Tom was about to interrupt but Hugo held up a hand. "Gravois rubbed his wrist a lot. He wore gloves and limped. Remember? He walked with a cane."

"The cancer."

"Cancer. No, it wasn't that. His whole appearance was off. I just didn't think any of it was connected. But he's had plastic surgery, his whole face is altered. I'm guessing whoever did the surgery also got rid of his hair, sucked fat from him, the whole nine yards. Hence the gaunt appearance. His face has literally been pulled out of shape."

"Gravois? That's pretty far-fetched. And what about the DNA and fingerprint evidence that says Dobrescu is dead?"

"Good question. That's why I called Emma, to check the reports to see exactly what they found."

Tom sat bolt upright. "Jesus, Hugo, they only found a hand and a foot, didn't they?"

"Bits of them, yes."

"And they assumed that bits of a hand and a foot meant the whole man was burned up in there, too."

"Right. Only I don't think he was. I think the Romanian rescue mission was a success—in part, anyway. Maybe he was burned in the fire, maybe that accounts for his surgery or his injuries, I don't know. But what I do believe is that he escaped, though not before he lost the use of his hand and his foot. Which is why he had to lean across and open a left-sided drawer with his right hand. Why he rubbed his left wrist and not his right one. And, of course, why he wears gloves and walks with a cane."

"Unbelievable." Tom drained his glass and signaled for another. "Gravois really is Dobrescu."

"It makes sense. It's why we couldn't find anything about his past, why he seemed to come out of nowhere. But he had the men, he knew the city. That guy Nica, he was one of them. I guess he started hiring Italians."

"Who the fuck is Nica?"

"The bastard who kidnapped Max."

"Oh? What makes you say he's Italian?"

Hugo cocked his head. "The name, of course."

"You dumb shit. You think that's short for Nicolas or something, don't you?"

"And you know better, of course."

"Damn right. Nica isn't Italian or a first name, not in this case. It's an Eastern European surname." Tom sat back, a smug grin on his face. "Romanian, to be specific."

"I should have known." Hugo shook his head. "A man like Dobrescu isn't going to shop abroad for his muscle. Too paranoid."

"No shit," Tom said. "A kingpin who's seen his men hacked to death, and maybe had his own hand and foot chopped off, he's gonna be pretty paranoid. And pissed. I bet after all that shit, knocking off bouquinistes is like downing hors d'oeuvres for him and his boys."

They locked eyes and Hugo smiled. "I know what you're going to say next," he said.

"You mean about having an awesome theory but no fucking evidence?"

"Something like that."

"Let's go get some. I'd be happy to go pluck a few hairs off the bastard's head for a DNA match. Oh fuck, he doesn't have any." Tom rubbed a hand over his face. "You're right, he is a smart guy."

"I'm afraid so. A great combination, smart and psycho."

"And if he's willing to come back and fight those who hacked off his foot, I'm guessing even I couldn't persuade him to talk."

"Fair assumption."

The floor beneath their feet started to vibrate, and the boat's engine changed pitch as the captain maneuvered toward the dock. Hugo looked out of the window, up toward the Quai de Conti. "I wonder. Maybe we can get someone else to talk."

"Let me at him, whoever the hell he is." Tom rubbed his hands together. "You got someone in mind?"

"Actually," Hugo said, "I do."

They opted for the subtle approach. Hugo left the dock and headed east along the Port des Saintes-Peres, while Tom trotted up to the Quai de Conti and sidled up to Max's old stall. He'd borrowed Hugo's hat and pulled it low down over his eyes. The plan was simple: a brief note for Jean Chabot to show up at a café in thirty minutes, signed "B. G." delivered with enough time for Chabot to get his stall closed up but, hopefully, not enough time to figure out whether the note really was from Bruno Gravois.

Hugo walked as far as Rue du Bac and then cut south, heading for the rendezvous point, a bar called Le Sanglier that sat yards from the Place Saint-Thomas d'Aquin. This was a quiet piece of Paris, a peaceful and relatively tourist-free section of narrow streets and old houses that Hugo discovered on one of his many wanderings. The square itself was home to the church of Saint-Thomas d'Aquin, an unremarkable building from the outside, certainly nothing to compare with the grandeur of Notre Dame or the ornate Church of Saint Chappelle. No, the beauty of this church was in its austere lines, its bare interior, and the cloak of tranquility that settled around the shoulders of the few visitors who crossed its ancient threshold.

Hugo looked at the church's entrance, tempted to spend a few minutes inside. He was, unashamedly, one of the many agnostics to appreciate, and sometimes need, the sense of peace and serenity that enveloped visitors to these old monuments. He thought hard for a reason not to go in, and found one: the church was reliant on natural lighting, which meant that *The Transfiguration* on the ceiling above the altar, the church's only original decoration, and also the painting of *Ste. Étienne Preaching to the Angel*, lost much of their luster after the morning light had passed. He would come back.

He turned and went into the bar.

Tom arrived three minutes later and peered into its dark recesses. Hugo sat at a table in the back, tucked into a corner. He had three bottles of beer open in front of him.

"He knows you." Tom said. "You better make yourself scarce until he sits down. If he sees you when he comes in, he might run."

"Good thinking. Have him sit where I am, so he has his back to the two walls." Hugo looked around the bar. "I'll be by the window with my back to the door. And give me my hat, I'll drop my head when I see him."

Chabot scurried into the bar five minutes later, checking his watch and looking around the dark interior. Hugo watched from under the brim of his hat as Tom waved him over. Chabot licked his lips before looking around once more and moving to the back of the room. As soon as he sat down, Hugo stood and walked quickly to the table, blocking him in.

Chabot's jaw dropped. "You!" He looked at Tom. "And who are you? You said Gravois—"

"Imagine that," Tom said. "I lied."

Chabot started to get up but Hugo put his hand against the front of the bouquiniste's knee and forced him back down. "We have some questions for you," Hugo said.

"I don't care," Chabot hissed. "You don't know what you are doing. Let me go and maybe I won't tell Gravois about this."

"We know who he is, Chabot," Hugo said. "We just want to give you a chance to come clean."

Chabot visibly paled. He stared at Hugo and then Tom. "Look, if you know who he is, then you know who I am. My background. You know that I am not . . . that I break the law, *oui*, but I don't kill. I don't."

"That's good," said Hugo. "The thing is, someone did kill Max."

"It wasn't me." Chabot licked his lips again.

"You were at his apartment," Hugo said. "Which means you lied to me once already."

"*Bien*. I was there." Chabot's eyes widened. "But only because I was

afraid. I was told that Max had agreed to move out, but . . ." He shook
his head.

"You didn't believe that," Hugo said.

"I didn't. He was one of those who had resisted. Several times."
Chabot started to rise but Hugo pushed him down again. "Please, *messieurs*, I was expecting Gravois at my stall this afternoon, he's supposed
to be coming by. That's why I thought I should come here." He looked
at his watch. "*Merde*, you have to understand. If I'm not there when he
arrives, if someone tells him I was with you . . ."

"Come with us to the police," Hugo said, "they can protect you if
you'll let them."

"Sure." Chabot's lip curled. "And if I testify against Gravois," he
said.

"Right," Tom said, "and if you don't, maybe Gravois will hear about
our little *tête-a-tête*."

"This is not a game." Chabot leaned forward and his eyes narrowed. "If he suspects that you know, you won't get within a mile of
him. Not alive, anyway."

"Monsieur Chabot." Hugo took off his hat and placed it on the
table, then sat with his hands open. "It's a matter of time. If you won't
help us, then I'll go talk to my friend at the prefecture, the man looking
into these murders. You know what he'll do? He'll come and talk to
you. And he won't pass you a note, he'll show up with half a dozen
police cars, sirens blazing and lights flashing. Then he'll take you into
custody and you'll spend a day or so in jail. Now, it doesn't really matter
whether or not you tell him anything at that point, does it? Because
when you get out, if you get out, Dobrescu will be waiting for you. Is he
the kind of man who'll take your word that you didn't say anything? Or
is he the kind of man to kill you just in case?"

They watched as the truth settled over Chabot, his shoulders
sagging under the weight of it. When he looked up at Hugo his eyes
were damp. "I want American custody."

"Why?" Hugo said. "I'm not sure I can promise you that. We're
not officially involved and the French would almost certainly object."

"Gravois has people in the prefecture," he implored. "If I go there I am no safer than staying on the street."

"What do you mean?" Hugo said. "What people?"

"I don't know. But I heard that a cop-friendly reporter was shot on Monday."

"What do you know about that?" Hugo leaned forward, his jaw tight.

"I know Gravois ordered it."

"What else?"

"How do you think Gravois knew where the journalist would be? The guy checked in with the prefecture, and someone passed on that information to Gravois."

"The journalist wasn't a 'guy,'" he told Chabot. "Your boss is not just shooting cop-friendly journalists, he's shooting female ones."

"Then you see why I don't want to cross him," Chabot said.

"Too late for that," Tom said. "Like it or not, you're on our side now."

"Only if I get American custody," Chabot said. "If not, I will take my chances." He sat back and crossed his arms in front of his chest.

"OK, fine," Hugo said. "But it'll take a while to arrange, a few hours. You should stick with us in the meantime."

"*Non*," Chabot shook his head. "If it will take a few hours, I will go back to my stall. You may think you are safe from him, but if he sees I am missing and we are together we'll make a big target for him."

"He's right, Hugo," Tom said.

"OK," Hugo nodded. "Go back to your stall while we take care of this. Tom, were you followed here?"

"Fuck you," Tom said. "You're the one who's out of practice, and I'm not a fucking idiot."

"Yeah, sorry," Hugo said. "OK, we'll leave one by one, Monsieur Chabot, you go first. Pick up a sandwich close to here, that'll explain your brief absence if Gravois comes by." Hugo wrote his cell number on a napkin and handed it to the Frenchman. "And memorize this, OK? Don't keep it on you. Remember and then destroy it. If anything spooks you, call or text me. A simple SOS will do. We don't want to let Gravois know we're on to him, but if I can't get to you quickly we'll send the police. Got it?"

"*Oui*," Chabot nodded. He put the napkin into his coat pocket with trembling fingers. "*Merde*. This is crazy."

"Do you have any family?" Hugo asked. Close family would also need protection of some sort, given Dobrescu's proclivities.

"*Oui*." Chabot looked at the floor. "I have a little girl. She lives with her mother and I don't see her too often." He sat up. "I have to tell her good-bye. Just in case, I have to."

"That's not a good idea. You need to be at your stall when Gravois comes by." Hugo remembered the public slap Gravois had given Chabot. "I'm guessing he's not used to people disobeying him."

"*C'est vrai, monsieur*." That's true. "But if I go into witness protection or if... I need my Nicole to know that I didn't leave without saying good-bye." Chabot spread his hands. "What would you do?"

"OK." Hugo frowned. "We'll need to change the plan, then. Don't go back to your stall at all. Do what you have to do, go see your daughter, and then come back here. And remember, call me if there's a problem."

Hugo sat and watched Chabot scurry out of the bar. He turned to Tom. "I'm no good at this secrecy business. Are we handling this right?"

"You never know until it's over." Tom sipped at his beer. "Hey, do you want me to stick with Chabot?"

"I don't know. He's going to piss off Gravois if he's not there for their meeting. That guy is pretty paranoid, so he may well set the dogs on Chabot. And if he does, you don't want to find yourself between them."

CHAPTER THIRTY-ONE

I t was three o'clock when Hugo walked into Ambassador Taylor's office. The ambassador already knew about Roussillon's death and he sat behind his desk, listening sympathetically and without interruption as Hugo articulated Chabot's request for US custody.

When Hugo had finished, he sat back. "Same question as always, Hugo. What is our interest in all this? Look, I may be the big boss around here but I have to answer to others, too. The secretary of state for one, and sometimes the president. If what you're saying is true, taking him into protective custody here is an admission that we think the French police are dirty."

"Only one or two of them."

"If we even suggest that, people will get upset. We spend a lot of time playing cop in the Third World, I'm not sure we want to be playing it in Old Europe, too. I need some genuine American interest to justify bringing him in here and keeping him from the French."

Hugo nodded. It wasn't an unreasonable position. "How about the fact that a US Embassy worker was shot at?"

"Nice try." Ambassador smiled. "The way I hear it you were the hero, not the target."

"That seems to depend on who you ask." Hugo stood and began pacing in front of the desk, his hands clasped behind his back as he thought. He stopped and snapped his fingers. "What if a member of the French police brought him here and asked for our help?"

"The French police . . ." The ambassador studied the floor for a moment. "Yes, I think that would do it. For a little while, anyway."

"Good enough." Hugo stood. "We're meeting this weasel at a bar across the river. I'll take a couple of my guys and bring him in."

"Hang on." The ambassador held up a hand. "If you do this, it's just you and the French cop. Otherwise it looks like we're running the show and that's the exact impression I have to avoid giving."

"Point taken," said Hugo. "I'll confirm the target has made the rendezvous and then call in my cop."

"Good idea." Ambassador Taylor walked to his door with Hugo. "So how is the wounded reporter doing?"

"Miraculous recovery. A little sore, of course, but physically pretty good, though shaken by her father's death."

"I'm sure. He was a good man, I can hardly believe it myself. I trust the French have someone looking out for her," Ambassador Taylor said. Hugo cleared his throat and looked at the floor, and the ambassador smiled. "Ah, I see. Then she's in safe hands."

Hugo left the ambassador's office and made his way down to the security section where he found Claudia and Emma in his office. Emma was running her finger over a map pointing out where she'd been stationed over the years. Hugo went straight over and gently put his arms around Claudia.

"Are you OK?" he said.

"Yes, I think so." Color had returned to her face and she looked more like the crime reporter he'd first met than a daughter who'd just stumbled over her murdered father. "I'm OK, Hugo, I just want to know what's going on, who did this."

"Me too, we're working on it." He looked at Emma and then Claudia. "Right now I need to ask a favor."

"From whom?" Emma asked.

"Both, actually. We've got some fun and games brewing with the locals. Probably be best if you sit tight here for a couple of hours."

"*Attends*," said Claudia. Wait. "What exactly is 'brewing'? Are you doing something dangerous?"

"It shouldn't be, no."

"Will Tom be with you?"

"Yes."

"Good, then you can take care of your nondangerous business while he looks after me."

"I'll tell you all about it tonight, I promise. But you're not coming."

"Why not?"

"Well, for one thing you just suffered a great shock. For another, you are still wounded." His voice was calm but firm. "I think those are pretty good reasons."

"And you think you're the one to decide that?" Sparks flew in Claudia's eyes, and Hugo saw he wasn't going to win easily.

He turned to his secretary. "Emma, tell her."

"I'm staying out of this." She turned and walked back out to her desk and closed the door on the way. Hugo thought he saw a smirk on her face.

"Hugo." Claudia stood with her hands on her hips, her hazel eyes flashing. "I'm absolutely serious."

"I know, but so am I. I meant it when I said it shouldn't be dangerous. And when I said I'd tell you about it tonight. But it's one of those times where if something does go bad, you don't want to be there."

"No, you mean if it goes bad *you* don't want me to be there."

"Either way." Hugo shook his head. "Look, I'm sorry, I just can't take the risk. It's . . ."

"It's for my own good?"

Hugo winked. "You bought that last night."

She rolled her eyes. "We're not talking about a spanking, Hugo."

He glanced at the door and gave her a "keep it down" look. "My plans involve coming back here anyway, probably in an hour or so. You're in no shape to be running around and neither Tom nor I will be able to babysit you."

"Hugo!" She refused his attempt at a peck on the cheek as he passed. He didn't stop to try again, but he felt her eyes boring into his back.

Outside the embassy, he called Tom. "Still in the Place de la Concorde?"

"No," Tom said, his voice low. "The Crillon."

"Jesus Tom," Hugo groaned. "What are you doing there?"

The Hotel Crillon, just across the street from the Place de la Concorde and within a quarter-mile of the US Embassy, was one of the world's oldest luxury hotels. Hugo had worked the place numerous times, as it was usually the first choice for visiting dignitaries. Everyone from Charlie Chaplin to Jackie Onassis and Axl Rose had stayed there. One of its greatest moments, as far as Hugo was concerned, was the day after Lance Armstrong won the Tour de France for the seventh time: the hotel flew the Texas flag to honor the achievement of their guest.

"What am I doing here? Are you kidding me?" Tom whispered. "I've always wanted to see this place, it's fucking amazing. Did you know they have seven different types of marble in here?"

"'In here?' You're in the restaurant? Great." The hotel's restaurant was called Les Ambassadeurs and had been serving fine and hugely expensive meals since the mid-nineteenth century. It was decorated in rococo style, with crystal chandeliers and marble abounding; his friend was right to be impressed. "And Tom, why are you whispering?"

"Why do you think? They don't allow cell phones in here."

"Of course not." Hugo chuckled. "So hang up and meet me out front."

"Jesus, this place is a fucking palace, you should see this furniture."

"It is and I have," said Hugo. "Now get out of there before I call and have you thrown out."

"You'd do it too, you bastard. I'll be right out."

They met in front of the hotel and walked slowly along the Right Bank, past the Tuileries and the Louvre. They crossed the Seine on the Pont des Arts and Hugo pointed out Francoise Benoit's stall, now occupied by a short, squat, and very dark-skinned man smoking a cigar. Hugo declined Tom's suggestion that they dump him over the bridge and play Poohsticks with him, but he smiled at the image.

Their route was roundabout, their plan to slowly circle into the bar, taking turns to dip in and out of stores along the way to see if they were being followed. It didn't take long to find out that they were.

"Easy peasy," Tom said, breathing hard as he caught up to Hugo. He'd slipped into a designer clothing store on the Boulevard Saint-Germain and had spotted the tail. "Want me to take her out?"

"Her?"

"This one's an amateur." Tom winked. "But as far as tails go, very nice. Have a look."

Hugo turned and saw, about a hundred yards behind them, a woman with short brown hair making her way toward them.

"Shit," he said. "Claudia."

They waited, and a few seconds later she spied them watching her. She stuck her chin out and kept going. "Shut up Hugo, don't say anything." She was a little out of breath, but defiant. "And you can't be mad at me, my father just died."

"Claudia, I'm not mad," Hugo said. He wasn't. In fact, he was impressed. "But you have to understand, I wasn't kidding, this isn't safe for you."

"Or for you."

"How about we don't play games?"

"How about you don't patronize me?" Her eyes flashed again.

"Yeah," said Hugo, "we've been over that. Just sit tight in a café and I'll call when it's over."

"When what's over?"

"Nice try."

Hugo frowned as his cell phone buzzed. He pulled it out of his pocket, planning to let it go to voicemail. But when he saw the incoming number, his stomach tightened.

"Tom, it's Chabot. Text message." He flipped the phone open and read the message: *21 rue veon vite*. He looked up at Tom. "Rue Veon, where is that?"

"How the fuck would I know?" Tom said. "This is your city."

Hugo looked at Claudia. "Any idea?"

"It rings a bell," she said. "Rue Veon . . . why is that familiar?"

"I'll call Emma." Hugo dialed her number and waited. "Dammit. Voicemail."

"Probably hunting for me in the bathroom," Claudia said. "Sorry."

"He didn't say anything else, Hugo?" Tom asked.

"No. The word 'hurry' isn't a good sign though."

"Yeah. Makes it unlikely to be just a new rendezvous point."

"Exactly." Hugo knew they were thinking the same thing.

Gravois has him.

"Call the cops?" Tom suggested.

"One of them, anyway." He dialed Capitaine Garcia's number and got him on the third ring. He explained the situation as fast as he could, listened for a moment, then hung up. "He'll be here in five minutes."

Tom nodded at Claudia. "And her?"

"She's staying with us," Hugo said. "If Gravois has Chabot he might know about us and have someone looking. My apartment doesn't seem to be the safest place in the world."

"A café might be," Tom said.

"Yeah, if she stays put, which I wouldn't count on."

"Hey," Claudia protested, "I'm right here, stop talking about me like I'm not. And tell me what the hell is going on."

"We were supposed to meet with this guy Chabot," Hugo said, "to take him into protective custody."

"Just you?" Claudia said.

"Yes. It's complicated. Jurisdiction and politics getting in the way of law enforcement."

"For once," muttered Tom.

Hugo put a hand on her good shoulder. "I don't need you in harm's way again, Claudia."

"I appreciate that," she said. "But I have my own reasons for wanting to come. This is important to me."

Hugo nodded. "I know. Look, you can come but you have to stay in the car, OK?"

"Fine," said Claudia. She added, with a tight smile, "I'm right-handed, so I can shoot if you need me to."

"No," Hugo said. "We won't need you to. Look, I'm hoping we're just going to pick him up, but I don't know how this is going to play out. I just don't. If you're coming you have to do exactly what I say, do you understand?"

"Yes, sure." Claudia nodded, serious now.

"And I mean exactly. None of this independent reporter crap, OK?"

"I said yes, Hugo, I understand."

They stood at the curb and watched for Capitaine Garcia. He was there in four minutes, pulling up in a plain black Citroen, his window sliding down as he stopped. Hugo went around to the front passenger seat while Tom and Claudia moved toward the back seat. Hugo started to introduce her to the capitaine, but they both ignored him, and she stooped by the open window to swap rapid *bisous*.

"You know each other?" Hugo asked.

"Get in," Claudia said. "And yes."

"We've worked together," Garcia said. "*Alors*, where are we going?"

"His message said Rue Veon, do you know it?" Hugo said.

"*Non*. I'll call my office." He dialed and, Hugo guessed from his tone, spoke to a subordinate. "*Oui*, Veon. V-E-O-N. What do you mean it doesn't exist? Look again."

"Wait," Claudia said, sitting forward. "Maybe he meant Rue Véron. With an *r*. He was texting, right? And in a hurry. Maybe he dropped the *r*."

"Where is Rue Véron?" Hugo asked.

"Montmartre," she said. "I had a friend who lives up there."

"What kind of street is it?"

"Small, narrow. Residential only. You know, the typical Paris street with five- or six-story buildings. All apartments, I'd guess."

"On my way," Garcia said. He revved the car and peeled away from the curb before she'd finished giving directions. He handled the car well, sliding past slower traffic without using his siren, using the accelerator to get him out of trouble more often than the brake. In minutes they were at Pont de le Concorde and speeding past the US Embassy. The thought flashed through Hugo's mind to drop Claudia there. But Chabot had said "vite," so time was against them.

Just past the embassy they hit traffic on Rue Royale, and Garcia swore under his breath. He then said what Hugo had been thinking. "This could be a trap."

"No shit." Tom sat forward. "Do you have backup available?"

"With about five minutes' notice," Garcia said.

"Don't call them in yet," Hugo said. "If Chabot was right about Gravois having someone in your office we don't want them to know where we're going. Not until we get there. We can call in the cavalry just before we go in."

The traffic broke up and Garcia stamped on the gas pedal. The car surged into a gap, then swerved across two lanes into a larger one. As they raced down Rue Royale, Garcia flipped his rear blue light on. "Don't want to get pulled over," he said grimly. "Don't worry, I'll kill it when we get there."

It took less than ten minutes and, as they approached Rue Véron, Garcia turned off the blue light and slowed. They turned onto Rue Lepic, everyone silent, eyes watching the street as if danger lurked behind the cars parked along the curb. Where Rue Lepic met Rue Véron, at its east end, Garcia stopped. He picked up the handset for the car's police radio and looked at Hugo.

"Time to call it in?"

"I don't think so." Hugo undid his seatbelt. "There's a chance that no one will be there. If that's the case and we call it in, we've tipped our hand."

"How about, if you're leaving me here," Claudia said, "I call after five minutes or something?"

"*Bon idée*," Garcia said.

"Yeah, good thinking," Hugo said. "And there's one other thing we can do." He took out his phone and dialed Emma. After reassuring her that Claudia's escape wasn't her fault, he asked for a favor. "Can you check number 21 Rue Véron? Find out who it belongs to."

"Sure, it'll take me—"

"We're there right now, Emma, it needs to take no time at all."

"Hold."

Silence settled over the car as they waited. Claudia fiddled with her handbag, taking out her phone and making sure it was turned on. Garcia stared out of the windshield, muttering and checking his watch every few seconds. Tom sat next to Claudia, his eyes closed and head back, impervious to them all. After a minute, he sat up and reached inside his jacket. He pulled out a small pistol. Garcia watched.

"You have a license to carry that here?" he asked.

"Nope."

"But you know how to use it?"

Tom just smiled.

Hugo saw Garcia open his mouth, so he spoke for Tom. "He's former CIA. I've seen him shoot the wings off a fly, drunk."

Tom dropped the magazine out of the gun's handle and checked it. "To be fair, the fly was drunk too."

Garcia hurrumphed and turned to look out of the front of the car.

"Hugo?" Emma's voice.

"Here. What do you have?"

"A lot of nothing. The house is like most, divided into apartments. It's five stories and the top one is empty. Fourth and third are owned by families, all clean, nothing of interest there."

"French?"

"French names is all I can tell you. Both families have young kids, so they're probably not operating criminal dynasties."

"OK," said Hugo. "And the first two floors?"

"Owned by a foreign company called Tepes Properties. I tried to figure out who the directors or principals are, but this company is tucked three or four deep inside corporations and partnerships. No luck getting through those layers, that would take a while. And no idea who's living there now. Sorry."

"That's what I expected," Hugo said. "Although, you said the company was foreign. Romanian by any chance?"

"That's right," Emma said. "I looked up the word and Tepes was the last name of Vlad the Impaler. A Romanian. But how did you know?"

"Lucky guess. Do you have a floor plan?"

"Yes, want me to fax it somewhere?"

"E-mail it, I can see it on my phone."

A moment's silence. Then, "Done. Hugo, are you doing something dangerous?"

"A little, but don't worry."

"Right, OK, if you're doing something dangerous but say not to worry, then I'll just make myself an egg sandwich and see if I can get a rerun of Oprah online."

"Emma, stop. I'm not doing this by myself, I have the French police here." *One of them, anyway.*

"What about the ambassador, does he know?"

"Most of it. I'll fill you in when we're done, OK? And when I said not to worry, I meant it. We'll be fine."

Tom frowned and tapped his watch.

"I gotta go," Hugo said. "Thanks for the help." He hung up, cutting off more admonitions to be careful. "No clean link from the house to Dobrescu. Sounds like we'll need a team of lawyers to figure out who owns the place, but that itself tells us plenty." He looked at Capitaine Garcia. "I've done this before, so has Tom. Do you mind if we take point? You'll get the credit if it works out, we'll take the heat if it doesn't."

"Fuck that," Tom muttered. "This thing goes bad, you're on your own."

Garcia gave a wry smile. "Yes, that's probably best," he said. "We don't do this cowboy stuff too much in Paris."

"Thanks," Hugo said. "And I'm hoping to avoid any shootouts. We go fast enough, we'll surprise them. Tom, we'll go in the front. Capitaine, cover the rear of the house and one of us will let you in that way. When we open the back door, capitaine, we'll bang on it three times so you know it's one of us. You hear three knocks, no shooting, *d'accord*?"

"*D'accord.*"

Hugo turned to Claudia and pointed down Rue Véron. "See where that street intersects? Our house is the one on the corner, on the right. Watch us when we go in. Tom will be behind me. If he waves his arm like a windmill, call in the cavalry. And Tom, you see one bad guy with a gun or any other type of weapon, even a butter knife, wave. OK? We don't want to take any chances."

"Fine by me," Tom said.

"One more thing, Claudia," Hugo said. "If we go in without waving and you hear firecrackers, or see even one person you don't recognize running from the house, make the call."

"So the only time I'm not calling for help is if the house is empty?" she asked. She was pale and her eyes flicked from face to face.

"Pretty much," said Tom. "Unless granny opens the door and offers us a slice of cake and a cup of coffee."

"Right. Now let's see where we're going," Hugo said, opening his phone. "Here's the floor plan."

The house was on the corner of Rue Véron and Rue Audran, and according to the plans Emma had sent, it had an old-fashioned, closed layout. The front door faced where the two streets met, opening into a foyer that serviced the whole building, including a staircase that led to the upper levels.

A double door at the back of the foyer, the one that led into what they assumed was Gravois's apartment, would be their first real challenge. Hugo raised an eyebrow and looked at Tom.

"Easy," nodded Tom.

"Easy?" Garcia protested. "You haven't seen the lock yet."

"I know," Tom said. "I'm assuming there's a key under the mat."

Once they were through the double doors, they would have to decide whether to split up or tackle the L-shaped floor plan together. A long hallway split the L into two distinct wings. On the left side lay three rooms, on the right side two more. Judging from their sizes and layouts, Hugo guessed that the rooms on the back left of the apartment were probably the kitchen and a bathroom. The room nearest the front of the house was likely a dining room. That would be the first door on their left as they entered the apartment.

On the right side of the L, Hugo guessed, was the living room and, behind it, the bedroom. From the schematic, he could see that the central hallway went straight through to the back door, which opened into a green space shared by all the houses on the street, roughly half an acre. A perfect escape route, he thought, giving access to the back door of every house in the street or, alternatively, to a gate at the back of the little park that led into an alleyway that curved around and opened up into Rue Audran.

"Interesting," Tom said. "Doesn't look like there's a way to get to the second floor from inside the apartment." He pointed at the tiny map. "You have to go out to the foyer and up the shared stairs."

"I don't understand," said Garcia. "Why would they rent two floors that aren't connected?"

"Insulation," Hugo said. "I'd guess the second floor is empty except for security cameras, maybe sensors." Garcia's face was blank, uncomprehending. Hugo said, "They use the first floor for whatever operation they are running. It's the easiest floor to escape from in case of an emergency. They use the second floor to make sure they aren't spied on. To make sure no one can overhear them. And possibly for storage."

"They may have built a ladder or makeshift staircase inside," Tom said. "Nothing substantial because they wouldn't want to attract attention, not if they can help it." He looked at Hugo. "So keep your fucking eyes open, just in case someone pops down from upstairs. You want to sweep the place together?"

"Yeah, sure," Hugo said. That meant they'd work back-to-back, clearing one side of the apartment and then the other. With no way to communicate, no radios or other equipment, splitting up to tackle a wing each would be too dangerous. "Everyone happy?" Hugo asked. He looked at Claudia, who was still pale and wide-eyed, her fingers working the strap of her bag. But she forced a smile and nodded that she was OK. "Good," he said. "Then let's go."

The three men stepped out of the car, closed the doors quietly behind them, and began walking.

CHAPTER THIRTY-TWO

Rue Véron was as Claudia had described it. Narrow, clean, and hemmed in on both sides by five- and six-story buildings, all with the gray stone façade that made up so many Paris streets.

They took the sidewalk on the same side of the road as the target house. Hugo led, with Garcia in the middle and Tom at the back. They walked in silence, the only sound their footfalls on the concrete, echoing softly off the stone buildings around them. Hugo scanned the street, looking for sentries. He felt confident that there wouldn't be any, simply because men lurking in residential streets attracted the wrong kind of attention. Gravois would probably rely on the house's anonymity for his security.

Number 21 sat on the corner of Rues Véron and Audran and was the only house with both a gate and greenery in the front. The gate was part of an iron railing that separated the sidewalk from the grass on both sides of the corner lot. Inside the rails, shoulder-high rhododendron bushes blocked the view out of, and into, the front windows of the first-floor apartment.

Hugo paused outside the gate and looked up and down the street. He pointed down Rue Audran to the alleyway between the houses that led to the shared park at the back of the apartments. Garcia nodded and made for it. Hugo waited until he'd disappeared from view and then swung the gate open and started down the short path. He was surprised to find the heavy front door unlocked. Behind him, Tom stuck two tools back into his coat pocket and shrugged.

They went into the small foyer, bare except for a worn rug on the hardwood floor. To their right a staircase led upward, just as the plans had shown. In front of them were the double doors to Gravois's apartment, and Tom moved quickly to them. He put his ear to the doors for a moment, then gently tried the handle. Locked. He pulled out a long, thin tool shaped like a dentist's pick and another, much like a flathead screwdriver. The pick and tension wrench, Hugo remembered. Just like old times.

Tom moved quickly and quietly. He inserted the tension wrench and turned it the same way he'd turn the key, offsetting the internal mechanism from its housing. He then went to work with the pick, locating the five pins inside the tumbler and pushing them into the lock's housing.

Five barely audible clicks and they were in.

Tom pulled his weapon and looked over his shoulder, making sure Hugo had his gun in hand, too. When Hugo nodded, Tom cracked the door and both men listened.

Nothing.

Tom stepped inside and Hugo moved in next to him, closing the door quietly behind them. A thick carpet ran the length of the hallway in front of them. Tom moved silently toward the dining room on their left, his gun extended, and Hugo followed, covering the hallway, his eyes on the closed door to his right, the door to the living room. The dining room was dark, the watery sunlight filtered out by a layer of grime on the windows. But it was light enough for the men to see a long table and a dozen chairs, all covered in a thick layer of dust.

They cleared the room in seconds, then swept through the kitchen and bathroom. The door from the bathroom to the hallway was locked. Rather than take the time to pick it, they went back through the dining room. Hugo led, checking that the hallway was still empty before moving to the living room door. It had a large glass knob. He rested his left hand on it, his gun up by his face. Tom squeezed his shoulder to tell him he was ready and Hugo slowly turned the knob. It rotated easily and Hugo held his breath as the lever slipped back and the door cracked open.

Behind him, Tom counted down in a whisper, "Three, two, one—"

Hugo kicked the base of the door. As it crashed into the inside wall, he moved fast. He went to the left, Tom to the right, both crouching, their guns extended. This room was darker than the others had been. A thin band of light around the window to his right told Hugo that the curtains had been pulled shut. With his back to the wall, he could see well enough to pick out the furniture and possible ambush spots. Opposite him was the fireplace, and between it and him was a long, low sofa.

Hugo looked to his right, where bookshelves lined the wall on either side of the curtained window. He saw Tom's silhouette in front of the shelves and watched as his friend crept forward for a clear view of the space between the sofa and the fireplace. Hugo covered that spot with his gun, in case of a trap.

When Tom gestured that it was safe, Hugo swiveled to his left and trained his gun on an armoire, the only other piece of furniture in the room. It was seven feet tall and sat in the corner of the room, but Hugo wondered whether there was space just the other side of it, space enough for a man with a gun. Out of the corner of his eye, Hugo saw Tom by the fireplace, covering the corner for him. The space cleared, they met by the closed bedroom door.

They paused for a second. If this was an ambush, Hugo knew, this was the last place it could be sprung. He nodded to Tom, who reached down and turned the door handle. Tom gestured for Hugo to move away from the doorway before they opened it, so he took a step back. Tom twisted the handle and shoved the door, moving quickly back himself.

Silence. The men met at the opening and Hugo noted that the door had only opened half way, despite Tom's shove. He looked down at the floor and saw that it seemed to shimmer in the dark. He put out a foot and heard the carpet crinkle. He glanced at Tom, who shrugged. Hugo held up three fingers and counted them down to one. Together, they moved through the door into the room, guns sweeping through the air. Beneath their feet the floor crackled. Plastic sheeting.

It was even darker inside, and Hugo struggled to make out any furniture in the room. But dark for him was dark for whoever else was in here, so he felt confident there was no ambush. Crouching by the door, he ran a hand over the wall behind him. His fingers hovered over the switch. He whispered to Tom in English, "Lights on," then shielded his eyes and flicked the switch. His eyes took two, three seconds to adjust, and he could see Tom blinking on the other side of the door.

He'd also been right about the lack of furniture in the room, with one exception.

In the middle of the room, in the center of the plastic sheeting that covered the floor, was a single, straight-backed chair. Bound to it with band after band of masking tape, was Jean Chabot.

At least, Hugo assumed it was Chabot. The man's face was unrecognizable. Both eyes were swollen shut and his nose was flattened. A river of blood stained his mouth and chin, completely soaking the front of his shirt, and his hair stood in clumps, soaked with yet more blood.

Hugo approached slowly, looking for signs of life. When he got close, he saw that the man's left ear was missing. He looked down and saw it lying on the floor beside the chair, nestled on a clump of bloody rags. It was white and waxy, like a fake ear sold on Halloween, except for the scraps of skin and blood that marked the cutting line. Hugo put his fingertips where Chabot's pulse should have been and shook his head at Tom. Nearby lay Chabot's cell phone and a scrap of paper. Hugo picked it up. His cell phone number.

"The idiot," Tom whispered. "You told him to get rid of it."

They looked around the room and Tom pointed to a trap door in one corner. A short rope hung down from the door, and Tom walked over and put a hand on it.

Hugo looked back at Chabot, but knew there was nothing to be done. He held up a hand, telling Tom to wait, then moved to the light switch and flicked it off. He walked back to Tom, his gun aimed at the trap door.

Tom pulled the rope and they both stepped back. A square of light opened up in the ceiling, broken by the silhouette of a man with a gun. Hugo dove one way, Tom the other, as the muzzle flashed and the sound of a gunshot echoed in the empty downstairs room. The man fired again, blindly, his targets having moved into the dark.

Hugo looked up and saw the man working his way around the hole in the ceiling. He gauged the shooter's progress then took careful aim at the plaster and fired. He heard a howl of pain as the man dropped through the opening, his right shoe, and much of his foot, blasted away by the bullet. As he hit the floor his left arm snapped and he cried out. Tom moved quickly to the man, leaned down, and swiped the butt of his gun across his head.

"Hush little man, go to sleep," he snarled.

Hugo went back to the rope and pulled the trap door all the way open. A rickety wooden ladder unfurled from above.

"Light, quickly," he said to Tom, and covered the opening with his gun. "I'll go up. Wait 'til I clear it." Leading with his gun, Hugo started up the ladder. At the top, he peeked into the room. It was dim, but looked empty. A musty smell enveloped him as he stuck his head through the gap. Mothballs? He heaved himself into the room and felt thin, worn carpet under his hands and knees.

Behind him, a sound.

He swung around and leveled his gun as a dark figure flitted across the back of the room. He fired twice and the figure dropped. Hugo pivoted to check for other hidden assailants, but saw no one. He moved to the fallen man, eyes straining in case he moved, his finger on the trigger. The man lay on his front and Hugo took a leaf from Tom's book and delivered a hefty kick. No response. Hugo flipped him over with his foot and kicked the man's gun into the corner. A quick check for a pulse told him the man was dead.

The darkness in the room had softened, and Hugo could now see from the back of the apartment to the front. Empty.

"I'm clear," he called, but Tom was already at the top of the ladder. Hugo looked around and noticed for the first time a windowless door not ten feet from the opening, set into the back wall of the house. A fire escape, and probably where the dead man was headed. There'd been no outside staircase on the plans Emma sent, so Gravois must have built one.

As Tom hauled himself into the room, Hugo turned his attention to the front of the house. If there had once been a wall dividing this space into two, it was now gone. It looked like an empty attic, devoid of furniture or decoration, just a stack of five or six boxes in the far corner.

Hugo started toward them, but froze when he heard the crackle of gunfire from behind the house. He turned and ran past the trap door to the fire escape. Tom was already there, wrenching the door open. Light flooded into the room and both men stood inside the doorway, waiting for their eyes to adjust.

"Let's go," Tom said. He ducked through the door with his gun up, Hugo right behind him. An iron stairway spiraled down into the shared garden. Hugo scanned the area, a rectangle of grass and a few bushes, privacy maintained by a stone wall. No one in sight. At the back, an iron gate stood open.

"Where the fuck is Garcia?" Tom said.

"No idea," Hugo replied. How many shots had they heard? Two? Three? They reached the foot of the fire escape without seeing any dead or wounded. "Let's go. Keep an eye on those bushes."

"No shit," Tom muttered.

They moved through the garden side-by-side. Once, Hugo saw movement in an upstairs apartment window a few houses down, the surprised face of an old man who quickly withdrew. As they reached the gate, they heard sirens. Hugo caught Tom's eye and knew they were thinking the same thing: Claudia. Hugo went through the gate first, dropping down to one knee, aiming left. Tom was a split second behind, covering the right side. The alleyway, the one Garcia had come down as they entered the house, was empty.

Almost.

"Look." Tom pointed at four shell cases on the ground. They both knelt to look, but not touch. From two different guns, Hugo saw, one a .40 and the other from a smaller .22. Hugo didn't know which was from Garcia's gun, if either.

They stood and moved quickly down the alley, sirens wailing louder now. As they neared the entrance to the alleyway, two more shots rang out. Hugo pointed downward to a pool of blood, but the men barely slowed, Claudia their concern now because the shots sounded close to the car. They turned left onto Rue Audran and ran up to the corner, in front of the house.

As they reached Rue Véron, Hugo looked down the street to where they'd left Claudia. The car was still there, but a dark form lay on the sidewalk about twenty yards away, between them and the vehicle. Tom covered the body with his gun as they jogged forward, Hugo covering the road around them. There were only two other parked cars on the street, on their right, but plenty of other places a gunman could hide.

Thirty feet from the figure on the ground, Hugo knew it wasn't Garcia. He strained to see inside the car, but couldn't. If Claudia was in there, she was either hunkered down or shot. He ran faster, and as they got within feet of the person on the ground, a figure rose from behind the car. Hugo swung his gun toward it and was about to pull the trigger when he recognized Claudia.

Hugo ran toward her as Tom stopped to check on the still form on the sidewalk, a man Hugo didn't recognize, a man who was dead. Hugo ran around the car and found a wounded Garcia propped against the rear tire. Claudia stood behind him, a gun in her hand.

"I think I killed him," she said, indicating the man on the sidewalk.

"Fucking right you did," Tom said, arriving breathless. "Dead as a doornail."

"I'm not sure that translates," Hugo grimaced. He turned to Garcia. "Was he the only one?"

"*Oui*," Garcia said. "I shot from the gate. I thought I'd knocked him down, but he disappeared into some bushes. As I was leaving the alleyway to look, he shot me in the back. I managed to get here, to the car, but I couldn't lift my gun." Pale lips gave Claudia a smile, the best praise he could muster. "I thought he would kill us both, but my friend here can shoot."

That explained the shell casings from different guns; they'd both fired from the same spot. Hugo looked at the wound, which had bled a lot but seemed to be superficial. It was either a deep graze or the bullet had passed through the flesh and kept going without hitting any arteries or bones.

"He got your shoulder," Hugo said. "You'll live." He turned to Claudia. "I had no idea."

She smiled weakly. "I'm just full of surprises."

"Tell me about it later. But nice work."

He took Claudia's scarf and folded it up, then put it into her hand and showed her where, and how hard, to press it on Garcia's wound.

Hugo stood and looked back toward the house on Rue Véron. The street was still empty, but he didn't want anyone popping up from behind to give them a last-second surprise. He saw Tom doing the same. As the sirens grew louder, the realization hit him. There was no legal justification whatsoever for his friend being there, especially with a gun.

"Tom." His voice was urgent. "You need to get out of here."

Tom looked at him for a second, then nodded. "Yeah, I was wondering how you were going to explain me," he said. He tucked his gun back inside his jacket and patted Garcia once on the head, winked at Hugo, then started down Rue Véron. They watched as he rounded the corner and disappeared out of sight.

"*Bon*," said Garcia. "It was just us. *Merci*. He would have been too much paperwork. And maybe my job."

Two police cars screeched around the corner from Rue Gemain Pilon, at the western end of the street, their lights flashing. They stopped beside each other thirty yards away, and four policemen piled out, guns drawn.

"Take out my badge, show it to them," Garcia said.

Hugo pulled Garcia's badge from his inside pocket and held it up. He'd already thrown his and Garcia's guns onto the sidewalk, visibly out of reach. Claudia also had her hands up. One of the officers appeared to recognize Garcia and holstered his weapon, then reached into his car and grabbed his radio. In the quiet that had fallen over the street, Hugo heard him order an ambulance to approach. It must have been waiting around the corner out of the line of fire, because five seconds later it turned into Rue Véron and lurched to a halt behind the police cars. The four officers and two paramedics ran toward them, two of the cops gesturing for them to lower their hands.

As the medics tended to Garcia, Hugo moved across the street with one of the policemen, a gray-haired detective who gave his name as Duguey. He told him what had happened, what to find in the house. As he talked, his mind flipped back over events, making sure there was nothing left at the scene that would point to a third person, to Tom. They should have thought of that before, he knew, but he was pretty sure Tom was invisible now. His main contribution had been quieting the man Hugo had shot in the foot. And he wouldn't be a problem because, even assuming that he'd seen who'd hit him, he could say what he liked and the police would call him a liar if Hugo and Garcia disagreed.

Hugo and the detective looked over as the medics loaded Garcia onto a gurney and began wheeling him toward the ambulance. They walked over to him and Claudia joined them.

"I'll be fine." Garcia's smile was thin, but genuine. "But let's not do this again, eh?"

"Fair enough," Hugo said. "You take care, capitaine. We'll send flowers."

"*Non*," Garcia said. "They make me sneeze, and that would hurt."

Claudia put a hand on his good arm and squeezed. "*Merci.*"

"*De rien.*" Garcia shook his head. "Just doing my job. And anyway, I should be thanking you."

They moved out of the way and the medics lifted the stretcher into the ambulance. They watched as it backed out of the narrow street and then took off, sirens and lights blaring, toward the Boulevard de Clichy and the hospital.

"Monsieur Marston?" It was Duguey. "My superior, Commissaire Delacroix, will be here in five minutes, would you mind waiting?"

"Not at all," Hugo said. He sat beside Claudia on the curb and put an arm around her.

"You going to tell me what this was about?" she asked.

"Yep," Hugo said. "But I'm not sure that it's over yet."

"What do you mean?"

"We got a couple of the bad guys, but there are more out there. One of them very bad." Hugo looked up as a white car pulled into the street. A uniformed gendarme waved it through, then saluted as it passed him.

Had he been a foot taller, Commissaire Delacroix would have resembled a bear. Round, with thick arms and legs, his face was half hidden by a dark brown beard. Intelligent eyes, thought Hugo, intelligent and curious. They shook hands, and Commissaire Delacroix led him away from Claudia.

"How is she? A shock for a civilian."

Some civilian, Hugo thought. "Not as bad as being shot, and she survived that."

"I recommend brandy. Now, you understand this is a serious matter. I have been supervising Capitaine Garcia on this case and didn't know about this raid. For that he will face some difficult questions."

Hugo went on the defensive, explaining the possibility of a leak and Garcia's reticence at abandoning protocol. The raid had been his own idea, Hugo said, and Garcia had come along to ensure the safety of French citizens and make sure Hugo didn't go too far. To Hugo's surprise, Commissaire Delacroix nodded and smiled.

"I trust Capitaine Garcia, and I'm glad you are able to speak on his behalf." He turned and looked at the house. "Now, we need to find this Gravois. He is our first priority," he said.

"Agreed," Hugo nodded, "and even if you do have a leak, we'll have to move fast."

"'We'?"

Hugo smiled. "You, with as much help from me as you require."

The commissaire nodded and called over one of the policemen. Hugo gave the man a detailed description of Gravois.

"*Bien*," said Delacroix, "I will send someone to his offices and his home. We'll have the train stations and airports watched, too, as best we can. You said he is crippled. Do you suppose he drives?"

"He might," said Hugo. "But I don't know what kind of car, and he'd probably need a driver."

"We'll notify the border authorities, flag his passport, not that that's much use these days. But on the off chance that he's stopped, we'll be notified. I'll call the US Embassy to let you know if that happens." They shook hands again. "If you would come to the prefecture tomorrow for a full statement, I would be grateful. For now, we will take Capitaine Garcia's car. One of my men can give you a ride to the embassy."

"No, thanks." Hugo wanted to walk to clear his mind and figure out his next step. Place Pigalle was a couple of blocks away, he could get the metro from there. "Claudia, do you want to walk with me or go with the police?"

"Go where?" she smiled thinly. "I'm fine, Hugo. Plus, if any more bad guys appear I may need to save your ass next."

"Oh, one more thing," Delacroix said. "I'll need your weapon."

Hugo hesitated. "May I ask why?"

"It's evidence for our investigation. Our ballistics people will need to make sure it matches with any bullets fired at the house. A formality, I'll have it back to you as soon as possible."

Reluctantly, Hugo handed it over. *The joys of international cooperation*, he thought. Ambassador Taylor would be proud.

CHAPTER THIRTY-THREE

I t was a downhill walk from Rue Véron toward Pigalle, and Hugo felt the adrenaline slowly drain from his limbs, his body loosening and his mind clearing as they got further away from the house.

Claudia was quiet, her hands dug deep into her pockets and her head down. He knew she was processing what she'd seen and done, trying to equate the violence and fear of the afternoon with all the previous experiences of her life. And he knew that no one, reporter, policeman, or even soldier, escaped their first armed and bloody confrontation intact, especially after what she'd been through just hours before. She was tougher than he'd imagined, so he'd let her deal with it on her own, for now.

She shivered as they turned into Rue Cousteau, a cobbled and narrow one-way street. Hugo put his arm around her, and she leaned into him as they walked. As they reached the end of the street, the sound of the traffic from Boulevard Clichy grew louder and seemed to disturb Claudia. On the corner was a small café, Le Chat Blanc, and he took her inside. Hugo nodded to the bartender and chose a table near the back of the café. He helped Claudia to sit, then went to the bar and ordered.

"*Deux cafés, et deux whiskies, s'il vous plaît.*" As he waited, he pulled out his cell phone and dialed Tom. On the fifth ring, his friend answered. "Where are you?" Hugo asked.

The phone clicked dead and Hugo felt a hand on his shoulder.

"Right behind you, buddy," Tom grinned.

"Jesus, what are you doing here?"

"Same as you." Tom held up a whisky glass. "Except you're two behind."

Claudia heard their voices and looked up, surprise at seeing Tom turning to pleasure. Drinks in hand, the men went to the table. Claudia took the whisky glass with a grateful smile and left Hugo to put the coffee on the table in front of her.

"Hot chick with a gun, it's like the movies, eh?" Tom said, a little too gleefully for Hugo's liking.

"Leave her alone."

"OK, OK." Tom's tone became serious. "I feel like an ass for letting Chabot get killed."

"Not our fault," said Hugo. "But me too."

"That fucking Gravois or Dominguez—"

"Dobrescu—"

"Whatever the fuck his name is. He's some psycho."

Claudia roused herself, suddenly alive again. "Wait, are you saying Gravois is Anton Dobrescu? Are you serious?"

"Yes," said Hugo. "Long story, but the bottom line is that he knows we're on to him."

"You think?" Tom said. "He may still rely on the fact we think he's dead. Or, he thinks we think he's dead." He waved a hand. "Fuck it, I'm confusing myself now."

Hugo smiled. "I know what you mean, but that's a risky assumption for him. He knows we're on to Gravois, and no disguise is perfect. First time he's fingerprinted, it's all over."

"So you think he'll disappear?" Claudia asked.

"Wouldn't you?" Hugo replied.

"Fucking right," Tom said. "Once those North Africans find out he's here, he'll be wishing he *was* burned alive." He emptied his glass. "So what do we do?"

"Nothing." Hugo shrugged and told Tom about his talk with Commissaire Delacroix.

"You want to leave it to them, then? Yeah, right." Tom looked around for a waiter, then saw Hugo's face. "Holy shit, you're serious."

"What can we do? The police are looking for him, they're watching the airports, train stations, and borders—"

"This is new Europe, dummy, they don't have borders anymore."

"Even so, what can we do that they can't?"

Tom muttered into his glass, but Hugo knew he had no answer.

Hugo looked at Claudia. She was sitting back in her chair, oblivious to them, her eyes half closed and her lips slightly apart. Hugo had an urge to kiss them but knew this wasn't the time or place. *At least she looks relaxed*, he thought. He put his hand on hers and said, "Quick question."

She opened her eyes and smiled. "Sure."

"David Durand. He's the dirty cop, and you were helping Garcia keep an eye on him, as he put it to me."

"That wasn't a question," she said.

"Am I right?"

"Aren't you always?"

"Sometimes. But always slow to get there."

"Then you know they were on to him," she said. "This little incident will be another nail in his coffin."

"How did you get mixed up in that?"

"A favor, really. The detectives I was interviewing had noticed his name come up every time a bad guy got away with something, or when evidence went missing. They had nothing hard and fast but figured if I spent time with him, flattering him, maybe he'd give me a different story than he was telling his bosses. Sometimes people like to brag when they talk to reporters." She shrugged. "Turned out he's not a bragger, but he gave me a couple of pieces of information he shouldn't have known."

"About?"

"Drug shipments. Les Pieds-Noirs. The deal was that I help the cops and they'd give me the first, and inside, scoop when Durand and his drug buddies went down." She looked up and grinned. "And they said they'd teach me to shoot."

"Seems they kept that promise." Hugo squeezed her hand again.

"They looked at you, too, for a couple of minutes, did you know that?"

"What do you mean?"

"When you started showing interest in a nonexistent investigation of Durand's, people started wondering."

"They made that assumption before figuring out it was a real investigation that he'd shut down."

"Right." She smiled. "Cops and their hunches."

Hugo nodded. "Let's head back to my place. Get a taxi, go home, light a fire, and open a bottle of wine."

"Am I included in this romantic evening?" Tom asked.

"Sure." Hugo frowned. "In fact, can you drop me at the embassy and take her home?"

"You reporting in to the boss?"

"Exactly. It'll sound better coming from me than the French police or, God forbid, the French news. I'll walk home afterward; it shouldn't take long."

After a five minute stroll along the busy Boulevard Clichy, they flagged down a taxi. They rode in silence, shuffling along in the rush-hour traffic as dusk began to close in around them. A few of the earliest Christmas lights flicked on in store windows as they passed. Hugo had forgotten that this was the festive season, when Paris was a place of enchantment, her boulevards and parks festooned with white lights and oversized red and green bows and ribbons, her store windows shimmering with baubles and tinsel. How festive would it be for him? Endless nights drinking with Tom? Polite embassy parties and then home to an empty apartment, most likely. He wondered if maybe Claudia would be around to share it, be willing to.

He hopped out of the cab by the Hotel Crillon and walked up to the main embassy entrance. He checked his watch: five thirty. Ambassador Taylor should still be there.

As before, the ambassador listened silently while Hugo talked. He again omitted reference to Tom, as much for the ambassador's sake as for his or his friend's. When he'd finished, Ambassador Taylor walked to the cart bearing drinks.

"Hell of a day for you. What would you like?"

"Actually, I'm fine," Hugo said.

"You know, most police forces put their men on paid administrative leave and send them to a shrink when they've shot someone." He poured himself a brandy. "I know what you're going to say, Hugo, but if you need time off for any reason, if you feel like it'd help to talk to someone about this, just say the word."

"Thank you, ambassador, but I'm fine."

"I'm sure you are. So we leave this to the French now, yes?" Hugo nodded. "I'll talk to some of the people at the prefecture, make sure they are happy, and let them know to take all the credit."

Hugo smiled. "Ever the diplomat, ambassador."

"We do what we can." Ambassador Taylor chuckled. "You shoot 'em, I make them happy about it. Quite a team." He looked at Hugo for a moment. "So tell me to mind my own business if you want, but I'm curious about something."

"Fire away."

"You told me before about a little windfall from the Rimbaud book. What are you planning to do with the money? I ask because I'm hoping you won't say 'retire.'"

"Oh no, despite the trials of today I like being busy." Hugo looked past his boss. The issue of the money had nagged at him, and for no particular reason, he now knew what he was going to do. "There are a couple of funerals I want to help pay for, if I'm allowed. And with the rest, well, I think maybe I'll buy myself a little apartment and some books to fill it with."

"You have one in mind, I assume?"

"Of course. It's on Rue Condorcet." Hugo smiled, mostly to himself. "I may even get a cat."

He stopped by his office before heading out into the cold and eyed a stack of mail waiting for his attention. He knew that Emma would get to it and that he could call tomorrow or the next day to see if anything important had come in. Urgent stuff came by e-mail or phone, so this pile could wait.

He sat down at his desk, rereading the instructions from Garcia's lieutenant for checking cell phone records. There was just one thing he wanted to confirm, an event he needed to be sure had happened. And after he'd clicked through the right steps, when he'd checked every possible data entry and realized that he was wrong, he sat there in silence, utterly bemused. He picked up his phone, hesitant to bother an injured man. But then he called Garcia anyway.

"Much better, *merci*," the capitaine said. "I'll be out tomorrow. Then they'll probably make me go back to work."

"Good, they need you. I have a quick question about the Roussillon shooting. I wanted to ask about the surveillance footage, whether you'd had a chance to view it."

There was silence for a second, then Garcia's voice was serious. "*Oui*, that system is hooked into a law enforcement program, some high-tech stuff I don't understand. Anyway, normally we can play those tapes back almost immediately."

"Normally?"

"*Oui*. Funny thing, there was nothing on his."

"Nothing on them? What do you mean?"

"The system had been switched off."

As Hugo stood to leave, his eye fell on a yellow envelope in the middle of his stack of mail. It was a padded envelope that contained something thick and square, the dimensions of a video cassette.

Or, Hugo thought, a book.

He shoved away the mail that sat on top of it and peered at the writing on the envelope. No return address, just his name and the address of the embassy. *I know where to find you*, Max had said.

Hugo's heart pounded as he ripped open the envelope. He knew all mail was screened before ever reaching his desk, so he didn't bother being gentle—it wasn't going to explode or poison him.

In any case, he already knew what was inside.

The walk home seemed long and cold, the evening breeze blowing up off the Seine, tugging at him as it tried to find a way through his coat. But it was cleansing, too, like a cold shower, blasting away the events of the day. It was rare for Hugo to leave a case unfinished, but he reassured himself that there was nothing more for him to do, that Gravois was the guilty man, and that if he were to be caught the police would do it. He now knew who'd killed Max and the other sellers, and he knew why.

The only remaining question was about Roussillon's death, and those pieces were falling into place, though the picture wasn't ideal.

On the plus side, though, he had two friends, one very pretty, waiting for him at home.

At the end of the Tuileries, he turned right and crossed the river on Pont Royal. He paused at the end of the bridge, eager to get away from the cold but curious to see Max's stall. It was past six o'clock, so he didn't expect anyone to be there, but somehow he wanted to go by and let his old friend know that justice was being done, that the man responsible would soon be caught or, at least, would likely never return to Paris.

Ten minutes later Hugo was within sight of the stall, the four metal boxes visible in a patch of light falling from a nearby streetlamp. He paused for a moment, then squinted, sure he'd seen movement. He had. Someone was there. He moved closer, and the man walked into the light.

Hugo didn't recognize him, his body shrouded by the long, dark coat that swept the ground every time the man stooped, his head covered for warmth. The man bent over a box, packing up, and Hugo stared. Had Gravois sent someone to close Chabot's stall, fearing an open one might look suspicious? But why would he care anymore? More likely, Hugo thought, a fellow bouquiniste had taken pity on Chabot, not wanting to leave the stall open all night. Come morning, there would have been nothing left.

As Hugo approached, the man bent over a box, trying to fill it with the stack of books in his hands. He lost his balance, just for a second, but long enough for the books to spill to the sidewalk. As the man grabbed at them his hat slipped from his head, revealing a shock of brown hair. He straightened and kicked the box in frustration, then started picking the books up. When he stood, the yellow light from a nearby lamp washed over the man's flat, comic-book face.

CHAPTER THIRTY-FOUR

Thirty yards away, Hugo's world closed in around him. The cold disappeared, the traffic blurred, and the only place in the whole of Paris with any light was the patch of sidewalk containing a thug who carried an ice pick and a silver pistol.

"Nica," Hugo whispered. He felt a rush of anger toward the man who'd all but committed murder in front of him, the man who'd rendered him impotent and who would have happily killed him, too. He started forward and then stopped. Ambassador Taylor's admonition rang in his head. "Leave it to the French," he'd said.

Hugo turned his back on the man as he dialed the emergency number for the police. He spoke quickly and quietly, giving the dispatcher enough information to propel her into high gear. He put the phone away, then crept forward.

As he got within twenty yards, a boat's horn sounded from the river, a long, low moan that was repeated twice more. Nica stopped what he was doing and looked over the low parapet toward the sound. Hugo did the same. A barge had changed course, plowing its way from the center of the river toward the bank, its wake a silver curve in the black water below. Nica looked away from the boat and started to work faster, and Hugo saw that he was loading something along with the books, plastic-wrapped bricks that had to be drugs.

Hugo clenched his teeth. This was Nica's escape route, the river. The same way his boss had planned to bring the drugs in to his bouquinistes. The damn river. Hugo shook his head in disgust. On their anonymous barge, Gravois, Nica, and whoever else remained could glide into central France among the industrial barges and pleasure boats and then go wherever the hell they liked. Hugo guessed that the books Nica was loading were expensive first editions, a currency as valuable as, and easier to trade than, the bricks of dope. All of them had been stashed at Chabot's stall, held in trust for just such an eventuality.

Hugo didn't let the Romanian's impressive cunning slow him down. He put his hand inside his coat and cursed. Delacroix had his gun, and he hadn't picked up another from the embassy's armory because this was supposed to be over.

He looked up and down the broad Quai de Conti for signs of the police but saw no flashing lights and heard no sirens. Nica was moving with more purpose now, and Hugo knew it was up to him to stop the bastard from escaping. He began to run, trying to close down the space between them as fast as possible, but he only got halfway before the man looked up. The flat face stared blankly for a second, then the mouth opened in surprise, eyes sparkling as he stood frozen over his box.

But Nica didn't hesitate for long. He leapt to the open stall and scrabbled under a pile of magazines. Hugo was ten feet away when he saw the gun swing toward him, a silver flash under the street lamp, and he launched himself, arms outstretched. His fist connected with the man's forearm, knocking the gun away. A split second later they were on the sidewalk, Hugo's shoulder pressing into Nica's chest. Hugo fought for a solid grip, but Nica bucked and kicked under him, cursing as wildly as he struggled. With a howl of desperation, Nica won himself enough freedom to roll out from under Hugo and clamber to his knees.

Hugo looked around desperately for the gun and saw it near his foot. Nica dove for it, and Hugo swung his leg as hard as he could. His toe connected with the barrel and the gun skittered along the sidewalk and disappeared over the stone steps leading down to the walkway beside the river.

Hugo scrambled to his feet, ten yards behind Nica, who lurched toward the top step, winded. When he reached it he glanced back at Hugo and started down, two at a time. As Hugo crested the steps behind him, the Romanian was halfway down and stooped over the gun, the fingers of his right hand closing around the butt. Hugo leapt toward him, and just as Nica began to raise the weapon, Hugo lashed out with his right leg and connected with his wrist. Nica lost his grip on the pistol and his arms windmilled for a second before he lost his balance and crashed down the remaining dozen steps. The gun clattered down after him and Hugo charged down, three and four steps at a time. He dropped on top of the Romanian, planting his left knee on Nica's wrist, pinning it to the ground, and drove his fist into his chest, knocking the wind out of him again.

From the street above, Hugo heard sirens approaching. He reached out and picked up the gun, then looked down at his captive. The dark eyes spewed hate, and his mouth twisted with pain and rage. "You had better kill me," Nica hissed. "If you think you will live past tomorrow, you are wrong."

"I'd love to." Hugo leaned in and they locked eyes. "Or maybe I'll arrange for you to share a cell with some Africans from the Seventeenth Arrondissement. That way you can slip out of jail piece by piece."

Nica let out a roar and bucked hard. Hugo steadied himself and drove the heel of his hand into the writhing man's throat. He stopped struggling and his face turned blue as he gasped for air.

"Now lie still like a good boy," Hugo growled.

The sirens grew louder and Hugo turned to look toward the main road, hoping to see the blue lights of the police. Instead, a light from the river flashed over them. Hugo looked back toward the water and tightened his grip on the gun. The light came from the barge, now less than thirty yards from the bank. Two men, silhouettes to Hugo, stood on the prow, one operating the spotlight. The other stood a few inches taller, the light gleaming on his hairless skull, his body propped up by a cane. Hugo raised the gun so the men would see it, then put the barrel right between his captive's eyes.

Five long seconds later, the silhouette with the cane shifted, Gravois moving away from the light. The sounds of a shouted order drifted over the water to Hugo and the barge's engine growled louder, its bow slowly swinging away, aiming back into the Seine. Still gasping for air, the man on the ground twisted to see what was happening.

"There goes your ride," Hugo said, and Nica cursed again.

Behind them, up on the quai, the blue lights finally arrived. Within seconds, Hugo heard a clatter of feet and shouts to drop the weapon. Four policemen, two in uniform and two in plain clothes, hurtled down the steps, guns drawn. Slowly, deliberately, Hugo put the pistol down beside him and slid it toward the foot of the steps, then raised his arms high. The uniformed officers ran up and grabbed his arms, pulling him to his feet. As his prisoner sat up, Hugo gave in to an impulse and landed the heel of his cowboy boot on the Romanian's nose, hard.

"That's for Max," he said.

Hugo didn't resist as the two cops wrestled him away, twisting his arms behind his back to snap on handcuffs. They deposited him on the bottom step, one standing over him while the other radioed for back up. He smiled as their plainclothes colleagues cuffed the bleeding and mumbling Nica. A uniformed policeman leaned over and put a hand inside Hugo's jacket, pulling out his embassy credentials. When he saw the crest and metal badge, the cop's face clouded with uncertainty and he took the wallet to one of the detectives, who turned his back on them both and opened his phone. A minute later Hugo was out of handcuffs and pointing to the barge that chugged against the westbound current, fighting its way alongside the Ile de la Cité.

"Call Commissaire Delacroix, right now. Tell him you're watching Gravois escape."

"*Comment?*" The detective hesitated.

"Delacroix. Call him *now*."

He watched as the officer connected to the prefecture and was put through to Delacroix. The detective talked hurriedly, his eyes flicking from Hugo to the barge, then he went silent, nodding as he listened. The policeman hung up and looked away to their left. Hugo and the three other officers did the same, and a moment later they heard the snarl of engines and the slap-slap of two police launches that raced out of the dark and skimmed past them. Within seconds they had reached the barge, their engines throttling back as they circled it, a dark figure on the prow of one launch shouting orders through a loud hailer for the barge's pilot to make land.

Watching intently from the walkway, a sudden roar from behind made Hugo and the policemen crouch. They covered their ears as a helicopter swept overhead, its rotors buffeting them. The spotlight on its nose blanched the water below as it searched for its prey, then locked on to the barge and pinned its occupants with a beam that drenched the deck with light. A chorus of sirens grew louder and Hugo looked up as a line of flashing blue lights strung out across the Pont Ste. Michelle, the bridge in front of the barge. Dozens of black silhouettes swarmed down to the walkway to await the surrendering vessel while dozens more stayed on the bridge, leaning over the parapet to watch the spectacle, their flashlights dancing in the dark like candles on a cake.

CHAPTER THIRTY-FIVE

Hugo trotted up the steps to his apartment, tired but exhilarated. Commissaire Delacroix had led the contingent of officers to the walkway, greeting Gravois and his men with an effective show of firepower and several sets of shackles. With the Romanians locked in separate police cars, Delacroix had told his men to hold Hugo until he got there. Without a word, the Frenchman had clasped Hugo's shoulders and given him a bear hug, apparently already aware of the American's tussle with the Romanian Nica. Delacroix released him and thanked him again before excusing himself. "I have a long interrogation ahead of me," he said. "If you'd like to observe, you are welcome."

"*Merci*. But I have a friend waiting for me." It was his way of reassuring the policeman that he respected their earlier agreement, that this was a French capture, and that Hugo wanted neither headlines nor accolades.

Delacroix offered him an escort home, but Hugo declined. He had Tom for the immediate future, and he expected a mass exodus of Dobrescu followers heading east for the border. If they weren't already on their way, they would be as soon as they saw images of their leader clapped in irons all over the front page of *Le Monde*. They would know they were beaten; they'd been slaughtered once by the North African syndicate, tried a comeback, and been shot up all over again. Hugo guessed that staying in Paris, for revenge or any other reason, was the last thing on their minds.

When he walked into the apartment, he found Claudia sitting on the floor beside the coffee table, the fire snapping and fizzing. A full glass of wine was in front of her.

"Your second or third?" he asked.

"First, actually." She smiled up at him. "I was waiting for you, though I wasn't going to wait much longer."

"I got delayed." Hugo dropped onto the sofa and worked his boots off with his feet. "Where's Tom? He'll want to hear about this."

"He tried waiting, then went to take a shower." She pulled herself up and wedged herself in the corner of the sofa, facing him. "Can we talk about something?"

"Sure. What's up?"

"Something's bothering me, and I need you to tell me whether I'm either insane or, well, whether I'm right."

Hugo nodded.

"It's about my father, the way he died. Something seems not quite right, but I can't explain it. I'm not even sure about it."

"Try me."

"When I found my father like that, I—" her voice wavered, then strengthened again. "I stared at him, I couldn't believe it. But part of me, I guess the journalist part, noticed some things. One thing."

"Which was?"

"Where he was shot. I mean, precisely there, the bullet hole. There was a kind of ring, red or brown, right around it."

Hugo nodded. He'd noticed it too. And he knew why it was there, but it was a conclusion he was afraid Claudia would not like. "Go on."

"You knew many things about my father, that he was rich, protective of me, and that he collected books. But there is something else. Did you also notice how trim he was, how fit?"

"Well, he certainly wasn't overweight, and now that I picture him, yes, I can see that."

"Jean started teaching him judo, probably twenty years ago. He had what he called his sanctuary in a small turret at the back of the house where they would train."

"Yes, he told me about that. He said he used it for meditation and exercise, I think."

"Right. No one except them was allowed in." She looked up, a wistful smile on her face. "I know what you're thinking, but it wasn't like that. Jean was quite one for the ladies. He'd been a martial arts instructor in the army; he was some general's bodyguard. Then papa hired him. But I spent enough time with him to know he had an eye for a pretty girl."

Hugo squeezed her hand. "I believe it, but either way I don't much care. Keep talking, though."

"OK, so Jean always joked that my father was fast and aggressive. He said papa was not so strong and not so talented, he'd never win the Olympics, but he was fast and aggressive, those were his words." Her large hazel eyes held his. "Hugo, that mark around the entrance wound, that means he was shot up close. That the gun was very close to his forehead, right?"

"I would say so. I'm not the expert, and neither are you, so someone else will check that out."

"But you think I'm right."

"I think you might be, yes."

"Then here's what I don't understand. There's no way in the world papa would have let someone hold a gun to his head, not in his own house. When I was a teenager he would make me try and poke him with a letter opener, or a butter knife. He even did it with guests after he'd been drinking, it was embarrassing. But he took the knife away every time."

"Fast and aggressive."

"*Exactement*. Even if he wasn't fast enough, there would have been a struggle, the shot would not have been so clean. It just doesn't seem right, it doesn't add up for me."

She sat back, and Hugo looked at her, not speaking.

"Tell me," she said. "Tell me what you know, what you think."

"When we spoke, your father reminded me that the truth can be painful, that revealing it sometimes does nothing but release the ghosts of the past into the present."

She cocked her head. "What are you talking about? What are you hiding from me?"

"I don't know if it's the truth, Claudia. I am not sure of anything. But I don't think Gravois killed your father."

"What do you mean?"

"He had no reason to. I thought at first that your father had confronted him about Max, maybe threatened to tell the police what he knew, go public somehow. But your father never called Gravois, he didn't call anyone between the time I left him and the time you found him. As far as I know, he never even left his library."

"What are you saying, Hugo?"

"I spoke to Capitaine Garcia less than an hour ago. There was nothing on the security tapes, nothing at all. They'd been switched off."

"Gravois did that."

"No, it's a sophisticated system. He wouldn't have had time to figure that out. And it hadn't been smashed or obviously tampered with."

"You're not suggesting Jean, are you?"

"Jean?" Hugo shook his head. "No, I'm not. Do you think he had reason to harm your father?"

"Of course not," Claudia said. "They were like brothers."

"Right. That's what I thought."

Claudia grasped his wrist, her voice urgent. "What are you suggesting?"

"Your father was distraught when I told him about Max, very upset indeed. He knew that the call he'd placed to Gravois had likely sentenced the old man to death. It wasn't his fault, he couldn't have known at the time, but he associates so much death and misery with that book. I think by getting his hands on it your father thought he'd be putting a stop to all that, not starting it all over again. I think, too, that your father knew that Gravois wouldn't care what he said, since he was no real danger. Gravois could kill him, threaten to kill you, even ignore him, and your father couldn't do a damn thing because he had no proof of Gravois's involvement in Max's death."

"So what are you telling me?"

"That Gravois didn't have a reason or opportunity to kill your father."

"So who did?"

They looked at each other, Hugo waiting for Claudia to catch up to him, to be at the same point of understanding.

When she got there, she began to shake her head. "No, no, it's not possible."

"It's possible Claudia, and I think quite likely."

"You think he killed himself and wanted the police to blame Gravois? That's ridiculous."

"No, it's not. If you'd seen his face when I told him about Max, you'd know. And then his illness, he told me about that."

Claudia nodded. "He was terrified of that. He didn't want to lose his dignity or to have me or Jean have to cart him around like a vegetable. His words, not mine. But to kill himself?"

"No one ever thinks their family members capable of it. And maybe I'm wrong, but it adds up. You yourself said he would have fought back."

Claudia chewed her lip, shaking her head every few seconds. She looked up, triumph in her eyes. "But there was no gun. I didn't see one and the police didn't find one. He can't have killed himself."

"And this is how we'll know the truth, if I'm right."

"What do you mean?"

"You father was a huge Sherlock Holmes fan, yes?"

"*Oui*. So what?"

"Well, so am I. Or I used to be. I read them all when I was in high school and college. I think they fueled my desire to get into law enforcement, to solve mysterious crimes and catch ruthless bad guys. Anyway, as I remember it, one of his stories is about a man who is found dead on a bridge. The murder weapon, a gun, is found in the possession of his mortal enemy. Open and shut case of murder. Except that Holmes sees a bit of the bridge's stonework chipped off. He does some thinking and some measuring, and he realizes that the gun the police found was one of a pair. The other was missing. The police couldn't find it and didn't much care, and no one else knew where it had gone. So Holmes jumps into the stream beneath the bridge and fetches it out."

"Hugo, I don't understand."

"The dead man had shot himself. He'd tied the gun to a rock, which he'd dangled over the edge of the bridge. When he pulled the trigger and fell to the ground, the weight of the rock pulled the gun into the water, chipping the stonework of the bridge in the process. Suicide designed to look like murder."

"The pond outside the library window."

"Yes, you remember that the window was open. Not what you'd expect on a freezing winter day. If I'm right, the pond is where the gun will be."

They sat in silence for a minute, and Hugo noticed Tom standing in the hallway near his room, listening. He walked in and sat down, saying nothing.

"But if you're right, why would he do that? My father was all about the truth, wasn't he?"

"Yes," Hugo said, "he was. And maybe he knew that sooner or later we'd figure out the truth. And remember that he was also about justice, and he wanted to make sure Gravois saw justice for what he did to Max. He told me that himself." Hugo smiled. "This time, maybe he was putting justice ahead of truth, just for a little while."

Claudia sat quietly for a moment, staring into the fire, before looking up. "One thing. You said yourself that there was no evidence pointing to Gravois, not directly."

"No, but once someone gets their interest, the police don't need direct evidence to investigate. He believed that once a spotlight fell on Gravois they would find some pretty ugly stuff."

"And he was right," said Tom. "That creepy fucker."

"He was trying to do the right thing," said Hugo, "and he was dealing with the guilt and the dementia at the same time. I'm sorry, Claudia, I really am."

Claudia folded herself over and lay down in Hugo's lap. Tom stood and moved to the whisky bottle, pouring three generous servings, which he handed out. "So Sherlock," he said, "now you just have to find the book and, if you're not too busy, Gravois. Together under a bridge somewhere?"

"No," smiled Hugo. "Not the book, anyway. That's at my office."

Claudia and Tom reacted at the same time. "What?"

"Max mailed it to me at the embassy. I didn't know until tonight because I've been on vacation and didn't check my mail. Emma only told me about the urgent stuff. She didn't know the book was important, so she didn't tell me."

"Why would he do that?" Claudia asked. "Why mail it to you?"

"I'm not entirely sure." Hugo frowned and shook his head. "Maybe because he knew it was valuable and would be safe with me."

"He could have given it to you in person, no?"

"I think he looked at it between the time I first saw it and the time I went back with the money I owed him."

"Why not just give it to you then?"

"Remember something about Max. He'd been dealing with Nazi hunters, collaborators, and then Gravois's men. He was probably pretty paranoid and he wouldn't have wanted to risk losing the book. And if he knew he was going to have to deal with Gravois, as your father said, he'd probably have known the bastard would take the book for his own ends and as soon as possible. Maybe he'd seen Nica lurking and was trying to protect me. There's a post office close to his stall, it would have been easy for him to run across the street and mail it off, make it good and safe immediately."

"But why not tell you?" asked Tom.

"I'm afraid I don't know," said Hugo, "but the unpleasant thought occurred to me that Max was going to play hardball with your father, to extort a significant amount of money for the book and for his silence. Retirement money. I'm just guessing, of course, but his mood did change in the hour between our meetings. And if I'm right about that, he wouldn't have wanted me to know about the contents of the book or his plans; he'd have wanted some time to think up a reason for mailing it to me. Maybe we'll never really know."

They sat quietly, all eyes on the fire, the ballet of orange heat entertaining them for a full minute, the crack and hiss of burning wood and occasional sips of whisky the only sounds.

Claudia sighed and slid to the floor, her back against Hugo's shins. He began to gently rub her good shoulder. Then she looked back at him.

"So why did you take so long to get here? You said Tom would want to hear about it."

"Yeah, and I'm next with the back rub," Tom said. "Where the hell were you? If I'd known you were going to be gone two fucking hours, I'd have taken her to bed."

"Somehow I don't think you'd last two hours with me," Claudia said.

They laughed, grateful for some humor, and Hugo began to tell them about his trip home. As he talked, Claudia turned so she could see him. The news that Gravois was in custody, and that Hugo had been the one to grab him, set off a round of toasts and hearty, soon drunken, congratulations.

After the fifth or six toast, Tom pulled himself to his feet. "I'll leave you two lovebirds alone. But before you go to bed, please make sure I haven't choked in my own vomit."

"Delightful," Hugo said. He pulled Claudia up off the floor onto the couch beside him. She draped her legs over his and snuggled in close.

"You know I couldn't tell you about Durand, right?"

"Of course, please don't worry about it." They sat quietly for a moment. "I'm sorry about your father, you know that."

"I do." She sighed. "He'd be pleased that I have my front-page story."

"About Gravois? He sure would."

"You know, I do have something else to write about now. I think that will be a whole book, though."

"Really? What's that?"

She looked at him. "You're tired, we can wait until tomorrow to talk about it."

"No, tell me now. What's the story?"

"It's about the Second World War," she said. "About the Resistance and the men who betrayed our French heroes to the Nazis."

"Ah, I see." He played along as she nuzzled him, her eyes closing. Hugo spoke softly. "You sure you don't want to stick to the Gravois story? There are already so many Word War Two tales that have already been written."

"No, this one has not been done yet."

"If you say so."

"I do," she said. "This one has it all. Intrigue and secrecy, trickery and deception. It features one of the most powerful men in French society, a count from one of the noblest of French families. It's a tale of great bravery and great cowardice, the tale of a terrifying secret that lay hidden for decades in the pages of a very old book."

"Wow," he whispered. "That's quite a story."

"If you're good, you might get a mention in the acknowledgments section." She settled deeper on the couch and her eyelids drooped.

"And when it's published," Hugo said, "I want a first edition signed by the author."

ACKNOWLEDGMENTS

This is my first novel, and it has taken the support and encouragement of many people for it to see the light of day. First, I need to thank my family and friends. My father, who passed away this year knowing I was going to be published but without getting to see the final product, was the inspiration behind my main character, Hugo Marston. Hugo gets his moral compass, his nonjudgmental nature, his humor, and his all-around decency from my dad. And beside my father, always, was my mother, who believed in my ability and never wavered in her support and encouragement, who read and critiqued my writing, and who may not have known that the best compliment ever was "this reads like a real book." And much love and gratitude to my brother, Richard, and sister, Catherine, always happy as clams when their brother does well, who have been supportive and eager to share this long and bumpy journey to publication.

I am particularly grateful to two fellow writers, Jennifer Schubert and Elizabeth Silver, for their tireless help and support and for their honest and invaluable critiques. Knowing you are there whenever I need support or a critical eye has been a godsend; you are both irreplaceable. And I'm grateful, too, to other writer friends who took the time to give me feedback as I was creating Hugo: Meredith Hindley, Cheryl Etchison, Vanessa Absalom-Mueller, J. E. Seymour, Todd Bush, Ken Hoss, Elena Giorgi, Ann Simko, and David Kazzie. And many thanks to these established authors, people far more talented than me, who were never too busy to give advice to a fledgling: David Lindsey, Jennifer Hillier, Steven Sidor, Carol Carr, and Bill Landay.

My thanks also to Glenn, of the rare booksellers Peter Harrington in London, for his help and advice on rare and used books.

Thanks, also, to my nonwriting friends who were as excited about this series as anyone and have been urging me on for, literally, years: Ryan Pierce, Conor Civins, Laura O'Rourke, Lisa Hobbs, Jessica Ghazal, Mark and Sheila Armitage, Todd and Allison Finch, Andy Baxter, Judge Mike Lynch, David Grassbaugh, Stephen Willott, Aaron Mueller, and two very gifted friends, the artist Donna Crosby and musical man Johnny Goudie.

Continuing thanks to Ann Collette, my agent, who has believed in me as a writer, in this novel, and in this series, from the very start. My small offerings of chocolate are in no way representative of my gratitude, they are but small tokens of my recognition of how hard you worked to knock Hugo into shape and then find a home for him. *Merci beaucoup.*

Likewise, to my editor Dan Mayer: thank you for plucking me from the pile and putting faith in me and in my writing. This is something of a new beginning for us both, a new journey, but long may it last.

To my three wonderful children, Natalie, Henry, and Nicola, who accompanied me on countless trips to the library or missed out on seeing me because I was there alone: I thank you for your patience and understanding. And, when you are old enough to read them, seeing one of my books in your hands will be a supreme delight, a reward in itself for all my work.

And, finally, my wife, Sarah, to whom this book is dedicated. There has been no stronger champion of my writing, no greater believer in me. No one has worked harder to bring Hugo to life than you. Year after year you gave me unqualified support and encouragement and you labored willingly and uncomplainingly through extra chores so that I had time to write, vacuuming around me, and just smiling when I failed to hear your question about dinner because I was lost in Paris with my imaginary friends. And because you are so unselfish in all things, you probably don't even know how brilliant you've been. Thank you, my love.